HOW THE STARS FALL

HOW THE STARS FALL

SARAH C DAVIES

Paperback ISBN 978-1-7635688-2-2

Cover Design by Lemon Design Studio
@lemon.design.studio
Editing by Sarah Davies & Megan G. Mossgrove
Line editing by Mossgrove Writes
Proofreading by Sarah Davies & Megan G. Mossgrove

To my Jared. My sun, moon & stars.

AUTHOR NOTE

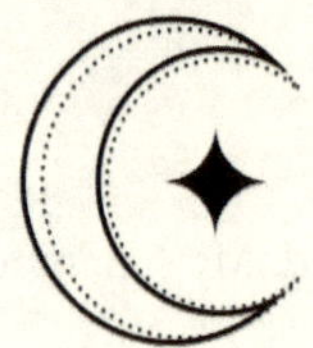

While this book does not focus on the following incidents, they may trigger some readers.
trigger some readers.
Accidental death
Physical abuse
Please keep this in mind as you read.

THE STAR PLAYLIST

Love Is Violence
Aaryan Shah

Blame The Moon
Hazlett

Amor
SayWeCanFly

Make The Angels Cry
Chris Grey

Restored
sod ven

My Poor Heart (Hushed)
Andrew Belle

What's Left Of Me
Grace VanderWaal

Memories
Conan Gray

What Was I Made For
Billie Elish

Those Eyes
Iris Jean

Floorboards
Noah Henderson

All Of The Stars
Hayd

I Don't Wanna Leave Just Yet
Thomas Day

Never Get Over You
Stephen Dawes, Dylan Conrique

THE STAR PLAYLIST

CONTINUED

Be Gentle With Me
yaeow

Come Home
Max Allais

Afterglow
Portair, WYNNE

The Storm In Me
Phineas

Even If It's Lonely
Hazlett

ONE

"**I** will give you five thousand gold coins to bring me the fallen star."

Hazel eyes stared intently at Ryker. The desire to look upon one of Earth's rarest beauties was evident on King Branoc's face. Everyone who dwelt in the lands of Emberfell knew of his greed, but none were brave enough to challenge him. It was best to stay in his good graces, because if you didn't, it was the dungeons—or the noose.

Ryker liked to poke the bear, though.

"What star?"

The king sneered. "Don't play dumb with me, Ryker. It won't end well for you."

Knuckles cracked as Ryker clenched his hand in his trouser pocket. He didn't mix well with threats. No one—not even a king—could make Ryker do something he didn't wish to do. He was a slave to none.

The idea of a large bag of coins was quite enticing, though.

"Ten thousand gold coins and you have yourself a deal," Ryker replied.

King Branoc's fingers idly stroked his long, grey beard, his gaze distant as he mulled over the bounty hunter's words. Behind his intricately carved throne, guards shifted uneasily, their tension palpable. He was an older king, and for the past few years, had called upon Ryker's services, however it had been a few months since he'd graced the king's home.

King Branoc smirked. "Eight thousand, and that is my final offer."

Ryker took his time answering as his gaze roamed over his surroundings. Fine oil paintings from well-known artists and blue and red flags—the kingdom's colours—filled the throne room of the palace. Warmly lit wall sconces cast shadows across the blood red carpet that ran along the floor, all the way to the platform that held the king's throne. While the room was beautiful to look at, it declared strength loudly, but was more a measure of ego than anything.

There was no queen's throne. The king had never married; Ryker could only presume it was because he didn't want to share his treasure with anyone.

Ryker folded his arms across his chest and eyed the king warily. "There will be bounty hunters in other regions looking for it. If you wish to have it all to yourself, it's going to require a lot of skill and effort from me."

King Branoc's lip curled in defeat as his hand clenched on the arm of his chair. "Fine . . . nine thousand. But you better bring it back to me in one piece."

Ryker shrugged at the king. "Depends on how I find it."

"Just don't get any ideas on keeping it for yourself, boy. If you take off with it, I will place a bounty on your head." King Branoc squinted at Ryker from his chair. "All your little bounty hunter friends would turn on you . . . I'll make sure you never know peace again."

"I have no desire to run off with your precious star," Ryker replied as he shifted his weight.

The king leaned back on his throne, fiddling with the large sapphire ring on his left hand. "You may be the best in the business . . . but it doesn't mean I can't make your life a living hell."

There goes those threats again. Ryker wanted to voice some of his own, but the thought of a decent pile of money kept his mouth shut.

"It already is."

King Branoc grunted and dismissed Ryker with the wave of his hand.

With a small bow, Ryker spun on his heel and strode from the room. If he was being honest with himself, he really had no desire to go after a fallen star. Especially with the amount of competition there would be.

The last time a star had fallen to Earth was a hundred years ago. In fact, it fell to Earth the same night Ryker's grandfather was born, a family tale shared down through the generations. In all his thirty-two years, Ryker had never once imagined he would live to witness it unfold before his eyes.

There was no denying the bright light that streaked across the night sky the evening before. Ryker had been keeping an eye on it for months now. It grew closer and closer with each passing day. At first, he thought it may have been a planet, but after last night, that theory was blown well out of the water. Because if it was, then the ground he now stood on would most likely not exist.

Now that the star had landed, others would race to claim it. Some would be curious to see if the stories were true. Others, like Branoc, likely just want bragging rights. The ability to show off a rare treasure that no one else could have.

Did the king even know what a star was? Did Ryker?

There was a good chance he would find a useless rock, yet if his family's stories were anything to go by, then the star in fact was in human form . . . not a rock from the heavens that, after a few years, lost its value and became a paperweight on someone's desk.

If Branoc suspected the star was indeed of human form, what did he hope to gain from it?

Courtiers and servants passed him in the halls—some fae, some human. Ryker nodded when he caught their eye, but remained silent.

Being a bounty hunter took its toll and for the last few months, Ryker had been considering lessening his work load. He'd groaned internally when royal guards knocked on his door this morning, summoning him to the palace. But after hearing the king's offer, Ryker knew he couldn't say no to such a large sum of money. He would send a portion to his parents and put away the rest for his retirement.

Ryker smiled to himself at the thought. He understood the challenges of living with limited resources, so despite the way he knew his mother would huff, he sent coin back monthly, alongside reassurances of his well-being and an elusive promise to visit as soon as he could.

His parents and sister lived in Sunriver, a quaint city nestled in the southern region. It sat along Emberfell's borders, but did not belong under the jurisdiction of King Branoc's reign.

The last visit, nearly two years ago, had been wonderful, yet painful. Memories he would rather not dwell on. Home had become a place of inner turmoil, prompting him to move closer to the palace four years ago.

The tiny, ruby pendant that hung loosely around his neck felt heavier with each turn of his fingers as he twisted it. He pushed the painful memories away as he reached the stone castle's massive doorway. Sunlight hit his face and warmed his skin as he stepped outside into the lush grounds.

Emberfell was nearing the end of winter. Though spring was but days away, the ground still crunched underfoot in the chill of early morning. Well-kept gardens and flowering trees bloomed as far as the eye could see. King Branoc certainly had enough money to keep the place tidy and visually appealing.

The smell of freshly cut grass reached him as he walked towards the stables. Groundsmen busied themselves in the gardens with shears, trimming hedges and rose bushes. Ryker arrived at the stone stable where the king's horses were kept, quietly stepping inside.

A stable boy recognised him and scurried off to fetch his horse. Moments later, a large, fully black stallion appeared, and Ryker smiled. For the past decade, Charlie had never left his side. Ryker had bought him with the first significant pay he earned—tracking down and returning an escaped prisoner at the behest of the local prison.

"Thanks," Ryker spoke as he took the reins from the boy. "I hope he behaved himself."

The stable boy nodded, grinning. "Yes sir, he did. He always does."

Ryker nodded as he ran his calloused hand down the length of Charlie's glossy mane. "Yes, he does."

As they left the stables, the rhythmic clop of hooves clamoured against the cobblestones beneath them. The castle fell away behind them, and they wove through the arching gates, emerging into the city of Emberfell. The air was alive here, not with the sterile silence of court, but with the pulse of life itself. Expansive, hand-carved fountains rose like jewelled sentinels, water cascading over precious stone, glittering beneath the midday sun.

They passed patrols along the well-maintained roads—guards casting brief glances their way before returning to their watchful duties. Elves mingled with humans, their ethereal grace catching Ryker's eye as they passed. A group of siren shifters lingered near a merchant's stall, displaying conch shells doubling as tankards. Even a lone half-orc shuffled by, half-forgotten beneath a heavy cloak.

The kingdom boasted residents from all over this portion of the world that they called Sapphire Vale. All but faeries, if they truly existed. Rumour claimed some walked unseen among the people. A myth, perhaps. Or, Ryker thought, with a slow exhale, a truth veiled by something far more dangerous.

Anyone with wealth lived here, and while Ryker could afford to live in such a grand place, he chose a quieter life on the outskirts of the city—deeper in the protection of the woods.

"It's the Hound," a small girl cried from the bustling crowd.

Heat rose in Ryker's stomach, making it hard to relax. He glanced over and offered the girl a strained smile. He was used to being recognised here, but the name still caught him off guard from time to time. Some looked at him sideways, usually offering him a wide berth, choosing to walk on the other side of the street.

With a swift glance, Ryker scanned his surroundings, his eyes catching the subtleties most overlooked. A young woman's face peeked from behind a lace curtain in a window high above, her gaze fleeting. Three buildings down, to his right, an elderly woman stood cloaked in shadow, her handkerchief slipping unnoticed into the dirt.

Charlie tossed his head. Eager to be free from the confines of the city as the pair turned down a side street paved with cobblestone.

A well-dressed gentleman—possibly a siren shifter by the looks of his angular facial features—opened the door of a shiny new carriage. Ryker observed the small strip of pale skin around the ring finger on his left hand. Either he recently separated from his wife or was keeping his marriage a secret.

"Fresh meat! Fresh meat!" the butcher called from his stall.

A female elf carrying a large basket of eggs on her head crossed in front of him as a human woman holding a bunch of freshly picked wildflowers met his eye and moved to make a space between them. Wealthy couples shuffled past arm in arm and young paper boys called out the headlines as loudly as they could.

He tugged the reins, guiding Charlie towards a narrow alleyway just as the smell of freshly baked bread wafted through the air. His mouth watered at the thought of a warm slice paired perfectly with a glass of rum. He should head for home to collect the essentials he needed for his trip, but there was one task he needed to do first.

Ryker exited the bakery with a lemon tart in hand and one for the road. Who knew how long it would be until he was back? He untied Charlie and pulled himself into the saddle, setting off down the road. As he left the hustle and bustle of the city behind him, Ryker eased Charlie into a canter. Dark green smudges streaked by, the trees dissolving into a blur of colour. The crisp air rushed against him, biting at his skin as Ryker shuddered in the saddle, the chill threading through the warmth of his jacket.

Soon, an ample wooden cabin came into view and Ryker tugged Charlie to the left of the trail, heading towards home.

"Woah boy!" Ryker hissed as Charlie pulled up sharply. "I know you're dying to go on a run, and we can do that soon, but for now, contain that energy a little longer."

Worn brown boots thudded on the ground as Ryker jumped down from the saddle. He held Charlie's head in his hands as he spoke. "I am going to get some things and then we will be on our way."

Charlie snorted in response.

As Ryker drew a large iron key from his pocket, he sighed, making his way up the four sturdy wooden stairs that led to his front porch. He unlocked the front door and pushed, its rusty hinges creaking as it opened. The comforting smell of home welcomed him, the room filling with light as he stepped inside. Ryker shut the door with a quiet click, slipping the key into his pocket before shrugging off his coat and carelessly draping it over the back of a small, worn wooden chair.

There was no spare minute to light a fire or sit down and rest his legs. Time was of the essence, and he really needed to get a move on. His cupboards weren't bursting, but he gathered what was left: cheese wrapped in wax, a small pot of butter, a few apples, some dried meat strips and a bottle of rum into a canvas bag. All of this, with the fresh bread and lemon tart, would last him a few days.

In his room, he packed out of habit, tossing what he got in with what he had. He'd be faster if he didn't bog himself down with supplies.

Ryker already had his longsword hanging around his waist and two daggers, one in each boot. All he needed to do was collect his bow and arrows by the door before he left.

He hesitated in the doorway of his room, drumming his fingers against the wooden frame before returning to his dresser to fish out a handful of handmade dreamroot darts. They didn't have enough dreamroot in them to kill, but one would certainly knock a grown man out for a few hours.

He closed the door behind him, gathering the food bag and glancing around the living room. Deer-hide rugs lay strewn over the wooden floor, and two large, dark brown leather armchairs faced the stone fireplace. His eyes rested on a framed picture of his family that sat on the mantle beside a cluster of sad looking candles. He would need to purchase new ones.

His home was modest, the kind built for a small family—three bedrooms, an outhouse, and a kitchen that was just the right size for quiet meals. His fingers reached for the ruby pendant resting against his chest, absentmindedly toying with it, feeling its smooth edges. Family wasn't in the cards for him.

After Ryker was satisfied that all the windows were locked and secure, he gazed at the large map on the wall next to his front door and drew a finger along a trail, the paper crackling softly beneath his fingers. The fallen star had landed roughly a three-day ride away, and there was a good chance someone would reach it before him—though he was not particularly concerned about that. If they did, he would simply hunt them down and take the star from them.

A sturdy wooden bow and a quiver full of arrows sat by the door. Ryker grabbed them as he headed outside. Charlie patiently waited as he strapped bags and ropes to the saddle.

Ryker sighed, giving his home a last look. Soon he would be able to stay for longer than a week or so . . . soon life would slow down and maybe he could finish that canoe out the back that he'd been carving out for the last few months.

With a heave of effort, he pulled himself into the saddle, then he and Charlie set off to find the fallen star.

TWO

THE CRASH LANDING

Nova didn't dare open her eyes. If she did, it would make it all too real.

A chill drifted over her skin as she lay against solid ground. The hard, rough surface was an unusual feeling. It dug into her, scratching like thousands of tiny splinters embedded into her flesh.

FLESH!

She had flesh—like a human.

Tentatively, she dug her fingers into the soil. It trickled between the gaps of her fingers.

Suddenly, burning pain bloomed inside of her chest as she clawed at her throat. Opening her mouth to scream, that cool sensation that tickled her skin rushed inside as her chest expanded to pull more of it in. After a few more mouthfuls of the cool air, her breathing slowed and her heart rate resumed its sturdy rhythm—she forgot humans needed oxygen to survive.

The scent of damp minerals and organic decay wafted all around. Flitting creatures she'd only ever viewed from the heavens sang their early morning song. She was definitely no longer at home in Ara.

It was all too foreign, the smells, the sounds and who knew what the sights looked like.

A sharp object poked her in the back, sending a piercing sensation through her spine. Nova was too afraid to move for fear the discomfort would only intensify. However, if she was going to look at herself, work out her surroundings and find some sort of shelter against the chill, she was going to need to see where she was.

With a slow blink, she opened her eyes. All around her was a blur as her eyes adjusted to the light. Shadows loomed overhead, swaying like otherworldly beings, and for a moment Nova wondered if she was still in the celestial realms, even if not in Ara. The gentle push and pull of her chest reminded her that she was definitely no longer home.

Feeling somewhat brave, Nova rolled onto her side, taking her time and allowing her body to adjust to her movements.

Trees.

That's what those looming shadows were.

Nova leaned on her elbow, pushing herself up into a sitting position. She blinked. The crater she'd left was enormous. No wonder her body ached. Did she really cause that?

Fingers—all ten of them—wiggled in front of her. Human fingers. Nova lightly dragged them over her face, feeling for her eyes, nose, and lips. She then dragged a hand down one arm, watching as the skin dipped beneath her fingers. It was smooth to the touch, yet warm and solid.

She was in a real human body—a completely bare one at that.

With a quick glance at her hands again, Nova wondered if she could use the powers she wielded in the heavens here in this part of the world. However, now was probably not the right time to find out.

Nova grit her teeth as she tried to get to her feet, but as soon as she moved her left leg, she cried out.

In Ara, the concept of pain was foreign. There, her form was light and untouchable, her existence a constant hum of illuminated energy. But now, as the sharp ache pulsed through her, her breath hitched—a sensation she had never experienced before. She pressed a hand to her ankle, her fingers trembling as they traced the unfamiliar sting. The discomfort was jarring. Nova rubbed her brow with the back of her hand. How long had she been here in this large, rocky pit? How would she find out where here was? Did it even matter? The last five years of spinning uncontrollably through the galaxy were finally over.

Before this ordeal took place, she'd been happily shining in the Ara galaxy, where the Creator had placed her. She'd looked down on Earth and watched humans for over a hundred years and secretly hoped one day she might actually experience what life would be like on the green and blue ball that hung on an invisible thread in the atmosphere.

This was not quite how she thought it would happen.

A phantom pain blossomed from the centre of her chest, and Nova instinctively reached for it. It was hard for her to see, but as she pulled her hand away, a star pattern glowed, imprinted into her skin.

It was pale blue—some of the star's auras in the celestial realms shone different shades of blue or green, others, pinks, golds or lilac. Now, she had a branding from the home she may never see again.

With a quiet groan, Nova lay back against the ground again and stared into the early morning sky above. Pale colours of lilac, pink, and yellow painted across it, promising that the sun would soon rise. She'd studied humans for years, but she'd never realised their sky looked like this from the other side.

Her sisters faintly twinkled amongst the lilac hues and the organ inside of her chest pulled against its strains. Would she ever see them again?

Something wet and warm escaped from the corner of her eye and ran down her cheek. Nova brushed it with her fingertips. Was this a tear? Is this what it felt like to cry?

She squeezed her eyes shut, her chest rising and falling with ragged breaths. Emotions surged inside her like a storm ready to break. She pressed her palms against the cool Earth, grounding herself in its steady presence. The rough texture of the soil and the faint pulse of life beneath her fingers slowed the chaos in her mind. With each inhale, the air filled her lungs, a little steadier, a little calmer, until the overwhelming tide of feeling began to ebb away.

She needed to get up. There was no point lying here. Someone would have surely seen her arrival. Perhaps she could seek refuge somewhere? Maybe a small town would be close by and she could ask for shelter.

Of course, before that, she needed to attempt to use her legs. Learn how to walk—if she could.

Her eyes shot open at the sound of stones skittering across the ground's surface above her. She wasn't alone.

There was nowhere for her to hide and there was no way of knowing if they were friend or foe. All she could do was lay as still as she could and watch as two hulking figures appeared over the lip of the crater before sliding down the crumbling walls, making their way towards her with heavy steps.

"Well, what do we have 'ere then, ay." The voice of a human touched her ears and Nova shuddered at its tone. It took a moment for the words to settle. Their language was strange, less melodious than what she was used to. The soft hum of her sisters, so gentle, so sweet—not the harsh, grating voice of a human.

Two sets of beady eyes loomed above her. Off-white teeth grinned in the early morning light.

Nova sat up, but before she had time to think or react, one of them reached down to smother her nose and mouth with some sort of cloth. The scent was choking, her eyes watered as she struggled to free it from her face. It was no use, and within moments, Nova succumbed to the darkness.

Nova stirred, her head lolling gently as her eyes fluttered open. Heat, more intense than she'd ever experienced, bathed her face. She attempted to raise her hand to shield her eyes from the bright light, only to realise they were tightly bound to the brown object she was seated on. Straining against the restraints, she tried to free herself.

Why was she tied to this . . . saddle? That's what humans called them, right? The buttery leather was soft under her hands. Warm from the sun's gaze upon it. Surely there was no need for her wrists to be tied to it?

The hard press of something solid pushed against her back. One of the strangers was sitting behind her on the horse.

Horse . . . she was on a horse.

Nova had awed at their beauty from her home in the heavens. She'd always wondered what it would feel like to touch one. Run her fingers through their silky manes.

"No need to pull at those bindings, love, you're not going anywhere." Warm breath brushed her ear and Nova squirmed away from it.

"I demand you let me go!"

"Not going to happen," the male chuckled.

The sound of his laugh sent a shiver down her spine. It wasn't a laugh of joy, but one that made Nova feel like the male was very pleased with himself. It infuriated her even more.

"Why do you have me tied to this saddle?" Nova yanked on her bindings again.

The male caught both her wrists in one of his large hands. "So ya don't run away."

"Why am I not allowed to be free? What do you plan on doing with me?"

"Well, a face as pretty as yours will sell for a handsome penny to the right person, but who you really are will get me and my brother a fortune."

Nova was aware of her heart rate rising as she swallowed slowly at the male's words.

In all her years of looking down at Earth and wishing she could walk amongst the humans, this isn't how she dreamed it would be. Not tied to the saddle of a horse, with a very painful ankle, a smelly brute of a man behind her and this weird feeling in her mouth, like she'd devoured a whole mouthful of sand.

"I don't think you have any right to sell me off, and how do you really know who I am? Unhand me at once!" Nova squirmed in the saddle.

"There was no missing your grand entrance last night. A rare occurrence around these parts of town, but we've heard the stories. We know you ain't a regular woman. A fallen star like yourself is worth thousands of gold coins. And you may think I have no right to sell you off, but around here it's first in best dressed and for once me and my brother would like to be the best-dressed men for miles around," the male spoke as his arms tightened around her waist.

"Well, I hope not all men are rude like you are," Nova huffed, giving in to her constraints.

The male on the second horse up ahead laughed. "I think you'll be sorely disappointed."

Nova glanced around at her surroundings. It was just her and the two males who looked almost exactly the same as each other, plodding along on horseback on a rough rocky road with rows of green trees on either side of them. Both males had short brown hair, cut close to their scalp. Their eyes were the colour of sad clouds. Neither held a smile for long, and their voices carried only crude words and harsh laughter.

Nova squirmed in the saddle. "Who are you anyway?"

"I'm Dante and that's Finnian, but most people just call us The Twins," Dante answered.

Nova could definitely see the uncanny resemblance in both males, good looking enough in an odd way, but not enough to make her flutter her lashes at either of them. That's what women did when they wanted to encourage a male, wasn't it? Secretly, she hoped, not all men looked like these two either, or Earth was going to be very disappointing.

"Can you at least tell me where I am?" Nova mumbled.

Dante shooed a flying insect away. "This part of the world is Sapphire Vale. And if you were to look at a map, this region 'ere is Emberfell."

Despite being tied to a horse, sitting with a male, she'd rather not be. Nova couldn't help but marvel at how beautiful Emberfell was.

Cold air whipped at her face, and Nova shuddered once again. Maybe it was normal to feel like this. They'd draped some kind of fabric around her shoulders and tied it loosely around her waist. She hadn't looked like this when she landed. Was this what humans considered clothing? If so, someone needed to show them how to dress properly, because this was terrible.

"It's getting dark bruv, we should find some place to make camp for the night," Dante called out to his brother.

"Yeah, alright," Finnian called back.

Neither man put her at ease, and Nova could sense something was off. The way their eyes kept drifting over her, sizing her up, sent a wave of heat through her stomach, while her skin turned cold and clammy.

Nothing about them felt good.

Finnian steered his horse to the right, off the beaten track and through the undergrowth, making a path with his horse's feet. Dante followed behind. Nova felt uneasy. Surely staying on a well-known road might give her the opportunity to cry out for help if someone came along. Heading into the dense forest would not allow for that.

Deeper in the woods, the brothers brought the horses to a halt.

"We rest here and then leave at the first sight of dawn," Finnian grunted.

"Obviously—I'm not daft."

Finnian snorted. "Could 'ave fooled me."

"Go lick a doorknob, Fin." Dante slid from the horse, but left Nova tied to the saddle.

Nova listened as the two men muttered quietly to each other, their voices rising and falling in a way so unlike the fluid communication she shared with her sisters in Ara. From her perch on the horse, she observed them closely. It seemed her celestial powers were translating their strange language into something she could understand.

"We will just keep her tied up over there by that tree. We can take turns watching through the night and before we know it, come morning we can be on our way again," Dante said as he moved away and squatted down to build a fire. Finnian grunted in response as he came towards Nova and untied her from the horse. With a rough tug, he pulled her down.

Fire speared through her leg as her feet hit the ground. Nova cried out, but did her best not to crumple on the spot.

"What's your problem then?" Finnian barked.

Squinting her eyes in distaste, Nova fired back, "If you must know, I have injured my ankle and I am in a lot of pain."

Finnian rolled his eyes as he scooped her up into his broad arms and carried her to the base of a large tree, sitting her down on a log stump before tying her against it.

"Don't move," he said as he walked back towards the horses.

He returned moments later with a small, round leather pouch—similar in feeling to the saddle she rode on earlier—and a piece of something that was white and brown. "Here . . . have this."

Nova eyed him warily. "What is it, and should I be afraid?"

"Only if you're not afraid of dying . . . It's water for drinking and bread for eating. Now take it before I change my mind."

Tentatively, Nova grasped it and brought the bread up to her nose. It smelled okay and looked okay, so she touched it to her lips, taking a tiny bite. It was crumbly and bland in her mouth, but her stomach growled in response as she slowly ate. If only she could get rid of the dry feeling inside her throat.

It took a few attempts to twist the lid off the container, but when she brought it to her nose, it had no smell at all. The inside sloshed strangely. Putting it to her lips, she let the cool liquid wash over her tongue and glide down her throat. Within moments, the dry feeling was gone, and Nova felt refreshed. Water was definitely a favourite of the two Earthly items she'd just inhaled.

She watched the pair intently as they set up a small camp. No shelters, just a fire and some food. Nova was grateful for the moon's gentle glow. Its beams seeped into the small parts of her exposed skin and rejuvenated her soul.

She wanted to test out her powers. Could she use them here on Earth like she could in the galaxy? If she could, would it work in her favour to free her from her captors?

Nova glanced at the twins as they scoffed down their bread and water, wiping the back of their hands across their mouths before using their trousers as a cleaning cloth. Nova shuddered. Something in her gut told her to keep as much of herself a secret as possible.

It was best to stay put for the evening, rest her body until she could use the sun's light to find a way to escape.

The rest of the evening was uneventful. Nova remained tied to a tree and the two men took turns watching their surroundings.

Orange flames from the fire put on a show. The flames produced inky shadows that danced along the forest floor, up the thick tree trunks and over Nova's shivering body.

"So star . . . can you grant me a wish?" Dante grunted across the flames.

Nova eyed the twins, both grinning from ear to ear. "No, I can not."

Finnian huffed. "I thought all stars could grant wishes."

"Well, you thought wrong."

Dante placed his hands behind his head and leaned back against the rotting log behind him. "Or perhaps you're telling us lies."

"Maybe she's more valuable to us as a magical tool rather than selling her to the highest bidder, bruv," Finnian muttered.

"You're a magical tool," Dante spat

Finnian smirked. "I've got one . . ."

"I know . . . We're twins." Dante said as he winked at Nova.

She closed her eyes at their conversation. The pair of them were insufferable.

"How do we know she's magical at all?" Dante spoke, his rough voice grating on her ears.

"She's a trophy, more like it. If she had powers, we couldn't have grabbed her so easily."

Nova opened her eyes and looked at the twins from her place against the tree trunk. "You're right. I don't have any powers. In fact, I'm very boring. You might as well let me go."

"Don't think so," Finnian grinned.

It was worth a try, right?

The twins muttered to themselves as Nova's eyes grew heavy. She wanted to stay awake and plot her escape, but the pain in her ankle begged her to rest, and the warmth from the fire sang to her a silent lullaby, and before she could fight it, sleep claimed her once again.

Walking. Walking. Walking.

That's all they ever seemed to do. Walking this way and then walking that way. Walking up a hill and then walking down a hill.

Nova felt like they might just walk all the way back to the galaxy at this point.

When she awoke in the early morning, the two men dozed, and she'd tried her best to summon her powers. All she managed to do was make her skin glow. Perhaps it would take some time for her body to adjust to the foreign atmosphere— or maybe they simply didn't work.

"Must I be on this horse for a moment longer?" she groaned softly.

"If you'd rather walk behind the horse . . . then by all means, be my guest," Dante replied, sarcasm lacing his voice.

Nova rolled her eyes. "To be honest, I think I would rather walk behind a horse right now than sit for one more second with either of you."

Dante pulled the horse to a stop and got down, violently pulling Nova behind him. His rough, calloused hands dug into her arm, and she uttered a cry as her foot hit the ground.

"Be careful, bruv. We don't want damaged goods, do we now?" Finnian hissed.

"Even as damaged goods, she'll still be worth more than we've ever earned."

"Doesn't mean we should break it before someone buys it," Finnian replied.

Nova rolled her eyes. Why did she have to be captured by these two idiots? Why couldn't it have been someone nice?

Dante was tugging her along when a rustling from some bushes nearby caught his attention. He stilled and Nova lightly bumped into his solid frame at his sudden stop.

"What are we doi—"

"Shut up," Dante hissed.

How dare he tell her to shut up? No wonder her sisters were never interested in coming to Earth like Nova had been—especially if this was how humans treated each other.

"Get your blade ready, bruv," Finnian whispered gruffly as he slowly got down from his horse.

Nova stood still, shaking. Something tightened in her chest, sending a shiver down her spine. Her skin prickled, almost as if every hair was standing on end. Her muscles tensed, ready to flee. She didn't know what was happening, yet she knew this feeling was horrid, and she didn't want to feel it again. Was something coming for them? Should she run and hide? If she did, where would she go?

With swift movement, Finnian slapped his hand against the side of his neck, looking shocked and red in the face. He dropped to the ground in a crumpled heap moments later.

Rough hands grabbed Nova around the waist, and she squealed. The edge of a blade found the soft skin of her throat and she winced as it pressed in, a warning..

"Come any closer and she's as good as dead," Dante threatened.

The pair encountered silence.

Nova's eyes darted back and forth. Whatever was out there was very good at blending in with the shadows of the forestry.

A soft, whooshing sound whistled past her ear, followed by a grunt. Dante's rough hands let go of her body, and the blade he held against her throat clattered to the ground.

He dropped in a heap, just as his brother had.

Nova trembled, still searching for the silent attacker. "Please . . . don't hurt me. I mean no harm," she called to the trees.

Movement caught her eye, and a figure stepped casually from the shadows. Loose gravel crunched beneath the male's boots, shifting slightly with each step as if he had not a care in the world. His expression was hollow, free of emotion.

Nova drew in a breath as he neared.

Black shaggy hair skimmed just below his ears, covering part of his forehead. Russet eyes trailed over her body from head to toe. He wore well-fitted black and brown clothing with a long silver blade hanging at his side. It glinted in the sun, and Nova thought it was breathtaking . . . seeing a deadly weapon for the first time.

His form was about the same size as the two brothers who currently lay unconscious on the forest floor, yet something about the way he walked made him different.

Instinctively, all she wanted to do was run. This male made her tremble more than the other two had. His eyes were cold and unforgiving. This was someone who shouldn't be tried or tested. Why was she attracting all of these unpleasant males?

"My lady." The stranger took a bow.

His voice washed over her body. Filling all the cracks with a soothing balm. It was deep and smooth—tickling her ears—making her cheeks feel warm.

"Who are you?" Nova questioned cautiously.

The man stood and placed his hands in his trouser pockets. "Ryker."

She stepped back until she bumped up against the warmth of the horse behind her, eyeing him. "Please go away . . . Ryker."

"Can't do that."

"Why not?"

"Because I've been ordered to take you to the king."

Nova stilled against the horse. "Why?"

"Because you're a very special guest here on Earth and King Branoc wants to meet you."

Was who she was that obvious to these humans?

"Who said I was special? What if I don't want to go?"

"Anyone with sight can see that you're the star that fell from the sky and . . . you don't have a choice."

What was with all of these humans presuming they could take her and do what they pleased? Surely there were other options.

As she quickly glanced around though, Nova could see that she really had little choice. Her wrists were bound and her ankle ached every time she moved. Even if she tried to escape, she wouldn't make it very far.

"Did you kill them?" Nova nodded her head towards the males on the ground.

Ryker flicked his gaze down towards the men and took a small step towards her. "Unfortunately, no. And if we don't get a move on soon, they will come to and I can't promise it will be a pretty sight." His eyes bore into hers the closer he came. His nearness sent a thrill through Nova's body, and her heart leapt into an erratic state.

Was it his scent that brought the wave of buzzing energy coursing through her veins, making her heart race and her breath quicken? Or perhaps it was the sensation she felt before—the one she never wanted to feel again. Something about this male told her she should be very careful.

"If I go with you, could you untie these ropes for me?"

"Like I said before . . . you don't have a choice and no I will not."

Nova held back the foreign emotions coursing through her body. "Is there anything I can do to change your mind?"

Ryker reached for the rope hanging from her wrists. "Behave yourself and I'll think about it."

Warm fingertips brushed against her cold, pale flesh as Ryker reached for the rope. Tiny bumps rose to the surface of her skin.

"Are you going to behave?"

"I guess you'll find out." Nova looked up at him.

Ryker's gaze held no sympathy for her situation. His heart matched the icy coldness of his eyes. How could anyone live like that?

For a moment, neither of them spoke.

Was this another man she needed to free herself from at the first possible chance? Did she even want to go with him to see his king? What if that was a worse fate than running away? Yet, where would she even go if she did?

It was Ryker who moved first. Clearing his throat, he placed the rope in one hand as he took the reins of the horse in the other. "Shall we . . . ?"

The way his words trailed off gave Nova the impression that he wished to know her name. Should she give it to him? What difference would it make if she did or didn't? With a small sigh, she answered.

"My name is Nova . . . Nova Seraphine."

THREE

THE CELESTIAL ENCOUNTER

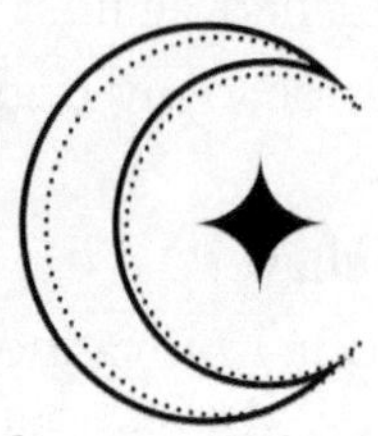

N*ova Seraphine.*

Even her name was beautiful.

From the moment Ryker laid eyes on his target, he'd struggled to breathe. In the last four years, no one had made his heart falter like it did when his eyes beheld the rare celestial beauty.

His gaze drifted to her hair, a cascade of pure white silk that defied gravity floating weightlessly around her. Each strand shimmered with a delicate glow, like threads of tiny diamonds suspended in the air. The sharp angles of her face carved a path to her pink lips, the fullness of them slightly parting beneath his stare. High cheekbones cradled eyes as vivid and green as the sea. Her ivory skin emitted a gentle hum of viridian light, as if she were encased in an ethereal fog.

Ryker's throat tightened. If gravity had no hold on her, then how did she pull him so irresistibly into her orbit?

It was almost unreal, seeing someone from a different realm. The family stories were indeed true.

Too bad she was a job. Another pretty thing to sit inside Branoc's castle.

When he had found the crater, it was empty—as he'd predicted it would be—but it hadn't taken him long to pick up the direction she'd gone. There'd been two sets of hoofprints, so Ryker stuck to the shadows, wanting to see what he was up against before approaching the group.

It wasn't his first encounter with the twins, and he knew from experience that a quick dose of dreamroot would knock them out for a few hours.

As the sun dipped lower in the sky, casting long shadows across the rugged terrain, Ryker led the way. The rhythmic clip-clop of hooves was the only sound in the quiet wilderness around them. Nova glowering on one of the Twin's horses—tethered to Charlie's saddle—behind him. He'd kept her wrists bound, harnessing her to the saddle. He couldn't afford to have her running off.

He pulled a small flask from his jacket pocket and took a swig of rum, careful to remain alert of their surroundings. He definitely didn't need to be surprised by an owlbear—also known as a Galanthor—or worse, a Lycan. The ancient mythical creatures, remnants of gods long forgotten, still prowled the Earth, rearing their ugly heads now and then. Ancient magic didn't seem to be in use anymore, but the effects of it still remained. One could never be too careful when venturing through the forests . . . Ryker would know.

He shifted, turning to look over his shoulder. Nova's glow was gone. Her diamond strand hair, limp against her delicate frame. She kept slipping in the saddle, her energy clearly waning.

It was too early, and they had too far to travel before they could camp for the night. Especially when they were in an area known for odd creatures whose teeth were sharper than the blade he carried at his side. Ryker knew he needed to do something, or he was going to have damaged goods on his hands. King Branoc would not appreciate that.

Ryker slowed his pace and turned Charlie around.

"Nova," he called, pulling up beside her. She looked at him, eyes heavy with fatigue.

"I'm fine," she murmured, but the droop of her shoulders and the paleness of her face said otherwise.

Ryker shook his head, dismounting swiftly. "No, you're not."

Without another word, he offered her a hand. She felt so weak and fragile as he helped her onto Charlie's back.

She's just a job.

Once satisfied everything was in place, he climbed up behind Nova, his arm wrapping firmly around her waist to keep her steady. "Lean back against me," he instructed, and she did, her head resting on his chest.

Red welts had already formed on her wrists, but he didn't want to unbind the ropes yet. Apart from her apparent fatigue, there was no guarantee that she would stay put, so for now, they would have to remain.

They continued for a few more hours. Ryker was grateful for the silence while the star slept. Soon, they should make camp before the daylight was completely gone.

Soft whimpers slipped from Nova's lips. Ryker glanced down at her furrowed brows, a sign that whatever images filled her dreams were far from pleasant.

"Nova . . ." Ryker nudged her.

The star remained asleep.

He pulled Charlie to a halt, brushing Nova's hair from the side of her face. "Nova."

She stirred and sat up sleepily. "What is it . . . are we there?"

Ryker's heart jumped at the sound of her sweet voice. "No, but you were crying in your sleep."

"Sorry. If it bothers you, you can just leave me here."

"You'd like that, wouldn't you?"

Nova shifted in the saddle, her hands fidgeting with each other. Ryker speculated that she probably did, in fact, wish to be let go. Most of the humans he caught and took back to their rightful places—prison mainly—would probably wish the same thing.

Her body shook against his chest as a brisk breeze blew through the trees. Too long had it been since he'd held a woman against his chest. The softness of her figure melted against his muscular body like honey on a warm tongue. It was very hard to focus on . . . anything.

"You're shaking," Ryker voiced.

"Is it not normal to shake like this?"

Ryker shook his head. "No, you're freezing. Here, have this."

He shrugged his cloak off and placed it around her shoulders. "This will help until we can get you something decent to wear."

He should have offered sooner. Of course, she was going to feel the temperature. It was still early spring, and she was only wrapped in a thin blanket that the Twins must have tied around her.

He found it surprising that they offered her that much courtesy.

Nova pulled the cloak close and nestled her back against his chest. "Thank you."

Ryker closed his eyes, drawing on every internal strength he had to push past the smell of her hair and the way her body fit against his.

This is a business deal. Nothing more. Besides, he wasn't interested in getting involved with anyone right now—or ever. Especially someone from a different realm.

"We are still a day or so away from the palace, but you need clothes and I need to drop these horses into town," Ryker said as they meandered along.

It was a few hours until sunset, but with the outfit she wore, if she didn't find something thicker soon, she could catch a cold.

Could a star catch a cold?

He was well aware of the risks he would take by entering a village with Nova. No doubt there were many people on the lookout for the star right now. But the extra horses were unnecessary and clearly she needed some clothing. Thankfully, neither her skin nor her hair was glowing like it had been earlier in the day.

She nodded softly. "I would love to wear something more than this odd design those brutes dressed me in."

Ryker smiled behind her. The innocence that oozed from her being was like a breath of fresh air, something he knew he should breathe in, but knowing himself all too well—he wouldn't.

The smell of smoke reached him, signalling there was a village close by. He knew this part of Emberfell well enough. Turning off the trail, he guided Charlie expertly through the forest. Moments later, sounds of metal clanging and wood chopping filled the air as the village came into view.

Goats frolicked in pastures, bells attached to their necks with rope. Logs were stacked by the side of the road, ready for builders of houses and barns. It was quite a large town.

Ryker's senses heightened as they entered. Get in and get out. And if she glows again, wrap her in his cloak tighter. Charlie slowed to a stop and huffed his appreciation. Ryker eased from his back and slid to the ground. "Here . . . we need to adjust your makeshift dress a little so you don't look like a . . . crazy person."

"What's a crazy person?" Nova asked, as she allowed him to lift her down.

"Ah . . . Well, never mind. We just need to make you look decent." Ryker motioned towards the fabric.

With inexperienced hands, Ryker tugged, pulled and tweaked the fabric until he was satisfied that what she wore resembled more of a dress than a blanket.

"Now, let's get one thing straight," Ryker spoke as he stood in front of her. "I'm going to untie these ropes, but if you even think about trying to run, the next few days are going to be very uncomfortable for you."

Nova's face paled and her eyes darkened. "What does that mean?"

"Muck around and you'll find out."

He tried not to let his heart sink as her gaze dropped to the ground, where it remained until he reached for her bindings. The touch of her soft hand against his rough palm was like a soothing balm upon a cut as he untied the ropes around her wrists. It was a feeling he didn't know he'd been craving until this very moment.

Dousing the fire that was scarcely a flicker inside his soul, Ryker steadied his breathing, and led them into town. He was painfully aware of every movement and every eye that glanced their way.

Thankfully, Nova remained close by his side. He glanced down, noticing the way she limped ever so slightly. His brows knitted. Perhaps she'd hurt herself? He'd have to ask her later.

Small wooden houses and grey stone shops lined the main street, their rooftops pitched and weathered by time. The town lacked the grandeur of the city surrounding the Emberfell Palace, but it had a quiet charm. The cobblestone paths were swept clean, flower boxes brimming with pansies and marigolds hung under the windowsills, and the air carried a faint scent of fresh bread from a nearby bakery.

Ryker's mouth watered at the idea of a zesty lemon tart.

They stopped outside a modest stable tucked between two shops. Ryker flicked his gaze towards Nova before handing over the reins of the two extra horses they'd collected on their journey. "Keep them," he said to the stable owner. "Consider it a gift."

The man blinked in surprise, but accepted with a grateful nod.

"Tell me, is there a dressmaker here in town?" Ryker asked the gentleman.

"About five buildings down."

Ryker nodded in reply before ushering Nova back into the crowds of people, his hand lightly gripping her upper arm.

Sideways glances were evident as the pair moved through the crowds with Charlie in tow. Ryker hurried them along, wanting to get Nova indoors and away from prying eyes—not that she seemed to notice any. She was too busy staring at all the colourful wares people were offering from their carts and store fronts. He felt his heart shift towards her as he watched the amazement of the human world written on her face.

Here was this innocent creature experiencing his part of the world—Sapphire Vale—for the first time, probably thinking that he was taking her to safety.

But he was taking her to Branoc.

Dread laced through Ryker's veins, turning to a searing heat in his blood. Usually it was so easy to find his target, hand them in, and finish the job. Not with this one, though. Something deep down inside of his chest was screaming to let her go.

Was being a pretty object in Branoc's possession better than being sold to the highest bidder that would do who-knows-what to her?

Pushing his guilt aside, Ryker quietly took a deep breath and focused on the task ahead. She wasn't his problem to worry about. She was just a job.

Nova halted, facing the cobblestoned area that housed a large fountain. He looked in the direction of her fixation. A skilled puppeteer manipulated a marionette, bringing it to life with practised movements. The wooden puppet, dressed in colourful fabrics, danced and twirled on the small stage, its joints moving with an uncanny grace. Children gathered around, their faces alight with wonder. Ryker wished there was time for pleasantries—unfortunately, there was not.

Her eyes tore from the sight, the light in them dulling as Ryker tugged on her arm. "We must keep moving."

The dressmaker's shop came into view and he steered them towards it, grateful for the quiet space as soon as the door closed behind them. Nova took a small step from his side and gently dragged her fingers along the edge of something pink and frilly, hanging limply from its hanger.

"Can I help you, sir?" a cool voice greeted them.

Ryker cleared his throat and nodded. "My—friend here needs a simple gown and some undergarments, please."

The woman—tall and slender—eyed both Nova and Ryker warily, but he couldn't blame her. It was certainly an odd sight—a rugged-looking man stepping into the store with a woman draped in nothing but a blanket following close behind.

"If we could do this swiftly?" Ryker's voice was smooth, yet forceful.

"You will need to give me a moment, but I think I have something out the back I could adjust for her," the woman replied.

Ryker nodded and ushered Nova to follow the woman, who was walking towards some dressing rooms.

Nova looked at him hesitantly for a second.

He lifted one corner of a brow. "Remember . . . don't try anything funny."

Nova squared her shoulders, her chin held high as she twisted and followed the woman from the room, her footsteps silent on the wooden floor.

Ryker stood alone in the small room. He felt odd being surrounded by all the female attire. Beautifully folded lace undergarments sat in piles on a round wooden table. Displayed on a shelf were a few rows of dainty brown leather boots and mannequins wearing elegant dresses of silk and ribbons lined the window front. Fiddling with the pendant around his neck, Ryker sighed and sat on the settee while he waited for Nova to return.

This would be the last time he'd accept a job where a female was involved.

FOUR

THE BROWN BOOTS

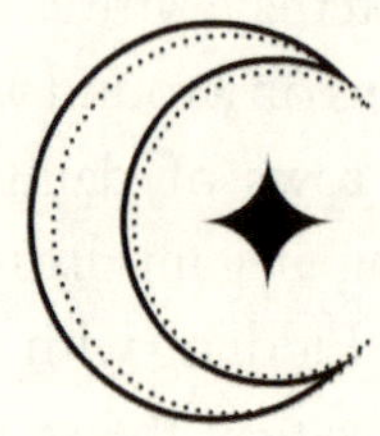

The woman ushered her into a change room, handing her some undergarments, with the promise of returning with a gown. Nova looked the lacy white items over and struggled for a moment to work out where to wear them. It was a struggle trying to work out where her legs went and where her arms went. At one point, Nova was certain she'd put the bottom half of the undergarments on her head. After a few minutes of fussing, she managed to get them on—in the right places.

"May I come in?" the woman called lightly.

"Oh yes, please do."

The woman slipped into the small curtained room and hung a simple gown from a hook on the wall. It was light teal and made from a plain fabric that was soft to the touch. Taking it from the hanger, the woman scrunched it in her hands and placed it over Nova's head. After Nova put her arm in the sleeves, the woman turned her around to button up the back of the dress. It gathered around her slender waist and hugged her upper body. Long sleeves encased her arms and instantly made her feel warmer.

Nova smiled at her reflection in the mirror as she smoothed down the skirt of her gown. This was a much better fit than that silly piece of cloth Dante or Finnian had dressed her in, although she was grateful they'd at least put something on her.

"There, all done. Are the undergarments to your liking as well?"

Nova nodded. "Yes, thank you."

Despite his gruff exterior, Ryker had been rather gentle with her, so why was she afraid to go back out to him? He'd warned her not to do anything she might regret, but finally being alone made her question even for a moment if she might try to escape somehow.

The woman opened the changing room curtain and stepped out of the way. Nova allowed the idea of trying to escape to play in her mind for only a moment. If she told the woman the predicament she was in, could she even trust the woman would help her? If she did, maybe she could find refuge somewhere in the village.

However, she was a star. A foreign being in a foreign place. There was no proof she could trust anyone at this point.

Maybe being with Ryker was safer than travelling on her own. He was certainly less offensive than the twins.

She offered the woman a smile and made her way to the front of the store.

Nova cleared her throat and Ryker looked up, his russet eyes dragging themselves over her figure. He was close enough for Nova to see the flecks of dark brown and gold in his irises. Yet they held no light.

"Is this alright?"

Ryker rose from the settee and ran a hand through his inky waves before turning to face the woman who now stood behind the counter. "She will also need some boots. Let me know what I owe."

Warmth rose in her chest. He'd looked at her like the dress pleased him, but he'd ignored her question. Clearly, he was not even remotely interested in what she wore. What did she care, anyway?

He moved to the counter to pay the woman, while Nova took a moment to glance around at all the pretty items in the store. It looked like it was fun to be a human woman. There were so many pretty dresses and colours to choose from. Fabrics in shades of the oceans, forests, barren lands and flower meadows she'd witnessed from the heavens.

Two young girls entered the store. Nova watched as the girls laughed together, holding up gowns and twirling them around, their smiles wide and carefree. The colours seemed to dance around them, a whirlwind of silks and lace, like petals caught in the wind.

Returning to her side, Ryker held a pair of shoes in his hands. "Sit here and put these on."

Nova glared at him for a moment before she sat down on the settee. Ryker folded his arms across his chest and watched her intently, which made her feel . . . Well, she didn't know what it made her feel. Being human was hard. The best she could describe it was—a wave of heat washing over her, while her heart raced. Whatever that emotion was, she was feeling it.

With one boot in hand, Nova tried to place it on her foot. Her heel caught on the back of the opening, making it hard for her to push her foot into the boot. It was no use. She didn't know how to put shoes on, especially ones with strings attached.

Ryker must have sensed that she did not know what she was doing, because he sighed and crouched down. After slipping on one boot, he then attempted the second one.

"Ouch," Nova winced with discomfort.

"What is it?"

With a scowl on her face, Nova pointed to her ankle. "This foot here hurts."

"Why didn't you tell me?" Ryker asked.

Nova shrugged. "Why? Is it important?"

Ryker smirked. "I guess not if you aren't complaining."

Nova rolled her eyes. Just because she didn't complain didn't mean it wasn't painful. She returned her gaze to Ryker's hands. They fiddled with the laces, brushing ever so lightly against the tender skin on her ankles. His touch was soft as feathers, yet the heat of it seared against her skin like a burning weight. He finished and stood, so she followed.

She waved as Ryker bid the lady goodbye, and the pair left the store. He moved with such silence and fluency, unlike the Twins who seemed to fumble over themselves and make a lot of noise. Regardless of the circumstances, she'd rather be with him right now than those other two brutes.

With his back to her, Nova couldn't help but notice just how well the clothing he wore fit his bulking frame. Arms the size of small tree trunks, broad shoulders that boasted well toned muscle covered by a layer of skin the colour of deep golden sunsets and hands large enough to engulf hers. He towered over her, but she didn't feel intimidated by him. More than anything, Nova was intrigued.

It had only been a few days since she'd arrived in Emberfell, but already there were so many differences that she'd seen. The climate was one of those differences. She didn't need to bother about temperature before, but here, as soon as the sun began its descent, the absence of its warmth on her body was certainly felt.

Nova's eyes grew wide at all the stalls, offering fruits and vegetables, wishing she could stop and view them all closer. There were too many to choose from.

They passed by a stall full to the brim of wooden buckets filled with an array of freshly cut flowers. Nova tried not to let her mouth hang open as her eyes dragged over every blossom. She couldn't name many of them, but one in particular drew her in. It was huge compared to the other blooms. Bright yellow petals, a thick green stalk, and in the centre was a colossal amount of black seeds. It reminded Nova of the eldest sister in the heavens—the sun.

She ran a finger along the yellow petals, a grin forming on her face. She wanted to scoop the entire bucket full into her arms and take them wherever she went—a reminder of what this part of the world could offer.

Ryker glanced over his shoulder, motioning her to move along, so Nova bid the flower stall farewell and kept walking down the bustling streets.

She passed the spice stall next. It was a riot of colours and aromas, with burlap sacks overflowing with vibrant powders and dried herbs. Among them, an unfamiliar object stood out—a jar of long, dark pods exuding a deep, rich fragrance that mingled with the sharper spices around it.

Nova stopped and bent forward to inhale it. The scent was soothing, like a soft breeze on a warm day, cutting through the sharper notes of the other displayed spices.

It was so familiar, as if she'd smelled it before.

Her gaze flicked to her captor's back as he stopped a few feet ahead. Ryker turned to face her. "We need a few supplies . . ."

"What is this?" Nova asked, pointing to the jar.

"That's vanilla."

"Do you put it on your body?"

Ryker shrugged. "I suppose it can be used for both its taste and its aroma."

Nova nodded and took the opportunity to reach for a peach as Ryker spoke with the stallholder. Its pale orange skin was fuzzy in her hand as she lifted it to her nose. She took a deep breath in. The most delicious scent filled her senses, and her stomach growled in response. Another delightful aroma.

"Are you going to pay for that?" a voice touched her ears.

As she looked up, she encountered the face of a young boy.

"I'm sorry . . . I."

"Here." Ryker's smooth voice answered as he handed the boy a small silver coin.

Nova's brow furrowed as they paid for the item and moved away from the cart. Ryker took her hand and pulled her aside, his voice low and brusque. "We can't touch food if we don't plan on buying it."

The feel of his warm hand on hers again sent shivers up her spine and made her body feel instantly tingly. Warmth spread to her cheeks as she locked eyes with the handsome, brown-eyed man before her.

"I was only going to smell it." Nova threw at him.

Ryker released her hand and gripped her upper arm once again, guiding her through the crowds. "Just don't touch anything."

With a huff, Nova shoved the food into her dress pocket. "If it bothers you so much, I'll pay you back."

"How? Did you happen to find a coin in that old blanket they wrapped you in?"

Nova ignored him, turning away to look at the sights. He truly was so pleasant to deal with.

With a shove, Ryker guided them through the busy crowds, stopping at a few stalls along the way. She watched as he purchased some bread—hopefully better than what the twins fed her—and a small selection of fruits.

Once he seemed satisfied with his purchases, Ryker steered her back towards the stables. Her ankle throbbed, but she refused to let it show. Gritting her teeth, Nova marched beside Ryker. They retrieved Charlie from where they'd hitched him and left the busy village behind—not before he bound her hands again.

Nova sighed at the peacefulness that the forest offered. She leant against Ryker's chest, allowing his muscular frame to support her. "All of that movement and noise is quite tiring."

"It can be," Ryker replied, his voice vibrating through her body.

He was quiet as they travelled back to the main road. "So Ryker, do you have a last name?"

"Thornbrooke," he murmured.

"What does Ryker Thornbrooke do?"

He paused. A beat too long. "I'm a bounty hunter."

She waited for him to continue, but no more words followed. "What kind of things do you hunt?"

The masculine wall behind her shifted in the saddle, and Nova welcomed his warmth as their bodies brushed together.

"People." Ryker murmured.

"Why would you want to do that?"

"Pays good money."

Nova stiffened. "How much is the king paying you to hunt me down?"

Ryker shifted in the saddle. "Not enough."

Why did it feel like the atmosphere just became colder? Maybe it was the hunter's confession that he was being paid to bring her to the king. The thought alone sent a chill down her spine.

Nova wrapped her arms around her body to retain some heat. Being as close as she was to Ryker's chest certainly helped. They'd be riding for a while now and the sky was darkening. Nova tipped her head towards the heavens . . . towards home.

Her sisters were appearing, shining their sweet faces upon the duo. A pang pulled on her chest, a ball of pressure sat in her throat and tears welled in her eyes. Nova wondered how they all were and whether they could see her here in this part of the world. Would she ever see them again? Could a fallen star go home? If she ever made it back to Ara, she would tell them everything she'd learnt and experienced on this foreign planet.

Sister Tierra would laugh at the twins and how ridiculous they were, while Sister Soleil would want to know all about the pretty dresses and trinkets that women wore. A small tear escaped, making its way down her cold cheek. It had been so long since she'd seen her family.

Nova brushed it away with the flick of her wrist. Reaching for a low-hanging branch, she plucked a few leaves to distract herself. Her fingers tightened around the velvet green foliage, crushing it in her palm. As her fingers peeled back one by one to reveal the leaves, a scent spilled forth.

It smelt like Ryker.

"What kind of tree is this?" Nova asked, pointing to the branches above them.

Ryker followed her gaze. "A cypress."

Nova looked back down at the crushed leaves in her hand. So this was the other layer of that familiar scent, blending with the sweetness of vanilla. His scent was like the forest after a warm day—earthy, rich, and alive.

"It's getting dark. We need to make camp for the night." Ryker spoke, his voice pulling Nova from her thoughts.

She simply nodded—too exhausted to ask questions. She needed the moon to regenerate the blood that coursed through her veins. That's how it worked back home in Ara, anyway. Surely it could do the same here? Without its beams, she felt weak and tired.

Ryker steered Charlie deeper into the forest towards a small clearing nestled amongst tall trees and pulled the glossy black horse to a stop. He slid to the ground and reached for Nova. Warm hands encircled her waist, and she drew a breath in. Holding his upper arms, he helped her to the ground, neither one breaking eye contact.

How did someone so beautiful become so cold?

"Sit over there." Ryker said as he let go of her waist and pointed towards a fallen log covered in a thin layer of moss.

"Yes sir," Nova answered.

Ryker didn't seem to be amused by her tone, so she scowled at his back and moved to sit on the log. She settled onto the rough bark, watching him intently as he worked. It wasn't long before he'd created some sort of fabric enclosure, which Nova could only presume was for sleeping in. Not even the twins had offered her that.

When Ryker was done, he worked on creating a fire—this she was familiar with. Large sticks, small sticks and a handful of leaves, plus a pair of rocks that Ryker struck against themselves, creating a small orange spark. His movements were fluid and efficient, every action carried out with the ease of someone who had done this a thousand times before.

"Do you need any help?" Nova offered.

Ryker glanced up from the fire and shook his head. "No. I don't need you injuring yourself further."

"Who said I would?"

Ryker didn't answer.

"Are you always this pleasant?"

Ryker caught her gaze over the crackling flames. "Usually I'm worse."

Nova lifted a brow. "Special treatment for me, then?"

"No . . . you've just got me on a good day."

With a huff, Nova rolled her eyes and twisted to face further into the forest. As she looked at her surroundings, she swore she heard Ryker chuckle.

The sky was darkening at a rapid rate, and Nova was grateful for the fire. Darkness didn't scare her—well, not in Ara, but here in Emberfell, it was different. Who knows what lurked in the shadows?

"Are there . . . creatures out there?"

"Many."

She swivelled back around to face Ryker. "Ones that might try and eat us?"

He shrugged. "Possibly."

Great. Just great. How was she supposed to sleep now?

"Tell me about them."

"Wild boars, mountain cats, Galanthors, Lycan."

Nova flicked her eyes to the darkness beyond their small camp. "Should we be concerned?"

Ryker glanced around. "I'm sure we'll be fine." His voice filled her with little confidence.

Nova may not know everything about this world, but she'd heard enough to know she needed to sleep with one eye open. She didn't want to become a meal to one of them.

Nova glanced across at her captor again just as he turned from retrieving food from one of the saddlebags. Ryker's eyes met hers, and before she could control herself, Nova beamed her celestial essence towards him.

Well, she hadn't even tried to do that. In Ara, glowing was to a star like breathing was to a human. Perhaps now that she'd adjusted to her surroundings, her new body was ready to let her powers manifest.

Her skin glowed with a pale blue light, illuminating a small boundary around her. Nova felt warmth creep up her chest, into her throat, spilling over her cheeks. One glance from him caused her body to react in a way that even she had no control over. Nova dropped her gaze and focused on the bindings around her hands.

Leaves crunched underfoot as Ryker approached the log.

"Here." Ryker offered her a rounded piece of wood. Nova reached for the bowl but didn't look up. Only a few items in the dish seemed familiar, apple and bread, though a few others did not. "What are these?"

Ryker stood by the fire. "Cheese and dried meat. That one is an acquired taste, but try it."

"Do you think you could remove these ropes so that I can use my hands?"

Ryker hesitated. "Do you promise to stay put?"

"Where am I going to go at this time of night?" she answered with a quizzical brow.

Ryker shrugged as he took the bowl from her hands again before he undid the rope. "Don't make me regret this."

Nova offered him a satirical smile. "I wouldn't dare."

He rose and left her side, but only for a moment. He returned to sit near her with his own plate of food. Nova rubbed her wrists, feeling the tender skin beneath her fingertips before she pulled the peach Ryker had bought her from her dress pocket. She held it up and looked at him. "Can I eat this now too?"

He threw her a sideways glance. "The peach? Go for it."

There were too many items to choose from, so Nova tried the peach first. Placing it to her lips, she bit into its flesh. Juices ran down her chin and onto her skirt. Nova looked wide eyed at the peach in her hand. "That is the most delicious thing I have ever eaten."

Ryker didn't smile, but reached for something from his trouser pocket. "Normally, we try to keep the juices inside our mouths," he said as he handed her a small cloth.

Nova wiped her mouth before placing the peach back onto her plate. "Sorry, this is all very new to me."

"Do you eat where you come from?"

Nova nodded. "Only one thing—and I would hardly call it food."

"What is it?"

"It's a starfruit."

Ryker's russet eyes flicked down to her mouth, then back up to her. "What does starfruit do for a star?"

"Helps us glow, regenerate. It's not like your fruits here."

"How is it different?"

Nova fiddled with her hands. "Well, for starters, the moon grows the starfruits in an orchard of cosmic magic trees. Whereas the sun helps yours grow here."

"I didn't think you would know much about Earth."

"Does that bother you?"

Ryker placed his plate on the forest floor and draped an arm over one risen knee, leaning back on his other hand as he stared off into the fire. "What you do is of no consequence to me."

Nova returned her attention to her dish of fruit. "I'm quickly realising that."

The surrounding forest was dark and quiet, with only the occasional rustle of leaves and the distant call of a night bird breaking the silence.

"Are you still in pain?" Ryker murmured.

His inky hair caught the golden glow of the firelight, his eyes also reflecting the light. Nova watched as he stared into the flames. He turned to look at her when she didn't respond.

"Your ankle . . ."

"Only when I walk."

Ryker nodded and turned his attention back to the fire. "Once we reach the king, he will have a healer look at it."

A healer . . . there was a small chance Nova could heal it herself. But the thought of Ryker knowing she might have powers kept her curiosity at bay. Only when she was alone would she test her abilities.

Nova stared into the flames, hypnotised by the way they crackled and snapped. Maybe things here on Earth weren't going to be as fun as she imagined from the heavens that it would be. People were after her and the pain in one's body was actually painful. Maybe life with this king in his castle would be better. Perhaps she would be able to lie down on something soft or even soak her body in a pool of warm water.

Nova could only hope.

Still, something tugged at the edges of her thoughts. She didn't know these humans—at least, not truly. What if the king wasn't the beacon of hope she imagined? What if neither he nor Ryker were people she should trust to have power over her?

Despite Ryker's kindness with food and clothing. Perhaps she should seek her own way out of the mess she was in.

They ate the rest of their food in silence. Once they'd finished, Ryker collected the plates and brushed off the crumbs before putting them back into a bag.

"You should sleep," he motioned his head towards the shelter under the trees.

"What about you?"

"The tent only holds one person, so I will keep watch." Ryker said. "Don't think about sneaking away."

Looking over at the tent and then back to Ryker, Nova stood with shaking legs. "You've been quite clear on that."

Nova moved towards the tent but stopped before turning to face Ryker with a smirk on her face. "I'm not sure why anyone would try to run away from your sunny disposition."

Ryker's gaze stayed on her face. "Stick around long enough and you'll find out."

With a last glance over at his figure, Nova disappeared into the tent, closing the flap behind her. Sinking down to the thin but soft mattress, she sighed as the weight of all the travelling eased from her body. She knew it wouldn't be long before sleep would claim her.

Tomorrow she would decide what to do—now that her hands were free. If the opportunity arose, Nova might just leave, sore ankle or not.

The weight of her aching body sank into the thin mattress and warm brown eyes were the last thing that filled her mind before darkness took hold.

FIVE

THE RUBY PENDANT

"Nova . . ."

The melody of birdsong filled the air, rousing Nova from slumber.

"Nova . . . are you awake?" Ryker called again.

Filtered light poured in through the flap of canvas. Her gaze traced the fabric dome above her as she blinked the sleep from her eyes. It took her a moment to piece together her surroundings. It surprised her to feel as rested as she did. The night before, she'd been utterly exhausted, her mind and body worn from the day's events. Though Nova usually felt most alive beneath the velvet expanse of night, she'd slept soundly and undisturbed.

She glanced at the tent's opening, her eyes catching the sliver of light between the flaps. "Yes, I'm awake."

"Time to get up," Ryker said, his voice husky and irritated.

Too bad a night's sleep hadn't changed his tune.

She sat up, rubbing her eyes before crawling from the tent. As she stepped outside, she noticed her hair drifting around her. With a swift pass of her fingers, she attempted to tame the unruly strands, smoothing them down.

A watery grey mist clung to the ground like a heavy blanket, swirling around her feet as her steps sounded across the dewy grass. Nova took a slow, deep breath, letting the fresh, crisp air fill her lungs. She glanced towards Ryker, her gaze lingering on him as he stood just a few feet away. His russet eyes lifted, locking with hers, and in that brief moment, the world seemed to narrow. Her heart stuttered in her chest, the sudden rush of warmth flooding her veins, catching her off guard and leaving her breathless.

Ryker abruptly lowered his gaze and walked past her, heading straight to pack up the tent. "We need to eat and get back on the road."

Nova turned to face him with her arms folded. "I had a wonderful sleep, thank you."

Ryker's gaze slowly travelled the length of her body, his eyes tracing every curve and detail. The intensity of his stare sent a rush of warmth to her cheeks, her skin flushing under his attention. "We don't have time for pleasantries."

Nova rolled her eyes. She moved towards the fire Ryker had maintained through the night, her steps snapping twigs and disturbing the leaf matter. She extended her hands, feeling the warmth on her fingertips. The air was still fresh, its cool edge biting into Nova's skin, causing a shiver to ripple through her.

Ryker tied the tent to the saddle. "Eat the food there while I pack up."

Nova took a plate of food. Her eyes focused on Ryker. "Does your horse have a name?"

Ryker paused. "Charlie."

Nova moved to scratch his shiny black muzzle. "Nice to meet you, Charlie."

She ate in silence, enjoying the early morning bird chatter drifting from the treetops. She slowly made her way through the simple yet satisfying meal—sweet fruit, creamy cheese, fresh bread, and cool water. By the time she finished, her stomach was pleasantly full, almost to the point of bursting.

Nova's gaze found Ryker again, his hands working diligently as he finished packing their belongings. "Is this king of yours the ruler of where you live?"

"He's not my king and yes, of Emberfell."

Nova folded her arms across her chest. "What gives him the right to stake claim to me?"

Ryker shrugged as he tied a bag to Charlie's saddle. "He's a king."

What a ridiculous answer. What did it matter if he was a king?

"How long will it take to reach the palace?"

She needed to gauge her surroundings a little. If she was going to form a plan of escape, the more information she had, the better. Not that she knew where to go. She just wanted to get away and see the world. Experience it without some brutish male telling her what to do.

"Another day or so."

Nova nodded. Perhaps she could go in the opposite direction from which they were going. Surely, there were other places close by where she could seek refuge. If she kept her glow hidden, she'd pass as an ordinary woman, would she not?

Surely, people would soon forget about her, and she could finally slip through the world unnoticed, exploring its hidden places and marvels. She'd wander from city to city, village to village, discovering each one with fresh eyes, free to let her curiosity lead her wherever it wanted.

A sound in the distance had Ryker moving swiftly towards her. Before she could argue, he pulled her to his chest and behind a tree, his muscular arms encasing her tiny frame as she settled into his warmth.

"What is it?" she whispered.

Ryker covered her mouth with his hand. "People. Don't move."

"Ryker—" her voice was muffled.

"Do as you're told," he whispered against her ear.

Nova noted the seriousness in his voice and as much as she wanted to fight against him, she did as he bade. His warm breath grazed her skin, each exhale a gentle caress that sent goosebumps down her neck. She could feel the rapid thrum of his heartbeat pressed against her back, pounding too fast for her to count. His scent of cypress and vanilla enveloped her senses, her heart hammering against its cage as she drank him in.

The only sound was the soft rustle of leaves as the breeze wove through the trees. Even so, Ryker stood motionless, his body taut and alert, ready for whatever might lurk unseen.

They stayed like that for a few moments until Ryker finally glanced around the side of the tree. His hold on her loosened as he carefully released his hand from her mouth, his other hand steady on her arm. Together, they moved cautiously back toward their small camp, each step quiet and measured.

"Stay beside Charlie and don't move," he commanded as he gently pushed her from his embrace.

Nova folded her arms. "Do you think it was the twins?"

Ryker shrugged before turning his attention to the black horse. "Possibly."

"Are they looking for me?"

"I would say so."

Nova glanced around the forest. "Are they the only ones looking for me?"

"You sure ask a lot of questions?"

She fixed her gaze, giving him a pointed stare. "You would too if you needed a lot of answers."

Leather strapping squeaked as Ryker tightened Charlie's saddle. "I'm certain there are others looking for you. Which is why I need to get you to King Branoc swiftly."

It seemed that even if she left Ryker's side; it would not be easy to evade someone else's grasp. Perhaps she should stay until they were closer to the city, where she'd have a better chance of hiding.

Ryker gathered the last of his belongings and helped Nova into the saddle before pulling himself up behind her. They headed towards the king—or so she presumed.

After a full day of riding without pause, Nova felt as though someone had thrown her down a jagged hill, and she'd hit every bump along the way. Her muscles screamed in protest, causing her to groan as she eased herself out of the saddle when, at last, Ryker announced they would set up camp once again.

The sky was growing unusually dark, and by the way Ryker's brows knitted together, casting shadows over his eyes, she could tell he wasn't pleased. His fingers toyed with the gold chain around his neck every time he cast his gaze skyward.

They stopped for the night along the banks of a wide stream, where Nova became bewitched at the sight of a fish in its crystal waters. Silver scales glimmered in the fading rays of the day's last light, and the longer she watched them, the more she felt she could remain there for hours, content and happy.

The trees there stood apart from those they had encountered earlier, their bark a lighter hue, their branches fuller, draping the forest in a denser, more vibrant canopy.

Nova pointed to a small chestnut coloured creature as it scurried by. "Is that a squirrel?"

"Yes."

"Are they friend or foe?"

Ryker flicked his gaze to the furry animal as it darted up a tree. "Pest."

A smile danced on Nova's lips. She thought they were quite sweet.

She sat by the fire, flicking her gaze towards Ryker. He remained preoccupied, fingers tracing the edges of the red jewel that dangled from his neck.

A loud rumble stretched across the sky. Nova knew exactly what was coming, having witnessed many storms from her position in the sky over the years. She had long admired the enormity of them, hoping one day she might feel the rain upon her skin. The thought of it approaching sent a thrill through her.

Ryker shoved a plate towards her. "Eat before we get soaked."

Nova reached for the plate, studying his face. "Is everything alright?"

"Yes," he said, his voice sharp, slicing through her.

She flinched, casting a wary glance in his direction as she lowered herself onto the forest floor. Silently, she ate her meal. Ryker stood near Charlie, his gaze distant, lost to the forest as he ate his meal.

Bright sheets of light illuminated the wind-tossed canopy, followed by a sharp crack of thunder that reverberated through the Earth. Nova grinned.

"The sky is about to open up, you'd best get inside the tent," Ryker called above the howling wind whipping through the trees.

"What did you say?" Nova called back.

Ryker cupped his hands over his mouth and shouted. "The tent. Get inside."

Nova wanted to refuse, but the thought of her captor's reaction kept her silent. Still, this was her first taste of rain, and the desire to feel it upon her skin outweighed her caution. While Ryker ensured Charlie was safely sheltered under the flowing branches of a large tree, Nova crept forward.

Thunder rumbled again, and the Earth grew thick with the scent of damp soil and musk, rising from the forest floor as if the ground had exhaled a breath. Nova tilted her head back, her eyes wide with wonder as the sky darkened, a single raindrop falling to kiss her cheek. She lifted her hand, brushing the cool droplet that felt more like a shard of ice, cold and sharp.

The rain fell in earnest, gentle at first, then steadily increasing in intensity. Nova stepped out from beneath the sheltering trees, her arms outstretched as if to embrace the sky. The rain washed over her in a cascade of tiny, sparkling drops.

She twirled slowly, letting the water seep through her clothes and run down her skin. Each drop felt like a delicate kiss, a sensation she had never known in the celestial realms. Her laughter bubbled up, light and joyous, mixing with the sound of the falling rain.

But it didn't last long.

Before she could protest, Ryker's arm swept around her waist, lifting her feet off the ground. He carried her to the tent, shoving her inside before stepping in after her. The low ceiling of the fabric shelter forced him to bow his head

"I told you to get inside the tent," he growled.

Nova narrowed her eyes, a hint of irritation twisting her expression. "You don't own me. I wanted to feel the rain."

Ryker ran his fingers through his wet hair, his skin glistening even in the darkness. His gaze remained unflinching, unwavering even under Nova's fierce scrutiny.

"Maybe I would consider your requests if you asked me nicely," she stated, a venomous edge in her voice.

Ryker played with the pendant. "Please . . . stay inside. Is that better?"

The downpour of rain pelted against the side of the tent, relentless in its attempt to knock it sideways, but the fabric held steadfast. Thunder rolled like a drum, shaking the ground beneath her feet, while lightning ripped through the sky, illuminating the shelter sporadically.

Russet eyes fixated on her, and Nova felt a slow, peculiar heat rise within, a sensation spreading low between her thighs. He waited, his silence thick with expectation. And for a moment, she revelled in the control she held over him.

"It's a start."

Ryker's gaze briefly lingered on her lips before flicking back up. Without a word, he dropped to the ground, settling on the mat, stretching out on his back, his eyes never quite leaving hers. "We may as well try to sleep. I think it's going to hang around for a while."

"Will Charlie be okay out there?"

Ryker closed his eyes and nodded. "He'll be fine. Lie down . . . please."

Nova blushed at the thought of lying so close to Ryker— not that it was any closer than sitting on a horse with him, but somehow this felt more intimate. The tent was cramped, as narrow as it was tall. Once she lay beside him, Ryker's hulking frame would most definitely press against hers.

She sat down on the mat. "You will not touch me while I sleep will you?"

Ryker huffed softly. "Little star, if I was going to touch you, I would make sure you were wide awake."

Nova caught his gaze. His mouth remained still, but something in his eyes glimmered—a tiny spark. She found herself drawn to it, whatever it was. The name he'd used for her sent warmth through her body, though she didn't understand why he called her that. Still, it brought her a sense of comfort.

With the storm raging outside, Nova laid down, turning her back to Ryker. Despite the warmth spilling from his body, Nova longed for the cold bite of the rain.

The commands of this stranger were becoming unbearable. She wasn't naive. Though Earth was new to her, she understood more than they realised. It was time to find a way out—time to make her own choices.

"What's the king like?" she spoke into the night.

"Like most kings, I suppose."

Nova rolled onto her side, facing Ryker's back. "Which is?"

His frame lay taller than hers. She felt small beside it. The heat from his body reached her, seeping into her skin as if warding off any chill that lingered in the night air. She leaned in just slightly, savouring the solid comfort he offered.

"I don't know . . . powerful—likes treasure." Ryker murmured.

"Is that what I am?"

Ryker hesitated. "Some would say you are."

Her stomach dropped. Was she truly that desired here in this part of the world? "Should I be worried?"

"Not if you do whatever he asks."

Nova's eyes travelled over Rykers' back. "And what if I don't?"

He sighed softly. "Then you should possibly be worried."

Nothing in his words gave Nova the slightest confidence in this king he spoke of. What if he was just as demanding as the twins, or as severe as Ryker had been—what if he was worse? The twins had planned to sell her to the highest bidder, and Ryker seemed focused on what he'd been paid to do. How would this king be any different?

If she got the opportunity tomorrow, she would take it—she would run. Her ankle was feeling much better. She'd had enough food and water that she could probably last a few days before she needed more. Surely someone in a town could help her find a way home—if that was even possible.

The steady rise and fall of Ryker's chest reassured Nova that he was asleep. She rolled onto her back, trying to find a comfortable position as the storm lessened outside. The rain continued, and she fought sleep for as long as she could before finally succumbing to the dark.

Warm, filtered sunlight licked at Nova's skin, stirring her awake. It was still a foreign feeling to have the oldest and brightest star in all of Ara kiss her human skin.

Instinctively, she reached out to touch Ryker's solid body, but her fingers only found coldness. She opened one eye, confirming that she was indeed alone. Sitting up, she crawled from the cosy sleeping space to find Ryker attending the camp fire.

He looked up as she neared. "We need to get moving."

"Good morning to you too, sunshine."

He raked his russet gaze over her dishevelled frame before throwing another log onto the hungry flames.

Nova looked around. Charlie was munching on some grass and the trees gently swayed in the breeze. Would she have an opportunity to find her escape this morning? Her ankle barely hurt, and after some food, she would be ready to run.

It was still early, the sun's rays barely brushing the ground. Her thoughts wandered to the stream where she'd watched the fish when they'd first arrived, her heart stirring with a quiet ache.

"Is it safe to bathe in the stream?" Nova asked casually.

Her captor stood, placing his hands on his hips. "It would be. However, you'll need to do it quickly."

Nova nodded. "Of course."

Ryker eyed her warily. Nova paused, her gaze lingering on him before she pivoted on her heel. Her boots sank into the soft earth with each step as she moved towards the stream. Long legs carried her with an effortless stride. The hem of her dress swirled around her ankles, catching the breeze.

Let him watch. She didn't mind. In fact, she was quite pleased with her human body.

Nova discarded her clothing to the grass banks before she strolled down to the water's edge. She dipped a toe in, shivering. It was indeed freezing; the coldness cutting at her skin like tiny razors.

With a held breath, Nova waded into the water until it lapped at her waist. Her skin pebbled as she sank beneath the surface. The feeling of being underwater reminded her of Ara. She felt weightless and free—like she was floating.

After a few moments, she broke through the surface and filled her lungs with air. This was exactly what her aching body needed.

"Do you mind if I bathe, too?"

The sound of Ryker's voice pulled her around.

Nova ran her hands through her wet hair, the strands clinging to her neck and down her back. "You can do as you please."

Ryker moved further upstream, the soft murmur of the water masking his quiet steps. He tugged his loose white shirt over his head; the fabric sliding against his skin before he let it fall carelessly to the ground. His fingers worked at the waistband of his light-brown trousers, pushing them down with a firm shove. He stepped out of the discarded clothing and stood still for a moment, exposed to the cool breeze.

Nova knew she should look away, but she found it difficult.

Her throat tightened as her eyes followed him to the water's edge, taking in every inch of his body. His powerful legs rippled with every flex of muscle as he drew closer, his abdomen taut, chiselled, displaying the grooves of muscle that undulated beneath his skin. Every inch of him called to her, beckoning for her to reach out and trace the rigid lines of his form.

Sun-kissed skin, faintly dusted with hair, gleamed in the light, and lower still, another part of him swung with each step, thick and half-hardened. The sight of him roused something deep within her—an unfamiliar heat that made her body react in ways she had never known before.

He dove into the water head first, surfacing a few moments later.

With a flick of his inky black hair, Ryker ran his hands over his face, wiping away the excess water. His muscular torso glistened in the soft caress of the early morning light. A slow warmth pooled in Nova's stomach, an undeniable pull at the sight before her.

Ryker caught her gaze, but his eyes soon drifted, travelling over the swell of her breasts where they broke the water's surface. A flush of heat rose to her cheeks under his attention. The seconds stretched between them. Unable to bear the charged silence any longer, she slipped beneath the glassy surface, the cool water swallowing her whole, before rising from the stream, breathless.

Perhaps it was best to put some distance between them. Ryker had his back to her as she waded to the water's edge.

A sudden thought occurred to Nova.

"I will change and meet you back at the tent," Nova called out.

He turned, his gaze roaming over her from a distance, taking her in with a silent intensity. Nova felt the weight of his stare as she stood before him, completely bare, her skin tingling under his slow inspection. His eyes travelled from the tousled strands of her hair to the bare tips of her toes, lingering in a way that made her pulse quicken. A slight grin tugged at the corner of her mouth as she raised a brow, her eyes sparkling with anticipation as she waited for his reaction.

Ryker sunk a little lower beneath the water, his chin grazing the surface. "Very well."

She offered him a soft, almost playful smile before gathering her clothes and heading back up the small hill toward their camp. The air was crisp, cooling her skin as she walked, a hint of satisfaction lingering in her stride. Charlie was still grazing nearby, his ears twitching at her approach.

While Ryker was in the water, naked and vulnerable, she could make her escape. At the very least, she would have a few minutes' head start before he realised she was gone. Despite her damp skin and dripping hair, Nova hurriedly put her clothes and shoes on. Should she take anything with her? Food or a blanket? Money?

Nova looked towards the stream one more time, but Ryker had not yet returned. She dashed inside the tent to search through his belongings. The small pouch of coins felt heavy in her hand as she shoved it into the pockets of her skirt.

Her fingers reached for the blanket but stopped just as the tips brushed the coarse fabric. It would weigh her down too much, so she left it.

With a quick glance around the forest, Nova made a run for it.

Her heart pounded in her chest as she bolted through the trees, her breath coming in sharp, ragged gasps. The dense underbrush scratched at her legs, and branches snagged her clothing, but she pushed onward, driven by the need to put distance between herself and Ryker.

She didn't know where she was going, only that she had to get away. The surrounding forest was a maze of towering trees and tangled roots, but she navigated it with a frantic energy, her feet barely touching the ground.

If she could get far enough away and hide until nightfall, maybe she could use the moon's glow to navigate her way to a village once the world fell into slumber.

Nova's lungs burned, and her thighs felt like lead, but she didn't stop. She couldn't. Not until she was certain she was far enough.

The forest grew darker as she ran, the canopy above thickening and blocking out the golden light. She stumbled over a root, the ground rushing up to meet her with a thud. Dirt and leaves cushioned her fall, but not enough to stop the jolt of pain that shot through her body.

She lay on the ground for a moment, trying to catch her breath. Get up, she told herself. Keep going.

Tears softened the dirt on her cheeks—exhaustion kicking in—as she forced herself to her knees, every muscle protesting. She had to keep moving, had to put more distance between herself and Ryker. The urgency of her freedom propelled her forward, but her body screamed for respite.

Finally, she burst into a small clearing, her strength nearly spent. A large, dark mound in the middle of the field halted her steps. With a shaking breath, Nova froze on the spot. What was it? Ryker had told her of some creatures that roamed these parts, but they were just rumours, right?

The creature lifted its feathery head, its beak pointed skyward as it sniffed the air. Despite its birdlike maw, its ears were oddly shaped, rounded like a bear's and twitching at every sound. Something in Nova's gut told her not to move . . . not even breathe.

She knew there were many creatures on Earth, but she didn't know which ones were dangerous and which ones weren't. Nova had no desire to stick around and find out, but uncertainty gripped her—she did not know which direction to take. At this point, Ryker would know she was missing and would not be pleased.

She took a small, silent step backwards, hoping to blend in with the shadows, when a rough hand encircled her waist and another covered her mouth, stifling her screams. Cypress and vanilla touched her nose, the familiar presence of Ryker's chest rising and falling against her back grounding her.

"It's a Galanthor," Ryker whispered.

The creature caught their movement, its massive owl-like head swivelling towards them. Black and auburn mottled feathers bristled along its shoulders, while its bear-like body tensed, claws digging into the Earth. Amber eyes locked onto them with predatory intent.

Nova's body shook as the Galanthor advanced with deliberate steps through the lush meadow. Ryker's grip was firm, guiding her backward with slow, cautious movements, but her instincts screamed to flee. How could two humans possibly stand against something so massive and powerful?

The beast moved.

"Hide!" Ryker shouted, pushing her to the side just as the creature launched itself forward, dirt flying from beneath its paws. Nova stumbled, hitting the ground hard, but Ryker's focus was already on the Galanthor charging toward him.

He unsheathed his sword with effortless grace, confronting the towering creature. Saliva dripped from his saffron beak, its yellow eyes wide with fury.

Brushwood clung to Nova's skirts as she scrambled from the forest floor to hide behind the thick trunk of a tree, her gaze never leaving the scene before her.

The Galanthor's wings spread wide, casting a dark and foreboding shadow over Ryker, and with a deafening screech, it lunged. He ducked as its talons slashed through the air, barely missing his head.

Nova bit back a muffled scream.

Ryker pivoted, bringing his blade up just in time to slice through the thick feathers on its side. The creature howled in pain, however, its rage only escalated. It reared up, its claws raking across Ryker's outstretched hand, drawing crimson blood.

Nova winced. This was all her fault. If she'd stayed with him, none of this would be happening.

With a swift movement, Ryker's arm drew back, and he drove his sword deep into the creature's shoulder. The Galanthor let out a piercing cry, its wings flapping violently as it staggered back. Ryker pulled the blade free, panting as the beast, wounded and furious, hesitated. With a final snarl, the Galanthor backed away, turning to flee into the safety of the forest, limping heavily.

Ryker's chest heaved, his hand dripping with blood, as he turned to face Nova. "This is why we don't go running off into the woods alone."

He was right. It was foolish of her to run away. But the idea of being shipped off to a king she didn't know didn't seem ideal either.

Nova stood, brushing forest debris from her trembling hands.

He stalked towards her, grabbing her upper arm and dragged them back into the forest. "You're lucky I caught you before he did." Ryker motioned his head towards the retreating creature. "It would have eaten you alive, little star."

Nova struggled in his grasp. "Please Ryker, I don't want to go to the king."

He pulled some leather binding from his trouser pocket and shook his head. "Like I've told you before . . . you don't have a choice."

She tried to resist further, but Ryker was too strong, and her energy was spent.

He tied her wrists and tugged her forward, their noses almost touching. "You run fast . . . I'll give you that much."

SIX

THE DIFFICULT DELIVERY

Petite hourglass figure. Full breasts with pale pink nipples. Milky white skin glistening in the morning light as water droplets rolled down her body. Legs that went on for days and arms that moved with such grace. Not to mention her ass. So perfect that one glance had him instantly hard. Ryker bit his lip as he tried to push the mental image of one very naked Nova from his mind.

She sat in front of him as they rode through the forest. The smell of her hair made him want to bury his face in it. Her scent was otherworldly, like tiny particles from a different realm. The closest thing Ryker could compare it to was lilac, the salty sea air, and something else he couldn't put his finger on. Whatever the combo was, it drove him wild and after this morning's ordeal, the combination of her smell and her incredible body had him grinding his teeth in self control. All he wanted to do was taste her.

Did her full lips taste as good as they looked? Would her skin feel like velvet beneath his hands? Would she make little noises while he rubbed his nose into the crook of her neck? Would this celestial creature even know what it was like to be pleasured?

He shouldn't even dance with these swaying temptations. Pretty creatures with pretty eyes and pretty lips weren't his to have, because when he did, he couldn't keep them safe.

Ryker closed his eyes and took a slow, deep breath in. This was a business deal—despite the small niggling of what if it wasn't?—that tugged on his chest. He needed to pull himself together and stop thinking about her naked or the evidence of it was going to show. There was very little fabric between them right now, which also didn't help.

He inwardly smiled at her escape attempt. She was daring. And boy, could she sprint.

It had only taken him minutes to realise she'd made a run for it. Thankfully for him, Nova had fled in almost a circle, making it easy for him to catch up—before the Galanthor could.

Horrid creatures, really. Massive, with the hulking body of a bear and the plumed head of an owl—powerful, yet lumbering in their movements. The kind of beast Ryker avoided at all costs. He knew all too well the pain one could inflict.

He carefully flexed his hand, wrapped in bandages. Luckily, the beast's claws had only grazed him, leaving a shallow wound that would heal in a few days. Ryker was relieved that the Galanthor hadn't caused more serious harm. It was the first time he'd seen one in a while.

Hopefully, it would be the last.

Farm lands stretched endlessly on either side of the winding road, golden crops swaying in the breeze under a sky streaked with hues of late afternoon. Herds of sheep and cattle grazed within the rolling grasslands, their contented sounds drifting towards Ryker's ears. He knew the palace was just hours away. Soon, he would leave her with the king, collect his money, and forget all about this beautiful creature in front of him.

At least he hoped so.

"You've barely spoken this afternoon," Ryker murmured.

"What is there to talk about?"

Ryker shifted in the saddle. "We could talk about why you tried to run away?"

"Can you blame me?" Nova huffed. "Would you want to be carted off like an item, taken to a place you've never seen, with no choice in the matter?"

She got him there.

"Trust me, you'll love living in a palace."

Nova huffed, her delicate shoulders dropping. "How would you know? You don't even know me."

Ryker caught her sea-green eyes as she glanced over her shoulder. "I know all women like fancy dresses and to be waited on hand and foot," he murmured.

"Maybe the women you know. I, for one, don't like that sort of thing."

Truth be told, Ryker did not know whether or not she would enjoy staying at the palace. Nor was he certain of Branoc's intentions with Nova. It seemed as if the king always got bored with new things. There was a good chance it would be the same with the star.

Who was Ryker to challenge a king, though? And there was no point in filling the poor woman's mind with worry, so he let the topic rest.

"Whatever you say, little star."

Nova fiddled with the pale green fabric of her skirt. "Why do you call me that?"

Ryker's brow furrowed slightly. "Call you what?"

"Little star."

He paused, uncertain of the answer himself. Maybe it was because she seemed delicate, like something rare that deserved care and reverence. And the name just seemed to suit her.

He shrugged. "Would you rather I didn't?"

Nova shook her head, a soft cascade of white hair falling over her shoulders. "Call me whatever you like," she murmured.

A slow smile curved his lips. He could think of a few other names he'd like to call her, but for now, little star would have to do.

The village on the outskirts of the palace borders came into view, and Ryker stiffened. Clusters of tents nestled beneath the canopy of trees, while makeshift camps littered the edge of the forest in a patchwork of rugged shelters. Children's laughter rang out as they chased one another, their clothing fluttering behind them in tattered rags. A few rough-hewn log buildings huddled together, forming the heart of the sparse village.

This particular camp sheltered many farmers who had little money to spare. Half-orcs, the odd elf, and a scattering of humans looked at Ryker with either fear in their eyes or a wariness that only came about because he worked for the king.

It tugged at Ryker's heart, seeing the children looking up at him with hungry, pleading eyes. The king should have intervened long ago, but his focus rarely strayed from his own desires, leaving these people to fend for themselves amid his indifference.

Other kingdoms he'd visited over the years seemed to flourish in all areas. Not just the cities, but the villages and farms too—obvious that their rulers actually cared about the people. Branoc was just a greedy pig.

There was no way around it—this path led directly into the city, forcing him through the familiar district. In past ventures, he would pause to buy food for the children. But today, Ryker didn't have the time for that. He needed to deliver the star to the king, before temptation overtook him—before he did something he would regret—like let her go.

Ryker moved swiftly through the cluttered tents and small log homes, ignoring the eager children who ran towards him. It nearly killed him to turn them away. He would come back to bring them sweet treats and stories after King Branoc paid him. It was all he could really offer.

"Why are these children coming to greet you?" Nova asked.

Ryker shifted in the saddle. "I usually stop and tell them stories."

Nova glanced over her shoulder. "The grouch can be nice—who would have known?"

"I can be many things, Nova."

The simple mention of her name on his lips shifted something in his chest. It wasn't often he called her by it.

Nova huffed in amusement. "Do they not have parents?"

"Some of them do. Some don't. Most parents are away all day trying to make money."

Nova's voice softened. "Why didn't you stop today?"

"I don't have time. I need to get you to King Branoc."

The quicker he dropped her off and took his money, the faster he would be free of this constant torment that had invaded his mind the moment he touched her.

Satisfied with his answer, Nova turned her focus to the road ahead.

The city loomed before them, and Ryker broke Charlie into a canter. Nova squealed as the black stallion took off, her glistening white hair floating behind her and tickling Ryker's face. He smiled softly at her excitement and pushed Charlie harder. The wind whipped over them, and Nova threw her arms out.

"Careful Nova!" Ryker said sternly.

"Of what?!" she called back. "I feel like I'm flying!"

Ryker pulled her tighter against his chest. His other hand tightened on the reins. "Just don't fall off."

Nova giggled as she nodded. "This is the most wonderful feeling!"

Forestry, farms, and wide open spaces flew past in a flurry of colour and textures, like the brush strokes of a painting. Birds sang overhead and for one fleeting moment . . . Ryker couldn't help but feel alive.

He eased Charlie to a slower pace as the palace came into view. Towering spires pierced the sky, their golden tips catching the afternoon light. The grand stone walls seemed to stretch endlessly, and the distant flutter of crimson banners waved in the gentle breeze. Bit by bit, the entire structure revealed itself, looming on the horizon like a silent watchman.

They passed villagers carrying their wares, the cobblestone streets alive with the hum of commerce. Stalls brimmed with vibrant fabrics and aromatic spices from distant lands, each watched closely by different fae races. Some with sharp, calculating eyes, others with smiles plastered on their faces and laughter bubbling from their mouths.

The savoury scents of roasted meats and spiced breads wafted through the air as they passed food merchants and bustling taverns. Yet, even after four years of living among these sights and sounds, the place still felt foreign to Ryker—never truly home.

Ryker steered Charlie through the main street towards the larger gates that entered the palace grounds. Wary people eyed them, gossiping, women whispering as they passed by. If he was honest with himself, he didn't think anyone would have noticed them as they rode through, but, glancing down at Nova, Ryker saw the reason they were staring wide eyed.

Nova was glowing.

It was the first time since he took her from the twins that her skin glimmered in such a lovely viridian hue.

Ryker wrapped his body around her a little more, trying to diffuse her celestial essence, but it was of little use. Her neck strained, following everyone's movements, and the more sights of the city she took in, the brighter she glowed.

If people didn't know what she was before ... they did now.

She gazed at everything with such awe and wonder, and something hit Ryker—an unexpected pang of regret ... No—something fiercer and far more protective. Maybe he should forego the bounty and simply find her somewhere else to live. This innocent woman did not deserve to be placed into the hands of King Branoc.

Yet, surely living in a palace was better than other fates, right?

King Branoc rose from the seat, his royal cape trailing behind him as he took long, confident strides towards the pair, grinning from ear to ear. "You did not disappoint, Ryker."

Nova drew closer to Ryker's side and reached for his hand. His first instinct was to take it and walk right out of the room, but he shoved it down. Surely living in a castle would have its benefits. She would be fed, have a comfortable bed to sleep in, and be out of the hands of other bounty hunters or even pirates.

Nova's already pale face was dull, and the glow she'd portrayed earlier was now gone. Even the strands of her diamond-like hair hung limp, clinging to her delicate frame.

"I rarely ever do."

"Ryker . . . please don't do this." Nova's voice touched his ears, trembling with fear as she gripped his arm between her bound hands. Her touch was like ice against the heat running through his veins.

Yet, he remained firm in his composure. He was hired to do a job and now that job was done. No matter what he thought of the king and his obnoxious grin. It wasn't up to Ryker to change the fate of the star.

King Branoc circled them, a sneer on his face. "Did she display any powers?"

Ryker furrowed his brow. "She did not."

Other than the schoolyard fables about stars granting wishes, it had never crossed Ryker's mind to ask if she had any powers. As a child, he had been enchanted by those tales, imagining that the shimmering lights in the night sky held secrets and magic just out of reach. But now, standing before Nova, the reality was far more intriguing than any childhood fantasy. He couldn't help but wonder if her celestial origins meant she possessed abilities beyond his understanding.

Branocs' brow creased with distaste. "I hope you're telling me the truth, Ryker . . . because if you are not—"

"I don't make a habit of lying." Ryker's voice was stiff.

The king stopped in front of them and grabbed Nova roughly by the chin. "Oh, the fun we are going to have . . . you and I."

Ryker bristled at Branoc's tone, his hand twitching towards the blade that rarely left his side. The urge to drive an uppercut into the king's smug face and snap his royal neck surged within him. But the thought of a guard's blade finding its mark—or worse, hurting Nova—stayed his hand.

He eyes the king. "Is that what you hope to gain from her—powers?"

King Branoc drew Nova's face inches away from his own. "She can't give me powers, but she can certainly give me something else . . . can't you."

Ryker's gaze flicked between Nova and the king. Was there something Branoc knew that Ryker did not? Perhaps he should have questioned Nova before handing her over.

Nova grit her teeth. "I will give you nothing."

A brittle laugh cut through the throne room, filling Ryker with more dread than he liked to admit. Nova clung to his side, trembling.

He needed to get out of this situation before he, or the king, wound up dead.

"If you'll pay me, I will be on my way."

King Branoc motioned to a servant who stepped forward with a large sack. The contents clinked inside as it was handed to him.

Nova took Ryker's arm and lifted her gaze to his, fear pooling in her eyes. "Ryker, please?"

Before he could answer, Branoc took hold of her hand and yanked her towards himself. "There is no need to worry. You will be very useful here."

Ryker swallowed, forcing down the emotions that bubbled to the surface as Nova clawed for him again. This was for the best.

"What will you do with her?"

The King chuckled as he tucked Nova closely to his side. "You have your money. You may go. Guards, take our lovely new trinket and show her to her room."

"No . . . please don't go, Ryker. Why are you doing this?" Nova cried.

This was a business deal, and now it was done. He had to walk away.

"You will be safe here. Goodbye Nova." Ryker turned on his heel, leaving the throne room, the sounds of Nova's shouts muffled as the doors closed behind him.

Pain filled his chest, and he winced. That will teach him to let his stupid heart get involved with the job.

He couldn't hurry from the castle fast enough. It was time to get home and put all of this behind him. A bath, good food, and a restful night. Charlie would appreciate his own stable, too.

Night had descended upon them, bringing with it the cool evening air as Ryker travelled. The air was thick with the intoxicating scent of night jasmine, its sweet floral notes wafting through the coolness. The fragrance stirred memories of Nova. He closed his eyes, trying to block out the haunting echo of her cries. He needed to put her from his mind.

They reached the lone cabin in the woods faster than ever and Ryker untacked Charlie quickly, wiping him down with a cloth before feeding him freshly loosened hay and a carrot.

After prepping a stew for dinner, Ryker placed it in the fireplace to cook while he bathed. He sank beneath the water's surface, Nova's cries ringing in his ears. He couldn't shake the image of her sea-green eyes filled with the pain of his actions, and Ryker knew she would never forgive him.

Once he was clean and changed, Ryker returned to the fireplace, drying his hair with a towel. The bag of coins sat on the table, silently goading him. Was it worth it? Was it a good idea to deliver an innocent woman into the hands of a king? Ryker clung to the hope that Branoc would be content to simply keep the fallen star as a trophy, but who was he kidding? Branoc was a greedy bastard, and if he thought Nova had powers, he'd be ruthless in finding and exploiting them.

His worn jacket lay over the back of a wooden chair. He fished through the front pockets, looking for his flask of rum.

Truthfully, it didn't matter what he thought . . . it wasn't his problem anymore.

SEVEN

THE KING'S DISPLAY

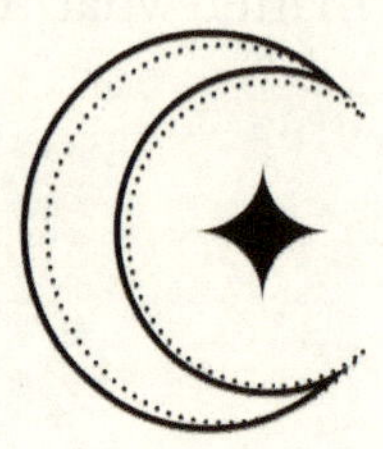

The post lady smiled as Ryker handed his letter over. She tucked it in a half-full basket near her side. "This will go out later this afternoon when the delivery man rides through," she assured him.

Ryker tipped his head in thanks and exited the post shop. As he promised himself, he enclosed some extra money notes inside an envelope to his parents, alongside a lengthy letter updating them on anything and everything he could think of that would satisfy their need to know all the details of his very boring life as a bounty hunter. He was certain his mother would be anxiously waiting by her letterbox soon. It had been nearly a month since he last wrote.

The sun was warm. Ryker blinked as he stepped outside, his eyes adjusting to the light. It was early afternoon, and he'd come into the city to purchase a few necessities for home. Candles, fresh meat, fruit, and some sugar cubes for his morning coffee.

On the way to the grocers, someone called after him.

"Ryker Thornbrooke!"

The voice had him spinning around. "Pete!?" Ryker said, extending a hand.

The man gripped his arm, grinning. Moss-green eyes peeked from under a wash of sandy hair. "How are you, friend? I haven't seen you in a while?"

"I'm well, and yourself?"

"Well enough, how's the hunting?"

"Wish it was deer or rabbits—not humans," Ryker replied, shoving his hands in his pockets. "How's the palace treating you?"

The light haired male with broad shoulders sighed as he folded across his chest. "Well, the workload is intense, but the pay is good, so I can't really complain."

Ryker had known Peter for a couple of years now, having met him in one of the city's many taverns one night as they both ordered the same drink at the same time. That moment birthed a friendship Ryker hadn't known he needed at the time.

"I hear you brought the king his prized star?" Peter went on as they stood in the shade of a store window.

Internally, Ryker winced at the thought of Nova. It had been three weeks since he left her with King Branoc. Three weeks of her haunting eyes invading his dreams. Three weeks of wishing he could undo it all.

"Yes, I did. Do you know of her wellbeing? I assume the king values her highly, and she's been treated with care?" Ryker asked with interest.

Peter shook his head. "I don't get to see a lot down in the kitchens, but the maids do chatter. Seems as though the king has been in a mood lately."

Ryker's jaw clenched briefly. "Do you think he is harming her in any way?"

He'd never seen it with his own eyes, but something in Ryker's gut told him that Branoc would forcefully do whatever it took to get what he wanted.

"I can't say, to be honest. But the maids ... as I said, they chatter. It seems no one has seen her since his most recent outburst. " Peter winced.

Fury built inside Ryker's veins. He didn't want to admit it to himself, but when he left her in the throne room that day, he knew it was a mistake. That he should have never freely handed her over to the king.

A trumpet sounded, bringing Ryker and Peter's conversation to a sudden halt. Crowds gathered in the streets, pushing them closer to the walls of the stone building. The sound of horses' hooves and the clamour of onlookers drew Ryker's attention to the approaching procession. His heart sank as he saw King Branoc at the forefront on top of a pure white horse, leading a parade of guards and finely dressed courtiers.

Then, Ryker's gaze locked onto a cage-like carriage rolling behind the king's horse. Inside, Nova sat, looking frail and depressed. Her once luminous skin was still as pale as the day he left her with the king. There was no celestial glow . . . her entire essence was dimmed. She appeared thinner than he remembered, her eyes hollow and filled with a deep sadness.

Branoc was parading her around like a prized possession—touchable only to him.

What had Ryker done—better yet, what was the king doing?!

This was not how he thought she would be treated. Sure, he thought the king might be demanding in his words as most kings are, but he'd hoped that living in a palace meant she was being treated well enough. "It doesn't look good, does it Ry?" Peter murmured.

Shaking his head, Ryker glanced at his friend. "No, it does not."

Fury surged through him like a wildfire. The sight of Nova, so vulnerable and mistreated, ignited a rage he could scarcely contain. His fists clenched at his sides, nails digging into his palms as he struggled to maintain his composure amidst the townspeople.

"King's like him should lose their heads," Ryker said through gritted teeth.

"If anyone hears you say that, friend, they will hang you for treason."

Ryker huffed. "He might be the ruler of Emberfell, but in my eyes, he's not a king. I'd like to see them try."

Peter gave him a wary look. "Don't be doing anything daft."

With a shrug, Ryker watched as the procession moved past them, stepping further into the shadows so he wouldn't be seen by the king or Nova. "Let's catch up for a drink soon."

Peter nodded and slapped Ryker on the back. "Yes, I best get back to it. A whiskey is on me next time. It's been too long."

Ryker tipped his head to the chef and spun on his heel. There were a few more items on his list that he needed before he went home. He'd relax for the rest of the afternoon, because come nightfall . . . he probably wouldn't rest again—for a while. He was about to throw out all his dreams of retiring early and go on his biggest undertaking yet, but this time he wouldn't be the hunter—he would be hunted.

Under the cloak of nightfall, Ryker watched the palace walls from the tree line, waiting for the guards to cross over. The moon cast a silvery glow over the stone fortress, its light intermittently obscured by drifting clouds. Torches lined the top of the castle walls, emitting an orange glow on the lichen and moss encrusted stone barrier. Only a few more seconds and the guards would switch posts. He could take them out with dreamroot darts. If he took both guards out, it would allow him a decent window of time that he could scale the barricade and jump down to the gardens below.

Was this the stupidest thing he'd ever done? To date, yes. Was he going to stop? Absolutely not.

He'd spent the rest of the afternoon drumming up a very loose sort of plan. Get into the palace undetected, find Nova, somehow try to convince her to come with him, and then escape back out of the palace without getting caught. There hadn't been time for the thorough research he'd usually relied on for a mission like this. Instead, he was forced to rely solely on his instincts and a bit of luck.

The guards began to move. This was his moment.

With silent movements, Ryker pulled his blowgun from the inside of his jacket pocket, loading it with a dreamroot dart. He aimed, finding his target within seconds. In the same breath, he loaded another dart and the second guard crumpled to the ground.

Ryker crouched low in the grass, waiting to make sure the guards were definitely unconscious. He slipped through the darkness like a shadow. Silent and swift, he slipped up and over the other side, landing on the ground with a gentle thud.

He didn't wait around to see if he'd been spotted—but no one was yelling or screaming. So far, so good.

Which room was Nova's. Ryker had no idea, but after seeing her in the city today, he'd made the decision to free her from Branoc's grasp, so he would search all night until he found her. Most of the higher up rooms that he could see from the ground were dark   empty. It seemed excessive to have such a large castle that didn't actually house any people. Especially when there were so many living in the streets. This type of royal ruling made Ryker see red.

A faint glow emitted from one of the balconies, and Ryker hoped it was hers. The last thing he needed was to stumble upon some courtier who'd wail from fright and give away his presence.

Finding a section of the wall partially covered by ivy, Ryker took a deep breath and began to climb. His fingers and toes found grip in the crevices of the grey stone, and he moved swiftly, the muscles in his arms and legs burning with exertion. Every sound, from the distant hoot of an owl to the rustle of leaves, heightened his senses.

Halfway up, he paused, clinging to the wall, as a pair of guards passed below. Their voices carried in the still night air, oblivious to the intruder above. Ryker waited until their footsteps faded before continuing his ascent.

Ryker pulled himself silently over the edge of the balcony, staying in the shadows. He wasn't prepared for what he saw as he peered around the corner of a rounded stone pillar.

There she was—Nova. Laying, curled up on the balcony floor—completely naked, her white hair sprawled on the marble tiles.

Clouds drifted past the moon, making the night darker, but he could see her glowing silhouette. The moon's filtered beams bathed her pale skin in light. Making her light up like he'd never seen before.

Movement caught his eye, and he held his breath as a figure stepped through the billowing curtains that separated the outside from the inside.

"My lady, would you like to come in now?" the maid offered.

Nova sat up and pulled her knees close to her chest, wrapping her arms around them. "No, thank you. Leave me here."

The pain in her voice was heartbreaking, a raw tremor that cut straight through him. Her usual warmth and light seemed stripped away, leaving only vulnerability laid bare. Each word she spoke wavered, catching slightly as though she were holding back a flood of emotions.

He should go to her. Pick her up and carry her away into the night.

The maid nodded and returned to the room. Once again, Nova was on her own.

A soft sniffing sound travelled through the air and Ryker almost ran to her side, but he would have to be cautious with his timing. There was no way of knowing who was inside and out of his view.

Nova shifted, and a heavy chime drew his attention to a silver chain attached to her ankle that ran its way back towards her room. Blood boiled in Ryker's veins. As the moon appeared from behind the clouds, her skin became clearer. Bruises mottled her skin in shades of purple, brown, and red. They spread across her arms, her neck, down her legs—marks left carelessly, thoughtlessly, by rough hands. Her whole body looked as if it had been beaten with a stick.

He wanted to kill Branoc for this. He should have known better than to leave her in the hands of the king.

There was still a chance he could fix this, right?

Ryker shook his head, took a deep breath in, and stepped out of the murky shadows.

EIGHT

THE UNPLANNED EXTRACTION

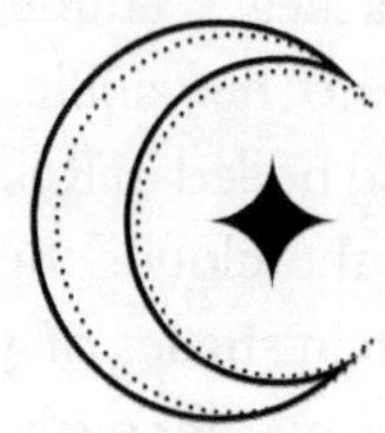

The sun had risen twenty-one times since Ryker left her with King Branoc.

Each day was the same as before. The maids would get her up, dress her in some ridiculous gown, and style her hair into some mass of frills and curls that gave Nova a headache by the end of the day.

She'd pick at her breakfast while they worked. Trying to find her appetite. It must have taken a liking to Ryker, because it left when he did.

Once the posse of women had finished their tugging and pulling, they would hand her over to the guards who stood posted at her door day and night. Then she'd be marched to the throne room and a waiting King Branoc.

Each passing day had brought new hope that Ryker would return to take her from this prison, but he was yet to come. Nova knew all along that he was leaving her at the palace. He'd never hidden that truth from her, but she'd harboured some hope that at the last minute he might have changed his mind.

Even if he came back, would she want to see him? Nova had pleaded with him, yet he'd left anyway.

Humans were depraved creatures, driven by their own selfish desires, and it seemed most of them were not to be trusted.

Now, as the heels of her boots echoed down the halls of the grand palace that had become a place of despair, Nova sighed. Mentally trying to prepare herself for whatever mood Branoc would be in today.

The heavy doors of the throne room swung open with a resounding creak, and Nova entered, her steps echoing in the vast, grand chamber. King Branoc sat on his gilded throne, watching smugly as she approached. The room was adorned with tapestries and finery, but the grandeur was spoiled by the oppressive atmosphere.

"Ah, my very own star. Come to use that magic for me again?" the king sneered.

Nova tried her best to hold her head high; she wouldn't allow him to see her in pain.

"What do you want?" she murmured.

Sister Tierra would laugh at Nova's boldness. Back home in Ara, she was always encouraging her to use her voice more. Perhaps here on Earth it was the perfect time to start practising.

King Branoc rose from his throne and sauntered over, forcing her to look up as he towered over her. His eyes brimmed with gluttony and pride—human traits Nova was quickly learning to recognise.

The king's smile widened, but it didn't reach his eyes. "Jewels, my dear. More jewels. I need you to replicate them with your magic. My treasury can never be too full."

It was the same thing he said every day, and every day she tried to resist the demand, with no luck.

Nova clenched her fists, her patience wearing thin. "What more could you possibly need? How can you hoard more when your people are starving?"

"My people have two hands and two legs . . . they can help themselves." He drew closer. "They are a stain on my kingdom. Perhaps I should be rid of them all together."

The threat hung in the air like a poisonous cloud. Nova's heart pounded with anger and fear. "You wouldn't dare," she spat, her voice trembling with rage.

"Disobey me and see what happens," the king sneered.

A salty wash of tears gathered in Nova's eyes. "You're a monster, and I hope you get what you deserve."

King Branoc's eyes darkened as he raised his hand and cracked it across her cheek. The force of the blow sent her to the ground in a trembling heap. A metallic taste, now familiar, blossomed through her mouth and Nova spat red blood onto the already crimson carpet.

The king crouched down and gripped her face in his hand. "See what happens when you don't behave? Shall we try again?"

Tears threatened to spill over, but Nova held them back, nodding in silence. Using her voice hadn't made a difference so far.

"Pick her up," Branoc ordered, and the guards stepped forward, roughly hauling Nova to her feet.

She stood, trembling but unbroken, glaring at Branoc with all the defiance she could summon. Her fists were clenched, every muscle in her body taut.

King Branoc pointed to the pile of glittering jewels spilling from a golden chest that sat on a small square table beside his throne. "Do it," he commanded, his voice cold and menacing. "Or we will see who pays the price for your disobedience."

Pitch black painted the skies above Nova. Her sisters glittering the realms from their heavenly places. Oh, how she wished to be with them. Would Soleil be watching her from the platforms of Ara? Can they see her in this bruised human body? Perhaps Tierra would chastise her, saying Nova's obsession with Earth would surely be cured now. Would Tierra make sure Soleil wouldn't get into too much trouble for trying to eat more than one starfruit a day?

The floor was like ice against her skin. Nova welcomed it. The sensation made her feel some sort of emotion as she lay naked on the floor.

After all her magic was depleted, Branoc would always send her back to her room. It was then that she would wait for nightfall so she could strip away the day physically and mentally.

Basking in the moon's glow.

Every minute that passed, she could feel her veins filling with her celestial powers. Pulsing through her like a life giving elixir—feeding her soul.

In her realm, she could summon handfuls of stardust to throw across the sky in a shower of tiny flecks. She could illuminate herself until she shone brighter than the sun shone in the Earth's sky. Auroras were created by her hands. Here on Earth, her powers had manifested differently. She could summon replicas of things she held, and then there was the whole glowing thing—not that she'd done a lot of that lately.

King Branoc had demanded she show him what she could do. He'd read the history books. He knew stars could perform magic on Earth and he wanted to see it for himself. At first, all she could manage was a faint glow. But after the fifth time enduring Branoc's rage, Nova became determined to find her powers, if only to make him stop hurting her.

Late at night, in the privacy of her room, she'd called upon them. Willing them to show themselves. Nova had begged internally—she needed to stay alive. What was the point of enduring five years of plummeting through space only to end up dead at the hands of a wicked man?

She'd been relieved to discover her power of replication, able to make an item appear in her other hand by simply holding it in her palm. Branoc, of course, had taken a liking to it as well.

With a soft sigh, thoughts of Ryker returned. Was he out there spending his sack of gold looking for his next victim? Basking in the glory of finding the star the king requested?

Truly, she shouldn't be shocked. She'd seen how cruel mankind can be from her place in the stars.

Tears pricked her eyes and started to flow down her cheeks. Wiping them with her hand, Nova sniffed and looked down at her body, covered in splotched colours of purple and brown—some new, some old. Never did she think falling to Earth would result in physical pain at the hands of a human.

Nova rested her chin on her knees as something moved in the shadows—halting her movements. "Who's there?"

No answer.

"Show yourself or I'll scream and the guards will come running."

A figure emerged, and Nova froze.

"Ryker?"

"Hello, little star."

The way her heart dropped to the bottom of her stomach at the sight of him brought a wave of heat that started at her feet and washed over her face. Nova scurried to stand, fully aware of how bare she was. Apparently, it wasn't common for a female to be naked in front of a male unless they were romantically involved—or so the maids said. Thankfully, her hair was long enough to cover her breasts. Though it didn't do much to cover the rest of her. She felt silly now for bathing with him when she did.

"Oh . . . oh . . . you do not get to talk to me. No, sir. Go away and don't ever come back." Nova choked back a sob.

It was the complete opposite of what she actually wanted, but the angry words spilled out, regardless.

Ryker took a few steps towards her, and she took a few back.

"Why are you here?" she asked. "Did you find someone who would pay you more for me?!"

"Keep your voice down. I just want to talk to you," Ryker pleaded.

Folding her arms across her chest, Nova scowled at the stupidly handsome man who blended with the shadows way too easily. "You have ten seconds to explain why you are here, or I will call the guards."

"I'm sorry, alright."

Nova stomped towards him, stopping just shy of him as the chain pulled on her ankle. "You're sorry!? I begged you not to leave me with him and you left me, anyway."

"I am a bounty hunter, Nova. It's my job to collect people and take them back to whoever has hired me to do so. I was just doing what I was being paid to do," Ryker explained.

A tear escaped down her cheek and she quickly wiped it away. "How's that going for you? Do you think this job was worth doing?"

"I don't. That's why I'm here. Let me take you away and truly help you find a way to get home."

"Why would I go with you?" Nova grit her teeth.

"Why wouldn't you?"

"Because you're just as likely to sell me off to someone else?"

Ryker tried to reach for her hand, but she pulled away, turning her back on him. "Please Nova. Surely coming with me is better than staying here chained to a bed?"

She turned to face him, sniffling as tears threatened to spill again. All these silly human emotions were so hard to juggle. She wanted to be so mad at him and at the very same time she'd wished for this very moment for the last twenty-one days.

"How do I know I can trust you?"

Ryker ran a hand through his inky waves and sighed. "You don't, but I am certainly going to try to rectify that. Starting tonight."

Nova thought for a moment as she looked out towards the darkened treeline. She certainly would like to be free from this abusive king and silly silver chain, but could she trust the man who put her in this position in the first place?

Ryker's gaze was softer than she'd ever seen it before. Those russet eyes that haunted her dreams. Ones she'd wished daily to look upon again.

"I will go with you only because I hate this horrid castle, with its suffocating clothing and greedy king, but so we are clear. I do not trust you."

Ryker hadn't let her finish before he was nodding in agreement. "I understand completely, and if you're done talking, we need to leave right now."

A commotion sounded from the hallway.

"Here, put this on . . . you need to cover up. And then we will see about that chain."

Nova's cheeks warmed at Ryker's words. She took the coat from his outstretched hand and put it on, wrapping it tightly around her body.

Ryker knelt down with a small knife in his hand and jammed the tip of the blade between the links of the silver chain and twisted until they bound against each, and with one more solid movement the metal gave way. She was free.

"Let me get my dress and shoes." Nova darted into her room and returned, shoving her arms into a fancy palace gown.

The gown Ryker had first bought her was long gone, but at least the maids had let her keep her boots. She'd worn them so often they'd become perfectly broken in, and she couldn't imagine trading them for new ones. She threw Ryker's jacket on again; she'd worry about the dress buttons later.

"We must hurry." Ryker spoke quietly as he took her hand and moved to the edge of the balcony.

"Are you expecting me to jump over the edge?" Nova whispered harshly, shoving her feet into her brown leather boots.

Ryker peered down at the ground below. "What if I promised to catch you?"

Nova simply glared in response.

"Fine, get on my back and I'll carry you down," he said as he turned his back towards her.

Nova rolled her eyes and sighed. There really weren't any other options. Placing her arms around his neck, she jumped up and wrapped her legs around his waist. The warmth of his back instantly seeped into her chest, making her body hum with that all too familiar glow.

"We're going to be spotted if you keep doing that," Ryker murmured.

Nova tried to shove her hands back into the jacket further. "I'm trying not to," she whispered back. She didn't want to admit that he was the reason she was glowing in the first place. Why did he have to smell so good?

With ease and light feet, Ryker had them over the edge of the balcony and down on the ground before Nova even had time to blink.

"How did you even get in here?" Nova asked as they slunk along.

Ryker glanced over his shoulder. "Sent the guards to bed early."

Nova shot her gaze towards Ryker's shadowed face. "You killed them?"

His brow knitted at her accusation. "No? I knocked them out."

"Oh."

"Do you think I just go around killing people?"

Nova shrugged. "I don't know you at all, but I certainly hope not."

Ryker huffed and pulled her close to his side, pressing them up against the stonewall of the palace gardens.

A few guards patrolled the grounds, so they waited until the coast was clear before moving on. They snuck through, making sure they stayed in the shadows as they ran against the wall. Ryker stopped halfway along and motioned with his hands that they needed to jump over the wall. Nova wasn't sure how she felt about this next part, but nodded. He knelt down and scooped her up, sitting her on his shoulder. With a stretch, she grabbed the top of the wall and put all her energy in, pulling herself up and over.

Ryker pushed her feet, and it was the boost she needed to sit on top of the wall. He took a few steps back and ran towards the wall. He hit it with his feet and almost ran vertically up it. Nova was thoroughly impressed.

"Hey! I think I just saw someone go over that wall!" a guard called from the other side, his voice filled with intrigue.

Heat washed through Nova's body, the glow from her hands fading. She was afraid they would be caught and she could only imagine what might happen to either of them, should Branoc find them.

"Don't be daft." A second male voice rang through the night air.

"I'm serious . . . I saw something."

Their voices became muffled the further Nova distanced herself from the castle. She huddled close to Ryker's side, grateful that they'd managed to get free without being spotted.

As they entered the dense forest, she smiled. Charlie waited patiently and snorted at their arrival.

"Well done, little star." Ryker winked at her.

Nova tried to hide her smile because she was supposed to be mad at him, but she couldn't help the corner of her mouth from sneaking up.

The next few minutes were a blur as they raced swiftly through the city and out into the forest. The air was crisp. Ryker gripped her tightly around the waist and, even though she was still angry with him, the touch of his hand on her body made her come alive.

The glowing light from a cabin window came into view, and Nova presumed it was Ryker's home as they neared. Charlie needed no direction as he aimed for the house, stopping short, just shy of the front steps.

"We must hurry. As soon as the king finds you're gone, he will send out a search party and we don't want to be around when he does."

Nova nodded as she slid down from Charlie's back and walked up the stairs to the front door. She waited patiently while Ryker unlocked it and then stepped inside as he held it open for her. His scent wafted over her and she instantly felt like she was home. The walls were unadorned, the furniture plain and functional. No soft fabrics, no delicate ornaments or flowers brightened the space.

"Is there anything I can do?" Nova asked, as Ryker rushed about.

"It's fine, you stay there; I only need a few things," he said as he paused in the doorway to a room. "I don't think you'll be comfortable travelling in that. Would you like a different dress?"

Nova looked down at the frilly palace gown and smoothed the fabric before fixing her gaze back on Ryker. "I only have this, so it will have to do."

"I think I have something."

His response drew Nova's brow together. Why did Ryker have women's clothing?

He disappeared into the room and returned with a bundle of dark blue fabric. "Here," he said as he shoved it towards her.

Nova looked at the ball of fabric.

"It's a dress . . ."

"I can see that. I'm just wondering where it came from . . . are you hiding someone back there?" Nova smirked, trying to peer over his shoulder into the room behind him.

His face was slightly redder than usual, and he fiddled with the pendant around his neck. "No. It was my sisters."

He seemed to stumble over his words, his shoulders slightly hunched, as his eyes darted around the room, avoiding her gaze.

Knowing they needed to get a move on, she didn't press further. "Thank you," she said softly.

Ryker nodded and pointed towards another room. "You can change in there."

Nova shut the door quietly behind her and took in the space. It was clearly Ryker's room. The bed was neatly made, and a couple of pairs of boots rested at the foot of it. A dark green rug, round and worn in places, covered the centre of the floor, while plain brown curtains framed the small window. It certainly didn't scream fashionable in any way, but to Nova it suited Ryker well. He didn't seem like the type to care for material things.

With fumbling fingers, Nova dropped the mass of ribbons and lace to the floor and drew the dark blue dress up and over her head. Despite the sleeves being a little too loose around her arms, it fit her quite nicely.

In the living room, Ryker leaned patiently against the kitchen table as he waited for her return. Inky black waves fell across his warm coloured face when he looked up as she entered. She itched to reach out and touch them. For a moment, she simply gazed at him. There were many men in the castle, but not one of them made her heart thud right out of her chest the way Ryker did when their eyes met.

"Would you mind helping me with the few buttons at the back?" she murmured.

Ryker shook his head. "Not at all."

Masculine fingers with a soft touch danced along her spine and Nova took a sharp breath in, trying not to imagine those exact same fingers dancing over other parts of her body.

"Done," Ryker spoke.

"Thank you."

He didn't linger long, instead reaching for the bags on the table and looking towards the front door. "We should really get going."

"Where are we going to go?"

"Anywhere but here."

They exited the cottage, and Ryker secured the lock to the front door.

After strapping the new bags to Charlie's saddle, he helped her up before pulling himself into position behind her.

"We will go in the opposite direction from where you landed. Fingers crossed they go looking for you there first," Ryke said as he pulled Charlie around. "Plus, I have a friend that I think might be able to help."

NINE

THE SMALL ROCK

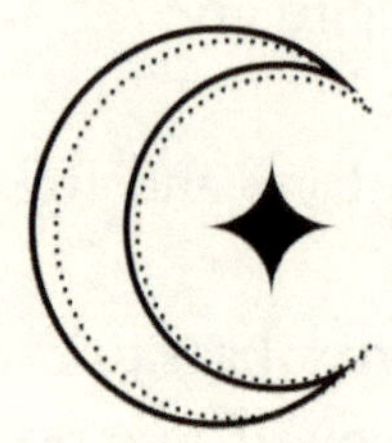

Three full days of riding. Only stopping at nightfall to rest Charlie and themselves. Ryker had suggested that they stick to the back roads and pathways deeper in the forests, avoiding open spaces and popular areas. Nova had politely agreed. She was still a little angry at him and no matter how many times their eyes had met over the crackling orange flames of the campfire or how many times their bodies accidentally touched when they retired for the evening in the very small tent, she was determined to stay angry a little longer.

It was late afternoon as they rode along. Nova closed her eyes as she breathed in the fresh spring air. There were no scents like this in her realm. Here in this part of the world, smells were different, sometimes not so good, but mostly quite desirable. Birds flit through the branches of the forest and Nova smiled as she watched them dance through the treetops.

As she looked towards the darkening skies, her thoughts travelled to her sisters. Soleil and Tierra would be stirring from their slumber, readying themselves for watching over Earth and taking care of the starfruit orchard.

Home in Ara was certainly peaceful and much safer than here, but here there was so much to see and do. Now that she was away from Branoc, she wondered if there was really any rush to get home?

"Are you warm enough?" Ryker's voice brushed the back of her neck.

She nodded. "Fine, thank you."

His arms shifted around her waist, pulling her closer to his chest. "Do you lie in the moonlight naked often?"

Heat rose to Nova's cheeks. In their rush to flee the castle, she'd forgotten that he'd witnessed her on the balcony.

Nova nodded softly. "It helps me regenerate my . . . powers."

"So, it's true? You have magic?"

Nova hesitated, then glanced over her shoulder and shrugged. "It seems as though I do."

Would he care that she could use magic? Would he see her differently? Could she trust him not to twist her abilities for his own gain, as others had before? Only time would reveal his true intentions, but for now, the question lingered, heavy in her mind.

"So how did you fall to Earth, Nova?" Ryker asked from his seated position behind her.

Nova looked towards the skies. "I was knocked from my celestial anchor by a small rock, which sent me off balance and spinning through the galaxies."

"What's a celestial anchor?"

"There are platforms in Ara spread across the galaxies. Each one holds a magical device that allows us to see Earth up close. It's our job to search for those who need our light . . . our guidance."

Ryker adjusted his position. "So, how did the rock cause you to fall?"

"Sometimes meteor showers come through. Usually they go around Ara, but this was different. The shower travelled closer to us than I'd ever seen before. It caught us off guard, and before I could raise my celestial shield, a stray rock hit me in the chest. The force of it broke my tether to the platform, and I began to spin out of orbit."

Memories from that moment rushed to Nova's mind. The pain of being wrenched from her home and projected into unfamiliar skies still fresh and unattended to. The dull ache pulled in her chest.

A gentle breeze blew through the tree branches of dark and light green. It rustled the leaves and danced over Nova's skin, playing with her hair. Ryker's grip around her waist tightened. His nearness warmed her body. Despite their short past, Nova felt safer with him than anywhere else she'd been on Earth so far. Glancing down at her hands, she saw the familiar viridian pulse of light radiating off them. She tried to conceal the glow, but it was near impossible.

"How long were you spinning?" Ryker's voice was low and gentle.

Nova was caught off guard by his question. He wanted to know more about her? "It took me five celestial years to reach the Earth's surface, but our time is different from yours. For every one of your years, it is five for us," she murmured.

Ryker shifted in the saddle and the warmth of his chest against Nova's back sent little tingles up her spine. "So, a whole Earthly year. How old does that make you . . . if you don't mind me asking?"

Nova pondered. "Well, I am one hundred and thirty years of age in the celestial realm, so I guess that makes me twenty-six in yours."

He softly blew air through his nose. Nova could tell he was smiling.

"My age amuses you?" she asked.

"This whole situation amuses me."

"How so?"

Ryker pulled Charlie to the left, taking a path deeper into the forest. "Stories of fallen stars are quite popular around here. There was a star who fell over one hundred years ago. They say she went into hiding and no one has seen her since. And now here I am with you . . . a star—on the run from a king."

"I'm sorry if my arrival has disrupted your busy schedule," Nova murmured.

Ryker huffed softly but didn't respond.

Nova glanced over her shoulder at the brooding man behind her. "How old are you?"

"I'm thirty-two."

Nova gazed forward again. "You said you had a sister? Do you have other siblings?"

Ryker sighed. "It's just my sister and I."

"Does she live around here?"

"No, she doesn't."

Nova noted the hesitancy in his voice. It seemed as though he didn't want to reveal too much about his family, so she let the subject drop.

The light in the woods grew lighter as they neared the edge. Shades of ginger, saffron, and bronze filtered through the branches as the sun set lower. It was the first moment Nova had been able to breathe since fleeing the grips of King Branoc. In this small window of time as she sat with Ryker upon Charlie's back, she felt peaceful—she could breathe in the fresh, earthly air without fear attached to it.

"Why did you come back for me?" Nova asked quietly.

Ryker cleared his throat. "Because I couldn't shake the feeling that I'd done the wrong thing, and I needed to make it right."

A small part of the anger she held for Ryker lessened. It was hard for her to hold resentment for long. The heavy weight of it swimming around in her stomach felt unnatural. Nova wanted to be rid of it.

Silence filled the air as Charlie meandered along.

"King Branoc is an evil man." Nova murmured.

Ryker's hands gripped the leather reins tighter, his arms firm against her waist.

"Tell me what he did."

Nova closed her eyes to the memories of Branoc's hand. "The first day he was almost nice. He seemed interested in impressing me with his possessions. Then he asked to see my powers. At the time, I told him I had none, which I thought was true. But the answer made him angry. He let me go hungry for the next two days, but returned smiling as if he hadn't locked me in my room. As such a close acquaintance, you must know how quickly his patience wanes. After the fifth time he hit me, I begged my powers to manifest, and one of them finally did."

"I'm going to fucking kill him." Ryker's voice was rough and low.

Nova fiddled with the saddle horn in front of her. "It's alright, I'm not there anymore."

"It's far from alright. He will pay," Ryker growled. "And I promise I am going to find a way to get you home."

As Ryker's words settled in her ears, Nova wondered how that was even possible. How was a star supposed to leave Earth and return to Ara?

Now that she was no longer at the mercy of King Branoc, maybe she could see the world a little before attempting to find a way home.

Nova nearly squealed out loud as they broke into a clearing outside the thick forest. A circular meadow, filled with wildflowers of every colour of the rainbow, grew at the edge of the forest's depths. It was the most magical image. Golden light filtered through the leaves, creating the illusion of gold dust falling to the ground. Butterflies danced along the flower tops and a few deer grazed in the distance.

Nova couldn't get off Charlie's back fast enough.

"Where are you going?" Ryker called to her as she ran.

"I have to see them up close!"

With light footsteps, Nova danced through the flowers, spinning and laughing at the butterflies that joined her. This was the part of Earth she longed to see. This is what she longed to touch and smell. This is where she wanted to stay.

The toe of her boot hit a small rock and, before she could collect herself, she went flying headfirst into the flora.

"Nova!"

Laughing, she rolled onto her back. Tears streamed down her face; It was so like her to once again be defeated by a small rock.

Ryker reached her side within seconds and slid to the ground. "Are you okay? You're crying. Are you hurt?"

Calloused hands gently checked her over and Nova softly smiled as she took in Ryker's concern. Warm brown eyes met her sea-green ones and, for what felt like an eternity, neither of them spoke.

"I'm fine. I'm only crying because I think your world can be so very beautiful, Ryker, and I'm not sure I want to go home just yet."

TEN

It was day four of their journey south, and Ryker was hopeful that they were far enough from the villages surrounding the palace that less and less people would recognise or care who they were. Only a few more days and they would reach his friend's house.

Chester Oak had been a friend to Ryker for many years. They'd met along their travels. Chester was a historian, which had him travelling all over the country filling journals with knowledge and stories passed down through generations. The hunter and the historian crossed paths often enough that Chester insisted it was a sign. Thus, a friendship was born.

Surely, he would have some answers.

The sun was setting, and Ryker could see soft smoke tendrils coming from the treetops ahead, confirming the town he'd expected to be nearby, just in time to replenish their rapidly dwindling rations.

Hopefully he wouldn't run into any . . . old friends. He'd managed to avoid Sable and her crew and if Branoc had sent men after them, there was a good chance they were still a few days' ride behind.

"We need to make a shortstop at this village up ahead. We need to replenish our food supply." Ryker said as they both dipped under a low-hanging branch.

Nova nodded, but remained silent. She'd been doing a lot of that. Could he blame her? Who knows what was swimming in her head? This whole entire experience must be baffling.

Just like it baffled him to have found her completely naked on the balcony.

There was no denying the attraction he felt for this woman. Every day he was finding it harder and harder not to reach for her and pull her close. Her scent was intoxicating. A mix of something from another realm and the lavender soap he carried. The way her body fit against his as they slept in the tent each night was almost like she was created just for him. He pushed down every feeling and thought. He wasn't looking for whatever she was.

His heart already belonged to someone else.

Nova glanced over her shoulder, a smile tugging at her mouth. "Is that all we are doing?"

The galaxies glittered in her eyes, and Ryker pulled his gaze away. He was losing his soul very quickly. Perhaps stopping in town would give him a little breathing space.

"That is all we are doing—I swear."

"I hope I'm not walking into some sort of trap."

Ryker shifted in the saddle. "I told you I would get you home."

"And how can I trust you?"

"Have I lied to you yet?"

Nova huffed with a smile and returned her gaze to the road ahead. "You certainly haven't told the whole truth."

Ryker sighed softly, "I didn't know Branoc would be so brutal."

Nova was quiet. The shoulder of her gown slightly slipped, revealing a few purple blemishes on her skin. Ryker's gaze skimmed over them before he pulled it away. He didn't like what the bruises awoke in him. Something was brewing deep within—something he hadn't felt in a very long time. He gripped the reins tighter in his hands, fighting the urge to turn the horse around and go back to Emberfell, where he would beat the living daylights out of Branoc.

He may still do it.

"He will pay for his crimes, Nova . . . I promise you this."

Nova sighed. "Don't make promises you can't keep."

A small crack formed in his already broken heart, widening with every breath he took. She was right. Who was he to make promises?

They broke from the safety of the forest into a small clearing between the woods and the small town. A modest tavern stood at the centre, its sign swaying gently in the breeze. The general store sat just beside it, stocked with essentials, while the small church, with its weathered stone, overlooked the square. The rhythmic clink of metal echoed through the air, signalling the presence of a blacksmith hard at work nearby.

A few people greeted them with nods or smiles, which Ryker returned sparingly. The less attention they drew to themselves, the better. He glanced down at Nova's hands and was grateful to find that she wasn't glowing. It was going to be hard to hide it in a crowd.

Ryker pulled up to the tavern, eyeing every possible escape route. Should they need one. There wasn't a pirate or guard in sight. Once satisfied that no one seemed to pose a threat, he slid off Charlie's back and hitched the black stallion to a railing before helping Nova down.

She was like air in his hands, a fragile skeleton of bones covered in a bruised blanket of skin. Did they even feed her at the palace? A few more days with him would see that she was eating well. Ryker was relieved that the long sleeves of her gown concealed the blemishes on her arms. Though the marks on her face were starting to fade, traces of them still remained.

"Will we stop for long?" she said as she glanced towards the tavern doors.

Ryker shrugged. "Long enough to eat, bath and gather supplies."

"And this place offers all of those things?"

"Food and bathing, yes. I will get supplies after we've eaten."

Ryker made sure all his weapons were in their right places before he took Nova's hand in his. It felt like ice on his skin. Hopefully, the tavern offered hot water in their rooms.

"Stay close."

Nova nodded, following him inside.

The inn was dimly lit and scattered with travellers. A pair of half-orcs sat at a corner table, their hulking forms hunched over steaming bowls of food and large pints of ale, their guttural laughter blending with the low hum of conversation. Beside them, a group of elves in finely woven cloaks exchanged quiet words, their delicate features betraying little emotion as they sipped from smaller goblets.

Ryker scanned the room for any threatening figures. A group of humans filled a table nearby, boisterous and animated, playing cards and shouting over each other in good-natured rivalry.

The atmosphere was alive, a mix of tension and camaraderie. Ryker's hand slipped to the small of Nova's back as they moved towards the counter, where a female, human barkeep with a round, joyful face gave them a nod, wiping a mug clean with a rag. She threw a glance Nova's way, her gaze remaining on the star's face a little too long. "What can I get you folks?"

Ryker hoped the woman didn't think he'd caused Nova's bruises. "What are you currently serving for dinner?" He asked, trying to sound calm.

"Pea and ham soup with a side of toasted sourdough. Oh, and we have an ale special on. Two for the price of one. Only lasts for another hour, though."

Ryker looked at Nova before answering the woman. "Does that sound alright?"

Nova nodded vigorously.

"Give us two servings of the soup, then please, and two ales."

"I'll bring it over to yer' table." The woman smiled at them and headed back towards the bar.

A few villagers watched as they made their way to a small table tucked in the corner of the room. Ryker was pleased Nova's glow was currently diffused. Most likely, they just looked like two travellers passing through. It seemed most occupants kept to themselves, so he allowed his guard to drop—just a little.

"Did you see those pirates who came through town yesterday?" a voice drifted through the air. "Loud bunch, I tell ya."

Ryker focused in on the conversation happening at the table behind Nova. He eyed the two males. One was definitely human, by the way his ear rounded at the tip. The other was elven. They looked like regulars.

"I didn't see them, but I heard they come through looking for supplies," the second male answered before taking a large gulp of frothy ale.

Nova's gaze caught his. "I want to see a pirate."

"No, you don't."

"Why not?"

"Because they are more trouble than they're worth," Ryker murmured, leaning back in his wooden chair.

Nova squinted her eyes as she looked at him from across the table. "Have you met one before?"

Ryker huffed. "Too many times."

"Tell me about them."

"You don't want to know the pirates I know . . . trust me," Ryker muttered. "Meddlesome bunch."

Ryker clenched his jaw, his thoughts circling around Sable Bloodfin, the notorious pirate captain from Corsair. She was always getting in his way, meddling in his bounty hunting business. Somehow, he'd earned her ire, and too often he'd got close to securing a big score, and she'd swoop in, messing up his plans.

Nova released a light laugh as she fiddled with the linen napkin on the tabletop. Ryker watched her as her eyes travelled around the room, taking in all the sights.

"Are those people kissing?"

"Who?"

Nova pointed to a couple at a table across the room. Ryker smiled quickly before returning his gaze to Nova.

"I suppose they are."

"It looks like they are enjoying themselves. Maybe we should do that?" Nova looked at him with such an innocence about her, that Ryker didn't have the heart to kill her joy, even if he felt a flush crawl up his face at the thought.

"That's something two people in love do."

"Only those in love?"

They were interrupted by the woman returning with their ale and soup. Ryker was thankful. He probably wasn't the best person to be having this kind of talk with. He'd never been great at expressing his feelings. More than a few people in his life would tell him that.

They thanked the woman, and she left them to eat.

"Well?" Nova pushed.

Ryker took a sip of ale before he continued. "Others do it just because it feels good."

"Have you done it before?"

"I have."

"Did you enjoy it?" Nova's eyes glittered with anticipation.

"Very much."

Nova sat back against the wooden booth and sighed. "I hope I can experience that one day."

An impulsive smile played across his lips. "How about we worry about getting some food into you first?"

With a nod, Nova picked up her spoon and ate.

Each savouring the taste of soup and toast in silence. They were two ales deep each when Ryker sensed that maybe the liquor was affecting Nova more than he thought it would.

"Are you alright?"

Nova smiled a sleepy smile. "I feel great. Why?"

Ryker huffed in amusement and signalled for the woman who had served them their meal. She hurried over.

"Do you know if there are spare rooms this evening?"

"Yes sir, we have a couple available, but all are only single sleeping arrangements."

Surely sharing a tent was the same as sharing a room, right? Of course it wasn't. Who was he kidding? A room with a warm bed—only one—was much more inviting than a thin mattress inside a tent on the forest floor. Especially when the company was as beautiful as Nova was.

"Are you alright with that?" Ryker turned to Nova and asked.

She simply nodded in response.

Ryker stood. "Perfect. Could I please purchase one for the evening?"

With a smile, the woman hustled back to the bar and returned with a key. "Room six, on the right as you head up those stairs."

Ryker thanked her and took Nova's hand in his.

The stairs creaked beneath their weight as Ryker led Nova towards the room. Unlocking it with one hand, he stepped inside and closed the door behind them. The room was small but tidy. A small vase of wildflowers, freshly picked, sat on a round wooden table by the window, their vibrant colours adding a touch of warmth to the space. The curtains, in a faded floral pattern, were already drawn against the approaching dusk, leaving the room bathed in the soft glow of the setting sun.

He released her hand and opened the bathroom door. "You can freshen up here while I go and get supplies."

"You trust me in this room all alone?"

Ryker glanced down at her full, soft lips, fighting the urge to bend down and kiss her soundly. "Are you going to run away again?"

She took a step towards him, her eyes holding his as she fluttered her dainty lashes. "Is there a reason to?"

"Let me warn you, little star, if you run away again, there will be consequences to pay." A smirk tugged at his lips.

She was enticing him—daring him to play.

A flash of mischief filled Nova's eyes, and she smiled bigger. "Maybe I'd like to see what those consequences are . . ."

Her words almost brought him to his knees.

Ryker steadied himself with a hand on the knob of the bathroom door, trying to still his mind. He was lost for words. This little star was creeping under his skin, and he didn't know how to react. No woman had had this effect on him in a very long time—four years, to be exact.

"It won't be me you should be worried about." Ryker traced her facial features, noticing her silvery skin sprinkled with tiny stardust like specks. Her hair was floating around her like glittering threads, lighter than the feathers from a dove. "Branoc will be looking for you. Not to mention the Twins. Possibly pirates."

"Pirates?"

"Yes, pirates."

Each time Nova took another step towards him, the glow from her skin grew brighter. She reached up to fiddle with a button on his coat. The simple act brought a heat to his core that he didn't want to acknowledge.

"Why would pirates be searching for me?"

He lifted a brow, unsure if he should dignify the question with a response.

She pressed her lips into a thin line. "Fine . . . I promise to stay in the room on one condition." Nova's eyes flicked to mouth and back up again. "Perhaps before I leave this Earth . . . you could kiss me?"

Ryker swallowed down the fire building in his stomach, fighting the urge of blood that wanted to harden certain body parts. She was too close. Too beautiful.

This wasn't the plan, though. He rescued her from the king. Now he needed to find a way to get her home so she would be safe and he would go back to his life—the one where he was responsible only for himself.

So why did the thought suddenly feel wrong?

He kept his expression even. "Perhaps you should bathe first?"

The light in Nova's eyes snuffed out, but her smile remained. "Rude," she called behind her as she moved into the bathroom.

"I will get supplies now. Lock the door behind me and don't answer it unless it's me," Ryker said.

Nova nodded, and Ryker left the room. The fresh air would do him some good.

The village was beginning its slow journey into sleepiness. Soon, all the stores would close, and everyone would retreat to their homes and beds for the night. Ryker wandered through the bustling marketplace, selecting a variety of food supplies: fresh bread, smoked meats, and a few ripe fruits. The aroma of spices and roasted vegetables filled the air as he navigated the crowded stalls. Once his pack was full, he led Charlie to a nearby stable, patting the horse's neck affectionately as he handed the reins to the stable master.

"I'll be back for him in the morning. Have him saddled and ready to go by sunup," Ryker said, slipping a few coins into the man's hand. With Charlie settled, Ryker made his way back to the tavern.

He knocked and announced himself. Relief washed over him when Nova warily opened the door. Her hair was still damp, and she smelt of the soap she must have found in the bathroom.

Jasmine and lemon.

"Did you get everything you need?" she asked, moving across the room to sit on the edge of the bed.

Ryker nodded. "It will do for the next few days."

He locked the door behind him. There was definitely no need for unannounced visitors throughout the night.

"Are you going to join me?" Nova murmured.

Ryker slowly moved towards the bed and looked down at Nova. The longer he stayed caught in her beautiful eyes, the brighter her glow seemed to grow. He wanted to do more than join her on the bed. He wanted to do things with her on the bed——if that's what she wanted too. Yet, he knew as soon as he opened that door, there would be no holding back the floodgates of consequences that would unfold if he did.

He didn't want to resist, but if he allowed even a tiny part of him to let Nova in, she'd have to join the ghosts of his past, and he wasn't sure he'd ever be ready for that.

Certainly not today anyway.

Ryker placed his hands in his pockets, taking a few steps back. "I'll rest in the chair over there. Sleep, little star."

Nova held his gaze for a few more moments before stifling a yawn. "Suit yourself," she said as she lay down and turned on her side, curling up in a little ball.

He reached for the blanket that hung over the edge of the bed and draped it across her body. Once he was satisfied that she was asleep, he sat himself down in the chair opposite the bed and pulled a flask of rum from the inside of his jacket pocket. His mind needed numbing, and this was the only way he knew how to do it.

Nova was nearly as intoxicating, and his body knew it.

He hadn't touched a woman in four years, and it was beginning to show. The hardness between his legs grew as he watched her sleeping form. The way her chest rose with each breath and how her dainty hands rested upon the bed had him wishing he could cover her entire body with tiny kisses.

However, sleeping with her would be connected with feelings and feelings were not something Ryker felt comfortable around. He had never been the type to fuck and run.

Nova stirred on the bed, a small whimper escaping her lips. It was at this moment; he knew that if he didn't stop now, he was going to fall into a place he was not yet willing to go.

A phantom pain pulled in his heart, a sore reminder of the last time he gave it away. He'd sworn to never again give it to another.

Yet just for a moment, he imagined what it would be like if he did. Could he do it?

His body ached from nights on the forest floor, but he knew if he gave into that desire, she would sidle up to him in her sleep and he would once again lay awake all night wishing he could touch her.

Ryker took another swig of rum. If he found a way to get her home and this torture will end. With that thought in mind, he finally drifted off to sleep.

ELEVEN

THE KING'S GUARDS

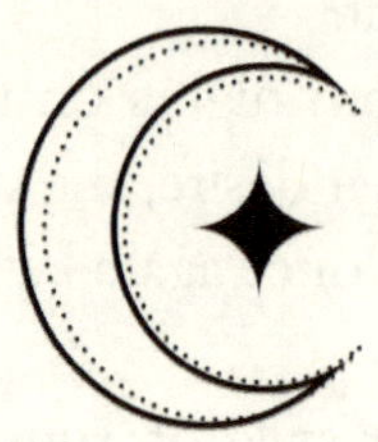

Like clockwork, Ryker rose with the sun. His body knew when it peered above the horizon, waking him as soon as the night was done. He slowly stirred so as not to disturb Nova, wanting to bathe before she woke. Ryker stopped, caught in the way she radiated as she slept, glowing like the star that she was. Ryker reached for the soft white tendrils of her hair and brushed it from her face—the touch of it sending shivers all over his body.

"Ryker," she softly murmured.

His hand froze at the sound of her voice, but she didn't wake. Drawing back, he eased from the bed and tip-toed across the floor to the washroom. He would freshen up quickly, so she'd have time after him. Then they needed to eat and get on the road. There was no way King Branoc would allow her to simply be taken from him. They couldn't stay put in one place for too long.

When he returned from the bathroom, he found Nova already up.

"Morning," he murmured.

"Morning. Did you sleep alright?"

Ryker nodded. "Well enough. But we should get a move on."

"Are you worried about something?"

Ryker moved to the small window and drew the curtain back, peering outside at the town below. "I just don't think it's wise to stay in one place too long."

Nova nodded and moved off to use the washroom. Ryker packed their belongings before they both went downstairs to pay for their lodgings and order breakfast. The woman from the night before greeted them with her joyful presence, ushering them to a booth, promising to bring them eggs, bacon, toast and coffee swiftly.

"I don't even remember falling asleep last night?" Nova looked at Ryker with bewilderment written on her face.

A smile tugged at the corner of his mouth at the memory of her soft snores echoing through the room. "That's because that ale knocked you out cold. How are you feeling this morning?"

Nova rubbed her head. "Things are a little foggy."

Ryker chuckled. "Once you eat, you will feel better. Though we must hurry."

Breakfast was brought over, and the pair dug in. It was good, just what they both needed.

Ryker finished his last mouthful of coffee when the tavern door opened with a thud. He glanced over his shoulder, his stomach falling to the floor.

Guards stood in the doorway—three of them—their uniforms red and blue, all too familiar. Branoc's men.

Not wanting to draw a single drop of attention his way, Ryker slowly turned back towards Nova. "Don't move an inch. I need to get us out of here," he whispered.

A wide-eyed Nova froze, and Ryker flicked his gaze towards the bar again. The guards had approached and were speaking to a gentleman there. He caught the eye of the woman who'd served them their meals and slowly pushed his jacket to the side, revealing a small pouch—one designed to hold gold coins—before he then looked towards the guards.

No words were spoken, but a mutual understanding was formed, and the woman nodded her head slightly to the doorway leading to the kitchen. Ryker bobbed and the escape plan was put into action.

The woman walked by them slowly and held out her hand down low by her side. He passed the small pouch of gold to her and stood. Then he took Nova's hand as the woman moved off to distract the guards. She greeted them loudly, offering any assistance. It was the perfect distraction for them to disappear out the back, exiting out the door into the morning sun. Townsfolk were already busy moving about and Ryker pulled Nova along as they blended in with the crowd.

His makeshift plan was working well until he glanced down at his fingers entwined with Nova's. Her skin was radiating with that delightful viridian glow, and each time he caught her eye, she would shine even brighter.

This was going to be a problem. The last thing he wanted was to attract more attention. He needed to find something to cover her body with—preferably something with a hood.

"Do you think you can control that glowing, little star?"

Nova quickly glanced down before meeting his gaze. "If you let go of my hand, perhaps I might."

Her voice was tinged with amusement and the flecks of playfulness in her sea-green eyes kept his hand at bay—if only for a moment. He didn't want to release it. In fact, he could quite happily hold it forever, but if he wanted to escape, she needed to keep her glow to non-existent. So, he gently dropped it, offering her a brief smile as he did so.

Ryker hugged the wall of the tavern and peeked around the front. Just as he suspected, there were three other guards on horses waiting outside.

Fuck

This was a lot more complicated than what he'd like it to be and the only way they were going to outrun the guards was with Charlie.

There was only one slight issue. The stables were located directly opposite the tavern, in plain sight to the red and blue-coated men. There was no way they would reach it at this angle. He'd have to approach from the other side.

Ryker looked in the opposite direction of where he needed to go. They'd have to circle around the town. He waited until a cart of straw and dung neared, then tugged Nova alongside it as the villager meandered along. He'd hoped the wooden structure would act as a barrier between them and the guards. Unfortunately, that was not the case. King Branoc's guards might not have Ryker's' keen eye, but they weren't completely blind and nearly everyone could see the woman whose hair was afloat and skin radiating.

"There they are!" came the cry.

"Quick, this way!" Ryker hissed, pulling Nova along. They sprinted towards the centre of the marketplace in hopes they might be lost amongst the crowds, but it was still early morning, so the sea of villages Ryker had counted on was thin.

"Stop, in the name of the king!"

"Not a chance," Ryker grinned as they ducked down a small street.

There was very little room and nothing to conceal them. Ryker's eyes darted around, searching for anything that might help them blend in. As they rounded a corner, he spotted a stall laden with various trinkets and accessories. Without slowing down, he snatched a wide-brimmed hat and jammed it onto his head before grabbing a cloak for Nova. She hurriedly wrapped it around her shoulders. Ryker tossed a few gold coins towards the shopkeeper as they dashed away.

The hat's brim cast a shadow over his face, partially obscuring his features. "Keep your head down," he murmured, pulling Nova's hood over her head. "You need to do something about that glow, little star."

This wasn't the first occasion he was chased through a village, and it certainly wouldn't be the last, but the times it had happened before, he was alone. Not carrying precious cargo.

"Ryker, I'm scared," Nova whispered as they scurried along.

He gripped her hand tighter. "We're going to get out of this. We just need to reach Charlie."

The shouts of the guards grew louder behind them. "There they are! Stop them!" one of the guards bellowed. Arrows whizzed past them, embedding into walls and wooden crates with solid thuds.

Nova screamed as one flew past her head.

Ryker ducked and weaved through the streets, trying to lose the guards, but they were relentless.

A surge of heat and pain seared through his shoulder as an arrow found its mark, but there was no time to stop and pull it out—it would only kill him faster that way. He'd deal with it later, despite the pain.

"Ryker, you're hurt!"

"Leave it be, little star, I'll be fine. Just stay close."

Ryker and Nova pushed through a side street, knocking over baskets of cabbages and corn, startling a group of children playing nearby. The townspeople's protests and shocked cries added to the chaos, providing a momentary shield against the pursuing guards.

"Over here," Ryker urged, pulling Nova into a small, darkened alcove behind a stack of barrels. They pressed close together, breath mingling, hearts racing. The guards' footsteps thundered past, fading into the distance.

Ryker's shoulder throbbed with pain, but he pushed it aside, focusing on the need to keep moving. Once the sound of the guards faded, he peeked out, making sure there were no threats.

"We need to get to Charlie," Nova whispered.

Ryker nodded, grimacing as he broke the arrow's shaft and discarded it. They waited a moment longer, making sure the coast was clear, before slipping out of their hiding place.

With cautious ease, Ryker moved, eyes scanning for any lingering threats. Finally, they reached the stable where Charlie was housed. The horse nickered softly as they approached. Doing his best to appear unhurried, Ryker thanked the stable hand before ushering the large black horse and the trembling star out the back of the wooden structure.

Pain flared through his shoulder as he mounted Charlie, then helped Nova up behind him. "Hold on tight," he murmured, spurring the horse into a gallop. They tore through the town's outskirts, the wind whipping around them, carrying them away from danger.

"That was so close, Ryker!" Nova exclaimed.

"Too close," he replied.

They didn't slow down for the rest of the day. Ryker refused to stop, despite the blood soaking his shirt. Only when the sun dipped low, and shadows lengthened did he finally relent. As the sky darkened, they stumbled upon a shallow cave nestled on the side of a hill. It wasn't much, but it offered protection from the elements. With the last of his energy, he guided them inside, his breathing ragged.

"Are you sure there won't be any . . . creatures in here?" Nova eyed the walls of the lowly lit hollow rock formation.

"I am certain. This area isn't known to house Galanthors. The only other creature that could be in here would be bats, but they will keep to themselves."

Satisfied with his answer, Nova slid from Charlie's back. She helped Ryker gather their belongings as they both stumbled into the cave.

Ryker built a fire and made sure Charlie was safe before he finally allowed his body to feel the full brunt of the pain coursing through it. He tried to keep the grimace from his face as he sat down, but mustn't have done the best job.

"Ryker, you're in pain. Let me help you."

He didn't refuse her offer.

She knelt close and undid his shirt, surveying the damage. "I'm going to have to pull it out."

"I can handle it. Just do it fast."

Thunder rumbled outside and Ryker instinctively reached for the pendant around his neck—his comfort, his peace of mind.

Her small hand trembled as she wrapped it around the snapped arrow shaft lodged in Ryker's shoulder. He clenched his jaw, bracing himself as she began to pull. A sharp, searing pain shot through his body, like his flesh was being ripped apart. The arrowhead scraped against his bone, sending pulsing waves of agony through his arm and chest.

Every nerve ending in its path felt like it was on fire. His vision blurred with the intensity of the pain, and he held back a scream, tasting blood as he bit down hard. As the arrow finally came free, the rush of relief was overshadowed by the throbbing ache that tarried.

"I want to try to heal it for you," Nova murmured.

Ryker held her gaze as the firelight danced on her skin. This woman had already endured so much in her short time on Earth. Yet, she remained soft. Taking each experience in her stride. She was incredible.

Sweat beaded on Ryker's forehead. The pain was intensifying, and he knew that if he didn't get his shoulder healed soon, infection would set in.

He nodded at Nova. "Can you do that?"

Nova shook her head gently. "I don't know, but surely my glow can do something . . . Will you let me try?"

Ryker looked down at his chest. The ruby red blood glistened in the fire's light. It was seeping from his body with every pump of his heart. He drew his gaze back to the star and nodded. He watched as she positioned her hands over the wound.

She went still with concentration. Nothing happened for a moment, but then a blue glow began to pour from her fingertips. The floating path of light was scattered with little glowing, golden dots that made their way into Ryker's shoulder.

Tingles began in his flesh and spread into his chest. The white glow surrounding Nova grew, intensifying until she cried out and light exploded all around them, illuminating the cave.

After the power diminished, Ryker looked down at the wound to find it completely healed. Not even a trace of blood could be found. It was surreal to experience magic from another realm. Here on Earth, there were tales of ancient magic that still ran through the Earth's core, feeding the creatures that tarried long after the gods had left. Ryker was yet to see the proof it was real.

"You're incredible, Nova." Ryker offered her a grateful smile. "Thank you."

"Might need to replenish after that one."

"Are you alright?"

She nodded. "Nothing a good dose of moon bathing won't fix."

Thunder rumbled outside and Ryker turned his head towards the sound. "Is that what you were doing the night I found you?"

"Yes." Her voice was barely a whisper.

"What powers was Branoc making you use Nova . . ."

She sat in front of the fire, hugging her knees. Ryker could see the pain in her eyes as she stared at the flames.

"The only one I managed to summon . . . replication."

"Does that cost your strength?"

Resting her chin on her knees, Nova tilted her head to look at him. "Seems like more than the healing powers, yes."

"What made you think you could heal my shoulder?" Ryker murmured.

Nova shrugged. "In Ara, we work together to mend those that are injured. It doesn't happen often, but I'd hoped I'd carried that ability here with me. All things are made of stardust after all."

The ground shook as the storm above them drew closer. Ryker did his best to ignore it by asking Nova about her gifts, but the familiar anxiety began to take hold.

He shifted closer to the fire. "What sort of things did he make you replicate?"

"More of his silly jewels and gold." Nova shrugged. "I tried to get him to help the poor with all of his riches . . . but that didn't turn out so well."

"I'm sorry, Nova. Truly."

She turned and flashed him a sad smile. "It's behind me now."

Outside, thunder rumbled again, and Ryker felt the shaking to his core. Cradling the pendant around his neck, he watched the flames dance, casting their shadows on the cave walls.

"Why do you always play with that when there's a storm?" Nova's sweet voice brought him back to reality.

"I don't."

"Yes, you do."

Ryker shrugged lightly. "Habit, I guess."

Nova stood to her feet and stretched. "I told you about my magic. Now it's your turn to tell me about your habit."

"There is nothing to tell. Just leave it be Nova," Ryker murmured.

It was true, there was nothing to tell that wouldn't bring up pain and trauma—something Ryker would rather leave buried deep in the past.

Nova spoke softly. "It's not nothing. Every time it rains, or a storm erupts, you fiddle with it as if the world is about to end."

Ryker pulled himself to his feet, dropping his arms to his sides. It was too painful to talk about. Even more than the wound the arrow had inflicted. It had been a very long time since anyone bothered to ask about his habit, and he liked it that way. Who was Nova to ask about it now? "I don't need to explain myself to a star."

He regretted the words as soon as they left his mouth. He didn't mean to snap. This is why he kept his feelings at bay. They had no business messing up his life. "Nova I'm sorry, I didn't mean—"

Nova flinched, and tears welled in her eyes. He wanted to pause time and pluck the words he'd flung at her from her ears. She didn't deserve any form of pain, mentally, physically, and certainly not verbally.

"You're right . . . I'm just a star. What would I know about humans." Nova twisted and headed towards the mouth of the cave.

"Where are you going?" Ryker called after her. "Nova?"

Her figure dissolved into the shadows, and Ryker sighed as he followed after her. He was such a brute, there was no need to hurt her feelings with his words.

As he rounded the corner, he found the passageway empty.

"Nova?"

Thunder rumbled again as the rain fell sideways outside. The lightning illuminated the forest, and he saw her standing beneath a tree, arms folded, and eyes closed.

"Nova please . . . come back inside."

No response.

Ryker gathered his composure. If she wasn't going to come to him, he would have to go to her. Taking a deep breath, Ryker jogged outside, straight into the storm. Nova didn't move when he reached her side.

"Please return where it's safe."

Nova shook her head. "I want to experience things as a human before I go back to being just a star."

Ryker ran a hand through his hair, droplets of water flung through the air, losing their grasp. "Can you experience it from the cave?"

Nova shook her head again.

A fork of lightning hit a tree not far from them, followed by a loud crack of thunder. Ryker did everything he could to hide the fear that was screaming in his mind to run. Could he call himself a man if another woman's life succumbed to nature's anger? He refused to wait around and find out.

Ryker picked her up, throwing her over his shoulder.

"Put me down, Ryker!" She kicked and screamed. "I demand you let me go!"

Once they were safely back inside, he placed her down near the fire so she would begin to dry.

"How dare you!" Nova hissed.

Even when she was angry at him, she was still breathtaking.

Ryker reached for her face, cupping it in his hands. "Don't ever do that again."

"Why not?" Nova demanded.

"Because . . . I can't . . . just do what I ask, please?"

Water droplets ran down her skin and glistened in the glow of the flames. Memories of another time when he saw her glistening with water had him feeling tight in his trousers. All he wanted to do in this moment was to kiss her and taste her skin. Flicking his eyes down towards her pouty lips, Ryker leaned forward.

"This conversation isn't over," Nova whispered.

"For now, it is."

He heard the breath catch in Nova's throat as he leaned towards her. A slight smile pulled at the corner of his mouth. Her warm breath touched his lips, and he almost blacked out at the pureness of it. The gentle glow of her skin began to pulse, mixing with the orange glimmer from the fire. With a thudding heart, Ryker's mouth hovered above hers, just as lightning outside the cave struck another tree.

Charlie neighed so loud in fright that Nova screamed and threw herself into Ryker's chest, burying her face against his jacket. A sudden overwhelming protectiveness came over him and he held onto her tightly, never wanting to let her go.

The feeling didn't last long before she gently pushed against him. "Goodnight, Ryker."

Their near kiss hung between them like a heavy weight. Ryker sighed quietly. Letting her go was easier than opening that door again. It was probably for the best. Whatever this was, there was no place for it in his life. Love had already cost him once, and he had no intention of paying that price again.

"Goodnight, little star."

Ryker kept an eye on her as she curled up on her bed by the fire. Charlie settled. The storm outside raged on as he retired to his makeshift bed on the opposite side of the fire. Nova had her back to him, but through the flames that licked the air, the gentle rise and fall of her chest confirmed she was asleep. He should rest, too. The morning would bring fresh problems, and the sooner they reached Chester's, the better it would be for everyone.

TWELVE

THE VELVET GOWN

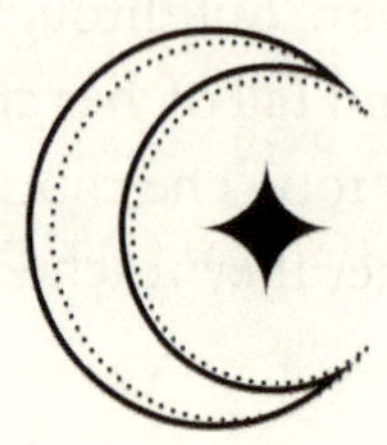

"Are you going to talk to me at all today?" Ryker asked from his spot behind her.

The forest was calm, bathed in the soft light of early morning, with the air still heavy from the night's storm. Droplets of water clung to every leaf and branch, glistening like tiny jewels in the fresh light of dawn. The scent of damp earth and pine hung in the air, rich and clean. Puddles gathered in the dips of the forest floor, reflecting the silver sky above. The trees, once swayed violently by the wind, now stood still, their leaves and needles dripping softly to the ground. Charlie's hooves squelched against the sodden terrain.

Nova had woken early that morning to pack her bed and get breakfast over and done with, just wanting to get on the road. These humans were too exhausting to understand with all their emotions. Especially Ryker.

If only she could talk to her sisters. Surely, they could see what she was currently enduring. No wonder humans struggled. Life on Earth was beautiful, but it was also chaotic.

She'd experienced the rage of nature, the brutal hand of a greedy king. Being chased through streets and shot at by arrows. Yet, on the other hand, she'd tasted the sweetness of nature and its beautiful flora. She'd met people whose laughter could change someone's day. Then there was Ryker, the male with the body like a god. Brown eyes that took her thoughts to places they probably shouldn't go, and a smile that set her soul alight when he decided to use it.

It was a lot to process, so she'd quietly kept to herself. Obviously, Ryker had noticed her silence.

"What would you like to talk about?" she replied.

As he shifted his grip on the reins, his arms grazed the sides of her waist, sending a warm thrill through her body. She closed her eyes, savouring the brief touch.

"We could talk about last night?" he suggested.

Nova sighed. If she was honest, she hadn't stopped thinking about it. Not about the way he'd easily thrown her over his shoulder and marched her right back into the cave like she was a feather in the wind.

She certainly hadn't forgotten how she felt when she ripped the arrow from his flesh or the pain that had flashed in his eyes.

"Was there something in particular you would like to talk about?"

"I'd like to apologise," Ryker answered softly.

The gentleness and endearment in his voice tugged on an invisible thread inside Nova's chest and she instantly needed to feel his warmth. Settling back against him, she spoke. "Go on . . ."

Ryker sighed. "I am sorry for last night. Storms bring back certain memories and seeing you out in the middle of it triggered me."

"Do you want to talk about those memories?" Nova asked softly.

Ryker shifted in the saddle. "I'd rather not . . ."

Nova nodded. Perhaps the pain was too much right now. Though she couldn't help but wonder who or what brought about such a deep wound inside his chest. Hopefully, he would share his past with her when he was ready. For now, she would leave it be.

Ryker shifted behind her. "Are you missing home yet?" His voice held a touch of compassion.

Nova shrugged. "I haven't decided."

She could hear the smile in his voice as he spoke. "That's a feeling I know well."

"Is it? You don't talk about your family too much. It must be lonely being a bounty hunter?"

Ryker hesitated. "My parents live in Sunriver, along with my sister and her husband. It's true I don't get to see them often. A lot of my work keeps me closer by the palace."

Nova glanced over her shoulder. "Is that why you own a cabin near the castle?"

Ryker nodded, his warm brown eyes catching hers. Nova's heart leapt, and she blushed beneath his gaze.

She cleared her throat, turning to face the direction they were headed. "Do you miss them?"

"My family?"

Nova nodded at his question.

"Yes, I guess I do. I write them every month."

"I'm sure they miss you." Nova softly added.

Ryker chuckled from behind her, and Nova grinned at the sound. She wished she could trap it and play it over and over. Because his laughter was few and far between. "I doubt it. I'm sure they are thankful my grumpy ass isn't around for them to look at."

Nova tipped her head back and let the early morning sun warm her face. "You're only grumpy sometimes."

"Hang around me long enough and I think you'll change your mind," Ryker stated.

"Don't tempt me with a good time." Nova turned to glance over her shoulder, grinning as she did so.

Ryker lifted a brow, but a smile tugged at the corner of his mouth.

Her gaze lingered on him for a moment. "What if I didn't go home?" she murmured.

The muscular arms wrapped around her tightened. "You don't want to?"

Nova shrugged. "I don't know."

A soft breeze blew over them, twisting knots into Nova's glimmering white hair. Each strand glittering like silver spider silk. She caught a piece between her fingers, twirling it around. There were definitely moments when she wished to return to Ara, then there were moments like right now. Sitting close to Ryker, on top of a horse, travelling through lush forests as they danced with the wind.

She brushed the thoughts aside. "So, who is this friend you are taking us to?"

"His name is Chester."

"And you think Chester can help me get to Ara?" Nova asked.

"I don't know. But given his line of work, he'd be the first person I would ask."

"What does Chester do?"

Ryker eased Charlie to the right as the ground beneath them became rocky and unstable. "He's a historian. He might know something about the star that fell one hundred years ago."

Before Nova could respond, Charlie's weight shifted, and Nova nearly fell over the horse's head to the ground below. Ryker reigned in the stallion, dismounting swiftly to inspect the issue.

"He's thrown a shoe," he muttered, running a hand down Charlie's leg.

"What does that mean? Is he okay?" Nova asked. It certainly didn't sound comfortable.

Ryker gave Charlie a reassuring pat on the rump. "He'll be fine, but we'll need to stop in town to get it fixed. I was hoping to avoid any more public places, but it looks like we don't have much of a choice."

Ryker ran a hand through his inky black hair and sighed. "We're going to have to walk the rest of the way. I don't want to damage his foot with our weight."

"I would love to stretch my legs anyway," Nova answered happily as she slid from Charlie's back.

Ryker agreed, and the pair set off on foot.

The hood from the grey woollen cloak Ryker snatched for her sat low over Nova's white gleaming hair. She leaned against the building's frame, her eyes drifting over the bustling village as Ryker spoke with the blacksmith. People hurried past, each caught in their own world, and she quietly observed the rhythm of their busy lives. She wondered if the smiles plastered across faces were honest and true. Were they happy, or was it a facade to hide how they truly felt inside? She bit into the apple she held, and juices spritzed into the air and fell against her hand. A moment of pure bliss—sunshine, sweet fruit, and a soft breeze dancing along her skin.

Movement and Ryker's warm voice brought her back to reality. "It's going to take a couple of hours before the blacksmith will be ready with Charlie. Let's find an inn and book a room for the evening."

"Are you sure that's a good idea?"

Last time they stayed in a tavern hadn't turned out so well.

"I'll ensure to mark the exits should we need to use them, and we won't dally long in the tavern."

Nova nodded as she followed Ryker into the crowd. He reached a hand backward, and Nova smiled as she took it in hers. His skin was warm and calloused. She shivered at the first brush of his fingertips.

The inn neared, and Ryker held the door open as Nova stepped inside. The rich aroma of hot food and the tang of alcohol filled the room, wrapping around her senses like a comforting embrace. They made their way to the front counter, boots tapping softly against the wooden floor. As they approached, a young woman behind the counter greeted them with a welcoming smile, her eyes twinkling in the firelight. "Good evening, travellers. What can I do for you?"

Ryker nodded his head towards her. "Can we please have a room for the night?"

"Certainly, you can. Will you be joining us for the local dance later this evening?" the woman asked as she opened the leather-bound book in front of her and started writing something down.

"What sort of dance?" Nova piped in.

The woman looked at her oddly. "The normal sort. You know, where people get together and dance to music. We all get dressed up in our best attire, laugh and eat food until the sun comes up. You should come along."

Back home in Ara, the spoken language—elirion—was hummed in a way that it sounded like the stars were singing. Nova knew of music, but the melodies on Earth were unlike anything she had ever experienced. In the palace, the king rarely played music, but when he did, the soft notes would echo through the halls. Those rare moments helped her to hold on to hope a little longer.

She switched her attention to the brooding male beside her. "Please, I want to see the dance."

Warm brown eyes locked onto hers and she dared not to look away, begging him with a single look.

"Not today, but thanks all the same," Ryker told the innkeeper as he handed a few gold coins over the counter.

"Please Ryker . . ."

"There is a dressmaker a few buildings down that sells lovely evening wear," the woman casually added.

Nova tugged on his hand. "Oh Ryker, please say yes."

Ryker remained stern. "Thank you for the room."

Nova could tell that he was done with the topic. Her heart dropped a little as he guided her towards the stairs. She knew he was only trying to protect her by keeping her out of the public eye, but the further they distanced themselves from Branoc, the more Nova wanted to see and do before she went home.

If he didn't want to go, perhaps she'd simply go without him.

Smoothing down the fabric of her gown, Nova smiled as she looked at her reflection in the mirror. After begging Ryker to attend the dance and promising to only stay for a little while, he'd reluctantly agreed. He'd then been very patient while she perused the racks of dresses at the dressmakers and generously paid when she'd chosen a velvet, burgundy coloured one.

As she stood in the washroom, adjusting the puffed sleeves on her shoulders, a small smile tugged at her lips. Her hair was styled half up, half down, with a few glowing white tendrils softly framing her face. The gown hugged her torso perfectly, the bodice tapering into a V as it met the gathered skirt.

Nova turned to glance over her shoulder at the mirror, noting the delicate rows of white pearls that lined the back, waiting to be fastened. She'd need Ryker's help with that—a task that was quickly becoming a familiar routine.

Nerves crept into her stomach as she opened the door, making it flutter as if a thousand tiny wings were trapped inside her chest. Her palms felt damp, and a subtle tremor in her fingers betrayed her calm exterior. Her heart thudded, echoing in her ears as her feet pressed against the floor.

Ryker was standing by the window, arms folded and lost in thought. At the sound of her steps, he turned to face her. His eyes grew wide, his mouth slightly parted.

Nova smiled and offered her back to him. "Could you help me with these pearls? I can't reach them myself."

He said nothing as he moved closer, each step deliberate. His rough fingertips grazed her soft skin, and Nova bit her lip, holding back a sigh. A surge of electricity seemed to spark between them, heat flooding her body, setting her nerves alight. She reminded herself to breathe.

"All done," he murmured when he was finished.

Nova nervously clasped her hands in front of her as she turned. "Thank you."

Rykers gaze raked over her body. Starting at her face, making its way down to her feet before it found her eyes again. "You look beautiful."

She smiled as heat flushed her already pink cheeks. "You don't look too bad yourself."

He still wore his usual attire, black cotton, loose fitting, button-up shirt with his brown leather harness that held his daggers diagonal across his chest, paired with his black trousers and brown leather boots that came up to his knees. The only thing that was different was that he'd combed his hair back. Instead of his inky black tendrils that formed a shaggy mop, he now sported a slicker and more refined image. Nova could stare at this man all day.

Warm brown eyes dragged their way up the length of her body again, and Nova felt heat pool between her legs. Whatever was happening right now, she didn't want it to stop.

Ryker shuffled on his feet. "Are you ready, then?"

Nova nodded. The moment was broken.

"Now remember," he said as he moved to the door, "we are only staying for a short time, and you must always keep me in your sight."

"Yes sir." Nova grinned.

"I'm serious—"

With a wave of her hand, Nova exited the room. "I know, I know, and we will be careful."

As they entered the inn lobby, the woman who served them at the desk winked at Nova as they glided past. Nova was determined to have fun, even if it was only for a short amount of time.

Gravel crushed underfoot as they crossed the street and made their way to the town hall, following a path lit up with jars of fireflies. Couples and groups of people ushered themselves through the doors, where beautiful music wafted into the street. It carried a sense of elegance, the kind of music that made you pause and listen, as if the world itself had slowed to savour its beauty. It made her feel as if she was going to burst with joy.

Inside was a flurry of colour and sound. Silken banners of deep crimson and royal blue draped the walls, their rich colours reflecting in the polished marble floor. Tables were adorned with lavish floral arrangements, their fragrant blooms wafting on the music notes.

She didn't know where to look first: at the tower of glassware flowing with a pale peach liquid or the group of musicians in the corner of the room playing on an array of stringed instruments.

Couples glided across the floor as if their feet were floating—void of gravity—just like Nova did in Ara. The reminder pulled against her chest. Would dancing give her a fleeting moment of feeling like she was back home?

"Oh Ryker, please let's dance."

Ryker shook his head. "I don't dance."

"What do you mean, you don't dance?" Nova exclaimed.

"I'm all clumsy on my feet. Trust me."

Nova sighed, but wouldn't let his sour disposition ruin her evening. They stood on the sidelines of the dance floor, watching couples twirl about. Waiters moved through the crowds with trays of what Ryker had informed her was called champagne, held high above their heads.

He grabbed two glasses as a waiter walked by and passed one to her. She took a sip and scrunched her nose at the bitter taste. Ryker chuckled as she handed it back to him.

"That looks better than it tastes,"

"All the more for me." Ryker winked.

Nova liked this side of Ryker. Maybe he was beginning to open up. Rolling her eyes, she returned to people watching. Music ebbed and flowed, and she couldn't help but sway on the spot. Her feet itched to glide across the floor to the sweet tunes.

Someone cleared their throat near her side, and Nova flinched.

"So sorry to scare you, my lady, I simply came over to ask if you'd like to dance?" The stranger had striking green eyes and neatly styled golden hair. He bowed before Nova, wrinkling his tailored navy-blue suit and waiting for her response. He was undeniably handsome, but in a polished, refined manner, the kind she'd seen among the castle elite. Not like Ryker, whose appeal was rugged and raw, with an untamed masculinity.

She quickly looked towards the broody protector. He didn't look pleased at all, but didn't stop her, so she extended her hand. "I would love to dance."

The male with the golden hair smiled, whisking her onto the floor. She lost herself in the music, swaying to and fro as if she was made only to dance. The skirts of her gown swished across the ground as she moved, and Nova loved the sound. She caught the eye of the male. He grinned at her, pulling her closer. He smelt of the fresh linen—like the ones in her room over at the tavern—and champagne, like the drink Ryker had offered her earlier. It wasn't unpleasant, but certainly not what she'd grown to prefer.

Nova strained her neck towards where she left Ryker. He was scowling and clearly displeased, but Nova didn't care. She was having the time of her life. Floating across the floor certainly did feel like she was home again—if only for a moment.

One song melted into the next, and Nova couldn't tell when one ended and another began constantly twisting and twirling about with a very warm hand resting on her waist.

Just as she thought she couldn't dance another step, the song ended swiftly, and Nova stilled to catch her breath.

"Would you like to go outside onto the balcony for some fresh air?" The stranger asked, almost out of breath.

"... *keep me in your sight* ..."

Ryker's words rang in Nova's ears, but when she looked around for him, he was nowhere to be found. She knew he would disapprove of her joining this man on the balcony, but the fresh, cool air did sound delightful. Nodding, she followed him outside. Besides—this man didn't look like someone to be afraid of.

Once the crisp evening air hit her face, she took in a deep breath and smiled. What if this is what life could be like? Spending evenings dancing. Dressing in fine attire and sipping on bubbling liquids that looked far prettier than they tasted.

The stranger took two glasses of champagne from a passing server and handed Nova a glass. "My name is Oliver, by the way."

She accepted the drink but didn't have the heart to tell her new friend that she found it horrid. "Lovely to meet you Oliver, my name is Nova."

She reached to squeeze his outstretched hand.

"Are you alright?" Oliver asked as he glanced down. "Are you . . . glowing?"

A wave of heat washed through her as her eyes fixed on her skin. The glow always started in her hands before travelling over the rest of her body. She'd been enjoying the dancing so much that her celestial essence had awoken.

"Oh dear . . ."

"Excuse me, but we were just leaving." Ryker stepped from the shadows and placed his hand on Nova's elbow. She shivered at his touch.

It only took one glance at his sullen face to know that he was definitely not pleased. In her defence, he'd vanished first.

Oliver stood tall and drew closer to Nova, reaching for her arm. He was certainly muscular, but she wondered whether it would be wise of him to challenge Ryker in any way. "I'm sorry . . . but who are you?"

Ryker pulled Nova towards his body. "Somebody who will break your hands if you think about touching her one more time."

"Ryker—"

"The lady is perfectly safe here with me. We were only enjoying some fresh air," Oliver said sternly, reaching for Nova's other elbow.

A low growl seemed to erupt from Ryker, who stared Oliver down. "Like I already stated, touch her and not only will you lose the ability to use your hands, I will also throw you off the balcony."

Ryker's face was laced with fury. He meant every word he spoke. Her heart fluttered as she watched him, the strength and intensity in his movements stirring something deep within her. There was an undeniable allure in the way he stood between her and the world, fierce and protective. But as her pulse quickened, her fists clenched. The frustration burned just as hot—why did he always have to destroy the peace with his brute force? The evening had been perfect, and now it was crumbling beneath his hands.

"I am fine Ryker . . . honestly," she assured him.

"Do you really know this man?" Oliver scoffed.

Ryker pulled Nova again. "Yes . . . she does, and we were leaving."

Without another word, Ryker turned and led Nova back into the hall, through the sizable crowd and outside into the street.

Nova's jaw tightened, her eyes narrowing as she fought to keep her expression calm. Inside, her anger simmered like a boiling pot, ready to spill over, but she refused to draw attention to them. In a crowded space like this, she knew better than to create a scene, no matter how much she wanted to. She stole a glance at Ryker, her fury growing with each heartbeat. Once they were behind closed doors, he'd hear every bit of it.

It didn't take them long, considering how fast Ryker was marching her back to the inn. Nova huffed, the skirts of her burgundy dress dusting the ground. They entered through the wooden doors and headed straight for the stairs. Ryker reached for the key in his pocket and unlocked their room. Nova pushed past him and stormed to the small window that looked down at the street below. Ryker slapped the door behind him.

"I told you to keep me in view." He growled, his voice low and commanding.

"How dare you," Nova muttered.

Ryker scoffed at Nova's back. "How dare I? You're the one who disappeared."

She couldn't face him right now, so she continued to look out the window. "I looked for you and you were gone."

"Well, it seems like you didn't look too far. Why is it so hard for you to obey me?" He all but threw the words at her.

The frustration she felt simmering at the surface spilled and bubbled over. Her? . . . obey him?

"I am tired of you telling me what I can and can't do. You don't own me. I was having a perfectly good time until you came barging in all puffed up—"

Ryker's footsteps pounded the floor towards her. She spun on her heel to face him, gathering her words for another protest, another battle. A fight she wouldn't win.

Calloused hands gripped either side of her face, cupping her cheeks as warm lips found hers in a hard kiss. Her knees buckled under the intensity, and she reached both hands out to grip his forearms. Her eyes fluttered shut as she inhaled the man before her.

His mouth moved over hers, running the tip of his tongue across the edge of her mouth, asking to enter.

With a gentle moan, she melted into him as he parted her lips. His warm tongue swept inside, teasing and taunting. She didn't know what she was doing, but it felt natural to kiss him back with equal passion, her tongue dancing with his. Heat pooled between her legs, and she whimpered as one of his hands cupped the back of her neck, the other gently wrapping around her throat. She grabbed the sides of his jacket and pulled her body into his. The kiss deepened, and Nova wasn't sure it could get better.

All thoughts of why they'd argued flew out the window.

No wonder the couple she saw at the tavern that day looked like they were enjoying themselves.

Kissing was most enjoyable.

Ryker's full lips were soft as they trailed across her jaw and down her neck. Nova crept her fingers to the back of his head, entwining them in his dark, unruly hair. She let her head fall back, allowing him access to her throat.

Slowly, he pushed her backwards until the back of her knees hit the bed, yet they remained standing. Nova was on fire, desire filling every crevice of her body. She wanted him.

Ryker's mouth found hers again, the kiss slower this time, like he was savouring her—should she disappear. Nova met him stroke for stroke, dragging her hands down his chest to slip beneath his shirt. He groaned softly as her fingers found his warm skin.

He was everything she dreamed a man would be.

Broad hands encircled her waist, Ryker pulled her against his body, kissing her deeper. Time and space no longer existed. Just her and Ryker.

The absence of his lips left hers cool from the air as he abruptly pulled himself away, His boots echoing on the wooden floor. He headed for the bathroom, leaving her dazed and confused.

"Ryker?" Nova reached for him. Adrenaline coursed through her veins, and her hands shook as they glowed.

He spun to face her, and she caught a glimpse of the anguish etched into him. His russet eyes were shadowed in a torment too painful to speak.

"I'm sorry Nova . . ."

She took a small step towards him. "Wait—"

With a gentle shake of his head, Ryker turned, and the door closed behind him.

Had she done something wrong? Maybe she didn't kiss well like other women, and he didn't enjoy it. Tears pricked her eyes. She didn't know if they came from the way he repelled from her embrace, or perhaps her tears knew the pain he bore and wished to grieve alongside him.

Her dull, icy hand wiped the salty droplets away. She didn't bother to ask him to help her out of her gown. She felt he needed the space.

Nova crawled into bed and pulled the covers up high. Her feet ached from dancing and now a new pain pulsed inside her chest.

THIRTEEN

THE MOONLIT STROLL

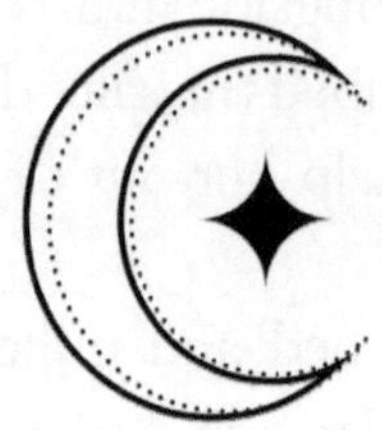

Ryker gripped the edges of the porcelain sink in anguish as he stared at himself in the mirror. Nova's scent was still strong on his senses, the feel of her skin lingering on his fingertips. She was made from stardust and cosmic essence. Velvet to the touch. Her lips were the taste of sweet nectar. Her moans like bottled moonbeams, threatening to send his mind into the galaxies.

He swore to keep his hands to himself, and he'd truly tried all evening. When Nova had stepped into the room at the beginning of the night wearing the deep burgundy gown, all sense left his mind. The red against her skin made the pale green of her eyes and pink of her lips pop. Joy had radiated from her soul as she looked at him for approval.

Then she'd gone and danced with that jackass of a stranger. How dare he touch her and pull her close? Ryker had wanted to cut the male's hands from his body right there on the dance floor, but Nova was enjoying herself with the male—too much for his liking—yet who was he to deprive her of some fun here on Earth? He'd already stuffed it up once. He wasn't willing to do it again.

So, he let it be. He allowed the man to carry the star across the floor in a graceful dance, purely to let Nova enjoy herself. Until he'd whisked her out of view.

Ryker had looked away for all of two minutes and when he turned back, she was gone. His heart nearly split in two. If something were to happen to Nova on his watch, he would never forgive himself.

He'd already lost a woman once.

He swore to never let her out of his sight again . . . not until he got her safely home—wherever that might be.

Then, in the room . . . all he wanted to do was make her understand.

He *needed* to taste her—he *wanted* to taste her.

And she'd been everything he dreamed she would be.

Tender lips that had never been kissed. His to bite and suck. His to trace with his own. His to memorise.

So why was his world crashing down?

He knew the answer . . . he just needed to admit it to himself. He didn't deserve pretty things.

He didn't deserve love because he held it dearly in his hands once . . . before he killed it. That love now haunted him. Following him everywhere he travelled. It didn't matter if he was awake or asleep because it would invade his mind every moment of his life—consuming him until he was nothing more than an empty soul of bitterness and pain.

Painful memories rushed in like a flood, drowning his mind one flashback at a time. The emotional gates that remained like an iron fort burst open and Ryker dropped to his knees—silent sobs racking his body.

"Yolanda . . ." he whispered between the gasping breaths. "I'm so sorry."

Ryker twisted the ruby pendant in his fingers.

It had been four years since seeing her sweet face. Four years filled with the absence of her laughter. Four years since he'd kissed her mouth. Four years of unrelenting torture trapping his mind in a constant, chaotic swirl of guilt-ridden thoughts.

Then he added to that blackness inside of him and tainted Yolanda's name by kissing another woman. Nova didn't deserve it, and neither did Yolanda. It couldn't happen again . . . it wouldn't. Pulling himself together, Ryker stood and wiped his jacket sleeve across his eyes. He knew better than to let his emotions speak louder than reason. He would apologise—something he seemed to be doing a lot of lately.

He quietly opened the door of the washroom and peeked through the crack. The room was quiet. Nova was already in bed, her soft glow adding to the illumination of the small, open space.

He moved with ease as he stepped into the darkened room to stand by the bed. Her face pulled together in a gentle frown. He was a mess, not fit to offer her anything, so why was he playing with her emotions?

The white-haired beauty that sat before him had been quiet all day. He couldn't blame her. Ryker would be surprised if she ever wanted to speak to him again.

When he woke this morning, she was already packed and ready to go. They'd exchanged minimal words. He knew he should try to explain the way he'd acted, but the words refused to form. Maybe some time in nature would help clear both their minds and they could pick up from where they were before.

That should be the most desirable outcome.

Seagulls screeched above the expanse of the Veridian sea, their white feathers striking against the bright azure sky. The ocean-blue waters glittered under the sun like shards of shattered glass trickling through an hourglass.

Ryker's stomach roiled as he neared the Oak's hometown of Pebble Beach. What if Chester didn't know anything about the last star that had fallen? Or how to get Nova home? What then? Or perhaps Chester would have answers . . . and Nova would be gone from his life forever.

That's what he wanted, right? To send her back to safety—away from the hands of greedy, violent men.

The air was crisp, carrying the tang of salt from the distant sea as they rode along the narrow, sandy path. In the distance, the seaside village came into view, small houses dotting the shoreline like tiny specks. The wind picked up, tugging gently at their clothes, while the scent of brine and wood smoke grew stronger the closer they got.

"Are you comfortable enough?" Ryker murmured.

Nova didn't move. "Yes."

"Are you hungry?"

"No."

Her voice was cold and distant. Ryker knew he needed to talk about the kiss.

She glanced over her shoulder briefly. "When will we reach your friend?"

"It's not much further. Just on the other side of that town, you can see up ahead."

She didn't reply, only looked to where he pointed.

"Nova, I—"

"And how long will we stay there?" she interrupted.

Ryker's shoulders dropped. "Perhaps a day or so. It will depend on what Chester knows and whether he can help us or not."

Nova nodded. Her glow was non-existent. Ryker ached to see it shine again. To be the one who made her radiate.

Yet, that wasn't to be.

They travelled in silence for the remainder of the journey, eventually arriving at the quiet, seaside village of Pebble Beach in the Eastborne region, a neighbouring land to Emberfell. Thankfully, King Branoc's influence didn't extend here; Eastborne had its own ruler. It should be easier to hide here—if only a little.

Ryker took in a deep breath of salty sea air, trying to stretch his back in the saddle. All this riding was starting to cause wear and tear on his body. His eyes flicked down to the star in front of him.

Despite their current situation, Ryker was still keen to introduce Nova to the Oaks. Their house was located through town and out the other side, just near the ocean shoreline. The smell of sea salt and fish hung in the air, a welcomed scent, one that reminded him of safety and comfort. He'd spent a good amount of time here a few years back when the pain of losing Yolanda had been too much to bear.

Chester had proved to be a steadfast anchor for him to cling to when the night got too dark.

"The Oaks just live on the other side of town. We will be there shortly," Ryker murmured softly.

She nodded.

Townsfolk smiled as Ryker and Nova passed by on the shiny black stallion—Ryker nodded in greeting. He'd always liked it here and thought on many occasions that maybe the seaside would be his place of retirement one day.

The small village hugged the rocky shoreline, its cobblestone streets winding between quaint cottages with weathered, whitewashed walls and faded blue shutters. Fishing boats, their sails tethered, bobbed gently in the harbour, while seagulls circled overhead, their cries mingling with the soft lapping of waves.

It didn't take them long to reach the other side of the town. Charlie followed the man-made trail towards a few houses scattered along the beachfront. Still, Nova remained silent. Perhaps some female company would help. He'd try to speak with her before they slept tonight.

He pulled Charlie to a stop outside a small cabin that sat nestled on a bluff overlooking the crystal-blue ocean. It was made of a pale white wood and had a thatched, gable roof. After easing down from Charlie's back, Ryker helped Nova to the ground. Together, they walked to the front door and Ryker stepped forward to knock gently. A few moments later, it opened, and they were greeted by a woman in her late twenties. She had long, wavy caramel-coloured hair, tanned skin and golden-brown eyes.

"Ryker!" she squealed with delight, throwing herself into his arms.

He chuckled at her enthusiasm, drawing her in for a warm embrace. "Hello Pippa."

"It's been much too long. Where have you been?" Pippa cried as she pulled back to look into his face. "Chester is going to be so pleased to see you!"

Ryker grinned as he stepped aside, revealing a very timid looking Nova.

Pippa's eyes widened. "Who is this, then?"

"Nova, this is Pippa, Pippa . . . Nova," Ryker introduced the two women.

"You are the most delightful creature I have ever seen. Is this your new lady . . . ?"

"No . . . she's not." Ryker interrupted a little too sharply. "Sorry, no. She is just someone I am helping. We've come to see Chester in hopes he will have some answers for us."

Pippa's eyes dulled a little but didn't lose their spark. "Oh, I see. Well, please come in. Chester will be home shortly. I'll put on some tea. There is much to talk about."

Ryker smiled as she ushered them in, this is what coming home felt like.

Chester didn't look a year older than his last visit: rich brown skin with a hint of his years, a mop of dark, curly hair, and a smile as infectious as his wife's.

"I can't say I've personally experienced a celestial being before. Though I've heard the stories that are whispered," he murmured softly before drawing in a puff of his cigar.

The men were on the back porch that overlooked the ocean below and a small forest in the distance. Both held a glass of rum in one hand and a cigar in the other. Ryker rarely smoked on his own, but in the company of Chester it was a ritual to trade cigars, then share both a drink and their stories.

"Do you think the previous fallen star still roams this Earth?" Ryker glanced across to Chester.

"It's possible."

Ryker sipped his rum, the liquor lightly burning his throat on the way down. "I wouldn't even know where to start looking for her."

"There is someone up in the Twin Peaks mountain range who is said to have known the fallen star. You could start there?"

The words piqued Ryker's interest. His brow knitted together as he caught his friend's eye. "Do you know exactly where?"

"All I know is it's rumoured she lives on the mountain on the left. I haven't seen it for myself."

"She?"

Chester nodded before taking a drag of his cigar. "I've heard she dabbles in darker arts. I don't know if she would have answers, but I fear she may be your only hope."

Ryker sipped his drink again. "How did you find out about her?"

Chester shrugged. "When you do the work, I do—you hear things."

"Ain't that the truth."

It was rare in this part of the world to wield magic. The darker kind was even rarer still. If this mysterious woman had found a way to tap into the ancient magic, perhaps she could give them a way to send Nova home.

Ryker pondered the new information. Would he risk it? What if this woman turned out to be evil? Killed Ryker with some spell or another and kept Nova for herself?

He let his gaze roam to the women in the garden. Nova was too full of hope and light for him to let her be taken by evil again—she was to be treasured.

The sun was setting, sending a warm orange glow across the ocean, though the dark clouds that scattered over the skies muted the orange tones. Its glittering surface turned from diamond and azure to amber and sapphire hues.

Ryker stood and leaned against the porch railing, watching Nova with a gentle smile. She knelt in the soft Earth, her fingers brushing over the leaves of a vibrant green carrot top. Her face lit up with childlike joy as she tugged gently, pulling the orange root free from the ground. "Look at this one!" she exclaimed, turning to Pippa, who was busy inspecting a row of plump tomatoes nearby.

Pippa chuckled, wiping dirt from her hands onto her apron. "That's a beauty, Nova. You're getting the hang of this."

Nova grinned, her eyes sparkling with excitement. She reached for another vegetable, her enthusiasm growing with each successful pull. The surrounding garden was lush and alive, rows of beans, squash, and leafy greens swaying gently in the late afternoon breeze.

His eyes followed Nova as she moved through the rows, laughing with Pippa, her energy infectious. He'd never seen her so carefree, her hands covered in dirt, but her essence glowing brighter than before.

Thankfully, here at the cottage there were no prying eyes to see her, so there was no need to cover her up.

Nova paused for a moment, brushing a strand of hair from her face and glancing towards him. She waved the carrot with a grin, her cheeks flushed with excitement. Ryker gave a small nod in return, his heart warming at the sight of her so at ease, surrounded by something as simple yet grounding as a vegetable garden.

It was likely one of the few moments of peace that Nova had been allowed since she fell to Earth.

Chester stood and moved to his side. "How's your heart holding up?"

Ryker understood the deeper meaning behind the question. He took a slow sip of the warm, sweet drink and shrugged.

"She would want you to be happy, you know?"

Dark brown eyes met his as he turned to face Chester.

"She would want you to keep living your life," Chester continued.

Ryker shifted uncomfortably on his feet. It was hard keeping things to himself. And the words wanted to come out—they sat on the tip of his tongue, waiting for the excuse to tumble from his lips in a cry of relief. "I kissed her. I kissed her, Chester. And now I feel as if I have danced on the grave of my love without caring for the consequences."

The truth settled between them for a moment.

His friend stood beside him, his hand resting on Ryker's shoulder. A gesture of support and love. "You've got to stop doing that to yourself, Ry. Yolanda is gone, but you are still here, and she wouldn't want you to live the rest of your life alone. You're allowed to love again," Chester murmured.

Ryker shook his head. "I'm not sure I can."

"Of course you can. It will be hard at first and your mind will scream at you to stop, but your heart needs this, friend. It's alright to find happiness."

Nova glanced up from the garden and caught his eye. Her glow grew brighter. So bright that Ryker feared it would be seen for miles around. He offered a gentle smile, a silent plea for forgiveness. The corner of Nova's mouth crept up slowly and Ryker's heart thudded in his chest.

Perhaps she would be his saving grace.

He didn't want to admit it to himself, but Chester's words seeped into his soul and found their home there.

Could he love again? Could Nova be his light in the dark?

The ocean lazily lapped against the sandy shore as Ryker and Nova walked side by side. Above them, the sliver of moon bathed the world in pale silver, casting gentle shadows and making the wet sand glisten under its light. The sky was a sea of stars, each one twinkling like a tiny beacon, while a few heavy clouds drifted lazily across, occasionally veiling the moon, hiding her from sight.

Nova's eyes were wide with wonder as she gazed up at the sky, the celestial display mirrored in her own starry gaze. Ryker's boots sunk into the sand. He was silent beside her, his hand brushing against hers now and then, but he didn't force the touch.

"I miss them, you know," she murmured.

"Who do you miss?" Ryker replied, though his gaze wasn't on the sky. He was watching her. The way the moonlight kissed her skin, making her glow like the stars above. She was a part of it all—the sky, the ocean, the endless night.

"My sisters."

"You have siblings in Ara?"

Silvery white strands brushed the shoulders of her gown as Nova nodded. "We are all one big family."

"You only have sisters?"

Nova glanced at him and smiled. "Yes. All celestial beings are female."

Salty sea breezes washed over them as their steps carried them further from the Oak's home. After dinner, Ryker had excused himself and Nova. He knew he needed to talk to her. The weight of their kiss sat heavy on his chest, so he'd taken her down to the ocean shores, hoping to free his mind of its tormenting remarks.

"Do you know all of your sisters' names?"

"Of course, but two in particular are my favourite."

Ryker studied her profile, captivated by the delicate curve of her lips, which turned up ever so slightly at the corners whenever she spoke of her home. Her high cheekbones framed her face elegantly, and her lashes brushed against her skin each time she blinked.

"What are their names?"

Nova stilled. Tipping her head back, she looked towards the dark velvet sky. "Soleil and Tierra. We share a dwelling together."

Ryker didn't want to tear his gaze from the star that shone beside him, but the way her voice carried towards the heavens with such raw love for her sisters had him staring into the galaxy.

He leaned closer so his shoulder brushed her arm ever so lightly. "Do they look like you?"

She glanced at him and shook her head. "I don't even look like me here."

Ryker couldn't imagine what Nova would have looked like as a celestial being in the heavens, but he knew for a fact that no matter which form he saw her in—she would be beautiful.

"Our bodies aren't like human bodies," Nova continued. "We can shift our forms to resemble humanoid figures when interacting with each other, but our essence is pure energy and starlight."

"No wonder the world wants you for themselves," Ryker murmured.

Nova looked up at him with a small smile. Her fingers brushed his briefly. "Tierra has the palest skin you can imagine, like fresh snow under moonlight. Her eyes . . . they're lilac, with flecks of gold. It's mesmerising. And her hair—jet black, darker than the night sky. She glows with this golden light, as if the sun itself is embracing her."

Ryker smiled softly, picturing the image. "And the other?"

"Soleil," Nova continued, her voice brightening as she spoke, "her skin is this rich mocha colour, like the raw soil at dusk. Her eyes are dark blue, like the deepest parts of the ocean. Her hair is caramel, flowing like sunbeams. And when she glows, it's this soft, warm pink."

There was a sadness in her voice as she spoke. Ryker knew all too well the pain the absence of a loved one caused. He wanted to reach for her and comfort her.

"I'm sorry you can't be with them right now." He shoved his hands in his pockets. "Perhaps we will find a way home for you soon and you won't miss them anymore."

"Did Chester have any answers?"

"He seems to think there is a woman who can help us."

Nova looked up at him again, her sea-green eyes filling with a morsel of hope. "Does she live near here?"

Ryker nodded. "See those mountains in the distance?"

Nova followed his gaze. "Yes . . . The two big ones?"

"Twin Peaks. She lives on the one to the left." Ryker ran his hand through his hair. "It will take us a day or so to reach it."

They continued to amble along the sandy shores for a short while. Ryker wanted to relish in the peace and quiet for as long as he could. It wouldn't be long before they'd be on the road again, avoiding guards, bounty hunters, and maybe pirates—especially in this area. The closer they were to the ocean, the more likely it would be that he'd run into Sable Bloodfin—they always found themselves at the same place at the same time, not least of all because he'd been paid to capture a member of her crew a time or two. With Nova in tow, he'd rather not run into her again.

Nova walked a little ahead of him, her feet sinking into the soft sand as the waves lapped quietly at the shore. The full moon shone upon the surface of the ocean, shaping a moon lit path ahead of them. The beach looked almost ethereal, as if they were walking in her world instead of his. She stopped suddenly, looking out over the ocean, her arms wrapped around herself.

Ryker stepped closer, sensing something on her mind. "What's going on in that head of yours?" he asked gently.

Nova sighed, brushing a strand of hair behind her ear. "I don't know what to do, Ryker," she said, her voice barely above a whisper. "I always thought Ara was my home, that it was where I belonged. But now, being here in this part of the world . . . things are different."

He watched her closely, his brow furrowed. "Different how?"

She turned to face him, her eyes reflecting the moonlight. "I'm starting to wonder if I want to go back at all. I miss my sisters, of course, but . . ." She paused, searching for the right words. "Earth feels alive in a way Ara doesn't. Here, I can feel the wind on my skin, the ground beneath my feet. I can taste the food, hear the music. It's real—tangible."

"Not everything is as beautiful as it seems, though."

"You of all people should know that I know that." Nova turned to face him. "But I want the good and the bad. I want to experience it all . . . I want to experience love."

She looked up at him in a way that made his heart erratic. Her face shimmered as though it had been dusted with the finest starlight. Her lips were full and slightly parted, inviting him to taste her again.

Ryker smiled. "I think the world would be honoured to experience you, Nova."

She huffed softly as she reached for his arm and gently squeezed it.

Ryker hesitated, scuffing the sand with his boot. "Nova, I wanted to apologise for the other night at the tavern."

Her gaze dropped to the waves lapping at the shore.

"It was wrong of me to kiss you and then leave you like that."

"Why did you leave?" Her voice was a whisper.

Ryker exhaled heavily, his hands slipping out of his trouser pockets. He raised them to his head, fingers combing through his unruly black hair. Talking about his past was like reopening old wounds, each memory cutting deep, like a dull, rusty knife twisting in his chest.

It was still too hard to tell the story.

"Because I frightened myself."

Nova dipped her toe into the cold water that continually reached for them before running away again. She looked at him, lifting an eyebrow. "Ryker . . . the bounty hunter . . . scared?"

A small grin played on his lips. "Beautiful women scare me—I'll admit it."

"I promise I won't bite."

The sudden laughter that bubbled from his stomach caused him to clamp a hand over his mouth. It had been too long since he'd laughed so freely. Nova seemed to be awakening parts of him that he believed were long gone.

"I'll remember that." She flashed him a grin and began to undo the buttons on her gown.

"What are you doing?"

The navy gown dropped to the damp glistening sand—soon joined by Nova's undergarments. "I'm going for a swim."

He felt his eyes widen as Nova stepped into the icy waters, her hair trailing behind her like pearlescent ribbons. The soft shimmer of the sea mirrored the stars, reflecting like a thousand tiny jewels scattered across the surface. With a playful grin, she took a step forward, letting the water rise to her ankles, then her knees.

The star marking in the centre of her chest began to pulse with a faint light. It wasn't the first time he caught a glimpse of it. But seeing it now, glowing against her naked skin, made Ryker's fingers itch to touch it.

"Nova, please be careful . . ."

She laughed, the sound light and carefree as she waded deeper, her hands skimming the water's surface. She splashed at the waves, twirling under the moon's soft glow.

Ryker bit his bottom lip as he watched the water kiss her body in all the places he wished he could. Her milky-white skin glistened with water droplets, each one trailing down her body like a tiny comet. Nova twirled around, beads of water catching in the air around her, sparkling like stardust.

He wished his body didn't respond in the way that it was. She wasn't just a beautiful woman that he wished to bed. She was a rare and unearthly thing, not of this world, yet here she was, playing in the ocean as though she belonged to the Earth, the sky, and everything in between.

FOURTEEN

THE BROWN RABBIT

Nova watched how Ryker interacted with Chester and Pippa as he said farewell. There was genuine love and respect between the males. She smiled. It was nice to see this side of the moody hunter she was used to. Beneath his tough exterior, his heart was soft—maybe he needed a safe place to use it.

Seeing Chester and Pippa love one another was the highlight of Nova's journey so far. That, and being taught about all the different food varieties, how to plant seeds, how to make bread. If she was to stay here on Earth, this is the life she wanted. The palace had been too much, but a small cottage in a village where she could plant her own food and flowers—that would be perfect.

Maybe she could convince Ryker that if he could help her find a little house, he could go on with his life and she could begin hers.

Ryker embraced Pippa, and the act brought memories of their kiss to the front of her mind. Rough but gentle hands grasping at her skin and the heat of his body warm against hers. The whole moment was almost like a dream.

He'd apologised for the kiss—said he was scared of her.

Nova knew that wasn't the whole truth though. Something was stopping him from stepping forward and embracing life. She wanted to pry it from his fingertips as they meandered along the beach, yet she'd seen the pain in his eyes, screaming from the depths of his soul. It begged to be released. That day would come, Nova was sure of it, and she hoped she'd be around to help him bear its weight.

Perhaps one day, Ryker would let *her* kiss the pain away.

In the decades of watching humans on Earth, love was the messiest and most beautiful act she'd ever witnessed.

Surely it wasn't love she felt with Ryker though, she barely knew him. Perhaps it was purely an attraction?

He caught her eye after he pulled from Pippa's embrace. The energy flowing in her veins pulsed as his brown eyes found hers. Her magic danced on her fingertips, so Nova tucked her hands behind her back. This was the effect he had on her. Love or attraction, whatever this was, Nova wanted more.

"It's been so wonderful to meet you Nova, I hope you find your way home and that the time spent here on Earth are memories you will never forget. I certainly won't ever forget the time I met a star." Pippa pulled her in for a squeeze and Nova hugged her back.

"Thank you for everything Pippa. You and Chester are such generous and kind people. I had a wonderful time," Nova answered.

Pippa beamed and she handed Nova a beautiful, light grey cloak. "It's meant to storm tonight, and I noticed you don't carry a coat with you, and that cloak won't be enough on its own. Take this one, please. I have many."

Nova ran her fingers over the fabric. "Thank you, Pippa. It's so lovely."

Ryker approached, fiddling with his ruby pendant. "We should get a move on then. Don't want the storm erupting while we're trying to find shelter."

Nova nodded and hugged Pippa one more time, waving to Chester before turning and pulling herself up into Charlie's saddle. Ryker followed, and the pair said their goodbyes to the Oaks.

Somewhere in the mountains waited their last hope. With any luck, the woman would have answers—even if Nova was still hesitant on going home.

Most of the morning was left in silence. Nova's mind was a whirlwind of thoughts. She glanced at Ryker every now and then, noticing the way he absentmindedly chewed his lip, his brow furrowed in concentration. He, too, seemed lost in his own world, eyes fixed on the horizon as if the answers to his troubles lay somewhere just beyond the distant hills. Though it was out of sight now, the wind still carried a hint of the sea.

It was past midday, and they'd just stopped at a small clearing off the main trail to rest Charlie and eat some food.

"How long have the Oaks been married?" she asked as she sat down on a small mound of tufted grass.

Ryker huffed in amusement and smiled while he loosened the girth on Charlie's saddle.

"You find me humorous?"

This time Ryker chuckled. "I find you inquisitive."

Nova looked at him and squinted. "Would you rather I wasn't?"

Warm brown eyes met hers. "I'd rather you be exactly who you are."

"Inquisitive it is then." Nova grinned.

"Perfectly fine by me." Ryker answered her as he placed himself down on the ground and opened their food bag. "They've been married a few years."

Nova reached for the bread and cheese he held out to her. Pippa had made the bread fresh this morning just for them and Nova could still smell its warm, toasty aroma.

Her gaze flicked to Ryker. His mind once again deep in thought as he stared at the ground beneath his boots. Perhaps he was thinking of his friends and the relationship they had.

"Have you ever been married?"

Ryker didn't answer, he simply shook his head.

"Do you want to get married?"

He lifted a knee and rested his arms around it as he cleared his throat. "I do not. Besides, marriage isn't on the cards for me."

"Why not?"

Ryker simply shrugged.

"Have you ever wanted to get married?"

She watched him fiddle with the pendant around his neck again. Something about storms and talk of love was tied to that glittering red ruby. Deep in her heart, Nova knew there was a side of Ryker she didn't know yet. A part of him that stayed locked up tight. If only she had the key to free him from his prison.

"I did once . . ." he murmured before standing to his feet. "Eat quickly, we don't want to hang around here for long.

She nodded and let the matter drop. They ate quietly, neither one breaking the silence, and once their meal was finished, they continued on their way without a word.

Ever since they walked along the beach together Ryker had been quieter than usual—his mind busier. The grip on the reins and around her waist tighter, as if he was waiting for something disastrous to happen.

They'd just reached a fork in the road when he stopped. Nova could see the two paths stretched before them.

"What are we doing?" Nova asked over her shoulder.

He shifted in the saddle. "The right path is well-trodden and will take us through the outskirts of another village."

"Is that a bad thing?"

"No, it would offer us safety, but it's predictable and easily tracked by those who may be searching for us."

Nova knew they'd already risked themselves in the last village, as well as in Chester and Pippa's home town. She wanted to stay out of sight just as much as Ryker did, especially when they were so close to reaching the woman who might have answers for her.

"So, what about that way then?" Nova pointed.

"That one . . . will lead into the Mordino Forest."

Its entrance was shadowed by ancient trees and thick undergrowth. It definitely seemed like the more unpleasant option.

"That way looks dangerous," Nova murmured.

Ryker nodded. "Dangerous, but no one will expect us to do it."

"Will both paths take us where we need to go?" Nova asked.

"Mordino Forest will get us to the mountain range faster but not without risk." Ryker gripped the reins tighter.

"And what pray tell, would this *risk* entail?"

"Galanthors, Lycan, rotten swamps . . . just to name a few."

Nova swallowed the fear that began to blossom in her chest. It wasn't that she didn't trust Ryker to keep them safe. It was more that she didn't particularly feel like facing large monsters or swamps. However, her time on Earth had already been quite the journey . . . why not add a few more experiences?

Nova bit her lip, considering their options. "Do you think we can handle the forest?"

He sighed, running a hand through his hair. "It's a gamble. The forest is a risk, but it might be safer in the long run. They won't expect us to take it, and we can hide better there."

"Then let's do it."

Ryker's arms tightened around her waist slightly. "Are you sure?"

Nova considered for another moment, then nodded. "The guards—if they are still pursuing us—will most likely presume we'd take the easier route. If they don't and follow us through here, well we'll just have to do our best to blend in—or hope a creature eats them."

Ryker huffed in amusement, and it tickled the back of Nova's neck. Small bumps rose over her skin, and she shivered.

"Such a vicious little star."

She threw Ryker a smile over her shoulder as he pulled Charlie to the left.

As they stepped onto the forest path, the trees seemed to close in around them, their branches forming a dense canopy that blocked out the sunlight. The air grew cooler and filled with the scent of moss and Earth. The sounds of the ocean faded away, replaced by the rustle of leaves and the distant calls of unseen creatures.

It got darker the deeper they went, and Nova wondered whether the storm that had been brewing on the horizon all day had already reached them.

Ryker had suggested they keep talking to a minimum as they made their way through the dense forestry—the less noise, the less likely they'd be eaten by something. Which was more than alright with her.

She drew her cloak closer, bracing against the sharp bite of the colder air as she surveyed her surroundings. Some parts of the forest were drenched in some sort of fog, she could only presume they were areas best left unexplored.

Thunder rumbled in the distance, the deep sound echoing through the air. Nova glanced upward, but the thick canopy of trees blocked any view of the sky. She was grateful for Ryker's solid chest behind her as they ambled along. There was no way to tell how long they'd been travelling, but the light around them grew darker by the minute.

She quickly glanced over her shoulder. Ryker's jaw was tense. His eyes darted to every shadow and flicker of movement in the trees. His hand hovered near the hilt of his sword, always ready. His other arm was firm around her waist. Their bodies brushed with every movement of the horse beneath them. She wanted to trace his lips with her own. She wanted to taste his tongue as he took her to a place she'd only ever dreamed of. Every part of her ached for him.

"Ryker . . ."

A hand flew to her mouth and silenced her.

"Don't make a sound." Ryker whispered in her ear.

Trembling at the intensity of his voice, Nova froze.

Something rustled to their left, even Charlie held his head high and turned towards the sound. Nova held her breath while looking around. She was waiting for *someone* or *something* to jump out of the bushes when a small brown rabbit ran across their path.

She felt Ryker relax behind her as he took his hand from her mouth.

"It's just a hare," he murmured.

She let her body relax. "I thought we were about to be atta—"

Something large flew at them both from the bushes, collecting Ryker and ripping him from Charlie's saddle. The moving smudge of vicious sound and dark colour disappeared into the dense flora and Charlie took off running in fright. Nova clung tightly to the reins as the horse charged through the forest, dodging low-hanging branches while sharp twigs grazed her skin.

"Charlie stop!" Nova cried. "You need to slow down, we can't leave Ryker."

The black stallion continued to run.

She tightened her grip on Charlie's mane, squeezing her eyes shut as if sheer willpower could bring the horse to a halt. The thought of Ryker lying injured and alone in the woods gnawed at her heart, filling her with dread. The kiss they shared couldn't be the last one, there had to be more than this.

Despite the little time she'd had to bathe under the moon, Nova called to her magic.

Tiny pin pricks began in her fingers, spreading their way into her hands. A white glow grew, and Nova could feel a hum of electricity running from her chest, into her shoulders and down her arms. The glow and hum intensified, and she cried out as light exploded around her. Charlie instantly reared and pawed the ground, uncertain. She turned him around and kicked him into a run, back in the direction they came from. As she neared the area Ryker went down, she saw him.

Nova's heart pounded in her chest as she watched the scene unfold. The forest around them seemed to blur, her focus narrowing solely on Ryker and the beast attacking him—fear froze her limbs and her mind.

Whatever it was, it was large. With four legs and a head as big as a small child. Sandy brown fur mixed with grey whipped through the air in a flash of colour. From Nova's limited knowledge of Earth creatures, it looked as if it was a large dog. Ryker battled the creature with his sword, a dance of claws, snapping jaws and saliva. But in a swift, horrifying moment, the creature sank its teeth deep into Ryker's thigh. His agonised cry pierced the air, sending a shiver down her spine. She wanted to scream, to rush to his aid.

"Ryker!" she managed to gasp, her voice barely a whisper.

He grit his teeth, his face contorted in pain, but he didn't falter. With a desperate, savage strength, he drove his sword deep into the beast's side. The creature let out a guttural roar, its grip loosening as it staggered back, blood oozing from the wound.

Nova's legs finally obeyed her, and she stumbled forward, her eyes locked on Ryker. He pulled his sword free and, with one final swing, severed the creature's head from its body. The beast collapsed, lifeless, at his feet.

She let out a distraught cry as Ryker took a step towards her, blood pouring from the wound in his leg. He staggered before dropping to his knees and collapsing onto his side. His breaths were coming in quick and shallow.

"It's alright." She dropped to the ground and pulled Ryker's head into her lap, brushing his inky tendrils from his face. "Ryker, stay with me . . ."

Warm brown eyes rolled back into Ryker's head as he grappled with consciousness. Tears formed, flowing down her face as she placed one hand on the wound on Ryker's leg. Ruby red blood pulsed from the gash; the skin torn in shreds.

"Ryker please . . ." Nova closed her eyes.

Now was not the time to go dying on her. She would certainly not survive alone in this forest. She needed to heal him. Yet she knew how depleted her levels were. It had been heavily cloudy over the past few days. The moon hadn't been able to refill her powers to full capacity. She used too much to stop Charlie from dashing off into the unknown. But she needed to try something—anything.

With a hand to the gushing wound, she drew in a deep breath and willed it to heal. She'd done it once before; she could do it again. She concentrated on the feeling, and tingles began again, and a hum travelled down her arms. In her mind she clung to the image of Ryker's skin knitting back together.

When she glanced down, it was actually happening. Even with him so close to delirium, Nova managed a smile. It was working. If she could just hold on until the bleeding stopped, Ryker might have a fighting chance.

She poured every ounce of her energy into the wound. With one last surge of power, Nova's glow flickered and vanished.

Flashes of light lit up the sky as Nova drew in shallow breaths. "Ryker . . . ?"

He remained lifeless, so she called his name again. "Ryker. Please come back to me . . ." she whispered.

Seconds felt like hours as she watched and waited to see if he would live. Her heart pounded against her ribs, breath hitching in her throat as her hands trembled uncontrollably. Every muscle in her body was tense, frozen in place. Eyes wide, she stared at Ryker, unable to move, her chest tightening with fear that seemed to grip her from the inside out.

Here she was alone in a dark forest, with a thunderstorm looming in the distance and a wounded man. If there were any more of those creatures out there, she was most definitely still a target.

Ryker moaned and his eyes fluttered open.

Nova let out the sob she'd been holding in as she pulled Ryker closer. "I thought I'd lost you."

He moaned as he tried to sit up. "What happened, how . . ."

"Careful, the wound is still fresh," Nova said as she wiped her eyes. "I didn't have enough power to fully heal it."

Ryker sat up and ran a hand over his face. "Nova, I'm so sorr—"

Nova shook her head. "Please don't. None of this is your fault."

"Are you alright?"

She nodded. "What was that creature?"

"A Lycan," Ryker muttered. "I haven't seen one in years."

"It nearly killed you."

He wiped his hand across his furrowed brow. "Some Lycan travel in pairs, so there's a good chance of another out there somewhere," Ryker groaned as he slowly stood. "We need to find shelter."

"The storm is nearing too," Nova added softly as she stood too.

Ryker held her gaze before reaching for her and pulling her into a crushing embrace. "Thank you, little star."

She melted into his embrace, feeling the tears build once more. Being human was exhausting, she realised—every emotion raw and relentless, the weight of physical strain, the ever-present danger of creature attacks. It was a constant, unyielding battle, each day pushing her to her limits. In his arms, she allowed herself to breathe, but even that felt like a challenge.

Ryker gently eased her from his grasp and helped her into the saddle, his hands steady as he guided her up. Once she was settled, he swung himself up behind her, wrapping his arms securely around her waist again. "Let's find shelter."

A deep rumble of thunder echoed through the trees, and Nova glanced over her shoulder and caught a glimpse of Ryker wincing slightly, as if the sound had struck his soul rather than the distant ground.

As Charlie took off into a canter, the grip around Nova's waist was tight and she smiled. Ryker could hold her forever and she wouldn't mind one bit.

FIFTEEN

Ryker navigated the dense forest, the leaves murmuring in the gentle breeze, the scent of Earth lacing through the air. Towering trees, aged and mossy, whispered secrets as he ventured further. The setting sun's light dimmed in the thick foliage. His head was still spinning from the attack. Usually, his keen eye never missed a beat, but that Lycan caught him off guard. The whole situation had him on edge and, to add to it all, thunder rolled in the distance.

Nova was quiet as she sat in front of him. Her use of powers had completely drained her. He needed to find shelter, and he needed to find it soon.

A subtle break in the green caught Ryker's eye. The forest parted slightly, unveiling a cave covered with vines and veiled in shadows. Ryker guided Charlie off the path and into the thick, untamed undergrowth, steering them towards the darkened den.

Outside, he pulled Charlie to a stop and carefully dropped to the ground. Pain shot through his leg, but he didn't let it show. He was grateful Nova had been able to stop the bleeding, but it would still take a few days to fully heal. "Stay here, I'll make sure it's empty and free of . . . animals."

Nova looked at him nervously, but nodded, remaining seated.

The mouth of the cave yawned at him as he silently scoped the entrance. It seemed as if it was empty, but he wasn't convinced, so he stepped in further. Water dripped from somewhere in the tunnel. Lichen clung to the walls and the air smelt of damp earth. As he contemplated, a distant rumble echoed, the air shifting with the scent of rain. Far off, clouds gathered, lightning flashes painting the sky. The distant storm cast an eerie glow, intensifying the hidden cave's allure. This was their only option for now.

He turned around and headed for Nova.

"We will spend the night here and wait out the storm," he said as he helped her down.

They gathered their belongings and entered the rock shelter. He made a fire and Nova laid out the bedding as close as she could without it catching alight.

Dinner was a simple meal of bread, cheese, and some fruit.

Ryker glanced at Nova now and then. She seemed to be in her head as she sat staring at the orange flames that cast dancing shadows onto the jaggard walls. If she hadn't been there for him today, that Lycan would have been the end of him. And that wasn't how Ryker had thought he'd depart from this Earth.

She'd saved him. This fragile and brave being . . . had saved him. And even though Ryker didn't want to admit it out loud. The act had changed things for him.

"Are you alright?"

Nova glanced across the fire to meet his gaze and smiled softly. "Yes. Though my body is aching from the absence of power."

"Is there anything I can do to help?"

She nibbled on the bread in her hand and shook her head. "I just need rest—and the moon once she decides to show herself."

Ryker huffed humorously. "She?"

"Oh yes. Moon is all femininity and grace. Her glow is all the stars need to twinkle." Nova smiled softly.

"She's essential to your wellbeing?" Ryker asked as he picked at his food.

Nova nodded her head, white gleaming strands of hair floating around her face. "Without her, I fear I would fade away."

Ryker swallowed his bite of food and tilted his head. "So, what exactly is it that you stars do?"

She set her plate aside, drawing her knees to her chest and wrapping her arms around them. "My sisters and I are made by the Creator to simply be. We exist to guide the adventurers, to shine bright for those who are lost and to twinkle for the dreamers. Born out of chaos into the galaxy. It is our beginning and our end, the place where our bodies will one day become part of the atmosphere, and the cycle will begin again."

The way she spoke about her home had Ryker feeling things deep inside his chest. Her eyes sparkled as she spoke about Ara and what a star's life purpose was. She went on with such a love for her own kind and the more she spoke, the more she glowed. There was no way he could take that from her. Ara was where she belonged, and despite the feelings that flooded his mind and soul, Ryker knew he had to get her home.

Did that mean he couldn't enjoy her company while she was here in this part of the world, though?

She'd stopped speaking and looked at him across the fire, eyes framed with dark lashes. He shouldn't be looking back at her the way that he was, but the thought of nearly losing his life today and the impending storm had Ryker wanting to seize the moment. Tomorrow wasn't promised. All they had was today.

Lightning lit up the cave and he fiddled with his pendant— thunder soon followed.

"Do you miss it yet?" he asked quietly.

"Home?"

He nodded.

She let out a soft sigh as she closed her eyes for a moment. When she opened them again, her sea-green gaze locked onto his, and his heart pounded, feeling like it might break free from its bone cage.

"I do . . . but if I'm honest, I like being here too," Nova answered. "As long as King Branoc and whoever else leaves me be."

Ryker placed his plate on the ground beside him and rested his arms against his knees. "He never will, little star. Ara is safer for you."

"I know. I just wish things were different." Nova sighed. "Why can't they let me be? I want to see the world."

Ryker's heart twisted as he took in her troubled expression, her brows furrowed, and eyes clouded with thoughts she wouldn't share. He wished he could ease the worry shadowing her face, but he knew he didn't have the answers she sought.

A cool breeze entered the cave, with the scent of rain riding on it.

"I think the storm is here," Ryker murmured.

Nova stood, stretching as she did so. She folded her arms, facing the mouth of the cave. Her mind was lost in thoughts. "Now that I've told you a little about myself, are you finally going to tell me why you're always fiddling with that pendant?"

Ryker swallowed down the instant heat that washed over his body at the mention of the ruby jewel.

Why was she so determined to dig into this part of him, the one he'd buried deep and left unspoken? Her questions coiled around him, tangling his stomach into painful knots as memories clawed their way back up, ones he'd fought hard to keep buried. Each word tightened the ache in his chest, making it harder to breathe. He knew she wanted to understand him, but opening those doors would be risking more than he was ready for.

Ryker rolled his eyes as he stood, tossing the remnants of his meal into the fire. "There's nothing to it," he shrugged. "I just don't like storms."

What was the point of dragging up old memories? They were better off where they were—in the past. He didn't need to relive memories that would most certainly tear his heart into a million pieces again. He'd only just begun to learn how to live with them. Though she really did deserve to know some things about him. She'd done her fair share of sharing who she was.

Yet the words wouldn't form.

"So, you won't tell me anything?"

Ryker caught her eye. "There is nothing to tell," his voice was gruff.

Nova eyed him, her gaze never waning before shrugging her shoulders. "Suit yourself," she said, as she took a few steps away from the fire.

The glint he saw flash in her sea-green orbs didn't go unnoticed. It wasn't one of playfulness or mischief—but determination.

"What are you doing?" Ryker asked.

Nova had started undoing the buttons on the back of her linen dress. Her cloak was already discarded to her bed. The dress dropped to the floor, and she stood there grinning at him with a mischievous smile on her face in only her undergarments.

"Nova . . . what are you doing?" he repeated.

"As we established before, I like storms, so I'm going out into the rain," Nova answered as she spun around and headed outside.

"Nova, please don't!"

It was too late, she disappeared into the darkness, Ryker paced the floor of the cave, both hands fisting the hair on top of his head. He couldn't go out there. It was too much. But he also couldn't let her be out there alone.

He moved to the mouth of the cave and called out, "Nova, please come back inside. It's not safe out there."

"Not until you tell me why you don't like storms!" she called back.

He watched her dance as the rain poured down. He wanted to smile at her joy. He wanted to experience it with her, but he couldn't. This was all just wrong.

"I can't . . . please Nova," Ryker begged.

Nova stilled. She turned to face him, standing her ground with her slender arms crossed tightly over her chest. The white of her undergarments had turned see through and Ryker struggled to stay focused on her face.

Nova's face was stern. "Tell me the truth. No rhymes or embellishments. No adjectives. Tell me and I will come back in."

Could he do it? Could he relive the moment four years ago that still haunted his mind day and night just so a woman he barely knew would come inside from a storm?

Nova wasn't just a woman, though, was she? This creature before him had somehow found her way into his heart and he'd refused to fully realise it until she was standing outside in the pouring rain. Ryker stood, battling his internal demons as Nova watched and waited.

"If I tell you, will you promise to come inside?"

A look of wariness flitted across her face, but she nodded.

Relief washed over Ryker, but it was quickly replaced with the dread of his past. Would he ever get over the internal pain attached to it every time he spoke it out loud?

Perhaps keeping his heart locked away was doing more damage than good. Perhaps it was time to open those gates.

"There was a storm four years ago," he said, loud enough so his voice would carry, though it laboured under the weight of both sorrow and remembrance. "Yolanda, my fiancée, was a spirited soul. We were childhood sweethearts. She loved riding with the wind in her hair, and the freedom of the open land. Her laughter echoed through the fields like music."

He paused, as waves of old ache crashed into his body. "We were caught in a sudden thunderstorm," he continued, his voice softer. "She insisted on riding back home despite the dark clouds looming overhead. I told her that it wasn't safe . . . but she didn't listen to me."

A sombre breath escaped him as he recalled the moment that changed everything. "Her horse spooked, startled by a clap of thunder. Yolanda tried to calm him, but he reared. She fell, struck her head on a rock, and . . ." His voice trailed off, the unspoken tragedy hanging in the air.

"We were to be married," Ryker murmured, his eyes meeting Nova's. "The storm took her away, and I've carried its echoes ever since. Every thunderclap, every raindrop, they remind me of that fateful night. It was all my fault. She was my love, and the storm took her away. I should have made her listen. It was my job to keep her safe."

A sob caught in Ryker's throat at the tragedy of all of it. "I won't watch it happen again . . ."

It was too much. The pain was too great.

One moment, Yolanda with her dark wild hair and deep brown eyes was with him, and then next she was not. Her last breath expiring from existence as he cradled her in his grasp.

Ryker's arms dropped to his side as he recalled Yolanda's last words.

"You worry too much . . ."

But in fact—he hadn't worried enough.

"And the red pendant?" Nova murmured, her once bright eyes, full of joy—now brimming with sadness.

Ryker dragged a hand through his hair. "It was Yolanda's engagement ring. My father had it smelted down into the pendant after the funeral and surprised me with it. I haven't taken it off since."

Nova's chest rose and fell with each steady breath as she watched him from outside the cave. Her face was etched with a deep empathy that struck right through his guarded walls. Her eyes, soft and unwavering, seemed to steal the breath right out of his lungs as they locked with his understanding in their depths. She didn't speak; instead, with a simple look, she beckoned him outside, silently offering him a reprieve he hadn't realised he needed.

Should he accept the invitation? Should he step outside into the heart of the fear that gripped his mind . . . body . . . soul?

Her eyes beckoned again, yet this time they were accompanied by an outstretched hand. One that glowed with an iridescent viridian. Illuminating the rain that tore from the heavens as it fell upon the land.

Ryker shook his head but made no sound.

Nova beckoned again.

He couldn't handle the pain anymore. His heart was broken, and he longed to find rest. Somewhere he could lay his heart down for a while. Just to take a moment to breathe.

Was Nova his heart's respite?

His mind told him no, but his heart screamed at him to say yes. She could be the very thing his heart had secretly been searching for. He just needed to trust it. Ryker ran a hand over his face, swallowing down the fear, and took one step outside of the cave. Then another. Then another.

Cold, stinging rain drenched him within moments as he slowly made his way towards the glowing star. With each step, the fear became duller, its voice no longer screaming in his mind. It wasn't gone completely—but it was quiet.

It was silenced the moment she ran from the embrace of the forest and threw herself into his arms.

Warm lips found his in a passionate kiss. Nova wrapped her arms around his neck and pulled him as close as she possibly could. Ryker wanted to resist. He knew he shouldn't be kissing her back, but she was intoxicating. Every nip of teeth on his lips, every tease of her tongue as she coaxed his mouth open, was another dose of a substance that he didn't want to stop taking.

His reflexes kicked in, and before he could tell himself to stop, he lifted Nova and placed her legs around his waist. Her glow grew brighter the longer they stood together in the midst of the storm, enduring it as one.

Not even the lighting was a match for her viridian light.

All thought drained away as he kissed her. And for once, the sounds of the external storm were louder than his internal one. The rain became just rain, the thunder just thunder. No screams. No crying. No sharp pain inside his chest.

Just Nova and the feel of her pliant body wrapped around him.

Ryker held her gently, cradling her close as he stepped back into the cave, his boots echoing softly against the stone. Without a word, he brought her over to the fire. He slowly eased them both to the ground just as his legs gave way. He leaned himself up against the wall of the cave, with Nova straddling his lap. Her skin glistened with water droplets in the firelight as he dragged his eyes over her body. There seemed to be a pattern here, Nova dripping wet and him becoming hard.

Ryker reached to brush his fingers across her collarbones. His gaze locked on hers, a silent invitation. She nodded in acceptance.

Her gaze was unwavering as he slowly eased the straps of her now sheer camisole down off her shoulders, where it fell and gathered at her waist in a damp heap.

His breath was ragged as his eyes caught the star imprint in the centre of her chest. It was pulsing with a faint blue light. Ryker reached and brushed the scar. It was warm under his touch and made his fingers burn. Nova quivered against his hand.

His gaze dropped to her shell-pink hardened nipples, his breath catching as he grazed his thumb over one.

"You're so beautiful, Nova."

She whimpered softly, arching her back and pressing her breast into his hand, filling it perfectly. He gently kneaded it in small strokes, drawing out her pleasure and indulging in his own. His other hand joined in, rolling her other nipple between his finger and thumb. Nova's head dropped back as a moan escaped her lips.

He needed more of her.

She dropped her head forward again, her sea-green eyes heavy with desire. Ryker cradled her face in his hands, drawing her lips to his in a possessive kiss. It was deep and hungry, tongues dancing together to a song only they could hear. Nova tasted like the fresh plum she ate for dinner, and Ryker wanted every bit.

His hands left the dampness of her face and traced lazy patterns down her back. It was warm from the fire. They found their way to the fabric that gathered at her waist and Ryker took it in his hands, gently lifting it up and over her head.

Nova now straddled his lap . . . completely naked . . . and glowing.

"Is this alright?" Ryker murmured.

"Yes," she whispered.

In the dim light of the cave, Nova shimmered. The droplets of water on her skin caught the flicker of the fire, while her celestial glow radiated softly from within. A faint hue of silver and blue thrummed from her body. Ryker reached out and ran his fingers through the thread of colours.

His gaze shifted to her face, where Nova watched him through the veil of her dark lashes. "Are you sure? Because if I keep going, it's going to be very, very hard for me to stop . . ." he said as his hands tenderly kneaded her thighs.

Nova shifted forward until her bare breast brushed against his jacket. She lazily brought her hands up and around his neck, her fingers tangling into his damp hair. "Definitely don't stop."

He didn't need to be told twice as he shrugged his jacket off.

Ryker's smirk grew as Nova's fingers deftly found each button on his shirt, one by one, slipping them free. She peeled the damp fabric from his shoulders, letting it fall away, leaving his chest exposed to the cool night air.

Delicate fingers traced a pattern on his skin, leaving a trail of bumps behind them. Every drag of her hand over his body was intentional and agonisingly slow. Her eyes drank in every part of him.

Nova's lips were the perfect shade of rose pink, soft and inviting, a subtle contrast to her pale skin. She caught the corner of her bottom lip between her teeth, a glint of mischief sparking in her eyes. When she flicked her gaze up to meet his, it was a look that pierced right through him, unravelling every ounce of his self-control. It wasn't just a look; it was a silent dare, an invitation he could feel radiating from her, tempting him closer.

Ryker groaned as he dipped his head and caught her mouth in a gentle kiss. His hands danced along the dip of her lower back before he cupped her ass and what a sweet, sweet ass it was. So perfectly round. It fit in his hands like she was made just for him.

The sound that escaped from Nova as he gripped her and pulled her closer had his cock hardening in his trousers. Her hands dragged through his hair as she kissed him with such a gentle force. For someone who hadn't been human for long, she certainly knew how to make him feel good.

Ryker pulled his lips from hers, tracing her cheek with his fingers. "You're so fucking a beautiful, little star."

Pink cheeks, swollen lips, and sea-green eyes stared at him as Nova rocked her hips. "So are you," she whispered against his mouth as she leaned forward to kiss him again.

He needed more than just the taste of her mouth; he needed to feel her too. He wanted to know her warmth on his fingers, what she would taste like on his tongue, or how she would sound as she came for him over and over.

As one hand cradled her back, the other reached between them and Ryker brushed his fingers against the wetness that pooled there.

Nova cried out as she ripped her lips from his. "What are you doing?"

Ryker stilled, his eyes glued to hers, heart racing and blood pumping. "Do you want me to stop?"

Nova bit her bottom lip and shook her head. The plea in her eyes had Ryker nearly coming on the spot. It had been too long since he'd been with a woman and his body knew it.

Ryker's hand moved again, a grin spreading across his face as Nova's head fell back. "Do you like this?" he asked as he slid a finger inside her warmth. Nova bucked against his hand, her breasts glistening under the firelight.

She brought her head back to look at him and nodded, lips slightly parted with the pleasure he was pumping into her. The walls of her warmth clenched around his fingers as he slowly dragged them out before pushing them back in. His thumb found her clit, and he circled it gently, which brought new cries from Nova's lips.

Ryker lifted his free hand and placed it on the back of her neck, dragging her lips to his as he kissed her. He sucked her bottom lip between his teeth, gently biting down as he slipped a second finger inside her warm, silky folds. Nova cried out and thrust against his hand. He kissed his way down her neck before taking a hardened nipple into his mouth and sucking it. She dug her hands into his hair as he drew his fingers out and pushed them back again.

She felt like a fever dream, and he never wanted it to stop.

"Ryker . . ." Nova whimpered.

"Yes, little star?"

"What is this? I feel like I'm going to shatter into a million pieces."

Ryker grinned against her mouth. "Then do it . . . come for me."

Ryker plunged his fingers deeper into her silky wetness one more time. Nova arched her back and cried out as she came all over his hand.

The star in the centre of her chest grew brighter and brighter with each wave of pleasure her orgasm created. It shone brighter than the sun itself, lighting up the cave like daylight for a moment. Nova's body jolted in ecstasy, her pleasure clamping around his fingers as her soft cries echoed throughout the cave. He melted under her gaze as her orgasm peaked and she came back down to Earth, her body limp against his.

With hearts racing, they sat on the floor, Ryker holding Nova close. Shadows from the flames danced on their bodies and for the first time in a long time, the storm that raged inside Ryker's head was calm.

"Whatever that was, can we do it again?" Nova whispered softly.

Quiet laughter erupted from Ryker's stomach. "I think one is enough for now. We need to sleep."

He reached over, grabbed Nova's cloak, and gently draped it around her shoulders. She was almost asleep, and he couldn't blame her. Most humans require sleep after seeing the stars. Who knew what an actual star needed after reaching for their own kind.

He hadn't found his own release, but that hardly mattered. Watching her come undone from the pleasure he'd given was more than enough. In a perfect world, there would be time for them to explore each other fully—if that's what she wanted, and if his heart would allow it. For now, he was more than content to see her blissfully happy.

"You should change before you get too cold," Ryker murmured into her hair.

Nova nodded sleepily, and Ryker eased her from his lap. He watched as she placed her dress over her head. Her cheeks were pink, and the smile that graced her lips was sweet and so unfettered. She returned to his side, dropping down beside him. Ryker encouraged her to lie down on the makeshift bed by the fire before placing himself behind her. He wrapped an arm around her waist and pulled her close.

"Goodnight, little star," he whispered into her soft white tendrils.

Ryker closed his eyes against the sounds of the storm raging outside. There was no going back now, whether he liked it or not.

SIXTEEN

THE STOLEN STAR

A smile crept across Ryker's face as he woke. It had been many years since he'd slept as soundly as he did. He may not have found his satisfaction last night, but seeing Nova experience hers for the very first time was more satisfying. Even though he shouldn't, he secretly hoped that there would be other opportunities for him.

Ryker silently propped himself up on his elbow. Nova lay tucked against his side, her chest rising and falling with gentle slumber. He watched her, wanting to keep her all for himself. She'd been the first woman since Yolanda to awaken his dormant heart.

Intricate lashes lay against her stardust infused skin. Her rosebud lips carried a glimmer of a smile as she lay sleeping. Ryker wondered if she was dreaming. Could stars dream? If they did, would they dream of Earth?

Nova shifted, curling tighter into his side, but did not wake. He wanted to brush the strands of diamond tendrils from her face, yet he was afraid to wake her. They had a long day ahead. She needed all the sleep she could get.

He slowly eased from the blankets, instantly regretting the absence of the extra warmth her body brought. Ryker placed another log on the dying fire. It would do well to keep it alight. He flicked his gaze towards the sleeping star. A soft smile tugged on his lips. If she was his, he'd swear on his life to protect her with every ounce of his being.

Such selfish thoughts didn't deserve to be spoken aloud. Best to keep them tucked away inside the part of his mind that required a locked door. He'd promised to find her a way home and there was still a very good chance that was exactly what she wanted—to go home.

Ryker couldn't blame her, and he certainly wouldn't let his feelings stand in her way.

The cave was still dark. Early morning light barely reached in, yet Ryker knew it was time to rise. He'd relieve himself outside and attempt to scout out a stream before Nova awoke.

He glanced at her sleeping form one more time before turning and heading for the mouth of the cave. Pale pink light bathed the entrance, illuminating the vines that hung from the top of the stony mound. Ryker glanced around, looking for anything or anyone who might be a threat, but all seemed clear, with only the usual sounds and movements of the forest waking up.

The crisp morning air bit at his skin as he made his way through the woods, the ground damp beneath his boots from the previous night's rain. Thoughts of the thundering storm still lingered. He'd been so afraid to see Nova out in the ferocious weather. What if it had claimed her too? Yet the moment her lips touched his, the world around him became silent . . . still.

She'd quietened his storm.

As he pushed through the dense underbrush, the faint trickle of water reached his ears. Ryker followed the sound until he came upon a narrow, clear stream winding its way through the forest floor. He knelt on the bank and cupped a handful of cold water to splash over his face, the shock of it waking him fully.

He glanced at his reflection in the water—tired eyes, tangled hair, and five-day-old scruff. He really needed to sharpen his blade and do something about the hair on his face.

With a sigh, he stripped off his clothing, the cool air rushing over his bare skin. He waded into the stream, the cold biting but welcome, washing away the tension that had built up over the past few days. He let the water run over his shoulders, soaking into him, clearing his mind. A slight pang from the wound on his leg reminded him it wasn't fully healed. Another scar to add to the story his body wore.

The sound of birds chirping in the trees above filled the morning air, but his thoughts drifted back to Nova, still curled up in the cave. He wanted to be back before she woke, but for now, he savoured the few minutes of solitude, letting the stream cleanse him of the weight he'd been carrying.

Ryker emerged from the water feeling refreshed. He'd offer her the chance to bathe once he returned to the cave. He threw on the clothes he'd discarded on the side of the stream and headed back.

His boots echoed on the rocky ground as he made his way to the cave and their makeshift camp. Ryker expected to see the ethereal presence that had become his constant companion.

But instead, all he found was an empty void.

Stones skittered across the floor of the cavern as he halted. He hurriedly looked left and right, searching for Nova. He dropped to his knees, his hands sifting through the dirt and leaves, as if she might be hidden somewhere within the earth itself. Maybe she'd left the cave to relieve herself in the bushes.

He swiftly moved to the entrance again and surveyed the forest, but the only movement was a light breeze rustling the leaves.

"Nova?" Ryker called.

She didn't answer. The only sounds were chattering squirrels and birdsong. How did she vanish into thin air?

Ryker dragged his hands through his damp hair as he spun around, searching for the lost star. He froze, realising the ground before the cave was littered with muddy footprints. Not one set . . . but many. He crouched low to the ground, his fingers brushing the soft earth as he studied the footprints in the dirt. He shifted to the side, looking for disturbances in the ground or broken branches nearby. There was a subtle drag in the dirt, a scuff mark where a foot had slipped.

Ryker's jaw clenched. He moved further along, his gaze sharp, scanning for any indication of a struggle. A snapped twig caught his eye, followed by the faint impression of multiple sets of footprints—larger, heavier ones.

"Fuck," Ryker cursed under his breath, berating himself for not noticing it in the dim light before. How did he not hear someone or somebodies entering the cave? Had he been so long at the stream? Why did he leave her in the first place? Already, fear ate away at his heart. He'd sworn to protect her, and now she was gone.

He swiftly returned inside the cave to shove all their belongings into bags. Kicking dirt and dust onto the fire, Ryker doused it. He was fuming, one because he let his guard down and he knew he shouldn't have, and two because he didn't like it when people took things that didn't belong to them.

It couldn't have been Branoc's men. They were always too loud and clumsy. No, this was someone trained, someone who knew exactly what they were doing. Another bounty hunter, perhaps?

Too many thoughts hammered in his mind. He needed to slow down. To breathe and think.

As soon as Charlie was ready, Ryker swung himself into the saddle and urged the horse forward, leaving the cave behind. The forest swallowed him up; the trees casting long shadows in the early morning light. He leaned forward, whispering encouragement as the horse's hooves pounding rhythmically against the forest floor.

Whoever took Nova couldn't have gone too far and they were going to be very sorry once he found them.

Because he was a damn good hunter.

SEVENTEEN

THE MEDDLESOME PIRATES

With a throbbing head and a funny taste in her mouth, Nova slowly peeked one eye open to survey her surroundings. Dull blue skies, fluffy white clouds that were dusted with pinks and oranges from the sunset painted the scene before her.

Last she remembered, she was in a cave, tucked up against Ryker's side. And just before that, the unexplainable feeling he'd given her with his hands before laying her down on the bed and joining her, sleep enveloping them both. She'd never wanted to move from that spot, instead hoping to repeat their desirable actions over and over again.

Ryker had kissed her with such urgency, like he wanted to devour every touch they shared. She could still feel him on her lips—a phantom kiss.

Nova wanted . . . no, needed more of him.

But now, however, she was flat on her back, her head resting on something somewhat soft and the world was too bright for her headache, so she closed her eyes against the morning.

There was a rocking, swaying sensation, as voices she didn't recognise floated through air that smelt like fish and salt. She tried to recall what happened.

A figure, tall and cloaked in dark leather, flashed across her mind. *"Careful, we don't want her waking up just yet."*

"Just grab her and run."

Rough hands had jolted her awake, dragging her from the cave and smothering her cries for help. That's when she blacked out.

Nova winced, cradling her head as she sat up.

"Captain! She's awake . . ." a deep voice called out.

Many sets of eyes peered at her from a small crowd, and Nova was very aware that everyone was staring at her.

"Hello . . ."

"Ahh, she awakens then! Sorry about the headache. Didn't want to scare you too much, so we knocked you out with a little dreamroot."

A copper-haired woman stepped between the crowd of people standing in front of Nova. She was wearing black trousers with matching, glossy boots that came up to her knees. A billowing white blouse peeked from beneath a dark-blue jacket lined with gold buttons. Diagonally across her chest was a wide brown leather strap that held a few small daggers. Tiny brown freckles peppered the woman's face, and her eyes resembled the colour of the ocean.

"You alright, missy?" the copper-haired woman asked.

Nova scrunched her brow. "Well, no. My head hurts. I'd like to know where you're taking me. And who you are?"

The woman took a bow as she took her black hat from her head. "The name is Captain Sable Bloodfin, pirate of the Veridian seas."

As Sable bowed, Nova took a moment to scan the crowd. Females and males of all shapes and sizes grinned at her and she smiled back nervously. How did she come aboard with this crew of misfits? And where was Ryker?

"Are you going to hurt me, sell me, or turn me over to the king for a large sum of money?" Nova sighed.

Sable straightened and placed her arms behind her back. "I figured you were valuable if the Hound had you. For now, I'll say none of the above. I only intend to get his attention. Though money is always handy."

"Hound? . . . Do you mean Ryker?"

Sable shrugged. "Well, that's his given name, yes. Most of us know him as Hound."

"What could you possibly need Ryker for?"

Sable shifted nervously, grinning at her crew, who gave a few obligatory chuckles. "He owes me a favour."

This must be the pirates that Ryker had been so worried about. *"Meddlesome bunch"*—his words.

"What could he possibly owe a pirate?"

Sable offered her a lopsided grin. "Safe passage to Corsair, of course."

Nova lifted her chin, trying to look as unbothered as possible. "And what if he doesn't come?"

Sable's eyes darted to those that stood behind Nova. Her hands twitched as if they wanted to grip the hilt of a blade. "He will come. If he knows what's good for him." She flashed another grin that didn't quite reach her eyes. "This ain't something he can walk away from."

Nova folded her arms over her chest. "So why steal me? Why not just ask him?"

Sable shrugged. "The man is hard to pin down."

Nova eyed Sable. "He will come looking for you."

The copper haired captain grinned. "That's what I'm hoping for."

Was it true, though? Would he come for her again? . . . a second time? Of course he would. He'd made a promise. They'd been intimate . . . he'd kissed her until there was nothing but all of his essence consuming her. He would come—and Sable would be sorry.

"I demand you take me back to the shore," Nova huffed.

"Sorry, love, can't do that."

Nova took a step towards the side of the ship. "I'll jump overboard and swim back then."

There was no way she was actually going to do it. She didn't even know how to swim—but Sable didn't know that.

The captain took a small step too, matching Nova's. "I wouldn't recommend that."

"Why not?"

Sable looked towards the skies. "It's nearly night."

Nova eyed the captain warily. "What has that got to do with anything?"

"Well, the leviathan is nocturnal," Sable added. "And nobody wants to run into one of those under the cover of darkness."

Nova flicked her gaze out to sea before returning it to the captain. "What's a leviathan?"

Most of the crew had returned to their work on the deck as Nova and the captain braced themselves against the edge of the ship. Salty sea water hit the sides, spraying into the air as they sailed along.

"A leviathan is a monstrous sea serpent, larger than any ship, with scales as tough as the strongest armour," Sable began, her voice lowering to a hushed tone as if the very mention of the beast might summon it. "It dwells in the deepest parts of the ocean, where the water is at its darkest."

Was the woman telling the truth? Was there a creature so great and dangerous that roamed the seas looking for its next meal?

Nova leaned forward, peering into the ocean. "Has anyone ever seen it?"

Captain Sable nodded slowly. "Few have seen the leviathan and lived to tell the tale. Those who have, speak of a creature with eyes like yellow suns and a maw that could swallow a ship whole. They say its roar can be heard for miles; a sound that makes even the bravest sailor's blood run cold."

"And you—you've seen it?"

"I've heard it cry on dark nights on the sea. Though I try my best never to travel under the moon," Sable murmured. "Too risky."

Nova shuddered and hoped that Ryker knew about the leviathan. She didn't want to lose him to the likes of that creature. She allowed her mind to ponder him for a moment. He would have undoubtedly presumed the worst once he found her missing.

This would not end well.

"So, we're all good then? You're not going to demand I take you back right now or . . .?" Sable eyed her warily.

Nova shrugged. "I guess I have no choice in the matter."

A few eyes still watched the Captain.

"Wonderful!" she retorted. "For now, it's all hands-on deck to get this ship home. Get to it!"

The crew scurried about, and Nova found herself fascinated at all the different parts of the ship, and how each person took their position with a smile plastered on their face.

"Land ho!" someone called from the crow's nest above.

Nova sighed, turning to rest her arms against the wooden edge of the ship and stared out at the sea. The ocean mist slapped her in the face and she inhaled the salty scent. At least she got to experience the sea before returning home, even if it wasn't in the best of terms.

The sun was descending as the ship pulled into port on a large island. It stretched to the north and south as far as Nova could see. The crew placed a plank down and everyone disembarked. Hesitating for a moment, Nova glanced back in the direction they'd come.

"If you'll follow me this way, my dear." Sable gestured towards land.

Nova hesitated. "Are you going to tie me up?"

Sable cocked her head to the side. "Not unless you plan on running?"

She'd like to. But Nova knew with the amount of water surrounding her, she wouldn't get too far. "No."

"No need for ropes then." Sable smirked. "We will feast and be jolly until the Hound arrives."

Gulls screeched in the air above them as the sunset across the horizon, spreading a vibrant orange glow across everyone and everything like a blanket.

As the pirate captain led her down the wooden plank, Nova's mind raced, but outwardly she forced herself to remain calm. Every step felt heavier with the weight of waiting for Ryker. She knew he would come for her, he always did.

Nova stepped onto the weathered cobblestone streets of the vibrant pirate village, and a riot of colours assaulted her senses. Pirate crews, each with their own style and garb, roamed the bustling market, exchanging tales of the high seas over tankards of grog in shanty-style taverns.

A woman with pea green skin brushed past her and threw Nova a wink. While a tall and elegant looking male with pointy ears and long golden hair that reached past his waist threaded his arm through the crook of the woman's elbow before whisking her away.

To her right, an old man hobbled along on wooden crutches, a black patch covering one eye and a few teeth missing from his grin. His ragged clothes fluttered in the breeze as he shuffled forward. The street was alive with colour and movement, an array of citizens that was a feast for the eyes.

The air was thick with the aroma of exotic spices, tropical fruits, and the unmistakable scent of the sea. Docked along the shore were ships with names like "Black Kraken" and "Crimson Tempest," their tattered sails casting shadows on the bustling scene. None were equal to the size of the ship she arrived on, though. That one was much bigger. The rhythmic sounds of shipwrights at work filled the air, and they repaired and enhanced vessels with, as far as she could tell, skill and ingenuity.

Nova was lost for words. She'd been in quite a few villages on this journey, but nothing prepared her for a pirate one.

Sable navigated through the bustling streets and Nova noticed the wide berth some of the folk offered her as she stalked through the crowd.

It was obvious that she was respected quite highly.

Nova's hands fidgeted in her dress pockets as they strode along. A part of her felt empty without Ryker by her side. She'd become so accustomed to his warmth. His presence gave her a sense of safety.

In a cluster of tattoo parlours, artists crafted intricate maritime-themed tattoos, and their customers proudly displayed their sea-inspired ink as badges of honour. Large flags adorned the establishments, showing the allegiance of the crews within.

Nearby, an oddly shaped fountain served as a central gathering point, surrounded by locals and pirates using it for various purposes. The figure had the top half of a human, but the bottom half sported a tail—like a fish. Nova tilted her head to the side, unsure what to label the figure.

Sable must have caught her staring at it. "It's a siren," she stated.

Nova ran her eyes over the figure again. She'd quite like to meet a siren. "Do they live in the water like fish do?"

Sable slowed her pace as they walked by the fountain. "They are shifters. They can live on land and water. I assume you've never encountered one?"

Nova shook her head. "No, but I'd like to."

"I'm sure some of them walk amongst us now." Sable gestured towards the crowds. "They rarely like to make themselves known, though. Quiet sort of creatures."

They continued their journey, and Nova eyed the citizens carefully in hopes of spotting a siren. Though she wouldn't know if she had any luck.

The aroma of grilled fish and seafood filled the air as vendors in the market prepared freshly caught treasures. Nova's stomach growled. This morning she'd missed breakfast, and the dreamroot had knocked her out well past lunchtime. Colourful boats, floating market stalls, bobbed in the harbour, selling trinkets, jewellery, and magical artefacts. Street performers captivated the crowds with acrobatics, fire-breathing, and musical performances, Earth trying to outdo the other and adding to the lively atmosphere.

Shouts erupted suddenly from the nearby tavern, and within seconds, the doors burst open as two men came tumbling out, fists flying. Their wild grins were laced with drunken rage, their movements erratic but fierce. One swung a bottle, shattering it against the other's head, sending glass flying across the dusty street.

The scene devolved quickly. More pirates joined the fray, turning the street into a chaotic whirlwind of fists and curses. Nova tensed, instinctively stepping closer to Sable.

She closed her eyes for a moment and pretended she was still in the cave, curled up to Ryker's side and not on an island filled with pirates far from his embrace.

"Get out of here, the lot of ya!" Sable cried out.

Nova flinched at the sound of the captain's voice. She certainly was loud.

Sable grunted and motioned to Nova. "Come on, let's be done with these nitwits."

The captain sauntered off towards a large tent that stood erect in the distance. Nova was hopeful that it would provide some peace and quiet—not to mention some food, too. She hoped to find some sort of solace while she patiently waited for the Hound to find her.

Under the sprawling canvas of a giant tent, the air buzzed with the clamour of merrymaking. Long wooden tables groaned under the weight of full tankards, overflowing platters of exotic seafood, and fruits plundered from distant lands. The tang of saltwater mixed with the savoury aroma of grilled fish and spiced meats, creating an intoxicating atmosphere. There was movement and sound everywhere Nova looked.

Clearly, there'd be no peace and quiet, but she did find food. Pirates sure knew how to make a tasty meal.

Dinner had been more than enough. Nova's tastebuds were almost yelling at her to stop. There were so many delights to choose from. It didn't take long for Nova to feel full to the brim.

She sat next to Captain Sable, the formidable figure with a tricorn hat and a cascade of copper curls, who presided over the festivities of a makeshift throne. They made eye contact and Sable grinned, revealing a flash of gold in her teeth, as a raucous sea shanty filled the air. Pirates and sailors alike pounded their tankards on the tables, caught in the infectious rhythm.

In a corner, a makeshift stage housed a lively band of musicians. Fiddles, accordions, and drums blended in a cacophony of joyous melodies that beckoned even the most stoic of pirates to tap their feet.

Nova couldn't help but grin at the sight before her. She'd wanted to dislike Sable for kidnapping her, but as the night wore on and the crowd got livelier, she was finding it very hard not to like this place.

As the music reached a peak, Sable rose from her throne of driftwood, coral, and seashells, gesturing for Nova to join her in the midst of the celebration. The captain's eyes twinkled with mischief as she led Nova to the centre of the tent.

"Ye' can't be a true pirate until ye've danced the Buccaneer's Waltz," Sable declared, her voice carrying over the music.

With a dramatic sweep, she launched into a joyful dance, her boots stomping in time with the lively tune. The creatures with green tinted skin cheered and clapped. A few elves with their pointy ears played on some instruments made of wood—that Nova couldn't name—creating a rhythmic backdrop.

A grin crept its way across Nova's face as she became caught in the contagious energy of the moment. She hesitated for a heartbeat before giving in to the call of the dance. With a light shrug of surrender, she matched Captain Sable's steps, mirroring the intricate footwork and twirls of the Buccaneer's Waltz. The tent seemed to blur around her as she whirled; the music carrying her away to a world of revelry and freedom.

The crew erupted into cheers as Nova and Captain Sable spun and dipped, their laughter merging with the lively song. As the music gradually slowed, the two women brought the dance to a triumphant close, bowing to the appreciative audience. Nova, breathless but exhilarated, grinned broadly at the captain.

Both women retreated to their seats and flopped down, chests rising and falling with heavy breathing.

"I have never seen a dance like that before." Nova spoke through short breaths.

Sable grinned. "If I'm not sailing the seas, I'm dancing. One can't go through life without it."

Nova returned the captain's smile. She was quickly becoming aware that she could quite happily live here on Earth amongst its array of people. There was so much diversity and culture yet for her to explore. Surely not everyone was like Branoc?

Her thoughts drifted to the Hound. He had claimed he didn't dance, but perhaps the lively tune filling the room could change his mind. Maybe, with a little convincing, she could get him to lower his guard and actually enjoy himself for once.

Though she had to admit that despite the colourful chaos of the crowd she dwelt in, she found herself missing the quiet that followed Ryker wherever he went. Like a loyal dog to its master. With Ryker, she knew what to expect. There were no sudden moves or loud outbursts. And certainly, no erratic behaviour like some of the pirates here displayed. She enjoyed dancing and music, but couldn't deny that he was peace. He was safety.

And right now, Nova wished he were here.

EIGHTEEN

THE OLD SLOOP

Ryker traced the collection of footsteps all the way to the shoreline of the Veridian sea. Crouching down, he picked up a handful of sand and let the tiny grains trickle through his fingers.

Pirates.

He knew exactly who it would be. Sable. How dare she think she could take from him?

As he stood, Ryker began to plan a course of action. First, he'd head towards the closest village. He needed a boat, and he needed one fast.

Once he reached the town, Ryker handed Charlie over to a stable for safekeeping. The stable master, a grizzled man with a weathered face, looked up from his work and gave Ryker a nod of acknowledgment.

"Good horse you got there," the man said, running a hand along Charlie's flank.

"I need to house him for a short while. Do you have room?"

The stable master nodded. "I'll take good care of him."

Ryker offered him a decent amount of coin, pressing the gold pieces into his calloused palm. "See that you do," he replied. "I'll be back for him on the morrow."

The stable master pocketed the coins with a satisfied grunt and led Charlie into one of the stalls, murmuring soothing words to the horse. Ryker watched for a moment, making sure his loyal companion was in good hands before turning on his heel and heading towards the docks.

He was careful to keep an eye out for unwanted trouble as he made his way through town. Guards, pickpockets, fellow bounty hunters—the Twins. Thankfully, he found none.

As he approached the shoreline, the sound of waves crashing against the pier grew louder, accompanied by the calls of seagulls circling overhead. Ships of various sizes bobbed in the water, their sails billowing in the breeze. Sailors shouted to one another, hauling crates and barrels onto the decks, while others repaired nets or mended sails.

He spotted a man by some boats and approached. "How much for that sloop?" Ryker pointed to the small vessel with a single sail. It wasn't in the best shape. The wood was weathered, and Ryker could see the sail had been patched more than once. It would, however, have to do.

"Do ye' plan on returning it?" the man asked, squinting up at Ryker.

"I do. I just need to make a trip to Corsair and then I'll be back."

The sailor turned his head to look out towards the setting sun before his heedful gaze returned to Ryker. "You're mad to sail at this time of night?"

Ryker shrugged. "How so?"

The sailor looked at him in disbelief. "I don't know, maybe there's leviathan's out there that would devour you like a snack?"

It's true. He'd be a tasty treat for a gigantic sea creature. But he hadn't heard of a leviathan in these waters for years. He wasn't going to let the possibility of a creature eating him stop him from reaching Nova.

"It's a chance I have to take," he murmured.

"Well, in that case, because I might lose me boat. It'll be forty silver coins." The man stood with folded arms.

"Fifteen." Ryker flipped his coat, displaying his sword as a threat. "And I'll spare you the steel."

The man eyed him warily. "Thirty. Fifteen gold for me, fifteen gold deposit that you'll get back when the boat makes it back to shore."

Ryker had no time to argue, so he nodded and fished coins from a small pouch in his trouser pocket, paying the man before reaching for the rope tied to the dock.

"I'll have it back to you by the morning."

The sailor tipped his hat back and scratched the top of his head. "I'll believe it when I see it."

Ryker grinned and proceeded to push the boat out into the water.

This was the last thing he felt like doing today. He'd hoped to awaken to a sleepy and satisfied Nova. Possibly explored her body more—should she have wanted that.

Yet here he was, chasing after Sable to fetch her back.

How could he have let this happen? How did he not hear a hoard of pirates trumping through the bush? Was he so indulged with his bathing in the stream that he didn't sense trouble? Did Nova have such an effect on him that all his usual sharpness had left his body?

This was exactly why he shouldn't have got involved with her, yet every part of him ached for her. Needed her. There was no point in denying it anymore. From the moment he first saw her, his heart had flipped in his chest, and now that she was gone, the truth was undeniable. He wanted more time—time to know her completely. Mind, body, and soul.

Ryker grit his teeth. He was determined to fetch her back. He'd made her a promise to return her to where she belongs— he wouldn't break it, not today, not ever. Nova would get back to Ara . . . if that's still what she wanted.

His arms burned with the drag of oars against the swirling waters. The setting sun was certainly a slight issue. Once it was set, he'd only have the glow of the moon to guide his way. Then there was the leviathan. Perhaps it was all a myth to keep humans from the waters, Ryker couldn't be sure. Either way, he'd stay on high alert.

There was no real way of knowing how far ahead Sable and her crew of misfits were. Their ship was undeniably bigger than the vessel he'd just acquired, but by his better judgement, it was going to take him all night to reach the island.

Corsair's Haven—home of Captain Sable Bloodfin.

It had to be her that took Nova. She made it a point to meddle in his affairs, usually freeing the prisoners he'd captured. He'd caught her attention one too many times— turns out pirates don't appreciate their crew or contacts being turned in. Now, she made his life more difficult for sport, no matter who he happened to capture.

He rolled his eyes and carried on. This time, he was really going to give her a piece of his mind. If she had so much as touched a single hair on Nova's head, there would be hell to pay.

Ryker reached the island by nightfall. He carefully navigated the small boat through the calm waters, keeping to the darker, unlit areas to avoid detection. The moon cast a silvery glow over the waves, creating an almost ethereal pathway that guided him to the shore. He was pleased she was so bright tonight.

He silently anchored the boat in a secluded cove, its hull barely making a sound as it kissed the sandy beach.

Ryker stuck to the shadows as he moved with the practised ease of a seasoned hunter. His footsteps were silent against the rough terrain. He moved carefully by the houses and taverns, his dark clothing blending seamlessly with the night. Occasionally, a drunk pirate would stumble onto his path, but Ryker would swiftly and silently slip past to avoid detection.

Most likely, he'd find Sable in her palace of worn leather and canvas held together by large rope stitching. The captain was the self-appointed leader of her lair, with many under her charge, be they human, fae, goblin, or any manner of creatures.

Ryker noted a few half-orcs staggering home from the tavern to his left. The sounds of laughter and music drifted across the street. A male elf with long, golden-wheat hair and a female with copper waves strolled along hand in hand. The female's bright green eyes lit up with joy as the male pulled her closer to his side, both looking adoringly in love.

If only it was he and Nova.

Ryker inched closer as he approached the back of the tent, but halted when he spied a pirate guard. Of course, there would be more guards. Unfortunately, he seemed to find them wherever he went.

Ryker pondered for a moment before he pursed his lips and whistled. The call of a nightingale. A sound that blended naturally into the night, but it caught the guard's attention.

The man's head snapped towards the source of the noise, curiosity and caution evident in his posture. He began to move towards Ryker, his steps slow and measured.

Ryker took the opportunity and pulled a dart gun from his pocket, loaded it with a dreamroot dart, and aimed for the small patch of skin exposed on the guard's neck. He was down to his last few, so he knew it better hit its target.

His aim was true. Within seconds, the guard crumpled unconscious to the ground with muffled sounds.

Ryker waited to make sure no one heard before he slunk from his hidden position and dragged the guard into the concealing shadows, his movements swift and efficient despite his tired arms and the pain that still throbbed from the wound on his leg. Luckily, the night swallowed the fallen pirate as if he were never there.

As the moon climbed higher into the sky, Ryker moved, making his way to the back of the enormous tent. The sounds of laughter and music grew louder as he approached. The heart of the pirate revelry was just beyond the canvas walls.

With a last glance around, Ryker slipped into the tent.

He was pleased to find that he'd emerged right behind the throne.

It was so loud and chaotic that no one noticed as he reached for the dagger in his boot—Ryker crept forward.

"There will be many more nights like this to come!" Sable cried as she lifted her glass to salute her crew.

"That's if you live to see tomorrow . . ."

Sable sucked in her breath as Ryker's swift motion brought his hand around the side of the chair and trapped Sable against it—blade to skin.

Nova squealed; her eyes wide as she first saw the blade on the Captain's throat.

The tent fell silent as he emerged from the shadows behind the throne.

Sable swallow against the blade. "Hound. Always good to see you."

"You've taken something that was mine . . . now I want it back," Ryker growled.

In a flurry of movement, a large half-orc, his skin the colour of algae, roughly pulled a shaking Nova from her chair and held her against his bulking chest—a blade to her throat.

Fuck.

This was not how Ryker planned the rescue would go.

Get in, tell Sable to stop meddling in his affairs, take Nova, head back to the mainland—not put Nova in the middle of it all.

"I see we're at an impasse . . ." Sable murmured.

Ryker's eyes narrowed as he stared Sable down. "Let her go."

Sable hissed as Ryker dug the blade deeper against her skin. "Maybe we could strike a deal?"

"Why would I want to do that?"

"Because I have something you want, and you have skills that I need?"

Ryker pulled the blade even closer and dipped his head to whisper in Sable's ear. "Why don't I end you right here?"

Sable swallowed. "Because if I die . . . she dies."

With a glance towards Nova, Ryker could see the plea in her eyes as the half-orc gripped her body tighter. If he drew crimson from Nova, Sable would quickly find herself with little to no crew—or without a head.

The air was thick with anticipation as the crew watched on, weapons already in hand.

"Tell me the deal," Ryker grunted.

With a nod, Sable spoke. "My brother, Captain Ratchet has something of mine and I want it back."

Ryker lifted a brow at her words. "Funny . . . seems as if we have the same problem?"

"I know, I know. Trust me, I stole her with this in mind, but let me go and we can talk about it." Ryker could hear the woman's grin in her tone. "Or I could always have her delivered back to Branoc. She mentioned there was a 'large sum of money' involved?"

Ryker hesitated for only a moment. There was no way he would allow Nova anywhere near the king again. He shoved Sable forward and stepped towards the half-orc. "Let her go . . ."

The green male glanced at Sable, who gave him a nod. In turn, the half orc released Nova. She didn't hesitate to stumble into Ryker's side. He hooked an arm around her with his blade still held out in defence in the other.

Sable straightened her jacket and motioned to her crew to resume the festivities before gesturing to Ryker to sit at the table. "Shall we discuss the finer details?"

Eyeing those who were slow to sheath their weapons, Ryker offered a curt nod, helping Nova sit before placing himself between the captain and his star. The sooner he got this conversation over, the better he would feel.

He turned to face Nova, reaching for her hand. "Are you alright? Did they harm you?"

Nova's body responded to his touch, a dull blue light emitting from her skin. Ryker pulled his hand away quickly. The last thing he needed was for Sable to find out—if she didn't know already—that Nova was a star.

Nova flashed him a gentle smile. "I'm perfectly alright."

He searched her sea-green eyes for a moment before he dipped his head and turned back towards Sable.

"So, what is it you need from me?" Ryker asked as he took a tankard of ale that a fae looking female offered him.

Sable settled in her chair with an ale in hand. Now that there was no blade to her throat, the cocky grin that usually adorned her face had returned. "My brother took something valuable that I need."

Ryker's brow knitted. "So why don't you just ask for it back?"

"Because we aren't on speaking terms."

"And why aren't you on speaking terms?" Ryker asked, not that he cared. Sable was always meddling in people's affairs and there were probably quite a few people who she wasn't on speaking terms with.

Sable's face turned a slight shade of red. "I may have taken something from him."

Ryker took a swig of ale before answering. "Why does that not surprise me?"

Sable flashed him a lopsided grin. "You know how it is, Hound. Anything is fair game for the right reasons."

Of course she would say that. It was her trademark. Sable liked to think of herself as the Robin Hood of the seas—just a little more . . . morally grey.

Ryker leaned back in his chair. "So, how is your brother my problem?"

Sable flicked her gaze to Nova, who sat quietly behind him. "You want Nova, and I want my treasure."

Ryker took a swig of ale before replying. "And where is this treasure?"

"Temple's Lair."

Great.

Another island. Hours away.

Temple's Lair was smaller than Corsair's Haven in size, but it was just as crowded with creatures of all kinds. Humans, half-orcs, elves and the odd faery—though those were few and far between. Ryker had never been to Temples Lair, but he'd heard the tales of scoundrels who lived there, and it certainly wasn't on his list of dream destinations.

"So, if I help you retrieve this item. You swear to me that you will let us go unharmed and you will cease to meddle in my affairs?" Ryker asked.

Sable nodded. "I swear on my life."

"I have requirements."

"What are they?"

Ryker shifted in his chair. "I'll need a disguise. You will come with me and so will Nova."

There was no way he was letting Nova out of his sight again. And if anything was to go wrong on Temple's Lair, Ryker would have Sable as a bargaining piece—or so he hoped.

Sable hesitated before holding out her hand. "Deal."

Ryker reached for it, and they shook. "We leave at first light."

As the crew got louder and Sable returned to her meal, Ryker glanced at Nova. He was reluctant to touch her again for fear of her glowing, so he gently brushed the fabric of her skirt under the table, hoping she might see his concern written on his face. "Are you alright?"

"I am fine. And though the circumstances are odd, I kind of like it here."

Ryker glanced around the room at the merrymaking. He too could admit that this particular lot of pirates were fun when they weren't being a giant pain in his ass.

Sea-green eyes found him once again. Nova was safe and unharmed. That's all that mattered to him right now.

A long-haired human woman with shark's teeth through the holes in her ears approached the table where they sat and placed a large plate of assorted food before him. Grunting his thanks, Ryker picked up a fork and chanced a bite. He wasn't too stubborn to admit he was starving. As the rest of the evening drew on, he became more and more aware of how much he needed some peace and quiet. Here, there was no resting easy. He couldn't trust that none of them might attempt to harm him.

Before long, bodies were collapsing on the floor in groggy sleep and people were stumbling from the tent, still singing their sea shanties.

Ryker turned towards Sable. "Do you have somewhere Nova, and I can retire, too? I will need time to form a plan for tomorrow."

Sable nodded and ushered to a pirate guard. "Toadie will show you where."

Ryker rose from the table and took Nova's hand. "Try anything funny in the night and you'll be sorry Sable."

The captain grinned before lifting her ale in salute. "Pirate's honour."

Ryker scoffed as he followed the guard from the room with a very sleepy-looking Nova gripped tight at his side. He wasn't taking any chances.

The guard led them down a rocky path, their footsteps sounding softly in the cool night air. Moonlight spilled across the sandy ground, lighting the way. As they descended further, the sounds of the village celebrations grew faint, replaced by the whispering of leaves and the distant calls of nocturnal creatures. The rocky path was uneven, and Ryker kept a watchful eye on Nova, making sure she didn't stumble or fall.

They stopped outside a small hut made from bamboo, canvas, and dried straw. Toadie's torch casting flickering light that danced across the hut's surface. "This is it."

"Thank you," Ryker murmured as he pushed the door open for Nova.

She stepped inside, with Ryker close on her heels. As soon as they were inside, he secured the door behind them. There was a good chance he wouldn't sleep tonight—or ever. Not until Nova was returned safely to Ara.

He turned to see Nova walking around the small room, taking in all the sights. A few shelves were adorned with books and sea shells. There was a large bowl of brightly coloured fruits that sat on a table to the left of the room, right under the window. He watched as she ran her fingers over the spine of the books, reading their titles silently to herself.

He'd had all these thoughts of what he'd do if he found her harmed, but hadn't thought of what he'd do if he found her completely well.

Should he take her in his arms? Should they talk about their time by the fire? Perhaps he should just tell her he was glad she was safe and then leave her be?

It was the first quiet moment they'd had together since Ryker found the star amongst the merry pirates. Too many thoughts swam around in his mind, so he opted for the last option.

"I'll guard the door all night while you sleep. We'll leave early." He motioned towards the small bed on the right of the room.

Ryker caught the brief flicker in Nova's eyes, the way her lips pressed together, the subtle drop of her shoulders. It was quick, just a moment, but enough to show the disappointment she tried to hide. He saw it, but said nothing, his gaze lingering on her a moment longer. Only her hands and face were visible beneath her clothing, yet he could see the familiar hum of light that radiated off her body any time her eyes beheld something that brought her joy.

He looked away. Too much had happened in the last twelve hours, he needed to give himself some time to sort through his thoughts.

"Will you not join me in sleep?" Nova asked.

Ryker shook his head as he moved to the door. "I'd feel better if I took watch outside."

Nova looked at him with a gleam in her eyes. "I think you should come here."

"Nova . . ." Ryker murmured.

"I want you in my bed tonight . . . Please."

How could he refuse her? She was glowing, illuminating the room . . . just for him. He didn't deserve to have any of her, but by the stars, he wanted all of it.

Ryker took a step towards Nova, her smile growing bigger each time his boot sounded on the wooden floor. "Are you sure?"

Nova nodded. "I am sure," she said as she reached for his hand.

Perhaps he could lie beside her until she lost herself to sleep. Then he would take watch. Either way, he wasn't sleeping tonight.

Together, they stripped their attire until they only stood in their undergarments before sliding beneath the cool sheets. Nova didn't waste any time cuddling up to his side. He smiled softly as she made herself comfortable. Maybe just for tonight, they could pretend the world was their oyster and that all of tomorrow's problems didn't exist.

The sound of the gentle waves lapping at the shore reminded Ryker of the long journey that awaited them in the morning.

They would never reach the mysterious woman in the Twin Peaks at this rate.

Ryker quietly sighed as he pulled Nova against his chest, tucking her close. The scent of her hair tickled his nose, filling him with a peace his body longed for. With closed eyes, he allowed his body to rest, though his ears did not.

He would not be caught off guard again.

NINETEEN

THE SLY SNATCHING

The boat rocked gently as it sliced through the early morning waves, carrying Ryker and Nova towards Temple's lair. The dawn was calm, the sea a glowing, citrus coloured expanse that stretched endlessly in all directions. Sable stood at the front of the small wooden boat, her keen eyes scanning the horizon, while two of her trusted crew members, Toadie and Marla, tended to the sails.

Ryker had woken as soon as the morning broke. He'd stayed in bed a while, transfixed on Nova's peaceful sleeping face beside him. Holding her through the night had brought a soothing balm to the ache inside his chest. One that only a certain type of person could bring.

She was the colour in his grey washed world.

He glanced across to Nova, who sat beside him, her gaze fixed on the water. He reached out and squeezed her hand, offering a silent reassurance. Being careful not to linger with his touch for too long. It made her glow brighter than he'd care for Sable to see. Ryker preferred it when she shone only for him—though he shouldn't.

Nova looked up and gave him a small, tentative smile.

He would do this for her. Find the item, get out of there and continue onto the woman in the mountains who could hopefully help Nova get home to Ara.

Sable's voice cut through Ryker's thoughts. "We're getting close," she announced. She turned to Ryker, her eyes narrowing slightly. "Remember, you need to get in, find the item, and get out without raising any alarms. My brother's residence is heavily guarded."

Ryker's jaw clenched, biting his tongue. He nodded. If he was being honest with himself, he didn't want to be a part of Sable's shenanigans in any way, shape, or form. But it wasn't about him anymore. It wasn't the Ryker show—he had someone else to take care of.

He'd borrowed some attire from Sable, hoping it would help him blend in with Ratchet's crew once they reached the island. A beige, loose-fitting, billowy shirt peeked out from beneath his black leather waistcoat. His pants were knee length, made of coarse cloth, tucked into worn leather boots that rose mid-calf. A wide, brightly coloured red sash wrapped around his waist. To complete his outfit, Sable had given him a headscarf—canary yellow.

The disguise felt ridiculous. Ryker was used to loose-fitting shirts, comfortable trousers and a coat. Unfortunately, his new 'get up' was a necessary precaution. "Remind me again what exactly I am looking for?" he asked.

Sable threw a glance over her shoulder. "It's a small, ornate chest with the emblem of two sea serpents wrapped around a sword on the lid."

"And you think it's in Ratchet's house?"

Sable nodded. "Most likely it will be in Rachet's study."

Ryker looked towards the approaching island. "And tell me again why you can't ask for it back?"

"Because my brother warned me if I stepped foot on his island again, I wouldn't live to tell the tale."

"Good grief . . . what did you take from him?"

"Does it matter?" Sable threw Ryker a grin.

Nova shifted on the wooden bench to his right. "Not if it's for the right reasons, right? Though, then you have to consider who decides what those reasons are." Her soft voice floated through the morning air.

Ryker smiled at Nova's boldness. She had a lot to learn about humans, but it seemed she'd learned enough to see through the pirate's flawed logic.

Sable huffed, shrugging her shoulders before staring back out to sea. "You catch on quick."

As they approached the island, the silhouette of rocky cliffs loomed ahead, dark and imposing against the early morning glow. Sable motioned for them to keep quiet as they neared the shore, the boat gliding silently into a hidden cove. Toadie and Marla skilfully manoeuvred the boat, ensuring it remained concealed from any patrolling guards.

Ryker mentally ran through his thrown together plan. Which comprised three things. Sneak in. Sneak out. Don't get caught. Simple right? Too bad Sable hadn't given him a shred of information about the layout of the island, claiming they wouldn't be able to trust any intel they got, anyway. She seemed to have great confidence in his abilities.

"Remember, bring it back, and you and Nova get off this island safely," Sable murmured.

Nova brushed his hand lightly just as he stood. He caught her eye and tried his best to offer her a reassuring smile. "I'll be right back," he murmured.

With a nod in Sables's direction, Ryker jumped from the boat. He turned to look at Nova one last time, and though no words were physically spoken, a thousand were said internally. She offered him a soft smile, one that gave enough courage for Ryker to see this through. She was trusting him to get her home.

Ryker adjusted his borrowed pirate garb, pulling the wide-brimmed hat lower over his eyes to obscure his features. As his eyes scanned the surroundings for any signs of danger. The sun was rising higher in the sky, casting his shadow on the cliffs, but Ryker remained undetected as he climbed higher, inching closer to Sable's brother's residence.

At the top of the cliffs, he paused, crouching behind a cluster of boulders. Ryker spied a large round hut nestled among the trees. Guards patrolled the perimeter, their sharpened cutlasses glinting in the early morning light.

He surveyed them for a while, forming a plan in his mind. Perhaps it would be the simplest to waltz right into the already bustling crowd. Surely no one would even look his way if he looked like he was a villager in the marketplace selling wares or buying goods.

With this in mind, Ryker began to scale down the rocky cliff face, slipping into the trees that sat on the outskirts of the village.

Temple's lair was a smaller island than Corsair's, which gave Ryker a disadvantage. It would be a lot easier to spot an unfamiliar face in the crowd than it would be over on Sable's island. So, despite his disguise, Ryker thought it best to stick to the side roads and the alleyways.

He slipped around the corner and spied Ratchet Bloodfin's grand hut in the near distance. Sable had described it as a too-big-too-grand-looking-round-wooden-hut-covered-in-dead-grass. Ryker couldn't stop the grin that crept across his face. Trust a sister to pick on her brother just because his house was bigger than hers.

His smile faded quickly. He needed some reason to be there—something that wouldn't make the guard's question him. Spying a discarded piece of paper on the ground, Ryker snatched it up and pretended to read it as he threaded his way through the crowds.

This was blending in . . . right?

His heart pounded in an abnormal rhythm, but his face remained calm, fixated on the hut ahead. There would be an opportunity for him to sneak around the side and try to enter through an open window.

The day was already quite warm, so there ought to be doors or windows open to let the morning breeze in.

To his luck, he was correct.

A small window halfway up the hut wall was wide open. Big enough to fit the body of a human. Even one as well built as he was.

Ryker slipped from the trees and snuck up to the side of Rachet's large hut with surprising ease, his eyes darting to and fro. The slight crunch of boots on rocks could be heard as the pirate guards began the changeover. He'd have a very small amount of time to jump up and slip inside.

Without any more thought, Ryker pulled himself up and over the windowsill. Inside was empty, so he jumped down to the floor with as little sound as physically possible.

The room was rather large. Maps hung on walls. Piles of books littered the floor and stacks of paper and journals were piled high on the table in the centre of the room. It could have been tidier—but who was he to judge?

Ryker began his search, his eyes scanning the room for the small wooden chest Sable had described. He moved methodically, checking behind books, inside drawers, and under furniture.

Just as he was about to give up, he heard the faint sound of footsteps approaching. His breath hitched, and he quickly darted behind a large tapestry, pressing himself flat against the wall. The footsteps grew louder, accompanied by muffled voices. Ryker held his breath, his hand instinctively reaching for the hilt of his sword.

"Someone said they saw a small boat approach the island this morning, but then it disappeared," one male grunted.

"Don't think the captain will be too pleased about that, will he?" came a second voice.

They must have been talking about the boat he'd arrived on. Nova.

Thoughts of her being discovered by Ratchet and his men sent his mind into a frenzy. Ryker knew he needed to get out of the room immediately. If only he could find the chest. No wonder Sable didn't want to get it herself. She probably didn't even know if it was here or not.

After what felt like an eternity, the guards finally left, their voices fading as they continued down the hallway.

Ryker exhaled slowly, stepping out from his hiding spot. He resumed his search, more cautious this time. After a few more minutes of searching, his eyes landed on a small, ornate chest hidden behind a stack of books on one of the shelves. He grabbed it, the sea serpent emblem gleaming faintly in the dim light.

"You better be worth it," Ryker whispered to himself.

He lifted the lid of the box to find a set of nesting dolls buried in a dark blue satin lining. A hand-painted design of a woman surrounded by orange, violet and sunflower yellow flowers lay smiling up at him. Ryker wanted to be angry. A wooden doll set? That's what Sable wanted?

She sent him into unknown territory with a high chance of being injured or killed . . . for this?

She was going to have some explaining to do.

With a shake of his head, Ryker pocketed the small wooden chest and headed for the window. But as he climbed, he couldn't shake the feeling that it had all been too easy. His instincts proved correct when, just as he exited the window, a guard spotted him. The guard's shout bounced off the exterior walls of the hut, and Ryker turned, ready to draw his sword.

Weathered skin and a flurry of movements were all Ryker saw as the guard lunged at him. He barely had time to react before the guard's sword came slashing toward him. The sharp clang of steel rang out as Ryker quickly blocked the attack, drawing his own sword in one smooth motion. The guard, a tough-looking male with a stupidly large moustache, came at him again, striking hard and fast.

Ryker danced away, the guard's blade just missing him. He deflected the next blow, using the opening to push the guard off balance. They circled each other between Ratchet's hut and the edge of the forest, the dry dust and sand creating clouds at their feet.

The man lunged, aiming for Ryker's chest, but Ryker sidestepped, slashing low at the man's legs. The guard grunted, stumbling, but quickly regained his balance. With a smirk, Ryker pretended to shift left before spinning to the right, disarming the guard with a swift blow. The guard's sword hit the ground, and Ryker placed his blade at the man's throat before knocking him out with the hilt of his sword.

"Too easy," Ryker muttered, before stepping back and slipping into the shadows, the wooden chest still safely tucked in his coat.

A commotion of sound and movement sounded through the air. His presence was fully known to Ratchet's crew. It was time for plan b. Escape the island.

Ryker made a run for it.

He darted through the trees in the direction of the village. Figuring it would be easier to lose any unwanted guests in the crowds than to try to hide in the bushes.

As he ran, Ryker spied a wall of bamboo scaffolding leaning up against a house. There would be a much better vantage point for him if he could get up off the ground—so that's exactly what he did. The wooden poles creaked under his weight, but he paid them no mind, his focus solely on reaching the rooftop above. With a final heave, he pulled himself up, his boots landing softly on the thatched roof. He sprinted across the rooftop, his feet barely making a sound as he ran.

"Stop!" came the cry below.

Ryker glanced over his shoulder and saw the small group of Ratchet's pirate crew chasing him in the streets below.

This would never do.

Quick thinking had Ryker jumping from rooftop to rooftop. Soon, the group chasing him were struggling to find their way through the streets without facing dozens of merchants and their carts overflowing with vegetables and fruits.

He reached the edge of the roof and leapt, his body sailing through the air—until it wasn't. One foot collapsed through the straw thatching, and before he could collect himself, Ryker crashed through the roof of the building.

Pain sliced through his side like a hot blade as he landed on the wooden floor. Knocking the air from his lungs. So much for avoiding more injuries.

He tried to sit up, but was quickly met with gasps and startled screams. Ryker glanced around, feeling quite warm in the face when he realised where he was—a brothel.

The women, all in various stages of undress, stared at him with wide eyes. He raised his hands in a gesture of apology, his face flushing with embarrassment. "Sorry, ladies. Wrong place."

He hurriedly exited onto the balcony, glancing over the edge to spot his next move. A cart full of hay sat below, a perfect landing spot. He took in a heaving breath and leaped, his body falling until he hit the soft pile with a muffled thud.

Thankfully, the landing was softer than the last.

The shouts grew closer, and Ryker knew Ratchet's crew were nearby. Best to stay hidden in the hay pile for a moment. It wasn't long before familiar screams carried down from where he'd fallen before. Those poor girls were getting quite the fright today.

Now was the time to make a dash for the rocky cliffs where, hopefully, Nova and Sable were waiting for him. Ryker rolled out of the cart and dashed towards the rock cliffs where the boat was waiting. His heart pounded in his chest, but he forced himself to remain calm, his mind focused on the escape.

"You won't get away with this!" came a cry behind him.

With a rushed look over his shoulder, Ryker spotted a male running after him, his red hair glinting in the sunlight. He was the male version of his sister.

"Take it up with Sable!" Ryker cried back.

His boots pounded the ground as he pushed himself harder. His body was going to need a really good nap after this . . . and a bath.

The sound of the ocean grew louder as he neared the cliffs, the salty breeze slapping him in the face as he scaled the rocks. Ratchet was close behind. With a final push, Ryker reached the top and began the descent down the other side.

"What's taking you so long?" Sable called out.

Ryker grit his teeth. "Shut up, Sable."

"Sable!" Ratchet's voice rang from the top of the cliffs.

One final glance back and Ryker was down on the rocks below, heading for the boat. Sable, Nova and Marla all scrambled out of the way, sending their weight to the back of the brigantine as soon as they saw Ryker scurrying down the rocks. Toadie held it as steady as he could, given the rocking waves as Ryker leapt aboard and collapsed to the floor of the boat in victory.

Sable peered over him. "You all good Hound?"

Ryker glared at the redhead. "Fuck you, Sable."

TWENTY

Nova had never been happier to see Ryker as he scrambled down the rocky cliffs, and once he was safely in the boat, she allowed her heart to slow.

Sable hadn't given him long before she was reaching for the chest still clutched in his hand. Nova was interested to see what treasure was so precious to the captain.

Ryker propped himself on the side of the boat as Toadie and Marla rowed through the choppy ocean waters of the Veridian sea. "I can't believe you sent me in there for that."

"You opened it and looked?" Sable cried out.

"You never told me not to!"

Sable huffed. "It could have been damaged."

"It could also still be in your brother's possession . . ."

The captain rolled her eyes as she drew out the object from the small wooden chest, letting it glint in the sunlight as she held it up. Nova watched, captivated, as Captain Sable turned it in her hands, inspecting every facet with a keen, assessing gaze.

Nova's brow pinched at the odd-looking wooden object. Its surface was brightly painted in a flower pattern.

"What's so important about it?" Nova asked.

"Pirate things . . . Most others wouldn't understand." Sable murmured. "Ratchet took it from me a long time ago."

Ryker huffed. "Maybe you could keep me out of your *'pirate things'* from now on. I don't want to be involved in sibling rivalry."

Sable shut the lid on the wooden box and shoved it into a pocket concealed on the inside of her jacket. "It's not sibling rivalry. It's just my turn to have it on my island."

Nova angled her head to the side "So what does it do?"

Sable sighed. "Whoever holds the wooden nesting dolls receives protection from the skimmers."

Ryker's gaze snapped back towards the captain. Nova could sense that skimmers was possibly a word to be feared.

"No one has seen them for years." Ryker eyed Sable.

"Just because no one has seen them, doesn't mean they ain't out there." Sable folded her arms across her chest. "And I'd like to keep my island and its citizens as safe as possible. Anything is fair game—"

"For the right reasons—I get it," Ryker huffed.

Nova glanced between Ryker and the red-haired captain. "Can someone tell me what a skimmer is?"

Sable sat back on the wooden bench seat, crossing her ankles. "Skimmers are a powerful and feared group, often referred to as the 'cartel of the waters'. They operate along the coastlines, harvesting rare, valuable pearls and coral from the reefs. Turning them into a substance that is both highly addictive and deadly."

Ryker eyed Sable warily. "What has that wooden doll got to do with the Skimmers?"

Sable reached up to adjust her hat. "Well, you see, skimming isn't just about taking from the ocean; it involves ruthless control, smuggling operations, and bribing officials to keep their illegal trade flowing," Sable murmured. "Their ships are sleek and fast, and their network reaches from hidden sea caves to the richest cities on the mainland."

The captain fished the wooden box from her pocket again. "This thing here—is a sign of protection. Whoever holds this is free from the skimmers route. If they attempt to skim in my reefs . . . I have every right to declare war. Though I would hope it never comes to that."

Ryker folded his arms across his chest. "How do the skimmers know who has the doll?"

"We raise the protection flag," Sable grinned. "No doubt Ratchet will have to pull his down now."

Nova couldn't believe what she was hearing. Were there truly others out there more dangerous than the pirates she was surrounded by? Not only did they have to be wary of the leviathan that prowled the waters at night, but now they also had to watch out for the skimmers who sailed the seas during the day.

Ryker must have sensed her unease. He reached for her hand and gently squeezed it, only allowing his hand to linger for a moment. Now was not a great time to begin to glow. She offered him a small smile in return.

They travelled back to Sable's home with little conversation. Ryker refused to sleep—even when encouraged, so Nova didn't push him. There would be time to rest.

Once they reached the familiar shores of Corsair's Haven, Ryker didn't waste any time, prepping their small rowboat.

"Are you sure you wouldn't like to stay one more night before making the journey back to the mainland?"

Ryker shook his head. "We've already been here too long."

Sable nodded, taking a step back. She removed her hat and took a small bow. "Well, it was nice to meet you Nova, and Ryker—Thank you, I promise it's the last you will see of me," Sable murmured.

Ryker's brow rose as if he didn't believe the words coming from the captain's mouth. A tiny smile hinted on Nova's lips. The more time she'd spent with Sable, the more she grew to like her. Secretly, she hoped that it wouldn't be the last she'd hear of Sable and her mighty crew.

They bid the pirates goodbye and Nova prepared herself for another long journey on the ocean. Sable had been kind enough to give them a basket of food and water for their trip as it would be a long one.

Deep blue ocean water stretched for miles. They'd been sailing for hours. Ryker sat against the small mast, letting his eyes drift closed as the wind pushed them forward. She couldn't blame him. The man had been through a lot in the last few days.

"You seem lost in thought." His words broke the silence.

Nova glanced at him and smiled softly. "I was just thinking how jolly the life of a pirate is. They all seem so content and happy."

"Probably because they steal everyone's money."

Nova hesitated, scrunching her nose. "I know her approach to life is—different, but I do think she means well enough?"

Ryker huffed as he rowed the boat through the dark blue water. "Either way. What do you think the chances are that she'll actually stop meddling in my affairs?"

"I do think she feels quite bad about that, and you must forgive her. I am completely fine and unharmed. The whole experience has actually been quite thrilling. Besides, I want to learn more about life here on Earth before you ship me off home and are rid of me forever." Nova grinned.

"It's not like that, little star. I don't want to be rid of you . . . I just think if you stay, you'll be running for the rest of your life, from those who seek to profit from you. You're safer in Ara."

Nova sighed as she leaned over the side of the wooden boat, letting her fingers trail through the cold salty water. "You could keep me safe though?"

"Living life on the run is not living. And besides, no one wants to live with me . . . I'm a grouch," Ryker replied

Nova eyed the dark-haired man before her with the warm-coloured skin and the kind brown eyes and smiled. "You don't have to be though."

Ryker shrugged and let his gaze dance across the large body of water.

"Why did Sable call you the Hound?"

The slow grin that crept onto Ryker's face had Nova feeling all warm inside her chest. It blossomed into her cheeks, and she couldn't help but smile back at him.

"I don't know how it started, but other bounty hunters in Emberfell began to call me that and I guess it just stuck."

"It suits you."

Ryker ducked his head, as if he were shy.

Nova lent forward with her elbows on her knees, her hands cradling her face. "Shall I call you Hound?"

The gold and dark brown flecks in his russet eyes sparkled. "Little star, you can call me whatever you like."

Nova glowed . . . she planned to.

As the sun began to sink below the horizon, casting a warm glow across the water, Ryker dragged the boat onto the shore. The rest of the trip had passed in a calm silence, broken only by bits of small talk about the pirates and their plans once they reached the mainland.

When the boat was firmly on land, Ryker effortlessly scooped Nova into his arms, carrying her across the sand to keep her boots dry. She leaned into the embrace, a pang of sadness washing over her the moment he set her back down.

"I just need to return the boat and then we will head into town to get Charlie," Ryker murmured as he surveyed the beach surroundings.

"He will wonder where we have been."

Ryker nodded. "Once we have him, I think we should ride into the night a little."

"Will that be safe?"

"Is it ever?"

Nova's shoulders dropped. "Is that because of me?"

Ryker looked at her with his warm brown eyes and shook his head gently. "Not at all."

They found the man Ryker had hired the boat from, and the two exchanged a handful of gold as the ocean gently lapped at the shore beside them. The man tipped his hat before he turned away, his boots crunching softly on the sand. Once Ryker had secured his money, they headed back towards the path that led into the woods.

The Hound took the lead, and the star followed.

"How far away is the mountain?"

"If we ride through part of the night, I think we can make it as early as noon tomorrow."

Nova nodded. "Then we best get to it."

Loud murmurs floated through the air, causing Ryker to stop abruptly. Nova, sensing the tension, wisely kept her questions to herself. She watched as his brow furrowed, his head tilted slightly, straining to catch the conversation. The tightening of his jaw told her everything—whoever was up ahead were those they'd prefer not to encounter.

"Something isn't right," Ryker whispered as he pulled Nova into the shrubbery. "I think it's Branoc's men."

Nova sighed. They'd just come from chaos and hadn't had a chance to rest before they were being propelled into it again. "How do you know?"

"I heard the name Branoc . . . and there's certainly enough clinking for them to be royal guards."

"Can we go a different way?"

"This is the only trail in this direction," Ryker motioned up ahead. "I could create a distraction, and you slip away. You could wait for me deeper in the forest and I will come for you?" Ryker spoke in a hushed tone.

Nova shook her head and frowned. "We only just found each other again, I'm not leaving you."

He reached for her hand and gently squeezed it. "I can't fight them and protect you at the same time."

"Then don't. I'll go on ahead and play innocent and you can ambush them. Do you have any dreamroot darts left?"

He checked the pocket inside his jacket. "I have two."

"Give them to me," Nova asked, extending her hand.

Without hesitation, he handed them to her.

Nova held the small darts in her hand and closed her eyes. There hadn't been a chance to bask naked under the moon to fully recharge, but she'd been exposed to the moon enough to feel a small amount of power simmering in her veins.

The humming sensation began in her chest and spread down her arms and into her fingertips. A small glow of light burst around her clenched fists, then it winked out leaving Nova with not two but multiple dreamroot darts.

Ryker's eyes were wide with amazement as he reached for darts. "No wonder Branoc wanted to keep you for himself."

With a raised brow, Nova placed her hands on her hips and stared at the hound.

"Too soon?" Ryker murmured with a grin.

Nova returned his smile. "Just a little."

The voices grew louder, so Ryker pulled Nova further into the shrubbery.

"What if there are only two of them?"

"There is never just two." Ryker surveyed their surroundings. "Perhaps creating a distraction is our only option. You go on ahead and I will hide."

She really didn't want to leave Ryker's side and place herself in the hands of Branocs' men again, but there was little choice. She'd trusted Ryker to come for her in Corsair, now, she needed to trust that he would get them out of this situation as well.

Nova nodded and started to walk off just as Ryker caught her hand. The feel of his warm calloused fingers against her soft skin sent shivers up her arm. All her senses stood to alert as his gaze locked on hers.

"Be careful," Ryker whispered.

"You be careful too," she whispered back.

Over the last few weeks, Nova was beginning to feel braver with each day that she faced. The world was huge and there would be times that it would all seem too much, but for right now, in this moment, she felt invigorated. Ready to face whatever she needed to. If it meant she got to spend a little more time with Ryker.

The hound moved silently into the underbrush and Nova picked up her feet, heading up the trail. She figured the guards wouldn't harm her, but the chance of Ryker being injured caused her heart rate to quicken. Or what if this all went pear shaped and the guards managed to ship her off back to King Branoc?

Nova's zest for life and all it had to offer suddenly came crashing down.

Maybe she wasn't cut out for this.

As she rounded the bend in the road, Nova wasn't expecting the small group of men waiting ahead. Ryker had been right—there were never just two. Six guards stood together, talking and studying a map. There was no way around them.

On either side of the group was a dense amount of trees and shrubbery and Nova wondered how Ryker would make his way silently. Maybe she could draw the men away from him long enough that he could form a plan of attack without the threat of them finding him.

She tugged the hood of her cloak further down, shadowing her face in hopes of blending in. Perhaps, if she appeared as nothing more than a weary traveller, she could slip by unnoticed. Her heart raced as she imagined waltzing right past them, her steps casual but her every nerve on edge, hoping they wouldn't pay her any mind.

"Hey . . . you!" one guard called; his voice harsh against her ears.

Nova swallowed and smiled cautiously as she took a few steps backwards. This drew the attention of all the men as they spun in her direction.

"We order you to stop in the name of the king!"

Frozen to the spot, Nova acted innocent. "Please help me, I have lost my way."

Three guards started towards her, but before they could get close, two of them slapped the sides of their necks as darts pierced their skin. Nova wondered where Ryker was hiding, but was pleased all the same that he'd managed to knockout at least two of them.

"Ambush! Take the woman and go!" one guard called.

The guard closest to Nova lunged forward and roughly pulled her by the arm and she let out a yelp. Trying to free his grip, Nova squirmed and pulled but it was of no use. The guard held fast.

Ryker appeared from the bushes, armed and ready with his sword and chaos erupted. The guard holding Nova dragged her towards a small horse drawn carriage as Ryker fought off the other three men. He managed to knock one male out almost instantly and it became two against three.

With as much energy as she could muster, Nova summoned her power from within, unleashing a burst of viridian light from her hands. The suddenness of it made the guard throw an arm across his face, but his grip on her arm only tightened to the point of pain.

"Unhand me at once you buffoon of a man!" she cried.

"You better watch it, lady. Keep talking like that and see where it gets you. The king wanted you home alive, he didn't say we couldn't teach you a lesson for running away in the first place." The guard's face twisted with a wicked grin and Nova felt sick to her stomach. Maybe allowing them to catch her hadn't been the best plan, but there was little time to think of something else.

The forest rang with the sounds of swords clanging and Nova strained to see Ryker as a flurry of bodies danced to the song of battle. Digging her feet in, she tried to slow the guard from shoving her into the carriage, but he was much too strong.

Nova punched and kicked, but with a rough grip, he shoved her up the stairs of the carriage. This was all going very badly, but she refused to be taken back to that fancy castle with its fancy dresses and abusive king.

She gave one last push off the side of the carriage door frame with enough force that it caused the guard to stumble backwards slightly but it wasn't enough for him to loosen his grip, instead it just made the guard angrier.

Sharp stinging pain lanced its way across the side of her face and lip as he backhanded her, and Nova cried out as her neck twisted jarringly to the side.

"I told you to watch it." The guard's rough voice warmed her ear.

Closing her eyes against the pain, Nova fought to remain calm. A familiar taste of blood washed over her tongue and she felt a warm sensation trickling down the corner of her mouth. Dread pooled in her stomach as memories flashed through her mind. She couldn't go back.

Ryker cried out and Nova lunged, but the guard used both hands to shove her inside the carriage and slammed the door, locking it securely.

"Ryker!" she cried through the bars on the window.

He whipped his head towards her cry, and it was enough to see him rage. Blades clashed and bodies twisted as the two guards he was in combat with finally fell to the ground. He dashed for the carriage and as he neared, Nova spotted a large, weeping gash across his upper right arm. The blood ran bright red, soaking into his shirt.

The guard who'd taken Nova captive lurched for Ryker and the two men fought furiously, but the male was no match for the Hound in single combat. Ryker slashed him across the face, and tears of red liquid streamed down his cheeks and neck. As the guard dropped to his knees in pain, Ryker hit him over the head with the handle of his sword, knocking him to the ground. He didn't rise again.

Relief washed over Nova.

Ryker wasted no time in freeing her from her wooden cage.

Leaping from the carriage, Nova threw her arms around Ryker's neck and squeezed him as hard as her arms would allow.

"I'm so glad you're alright," she whispered.

Ryker held her tight before gently pushing her to arm's length. "He hit you?" The look that crept across Ryker's face was one of pure madness.

Nova stepped towards him again and cupped his face. "I'm alright . . . we're okay. Let's get out of here before anyone comes to."

Ryker nodded, taking her hand in his as they hurried off through the woods.

After collecting Charlie from the stablehand who looked at them oddly, the star and the Hound took to the forest.

"I think we need to find shelter for tonight and lay low for a few days. I didn't think the king's guards would actually be that good at finding us but it seems as if I have underestimated them," Ryker said as he trotted along the road.

Nova studied the way his fingers gently held the reins. "That was a close call, I thought I was going to lose you for a moment there."

Wrapping an arm around her middle and shifting in the saddle so his body was pressed up against her back, Ryker answered, his voice confident, "It's going to take more than six guards to take me down."

★ ◆ ★ ◆ ★

The fire's flickering light cast dancing shadows across the cave walls where they'd made camp for the night. After hours of navigating the dense forest in search of a well-hidden spot, they'd finally stumbled upon a cave free from any lurking creatures. Once inside, they brought Charlie in, pitched a tent, and built a crackling fire to warm the space.

Nova had grown so accustomed to setting up camp that it felt instinctive. She moved through the motions effortlessly, no longer needing to ask Ryker for help. Even building the fire, something that once felt foreign, was now a task she could handle with ease.

The warmth on her skin was welcome as she sat by the fire with her arms wrapped around her knees. Her body ached from the rough handling from the guard, not to mention the dull throb of her swollen lip. Painful memories from Branoc beating her surfaced again and she closed her eyes against the phantom slap that echoed in her ears.

Nova's eyes flicked to the male across the cavern. Ryker was busy sorting Charlie and gathering some food from their bags. His brow was pinched, his mouth pressed in a thin line.

Ryker's steps were soft as he approached her with a canteen of water and a small piece of cloth. He sat beside her and gently reached for her chin, turning her face towards him.

"Let me clean this up for you." He motioned towards the water.

"I'll be alright," Nova murmured.

Ryker tugged her chin closer to his face. "You've cared for me many times. Let me do it for you."

His eyes pleaded with her and before she could stop herself, Nova found herself nodding.

Soft hands dabbed at her lip, and she hissed in pain at the first touch of the cool water against her skin.

"Sorry . . ." Ryker said softly.

He dabbed her lip a few more times and, once satisfied, put the lid back on the canteen. "It will hurt for a few days."

"I can't be any worse than the wound on your arm. Let me heal it for you."

Ryker shook his head. "I'll be fine. It's only a surface wound."

"I'm sure I have enough power in me—"

"You need to rest." Warm brown eyes gazed into hers for a few moments before he sighed and started to undo the front of his shirt, shrugging out of it and letting it fall to the ground. "No powers, but I'll let you clean it."

Nova shifted so she was sitting on her knees with Ryker's bare chest gleaming in the low light of the orange flames.

By the stars, Nova thought as she trailed her eyes over his torso. He was utterly divine to look at. The grooves along his hardened stomach glistened with sweat, each droplet like melted gold as they beaded on his skin. Veins in his arms slightly bulged each time he moved or flexed his hands.

The dark tendrils of his unruly hair hung loosely over his forehead. And over the past few days his jaw had produced light stubble. Nova found him utterly desirable, wishing she could climb into his lap and do the things they'd done the other night.

Before pirates and guards.

"Hand me that cloth," Nova murmured.

Ryker handed it to her, and she splashed it with water from the canteen beside her. It was the Hound's turn to wince in pain as she gently wiped away the blood and grime. His arm felt huge beneath her small hand. She fought the urge to run her fingers along his muscles.

"I think that's as clean as we will get it."

Ryker nodded.

Before he could move, Nova placed her hand on his arm just below the wound and closed her eyes.

"Nova . . . what are you doing?"

"Shh," she hushed him.

Nova concentrated on the feeling of her magic, she called it calmly, willing it into being. At first, nothing happened, so she took a deep breath and let it out slowly, internally calling to it again.

A slight buzzing sensation rippled down her arms and into her hands. Her body began to glow, and, with a push, Nova expanded her power out through her hands. The golden essence flowed to Ryker's wound and began to knit the skin back together with invisible threads of light.

Within moments the wound was a faint red line.

She pulled the power back into her body, opened her eyes and met Ryker's. He was watching her with awe and wonder.

"There you go . . . like new." Nova grinned.

The Hound couldn't help but crack a smile at her words. "Thank you, but you really need to rest."

Nova moved back to face the fire, warming her hands. "Now I will rest. If you're so concerned, perhaps you should keep yourself from harm, so I don't have to keep healing you."

Ryker huffed as he stood and reached for his shirt. "Perhaps you should stop getting taken by pirates, so I don't have to keep rescuing you?"

Nova flashed him a smile as she shrugged. "Can't promise."

Ryker shook his head but smiled as he started to place his shirt back on.

"Where did you get those scars?" Nova asked as she eyed the three large, darkened lines across his left pectoral muscle. She'd seen them the first time they bathed together, but was too shy to ask.

Ryker paused; his shirt gathered in his hand. He glanced down at the old wound and ran his hand across the ridges in his skin. "A Galanthor."

"Like the one I saw that day I ran away?"

The corner of Ryker's mouth pulled up. "Yes."

Nova felt warmth crawl up her neck and into her cheeks at the thought of what might have happened had Ryker not found her in time. "Tell me the story."

"I was out hunting deer one day in the deeper parts of a wood near home. Galanthor didn't like that I was taking his food."

"Obviously you lived." Nova threw him a playful smile.

Ryker chuckled. "I certainly did, but the Galanthor met a different fate, unfortunately."

Nova stood and closed the distance between them, her steps faintly echoing through the space. She placed her hand over the scar, right above his heart. His skin was warm under her hand. "I'm glad you're still here."

The feeling of his heart rate quickening brought a prickling sensation over Nova's entire body. She went from looking at his chest to looking at his soft, full lips that beckoned to her. She wanted his mouth on hers, but she wanted him to want it too, so she stilled and waited for him to pull closer. Silence rang loud as the star and the Hound held each other's gaze.

Disappointment replaced desire as Ryker slowly took a few steps back.

"Sometimes I'm glad too." He moved towards their bags as he shoved his shirt over his head. He fished around inside one of them before pulling out their rations. "We should eat."

Nova dropped her hand to her side and nodded in response. Maybe he was beginning to regret their moment the other night. Maybe it was for the best. He was so determined to get her home that perhaps she should be focusing on that too, even though she was becoming more and more certain that home was possibly not a place.

TWENTY-ONE

THE FAMILIAR ACHE

Ryker leaned against the mouth of the cave, watching the forest come alive in the early hours of the morning. Little squirrels darted here and there. A young doe silently moved through the underbrush and birds had already begun their morning song.

His mind was restless. All night he'd tossed and turned. Not wanting to wake Nova just yet, he'd left her sleeping peacefully by the fire.

When she'd touched him last night with her delicate hand, it took all his strength not to reach for her, to kiss her. But if he did, then he wouldn't be able to stop himself from taking her right there and then. The moment he stepped away from her, her face fell. Her disappointment pulled on his heart. Before, he'd let his hands take it too far, and it had been the most incredible feeling, but he shouldn't have done it in the first place. He should have kept them to himself. His heart couldn't take saying goodbye to another woman.

Get her home to Ara—go back to your canoe. That's what he kept telling himself.

But every time she looked at him with those sea-green eyes scattered with tiny fragments of stardust, it got harder and harder to stay away.

Deer called to one another through the forest and pulled Ryker back to the present. Before they continued their journey, he wanted to wash some of their spare clothes, including the ones they were wearing, down by the stream. Though, last time he'd done something similar, he'd come back to an empty bed. He wouldn't make the same mistake again.

Ryler pushed off the side of the rocky wall and headed back into the heart of the cave. Nova was up and stretching as he returned.

"Morning, star," Ryker smiled at the sleepy, glowing female.

Nova grinned back and stretched again. "What I would give to not sleep on a hard stone floor."

"I do apologise for the less than comfortable sleeping arrangements, but it's better than a prison cell," Ryker added as he moved to their food bag.

"You are quite right. I shouldn't complain. Although, the thought of staying in that cosy cabin back on the island with Captain Sable and her crew does sound even more appealing."

Ryker twisted to look at Nova, who was now standing, brushing her fingers through her waves of hair. She had a sparkle in her eye, and Ryker couldn't help but smile.

"I thought you'd had your fill of the pirate life?"

"I guess so, but I certainly haven't had my fill of cosy cabins," Nova challenged, lifting an eyebrow as if daring him to speak against the idea.

Ryker huffed in amusement and returned to the food bag. "You would get over that pretty quickly."

"Doubt it," came the softened reply.

A smile tugged at the corner of his mouth. Ryker pulled two apples, some crusty bread, and wax wrapped cheese from the pouch. "Let's eat. I think we should wash our clothes and ourselves before we leave this morning, or people are going to smell us coming before they see us."

Nova grinned as she bit into the fruit. Juices spurted into the air and she locked eyes with Ryker as they did so. Swallowing his mouthful of food, Ryker cleared his throat and turned his gaze away. She was getting too good at the eye thing, and it made his pants feel way too tight each time. Damn those eyes and the way they looked into his soul as if they already knew all his secrets, good and bad.

"I promise I won't run away this time," Nova said casually.

"If you do, I can promise you won't get too far."

"Why? Will you chase me?"

Ryker's gaze travelled over her body. "I would," he replied before taking a sip of water.

Nova bit into her apple again, delaying her answer as she chewed it. "Sounds like something I'd enjoy."

Ryker raised his brow. "There would be consequences when I found you."

Nova lightly shrugged as she bit into the cheese next. "I'd probably enjoy that, too."

Sea-green and russet met across the distance. Smiles dancing on hungry lips. A wave of heat pulsed through Ryker's body, and he fought the urge to stretch his limbs out from the pent-up pleasure battering against the inside of his skin. Not only was she looking at him with a desire that made his cock jump at the sight, but she was also teasing him in a way that made it very . . . very hard to function.

The respectful, disrespectful things he would do to and for her if she allowed him the pleasure. Better yet, if he allowed himself.

Ryker huffed in amusement. "Let's eat."

They finished their light breakfast before gathering their clothing, feeding Charlie their apple cores, and heading down to the stream. Ryker stayed a few steps behind Nova as they walked and couldn't help but glance at her ass a few times, attention catching on the way it swayed gently as she moved.

His pants felt tight again. If he didn't get himself together, there was no way he would be able to bathe in the same stream as her without very hard evidence making itself known. Who was he kidding? It was going to be hard regardless.

They reached the water's edge and dropped their clothing on the ground. Ryker had brought down the small bar of jasmine soap he carried for all their washing needs. He passed it to Nova to use first as he kept an eye on their surroundings.

Movement from Nova had him glancing her way. She was stripping down to her undergarments.

"Are you bathing first?" Ryker asked.

Nova nodded as she pulled her gown up and over her head. "If I'm washing these other items, I may as well wash my dress, too."

Ryker nodded and returned his gaze to the forest. Anything to keep from looking at Nova in her barely there outfit. Every sound or flick of movement had him hypervigilant, not wanting anything or anyone to catch him off guard. He'd let her wash first.

It should only take them the day to reach the base of the Twin Peak mountain range, where the woman Chester had told them about resided. Perhaps they would even reach her sooner if they didn't face any problems along the way. Knowing his luck, though—

Cold water hit Ryker in the back of his head, and it took a moment for him to register what was happening.

The sound of Nova's laugh rang through the trees like a magical song.

Another handful of water hit him in the back, causing Ryker to spin on his heel to face her. He looked at her with a cocked brow. "You do realise what you've just started?"

"I slipped . . . sorry." Nova smirked.

Ryker shook his head but couldn't stop himself from grinning at the beautiful creature before him. Taking a deliberate step towards the water, he kept his eyes locked on hers as he crouched and cupped his hands under the surface. With one swift motion, he tossed two handfuls of icy cold water in Nova's direction. Squealing at the temperature, she dashed into the water further, then spun around and splashed water back at him.

"Oh, you're going to get it now." Ryker smirked.

Nova laughed as she backed further into the water. He hadn't planned on dallying by the stream, but his heart longed to do something other than running.

Fuck the world and the people looking for them.

Ryker stripped down until he was only wearing trousers. He moved into the water, sucking in his breath at the sting of its coolness.

When he was waist deep, he sank beneath the water's surface, but as soon as he emerged Nova splashed him again, laughing as she did so.

He lunged for her and caught her ankle just before she slipped from his reach. She fell under the water, and Ryker went with her. Wrapping an arm around her waist, he stood, dragging her up, still laughing and spluttering. The feeling of her body against his was electric. Her white undergarments had become see through from the water and her shell-pink, peaked nipples poked through the wet fabric against her skin.

Oh, how he wanted to take them in his mouth and taste them again.

His gaze darted from her breasts to her mouth, to her eyes. Ryker took a breath to steady his racing heart. "How's that bath going for you?"

Nova's chest rose and sank as the pair stood waist deep in the water, the palms of her hands resting against his bare chest. "Best one I've had yet."

If he didn't let go of her soon, there was no way of stopping what would happen next. So, he swooped down to pick her up, supporting her under her knees. He grinned. "How about now?" He didn't wait for her to answer before throwing her into the stream.

Her squeal silenced as she disappeared beneath the water's surface.

Still beaming, Ryker made sure she was okay before he headed back towards the bank. The sound of water splashing behind him told him that she followed.

"Why won't you kiss me again?"

Her question hit him right in the gut.

Ryker drew in a breath before spinning to face the dripping wet star. The fabric of her garments plastered against her skin and her hair slicked back from the weight of the water. She embodied femininity.

"Nova . . ."

"No, don't do that. Answer the question. Why won't you kiss me?" she asked again.

"It's complicated," Ryker answered.

"Uncomplicate it then."

Ryker ran his hands through this wet hair. "It's not that I don't want to star . . . I do. It's just I can't have you. It's selfish of me."

Nova stood in front of him. "What do you mean? Why can't you have me?"

"Because . . . because you're going to go home and I will have to stay here and I don't think I can say goodbye," Ryker answered.

He wouldn't allow his heart to fall for another woman that would leave him.

"You wanted me the other night . . ."

Ryker looked into Nova's eyes and all he could see was pain and confusion. He shouldn't have done anything with her in that heated moment all those nights ago, but before she returned to Ara, never to be seen again, he'd wanted just a taste of her.

"And I want you now. I would take you against that tree over there if I could." Ryker spoke in a low tone as he flicked his gaze between her eyes and her lips.

Nova took another step closer. "Then why don't you?"

Ryker ran a hand over his face in frustration. "I just can't, Nova . . ."

"I don't believe you can't . . . I just don't think you're ready yet. So I'll wait, because I want to experience human things between a man and a woman, but only with you."

Ryker didn't answer as she moved to the water's edge, retrieved her clothing, and began washing.

That familiar ache he schlepped inside his chest—the constant companion he didn't allow to leave—clawed at his heart. Would it ever end?

Perhaps if he bid it farewell.

The rest of the morning was quiet as the pair allowed their clothing to dry before packing their belongings and leaving the cave that had become a safe haven for them both. The atmosphere between them wasn't unpleasant, but Ryker knew that Nova was somewhat upset, and he didn't want to make things worse by opening his big mouth.

They rode for a few hours through dense forestry and rocky open spaces. It was late afternoon when they reached the base of the Twin Peak mountain range, where the woman supposedly lived. The sun cast long shadows across the rugged terrain, and the peaks loomed above them, shrouded in mist. Ryker dismounted and looked up the steep, rocky trail, his eyes narrowing as he considered the journey ahead. He wondered what lay at the top. Would they find the woman they sought? Would they find danger instead?

He knew Chester wouldn't send him on a journey filled with peril on purpose, but there was always a chance of unexpected dangers. They could encounter creatures lurking in the shadows, hostile humans, or even the more elusive of the fae kind who were known to inhabit these remote regions. Environmental dangers could also strike without warning, adding another layer of uncertainty to their quest. Yet, the only way he was going to find out was to travel it.

Ryker took a deep breath, the crisp mountain air filling his lungs, and glanced at Nova. The star-turned-woman met his gaze with a determined look.

"Is everything alright?"

He nodded.

It wasn't, though.

If the woman they were looking for turned out to know how to send Nova home, it meant that their time together here on Earth was nearly at its end.

And Ryker didn't like it . . . not one fucking bit.

"Are you ready?" Nova murmured as she leaned into his chest.

"If you are?"

Nova nodded. "I think so."

Ryker relished the feeling for as long as he could. The scent of the jasmine soap she'd used earlier filled his senses, the softness of her skin in his arms, the sound of her voice when she asked about nature. Or the way she laughed each time Charlie whinnied or shook his mane.

He wasn't ready to say goodbye, yet he urged Charlie on.

The trail leading up was steep and treacherous, the ground uneven, strewn with loose rocks. Ryker led Charlie carefully, the horse's sturdy hooves finding purchase on the rocky path as the mountain range rose before them like a wall of stone and forest.

As they ascended, the air grew cooler, and the sounds of the valley below faded into the distance. The trail wound its way through dense thickets of trees, their branches forming a canopy overhead that filtered the late afternoon sunlight into dappled patterns on the ground. The forest was alive with the sounds of rustling leaves and distant bird calls, creating a symphony of nature that Ryker found a welcomed comfort for his chaotic soul.

Hours passed before the trail halfway up the mountain came to a stop. Ahead of them lay a wall of thick, entwined branches that climbed all the way to the sky, almost blocking out the sun.

Ryker pulled the black stallion to a halt and jumped down. "Surely this isn't it?"

Nova slipped from Charlie's back. "There is nowhere else to go, though?"

Retrieving the sword from his side, Ryker hacked at the limbs and branches of the trees and shrubbery, but each time he cut through, they would instantly knit back together as if bound together under a spell of enchantment.

"I don't think this is the right place, Nova. I can't even cut through," Ryker said, sheathing his sword back at his side.

Nova stepped closer to the rough, woody branches and brushed a hand over it. "It has to be—it's enchanted, Ryker. I can feel it."

"So how do we get through if it is?"

"Maybe my magic can do something?"

"You haven't bathed in moonlight, though. You'll exhaust yourself." Ryker reached to still her glowing hand.

"Ryker, I have to try."

He didn't want to see her overexert herself. Yet, what other way was there? They'd come so far, endured too much for them to turn back now. If the woman truly dwelt on the other side of this murky forest, then some sacrifices must be made.

Ryker just wished it was he who bore such sacrifice.

"Perhaps we could just ask it to move?"

Nova smiled at his attempt at humour. She brushed her fingers over the foliage and closed her eyes. "Can we please pass through?"

As soon as she spoke, the branches parted and created a long, dark passageway straight through the trees.

Ryker's mouth dropped open. Never in his wildest dreams did he think asking the forest would actually do anything. "How did you do that?"

She shrugged, offering him a smile as she disappeared inside.

"Nova, wait!" Ryker called as he hurried to gather Charlie and follow her.

It was shadowed and eerie as they entered the entanglement of twisted trunks and branches, the large black stallion trailing behind them. There were no sounds, no rustling of leaves or calls of birds, just a pervasive silence that hung thick in the air. The trees loomed tall and gnarled, their bark rough and charred, as if scorched by fire long ago. Grey and black trunks stretched out in all directions, the occasional muted green patch of moss clinging desperately to life. The underbrush was sparse, littered with tangles of thorny bushes and brittle branches, all cast in a dull, lifeless hue.

It reminded Ryker of a burnt forest, stripped of its vitality, as if nothing had dared to grow back. Desolation surrounded them, and even the wind seemed reluctant to pass through.

A small slit at the end of the path glowed yellow, and Ryker hoped it was sunshine. As they neared, Nova held her hand out once again. The branches parted, and they had to squint against the gleam.

Ryker inhaled sharply; eyes wide at the sight before him. A small cottage sat on a grassy knoll in the distance, nestled amongst a meadow of brightly coloured flowers. Each blossom bobbed their heads in welcome as Ryker and Nova unhurriedly dragged their eyes across the scenery. It was a striking contrast from the dark forest behind them.

"Well, I think we found her," Nova whispered.

"I think we did," Ryker agreed.

TWENTY-TWO

THE STAR CARVINGS

A figure stood on the porch of the cottage; her silhouette framed by the warm glow of the setting sun. She watched them walk up the hill towards the home, her cool grey hair blowing gently in the light breeze. Even from a distance, Nova could see the brilliant blue shade in her eyes, like twin sapphires catching the last light of day. The woman's posture was relaxed yet alert—she had an air of wisdom and strength about her.

As they drew closer, Nova noted the details of the cottage: it was a quaint, rustic structure, nestled comfortably against the hillside, with wild roses climbing up its stone walls and colourful flowers blooming in the garden. Smoke curled lazily from the chimney in a cloudy dance, adding to the homely atmosphere.

The woman smiled warmly as they approached, her eyes crinkling at the corners. Something inside Nova reached for her, as if she knew her in another life. Everything about her was so familiar, yet strange. Nova felt a sense of relief wash over her; they'd come to the right place. There was an unspoken welcome in the woman's gaze, a silent assurance that they were safe here.

"You've travelled a great distance, young ones," she said, her voice like a song. "Come, you must be weary. I have food warmed by the fire."

Nova glanced at the Hound to see his complexion. His eyes darted around, making sure, likely on the alert for some kind of trap, but his posture remained relaxed. "You were expecting us?"

The grey-haired woman nodded. "I was."

Nova was in awe. The way she moved and talked was as if she was floating through the air.

"Nova . . . you're staring," Ryker whispered beside her.

His voice broke her trance, and she felt warmth creep into her cheeks. "I'm terribly sorry, you're just so beautiful."

The woman laughed. "No one has called me that in quite some time, but thank you . . . ?"

Reaching out to clasp the woman's offered hand, Nova fumbled over her words. "Nova . . . Nova Seraphine and this is Ryker Thornbrooke," Nova quickly answered.

The woman smiled at them both. "I am Astrid Vespera."

A loud ringing sounded in Nova's ears. Her vision hollowed, distorting the image of the woman before her. Stories from her sisters in Ara hammered at her mind as Astrid's name imprinted on her thoughts. Nova knew who this woman was, and her heart nearly fell from her chest. Yet shock held her tongue in its grasp.

Astrid ushered them inside before Nova could find the courage to speak.

The room was warm and welcoming. A fire crackled inside the fireplace and the smell of a delicious stew wafted through the air. The kitchen table was laden with fresh bread, butter, and a bowl of what looked like freshly picked wild berries.

She truly was expecting them.

The sight of it all had Nova's stomach growling, and she couldn't wait to eat.

Astrid motioned for them to sit as she busied herself with the iron pot bubbling over the flames. Nova took the opportunity to look around the room. She noticed a recurring theme throughout it.

Little wood carvings of stars and moons found their home upon windowsills, shelves, and the fireplace mantle. Some were painted butter yellow and azure blue. Someone very creative must have spent a great deal of time on these ornaments, and Nova wondered who.

Ryker's warm brown eyes found hers, silently asking if she was alright. Nova smiled at him with a nod. This was the first time since falling to Earth that she actually felt like she was home.

Astrid placed two steaming bowls of stew on the table in front of Nova and Ryker before returning to the fire to dish out her own.

"Please, eat." Astrid smiled at them. "And once you've had our fill, you can tell me why you're here."

"How did you know we would come?" Ryker murmured as he fiddled with the napkin on the table.

"I have my ways." Astrid winked at him. "Now, eat."

Ryker didn't need to be told twice and hungrily dug into his food. Nova followed suit, her eyes fluttering shut as she brought the spoon to her lips. A soft sigh of delight escaped her, the warmth of the food melting against her tongue. Savoury meat and vegetables with a delightful helping of bread and butter.

"Thank you, Astrid, this is the most delicious meal we've had in a long time." Nova spoke.

Astrid offered her a smile before sipping at her tea. "Tell me, what is it you two need?"

Ryker sat back and let his spoon rest on his plate, his gaze flickering to Nova before answered. "We've been told that there is a chance you could help Nova get home."

Astrid turned to her. "And where is home, Nova?"

Nova leant forward and rested her arms on the tabletop. "Home for me is not on this Earth. It's a place that I feel you might know all too well?"

Ryker's brow scrunched as his eyes darted between the women at the table.

Astrid smiled softly. She'd never served herself a bowl of stew, instead nursing her tea as they ate. "How did you know?"

"Your name is still spoken of in Ara." Nova lifted a hand to all the star carvings. "I haven't felt this at home since I got here."

The room was silent.

"You are the last star who fell to this part of the world one hundred earthly years ago, aren't you?" Nova murmured.

Ryker's face looked as if he'd just seen a ghost.

A smile broke across Astrid's face, and she nodded. "I am she."

Nova's heart swelled in her chest. The stories flooded her mind. All newborn stars were told of the beautiful star who fell to Earth just over one hundred years ago and never returned. These stories told of how she had fallen in love with a humble farmer and chose to stay on Earth.

"What are my chances of sitting between two stars? I was struggling to believe I'd ever see one, let alone two," Ryker murmured in dismay.

Astrid reached across and squeezed his arm. "We are as real as they come."

"I've heard your story, Astrid, but I would love to hear it again from you," Nova said softly.

The woman sat back in her chair and sighed. Her gaze drifted to the horizon beyond the small window by the front door, lost in the memories of what once was. "One night, a cosmic peculiarity unfolded, and I found myself hurtling towards the unknown expanse of Earth. The descent was both terrifying and exhilarating as I plummeted through the celestial veil, leaving streaks of stardust in my wake. It took me what felt like years to reach Earth's atmosphere."

A feeling Nova knew all too well.

Astrid's brilliant blue eyes shimmered with fondness. "I landed in a large open space right here on this mountain. As I touched the Earthly soil, I realised the beauty of mortal existence. It was here I encountered a humble farmer named Eli, whose crops I had landed in. His heart resonated with a simplicity and warmth that mirrored the sun-kissed fields he tilled, and I never wanted to be apart from him again."

A tender smile graced Astrid's celestial features. "As a hundred years passed, I watched seasons change, witnessed the ebb and flow of life on Earth. Eli and I discovered a love that defied the boundaries of time and realms. His laughter became my celestial melody, and the tenderness in his eyes became my anchor for this terrestrial haven. When he passed, it felt as if my soul was ripped right from my body. And even though I knew I could go home; this part of the world had become such a part of me that I couldn't bear to leave."

With a sigh that held the weight of a century's worth of stories, Astrid concluded, "So, in choosing love over Ara, I forsook my home to be with Eli, embracing the fleeting beauty of human existence. Here, among the emerald fields and beneath the boundless sky, I found a love that transcended the stars."

Nova sniffed, wiping the tears from her eyes. "Oh Astrid, your story is tragic, as it is beautiful. How do you still look so young?"

Astrid chuckled, then sipped her tea. "Us stars age very slowly here on Earth. In human years, I am one hundred and twenty-five and yet I feel as if I could run and dance for miles." A mischievous grin appeared on Astrid's face, and Nova beamed.

"This is all so unreal," Ryker whispered. "I heard stories from my late grandfather about a star who fell the night he was born and here you are."

"Your grandfather was a blessed man. When stars fall to Earth, they bring with them a blessing of radiant joy for all babes born that day." Astrid nodded and brought her cup to her lips.

Ryker went back to his stew with zeal. "In the few years that I knew him, he certainly was a joyous man."

"So, I brought joy with me when I landed?" Nova whispered, her eyes clouding with tears once again as she looked to Ryker.

Astrid's voice was gentle. "You did."

Ryker's gaze remained locked on Nova from the opposite side of the small wooden table, and she couldn't look away. She may not know every soul that was touched by her joy, but there was one she hoped she'd given the most to.

The room was silent for a moment as all three were lost in thought.

Astrid spoke first. "Do you want to go home, Nova?"

Nova hesitated, shrugging her shoulders. "Some say it is safer for me there than here on Earth, but now that I know you live here and love it. I am beginning to wonder if I might like to stay."

"What does your heart tell you?" Astrid asked softly.

"I'm not sure I can trust anything my heart says, we haven't been acquainted long."

Astrid offered Nova a smile. "I understand completely, though you will have to make the decision before you enter the pool."

Nova's brow knitted. "What do you mean?"

Astrid stood and cleared the empty dishes to the sink. "Once you enter the place where the two realms meet and speak the celestial saying, you will be transported right back to Ara. You won't be able to change your mind."

Ryker ran his hands through his hair as he leant back in his chair. "It's that simple? How has no one discovered this magical pool?"

"Well, it's only magical to those of the celestial realm," Astrid answered softly. "To the people of Earth, it's just a body of water."

It was Nova's turn to rise from the table. She moved to the cottage window, looking at the evening sky that had caught them unawares.

Why was it so hard to decide what to do? Surely she wanted to go home? She didn't choose to fall to Earth. In fact, before arriving on this planet, she was happily existing in the heavens . . . Until that small rock came along.

Nova glanced over her shoulder at Ryker. His eyes met hers, unwavering, yet his expression remained serious. No smile touched his rugged features; instead, his face seemed conflicted, as if battling an internal storm of emotions beneath the surface.

As she turned back towards the window, Nova spoke. "What is the saying?"

Astrid sighed before placing a hand over her heart. "Veliar silea mynaris," she murmured in the native tongue of elirion.

"Take me to the heavens," Nova whispered. "And will you tell us how to get to the pool of reflections?"

Astrid nodded as she ushered them to sit on the large, soft chairs in front of the fireplace. "I will draw you a map and then you must sleep. Your journey doesn't end here."

The rest of the evening was spent in front of the warm fire, with Astrid drawing a map and explaining to Ryker how to get there.

Nova zoned out after a while. All this talk of going home made her feel sad. If Astrid loved living here on Earth, why wouldn't she? Why was Ryker so afraid to let her stay, and why was she allowing him to tell her what to do? He meant no harm, he just wanted to keep her safe, but maybe safe was dreary. What if she wanted adventure? Or to find a passionate love like she'd seen from her place in the stars as she gazed down on Earth?

Maybe it was time to really decide what she wanted to do.

"Nova. . . ?" Ryker's gentle voice touched her ears.

"Oh sorry, I was just thinking, and this fire is making me sleepy," Nova answered as she glanced between the two faces staring at her.

Astrid seemed to agree as she snuffed out some cream wax candles sitting on the fireplace mantle. "It's time for sleep for all of us."

She moved towards a small closet, returning with a few folded blankets, offering them to Ryker. "The washroom is in here and the spare room is opposite. I only have one double bed in there, though . . ."

"It's fine. I'll sleep in the chair here by the fire," Ryker answered before Astrid could finish. "I'd like to keep watch through the night if that's alright?"

"No one has breached my wards yet, but you are welcome to do as you please," Astrid said.

"Yes, that forest wasn't keen on letting us in until Nova touched it."

The woman nodded. "It allows only those I allow in. I saw you coming from the bottom of the mountain, but wanted to make sure it was Nova who wanted to enter before dropping a part of the ward."

Nova hovered at the washroom door. "Do you think I could do that with my celestial powers?"

"Of course. If you decide to stay on Earth, I will teach you." Astrid glanced over at Ryker before returning her gaze and winking at Nova.

Warmth filled her cheeks at Astrid's insinuations.

Nova opened the washroom door. "I'll say goodnight here then—and Astrid? Thank you for everything."

The woman smiled with a nod. "It's my pleasure. I'll see you both bright and early in the morning."

Astrid closed the door softly behind her, leaving the star and Ryker looking at each other from across the room. Nova wished he would reach for her, show her some sort of sign that he really didn't want her to leave. She searched his eyes for a sign—a glimmer of hope. But she was met with emptiness and pain.

"I'll wash up then," Nova said softly.

Ryker nodded.

As she closed the door behind her, Nova leaned against the wood. Tonight, she needed to decide on what she wanted to do. Either she leaves with Ryker and goes home, or she asks to stay with Astrid. Maybe they could become spinsters in the woods with lots of cats.

Nova smiled at the thought before she pushed off the door and began to wash her face. Once she'd cleaned up, she found the space she'd left Ryker empty.

The front door was slightly ajar, and a soft breeze whispered through the gap. Nova stepped forward, catching a glimpse of him leaning heavily against the balcony post. His broad shoulders were slouched in a rare moment of vulnerability, his back curled, he carried the weight of the world. His gaze was fixed on the vast galaxy above, the starlight reflecting in his dark eyes, making him appear lost in thoughts she couldn't reach.

Ryker turned when he heard her. "Are you all done in there?"

Nova nodded. "Are you alright?"

"Yes," Ryker murmured. "You?"

Nova wrapped her arms around herself. "I'm scared, Ryker."

A small hitch in her breath had Ryker pushing off the post to take one of her hands in his. He squeezed it tight, rubbing the back of it with his thumb.

"What are you scared of?" he murmured.

Nova looked up at him, a sob catching in her throat. "I don't know . . . all of it."

"You can talk to me . . ."

His voice was earnest. She truly felt she could talk to him as if she'd known him for a thousand years. Yet tonight, all of her words just seemed hard to articulate. Her mind was a flurry of thoughts and emotions.

Nova wiped her tears and forced a smile. "I know."

She turned from his face to look up into the velvet skies. The moon was in its waning crescent phase, yet enough of it shone that Nova felt its pull in her blood. Her body ached to be restored once again.

She flicked her gaze to Ryker. "Watch over me while I bathe?"

His brow pinched. "You want me to watch you—"

"Under the moon, Hound." Nova flashed him a grin.

A pink tinge flooded Ryker's cheeks. "Do you mean right now?"

Nova shrugged. "It's the perfect night for it."

Ryker looked towards the field of flowers. "I will watch out for you if that is what you wish."

Nova smiled again before turning her back to him. "Help me with the buttons?"

Calloused fingers brushed at the nape of her neck. The gentle touch against her skin made her body shiver as he dragged his fingers down her spine, one button at a time.

"All done."

Nova glanced over her shoulder, catching his russet gaze as she pulled her brown leather boots from her feet. They clunked as she dropped them on the wooden floor. She danced down the steps, the grass cold against the soles of her feet. She dug her toes into the emerald blades and sank to her knees.

With intentional movements, Nova peeled her sleeves away, dropping the bodice of her simple gown down to her waist. She pulled the leather ties that held her diamond strands captive and shook her head, freeing them to play in the breeze.

From the waist up, she was bare. Her skin glistened under the face of the moon. Nova drew in a deep breath and tipped her head towards the star-dusted sky. Her eyes closed, and she basked in the moonbeams.

Every fibre in her body came alive as the silver light seeped into her skin, filling her blood with the magic of Ara. Her mind became clearer with every second that passed. Sounds became sharper, and the scent of the surrounding blossoms infused with the wind. Marigold, buttercups and wild basil.

Nova opened her eyes, turning her head to look over her shoulder. "Care to join me?"

A smile played on her lips when she heard Ryker chuckle.

"I quite like the view from here."

Nova tipped her head back. "Suit yourself."

She drank in the magic as if it would be her last. The moonbeams kissed her skin, leaving pulsing spots of vigour in their wake. Her fingertips brushed the grass at her sides. She gripped the smooth blades in her hands and grounded herself to the Earth. Energy hummed all around her as she lost herself in creation.

Blossoms dabbed at her skirts as the breeze danced through their stems. Long blades of grass reached for her as she sat back on her feet. Nova had never felt more alive than right now at this moment.

Yet, it could not last forever. Humans still required sleep, even celestial ones.

With a sigh, Nova stood to her feet and turned to face the hound. His arms were folded across his chest as he leaned against the wooden post.

Nova was fully aware of her nakedness as she strolled towards him. His face was emotionless, yet she saw the desire flash in his eyes the closer she came. His gaze travelled from her navel all the way up until it reached her lips. He lingered there a moment before captivating her eyes with his own.

Nova placed her arms into the sleeves of her gown as she slowly ascended the wooden stairs. One at a time. When she reached the top, she turned her back to him.

Ryker eased off the post and did the buttons of her dress up in silence, though his fingers remained longer than needed. Nova wished they'd stray . . . found their way entangled in her hair.

"Do you feel refreshed?" Ryker murmured.

She faced him. "I feel as if I could run down the mountain and back up again."

He chuckled. "You'll have to go alone—I'm pretty knackered."

She grinned and lightly shoved his arm with her shoulder.

Both of them returned their attention to the world above. Nova closed her eyes and thought of Soleil and Tierra.

"I miss them so much, Ryker."

"Your sisters?"

She nodded. "What I'd give to talk to them again. To drift through the starfruit orchard, picking fruits and eating them."

Ryker shoved his hands in his trouser pockets, scuffing the toe of his boot on the wooden floor. "You could see them? If you go home, you could be with them again?"

"What if I don't want to go home?"

Nova heard the catch in his breath. Ryker hesitated before he turned to look at her. He drew his hands from his pockets and cupped her face, wiping the tears that had formed on her cheeks. He held her there for a moment, his russet eyes searching hers. "If that is truly what you want, then we will find a way to keep you safe." Ryker wiped a tear.

Calmness washed over Nova as she stood captured by Ryker's hands. She nodded and nearly burst into a fresh stream of tears as Ryker leaned down and kissed her forehead.

It was the most innocent act, but it spoke volumes to Nova.

As he pulled away, she gripped one hand on the front of his shirt. The other stole its way behind his neck as she brought his head down to hers. She was done waiting for him to kiss her again. If she was leaving, she wanted to taste him.

Feel his lips upon hers. She wanted to run her fingers through his inky tendrils.

Nova caught Ryker's mouth in a tender kiss. He groaned softly as their lips moved together like a well-rehearsed dance. His hands circled her waist, pulling her tight against his body—as if they were one.

The scent of cypress and vanilla consumed her as his tongue dipped between the seam of her mouth. Nova sighed as she opened for him, melting into his taste. He was so gentle with her, yet his hands and his body held her with such strength. Everything about him was addictive, and Nova didn't want to give him up.

Her breath became hers again as she tore herself from the kiss. Ryker's hands still gripped her hips—the heat of his touch searing through the fabric of her gown. His eyes sought hers, yet no words were exchanged.

This was goodbye. Nova could feel it in his silence. He knew that home was safer for her. Earth never would be.

And maybe he was right.

She stepped out of his embrace—her hand lingering on his chest. "Good night, Hound."

For a moment, she thought he would ask her to stay.

"Good night, little star."

Nova turned on her heel, slipping quietly back inside and heading towards the bedroom. A smile crept onto her face as she discovered a large, inviting bed draped with a cheerful yellow blanket and piled with plush pillows. The window framed a breathtaking view of the mountain peaks above them, leaving her momentarily stunned. Standing beside the bed, she gazed up at the moon, its silvery light spilling softly across the room, illuminating the space in a gentle glow.

"Oh sisters . . . what shall I do?" Nova whispered to the glittering sky. It shimmered in response, and Nova smiled. Maybe going back to Ara wouldn't be so bad—especially when it looked like that.

She pulled the blankets down, climbed into the softness and lay down, bringing the covers up to her chin. Sleep claimed her quickly, but not before her mind wandered back to the hound.

Everything about him felt so right. And there was still that lingering thought, that maybe she was already home.

TWENTY-THREE

Early morning light spilled across the meadow and crept up the stairs, warming Nova's feet as she stood on the porch of Astrid's cottage. Breakfast had been a simple meal of oatmeal, fresh fruit, tea, and coffee.

"We can't thank you enough for everything, Astrid," Nova whispered as she squeezed the grey-haired star.

"You are both always welcome here," Astrid murmured. "If you decide to stay, come and see me again. I'll make us something delicious."

Nova nodded with a smile. "I would love that."

Astrid fixed her gaze on Ryker. "What's your favourite treat?"

A boyish grin spread across his face. "Lemon tart."

"Oh, good choice. I will make you one," Astrid said, her eyes brimming with delight.

It was so easy to watch Ryker and Astrid talk, like they'd known each other for so long. Nova fought back the wave of tears that threatened to spill. This was what her future could look like. However, on the other side of Astrid's protective forest lay a world that would never allow her to be at peace with Ryker. She'd forever be hiding with him—was that the life she wanted?

"Again, thank you for everything," Ryker added. "Now let's hope the forest won't try to eat us alive on the way out."

Astrid laughed. "I assure you it won't. Now that it knows who you are, it will let you pass. The forest is now your family."

Nova pulled her newly found friend in for one more embrace. "Until the cosmic currents bring us back into the celestial embrace," she whispered.

Astrid rested her forehead against Nova's and closed her eyes. "Stay safe, little one."

Ryker had brought Charlie around from the back pasture and had him all tacked and ready to go. As she departed down the stairs, Nova turned to wave goodbye to Astrid.

The elderly star took a small step forward. "Don't forget . . . the words as you step into the pool."

Nova nodded. "Veliar silea mynaris."

Astrid's eyes smiled, crinkling in the corners as her mouth pulled up.

This was the right thing to do, though. Going home would make it easier for everyone. Ryker could go back to his life and Nova would be safe in Ara.

"Thanks again," Nova whispered.

Ryker helped Nova onto Charlie's back before he pulled himself up behind her. They waved to Astrid and set off down the hill. The small walk to where the meadow met the forest felt like eternity. Glancing back, Nova smiled. One day she hoped to see Astrid again—whether on Earth or once they both passed into the celestial heavens to shine for the rest of eternity.

They stepped into the trees, and it was like stepping into a dream. Where dark-grey, dead-looking branches had greeted them the day before, there now stood a sea of white blossom trees, their delicate petals shimmering like snow in the soft light of dawn. The transformation was breathtaking, a stark contrast to the desolate landscape they had encountered earlier.

Branches parted and made a way for the trio to pass through.

The air was filled with the sweet fragrance of blossoms, each breath Nova took infused with the scent of spring. The ground beneath Charlie's hooves was carpeted with fallen petals, creating a soft, white pathway that led deeper into the enchanted grove. Sunlight filtered through the canopy, casting a warm, golden glow that made the blossoms sparkle as if dusted with diamonds.

Nova laughed and tipped her head towards the morning sun as petals kissed her cheeks where they fell. This certainly wasn't helping her decision. There was nothing like this in Ara.

"I saw a lot of similarities between you and Astrid." Ryker's words interrupted her thoughts.

"You did?"

Ryker nodded. "You both shine when you talk about things you love and the blue-green eyes you both share are uncanny. Are all the stars in your world like this?"

Nova glanced over her shoulder and smiled. "All stars have eyes that reflect the colours in the galaxies. Blues, purples, pinks, silvers and golds."

"It must truly be a beautiful place . . . Ara."

"It certainly is. So different from this part of the world."

Charlie snorted softly, and they continued in silence. Nova inhaled deeply, savouring the crisp air and relishing the feeling of Earth's atmosphere. When she first arrived, she'd instinctively clawed at her throat, not realising that breathing was something this form needed. It had been terrifying at first, the unfamiliar sensation of needing air.

Now, breathing felt second nature to her, something as natural as any other part of her day. The thought of losing that sensation, of not needing it again, made her feel a strange sense of longing. She knew she was going to miss it once it was gone.

They broke through the heavily flowering trees and stepped onto the road they'd arrived on yesterday.

"Astrid said we need to head back down the trail, make a left about halfway down," Ryker murmured as he looked around. "It's a shortcut that will get us to the road that leads up the other side of the mountain, where the cave is located."

"Lead the way, Hound." Nova smiled over her shoulder.

The morning sun warmed their backs as they travelled back down the mountain along the route Astrid had marked on her hand-drawn map. Ryker kept it tucked safely in his trouser pocket as they followed its guidance.

They found the second trail easily enough and started the venture upwards on the opposite mountain peak. Charlie carried them both with ease and Nova was glad to feel the warmth of Ryker's chest against her back, even if it was for the last time.

She'd been through much. Dante and Finnian—The Twins, King Branoc and his punishing hands. Branoc's guards and pirates on the sea—Lycans. Galanthors. So many situations that brought fear and anxiety into her life that Nova was more than happy to never experience again.

However, there were also such beautiful moments she'd encountered too. The warm sun on her skin. Fields of flowers filled with butterflies and bees. Dancing with strangers to music, rain on her skin from storms.

And all of it, she'd experienced with Ryker. Memories she hoped would carry with her on her return to Ara.

As they rounded a bend in the road, Ryker spotted a dark shadow on the side of the mountain. "There it is."

The mouth of the cave yawned in the distance. Astrid had said they wouldn't miss it due to its size, and she wasn't wrong. It didn't take them too much longer before they reached it. Ryker pulled Charlie to a stop and climbed down from his back, helping Nova once his feet were planted firmly on the ground.

Their eyes caught and Nova swore Ryker's hands lingered a little longer than necessary on her waist. Her eyes begged him to ask her to stay, yet he simply smiled and moved to settle Charlie. He was too large to come inside.

"Goodbye, Charlie boy. Thanks for always keeping me safe." Nova rested her forehead against the horse's black muzzle, squeezing his head one last time.

Tears welled in her eyes, but she didn't let them fall. She could do this; she could be brave. Ryker had promised to help get her home, and he was fulfilling that promise. The resolve in his eyes gave her strength, and she took a deep breath, pushing back her fear.

They walked into the dark cave cautiously, their steps echoing in the silence. The entrance was wide and foreboding, but as they moved deeper, the cave seemed to swallow them whole. Once inside, their eyes adjusted to the dim light filtering through cracks in the stone, and Nova could see that it was very similar to all the other caves she'd seen. Damp walls, uneven ground, and a faint, musty smell that clung to the air.

But that sight didn't last long.

Round the bend, they came face to face with something so beautiful that Nova caught her breath in awe.

Deep within the heart of the cave, a hidden pool lay veiled in allure. The cave's ceiling, adorned with an array of iridescent crystals, mirrored the world of Ara above. These luminescent gems, when touched by the gentle breeze that whispered through the cavern, emitted a soft glow, creating the illusion of a star-studded night sky.

Beneath the celestial display, the pool, like a liquid mirror, embraced the magic of its surroundings. Its surface was alive with a dance of ethereal lights mimicking the far reaches of the galaxy. Glowing little creatures, akin to celestial fireflies, flitted across the cave's ceiling, casting their radiance upon the water below. As these tiny beings darted and shimmered above, their glow painted constellations on the water's surface.

"A place where two worlds meet," Nova whispered.

She stood at the water's edge—feeling the celestial energy coursing through the air. All she needed to do was to step into the water, right?

Did she want to?

Here it was . . . the place that would send her home. The place they'd been searching for these past few weeks. All of it led to this moment. But when Nova turned to look at Ryker, his face was filled with pain, like he had so many words to say and yet none came out.

Too much had been left unsaid between them and it was now or never. She needed to tell him how she felt before she never got the chance to again.

She needed to kiss him one last time.

"Ryker . . ."

With a hurried step, Nova flung herself into Ryker's chest, wrapping her arms around his neck before bringing his lips down to hers in a heated kiss.

At first Ryker felt stiff against her body, but within moments he relaxed, drawing his arms around her waist, pulling her closer. Nova sighed against his mouth as he kissed her deeper than he ever had before. The taste of him on her tongue brought Nova onto the tip of her toes.

They stood tangled together, teasing and tasting in the quiet sanctuary of the cave. But it wasn't enough. She craved the feel of his taut skin, stretched across his muscled frame, beneath her fingers. She needed to memorise every inch, so she'd never forget him. Too many nights together beneath the velvet skies had left her aching for him in ways she was only beginning to understand. If he'd let her, she wanted to touch him, taste him—feel him fully.

Her hands found the buttons on his shirt, undoing them one by one. This brought a small hesitation from Ryker as he kissed her. He pulled back ever so slightly. "What are you doing, little star?"

"Let us have one more night together," Nova whispered against his lips.

Ryker gently cupped her face, resting his forehead on hers. His touch was full of tenderness, which spoke to the longing inside of Nova's human heart. It yearned for the intentional touch that only two souls could offer each other.

"Are you sure?" Ryker murmured.

Nova nodded. "Yes."

Russet eyes bore into hers before Ryker gently took her hand and stepped away from the pool's edge. His thumb brushed over the back of it, leaving bumps on her skin in their wake. "I'll fetch our things."

Nova watched as he strode towards the cave mouth, his body swaying with his usual confidence. He was all man. Rugged, strong, protective, and yet every time he touched her, it was tender, thoughtful, and thrilling. She wanted to capture the way he moved, so she'd never forget.

He returned moments later. Together they made a small fire, laying their makeshift bed of a few woollen blankets beside it. Nova didn't even care that it wasn't a bed of luxury. All that she cared for—was Ryker sharing it with her.

She had grown to love the familiar rhythm of setting up camp with the Hound. Travelling through the different areas of Sapphire Vale—even with the frequent encounters with danger or unwelcome guests. It was an adventure. Each time they made a temporary home, they created fleeting memories that felt precious, even if just for a short while.

Her gaze fixed on Ryker over the crackling, orange flames. Their final meal was cheese, dried meat, and slices of fresh pumpkin sourdough that Astrid gave them.

The flames danced in his eyes; the shadows licking at his skin. The food was bland in her mouth compared to the view. His inky waves glistened with a tinge of gold as the fire reflected off it. Warm tinted skin, like honey, blanketed his frame and Nova hoped soon that she would see more of it.

Rykers' brow rose, amusement dancing on his lips. "Tell me what's your favourite food been to eat here."

Nova's cheeks warmed. "Probably the peach."

The taste of it was still vivid on her tongue. She pictured biting into its flesh, the velvety skin giving way to the fruit's succulent flesh. A burst of sweet, floral notes mixed with a hint of tartness, especially closer to the seed.

Ryker chuckled softly. "Good choice. I quite like them too."

She offered him a smile before biting into her bread.

"And what about your favourite animal?"

Nova tilted her head to the side while she finished her mouthful. "Definitely Charlie, but I would have to say the fish in the streams come in as a close second."

"Why the fish?"

Nova shrugged. "There is just something in their freedom of moving through the water, weightless and free."

"Sounds like someone else I know."

The corner of Nova's mouth turned up as she held Ryker's gaze across the fire.

He threw his crust into the hungry flames as he stood beside it. "And what is one thing you've experienced that you loved the most?"

Heat pooled in Nova's stomach. That familiar ache between her legs blossomed as she eyed the Hound. It travelled through her body with a speed that had her heart pounding against her chest. "I haven't done it yet."

Ryker's eyes darkened at her response. "What are you saying, Nova?"

Nova set the food beside her, brushing a few stray crumbs from her lap as she rose. She watched Ryker for a moment, a soft smile playing on her lips before she took a few small steps towards him. He placed his own plate down and turned to meet her. Her steps were slow, unhurried, savouring the simple act of walking toward him.

"What do you want to experience before you go?" he murmured, looking down at her with adoration.

Nova reached up to brush the curls from his forehead. "Let me experience you before I leave . . . please?"

Ryker grazed his thumb over Nova's bottom lip and the ache between her legs grew stronger. "Are you sure?" he whispered.

"I've never been surer of something in my life, Hound."

Ryker's eyes glittered with a silent joy that Nova had only dreamt she'd see one day. With a boyish grin on his face, he leant down and planted a quick kiss on her mouth. "If we do this, will you promise to go home after, so I know you are safe?"

"I promise."

He swallowed. "And do you know what can happen between a man and a woman when they come together?"

Nova pondered for a moment. "Are you referring to creating human life?"

Ryker nodded.

"I don't even know if I can do that Ryker, besides I will be returning to Ara, so I'd say we would be safe in regard to that."

"As long as you're sure?" Ryker murmured, tracing a thumb over Nova's cheek.

She pulled him closer, pushing his shirt from his shoulders, watching it as it dropped to the ground. "I want to feel this with you before I leave. Are you alright with that?"

"Very much so."

Nova grinned as she placed her arms around his neck. "Then please undress me."

Ryker groaned at her words, spinning Nova so her back was to his chest. With gentle hands, he undid the buttons, letting her dress slip to the floor in a pile of navy cotton. She was left standing in only the bottom half of her undergarments.

The cool air in the cave coated Nova's bare skin, sending a small shiver across her body. Soft, bright white locks of hair brushed against her back as she glanced over her shoulder to look at a very silent Ryker. His eyes were darkening by the second as they travelled up her back, finally reaching her face.

With a slow smile, Nova turned to face him.

"By the stars, Nova," Ryker groaned as he ran a hand through his inky waves.

Nova couldn't help but feel very vulnerable under his gaze. "I don't know if this human body is to your liking—"

The hound moved with swift ease, as he caught her face between his hands and silenced her with a kiss that sent Nova into a different universe. It was full of desire and passion. His tongue brushed against hers. Sucking. Biting. Teasing.

Nova's legs trembled as he pulled away.

"I don't have a type," Ryker said before he placed a tender kiss on the tip of her nose. "But you're fucking perfect."

Before she could respond, Ryker dropped to his knees and began to pull her undergarments down slowly from her hips. His broad hands clasped the thin white fabric, dragging it down her thighs, before discarding them into the pile of fabric on the floor. A pleasurable ache throbbed between her legs, travelling up into her stomach, where it then spread into every fibre of her being.

Ryker's gaze found her beneath the veil of his darkened lashes and Nova could no longer deny the desire she felt for this man. It wasn't a figment of her imagination. It was true, and it was real. He'd rescued her time and time again. He'd kept her safe and shown her parts of the world she never thought she'd see. Experiencing this with him was exactly what she wanted to be doing.

"I'd like to pleasure you, little star," Ryker said as his mouth trailed over her hips, his warm breath licking at her skin.

"If it will feel as good as it did that first time in the cave, then please . . ." Nova traced a finger across Ryker's bottom lip. "Show me everything."

Ryker grinned up at Nova before burying his face between her legs, lapping at her warmth. She uttered a soft cry as his hands dug into her thighs, pulling her closer as he kissed and gently sucked at her most sensitive parts.

It was even more thrilling than the first time he'd touched her there. Currents of pleasure pulsed through her body over and over again like static electricity. Nova could barely stand as Ryker's tongue had his way with her.

She gripped his head and thrust her hips into his face as he gently nipped at her. With a primal growl that vibrated through her core, Ryker slipped two fingers into her wetness.

"Ryker!" Nova cried, her voice echoed through the cave, bouncing off the blue illuminated walls. She dropped her head back, closing her eyes against the waves of pleasure his tongue brought her each time he dragged it up her centre. Or every time he slowly drew his fingers out, only to pump them back in with gentle force.

He pulled back. "Yes, little star?"

Nova brought her head back. His lips glistened with remnants of her and that heat that was building in her core doubled. He was the most beautiful man she'd ever laid her eyes on. Nova hoped that as he looked at her, he could see just how much she wanted him.

"I don't think I can stand for much longer." Nova's voice was heavy with desire.

Ryker's chuckle echoed through the cave as he stood. "We can take as long as you need."

Nova shook her head. "I don't want to slow down. I would like to undress you."

"I'm at your mercy," Ryker murmured.

He gripped the sides of her face, his rough hands cradling her soft skin as he brought his lips to hers in a heated, desperate kiss. She tasted herself on his tongue, a sensation that sent a wild thrill down her spine, igniting her core. The kiss was raw, primal, as if their very souls were being fused together with each fervent motion. It wasn't just passion—it was something deeper, something that altered her very being. The kind of kiss that whispered promises of forever, knitting two hearts and souls together for eternity.

Ryker pulled his lips from hers, their breaths coming in shallow gasps. Nova's head swirled, her heart pounding in her chest as she fought to steady herself. The thought of being even a moment apart from him felt unbearable—she craved every piece of him, desperately needed more.

One by one, the buttons on his shirt gave way. Ryker was patient, his hands resting on her hips, the warmth of his fingers seeping into her skin. The last button freed itself, and Nova pushed the fabric from his shoulders.

Her fingers traced the taut skin that stretched across his chest as it rose and fell with his breath. His heart was thumping under its bone cage. Muscles rippled under the glistening canopy above them. Ryker remained still as she traced her fingers over the plains of his stomach. It was her turn to please him—if she could. Nova had no idea what she was doing, but she figured all she had to do was follow Ryker's example.

The laces on his trousers gave way as Nova tugged at them. She could visibly see the hardness straining against the fabric, so she pulled it down his hips, releasing his cock. It bounced free, and she swallowed as she took in the sight of it. All of that was supposed to go inside her, right?

She had no way of comparing his size because she'd never been with a man before, but she certainly wasn't naive enough to think that he was small.

Because he certainly wasn't.

Nova reached for it, softly dragging her fingertips over the length of it. It felt like silk to the touch. Softer than any other part of him she'd felt before. Yet it was big and powerful like the rest of him. Flicking her gaze up to meet his, Nova was met with russet eyes that were darkened with desire. Ryker didn't break the stare as Nova wrapped her hand around his cock and gently squeezed.

He may not have said a word, but he certainly was having trouble breathing as she slowly tugged on him.

"You're doing so good," Ryker uttered softly.

"Can I pleasure you with my mouth as you have done with me?" Nova whispered before reaching up on her toes to plant a tender kiss to his mouth.

Ryker wrapped his arms around her waist and kissed her back. "I would beg you to, but I only want you to do things that make you feel comfortable."

"I want it all, Ryker . . . teach me."

His thumb grazed her bottom lip. "Then yes, you can, little star. Now on your knees."

He groaned softly as Nova slipped to the floor in obedience. Her hand gripping his hardened length. Flicking up her gaze, she studied his face for a moment. "Like this?"

He nodded without words.

Nova smirked, dragging her gaze back towards his cock. There was a bead of moisture on the tip of it, glistening in the blue glow of the cave. It tasted salty on her tongue as she wrapped her lips around the head of his cock and gently sucked.

"By the stars, Nova—" Ryker uttered.

She drew back and forth a few times, her teeth gently grazing the underside of his rigid length. From this angle, as she looked up at Ryker, she could tell he was thoroughly enjoying himself by the soft moans he was making and the way he bit his bottom lip. She kept her gaze fixed on him as she drew her head back and forth.

Her lips popped as Nova released him from her mouth. "Is that how you do it?"

"Yes, little star, . . . that is how you do it."

Nova grinned up at him. She was pleased that, in her lack of experience, she was still able to please him. "Is there anything I could do differently?"

Ryker shook his head, reaching down to stroke her cheek. "Your mouth feels like silk Nova. I want you to wrap me in its woven threads."

His voice was low—commanding. It sent a shiver up Nova's spine, peaking her nipples and making the slick between her legs thicker. She longed to touch herself—anything to ease the friction building there. But it was his turn first.

Nova grinned at Ryker. Parting her lips, she held her mouth open for him. "Fuck," Ryker whispered. He held her head, guiding himself between her lips. The salt from the glistening bead on the head of his cock brushed against her tongue, sending a twang through her jaw as it spread over her tongue.

Ryker gently thrust his hips into her mouth in slow, sensual strokes.

He was holding back, Nova could tell, and even though she appreciated the caution, she wanted to see him undone, so she grabbed his hips and took him deeper, sucking him down her throat as far as she could go.

"Nova!" Ryker cried out, throwing his head back.

With a sense of triumph, Nova dragged her mouth over his length again and again. She could feel it twitching with each stroke she made. Never did she think humans could find pleasure this way, but she was certainly wrong. This was beyond her wildest dreams. Nova only wished to feel Ryker's mouth on her skin once again.

He stilled her strokes, pulling from her mouth before he bent down, cupped her face and kissed her soundly.

"I need to be inside you," he murmured against her lips.

"Show me how."

He didn't hesitate after that. He took her hand and drew her towards the bed they'd made beside the warm fire. Then he gathered their discarded clothing from the rocky ground and added them to the bed, softening it further.

Nova watched him as he moved. His muscled legs and torso, the v-shape that pointed right to his cock that bounced free as he tried to make the bed as comfortable as possible. She smiled to herself. Just wait until her sisters heard about this. She was going to burn every taste, every touch, every feeling into her mind, so once she was home in Ara, she could play it over and over again.

"Come here," Ryker whispered, reaching for her hand.

Nova took it and followed him to the bed. He guided them gently to the ground. He settled on his back, beckoning to her.

"What if I don't know what to do?" Nova hesitated.

"I promise I will guide you."

Russet eyes that haunted her dreams and melted her soul met her as Nova lowered herself down to straddle Ryker's hips. His rigid length lay right against her core, right between her thighs. Both Nova and Ryker drew in a gasp at the first touch of it against her wet warmth. Her body felt like it was on fire. Every place he touched her burned with desire.

Ryker gripped her hips, his gaze never leaving hers. "There will be a little pain the first time, but we will go as slow as you need."

Nova nodded, her pulse fluttering as Ryker reached between them and guided the tip of his length into her. The head of it stretched her inner walls, filling her with a slight sting as she sunk down inch by inch.

"Oh Ryker—"

"Yes, little star . . . you're taking me so well."

Her mind and body were buzzing with pleasure, crying out as his size stretched and filled her.

Celestial beings might have powers to create in the heavens and on Earth, but nothing compared to this feeling she was currently experiencing. Nova was not in her body, but floating above it as Ryker guided her hips into a gentle rocking motion. It was only her and him. Nothing else existed.

"You're glowing," Ryker murmured.

Nova's voice was barely a whisper. "Don't I always when you're near?"

The hound grinned at her. "This is a different kind of glow . . . look." Ryker pointed to the star-shaped scar in the middle of her chest.

"It must like you," Nova smirked.

Ryker's fingers dug into her skin—possessing her. "It's going to like me even more in a moment."

With a purposeful smile, Nova grazed the scar with her fingers as she rocked her hips. Each time she did, the sea-green star in the middle of her chest grew brighter. It fuelled them both into a frenzy of passion. Ryker was moving her faster and faster. Nova's back arched, baring her breast, her throat, her soul to him—all for the taking. Which Ryker happily did.

As she circled her hips, feeling every twitch of his cock inside her, Ryker sat up, leaning on one arm. He leaned down to take one of her breasts into his mouth. His warm tongue circled around her shell pink nipple, sucking and teasing.

"By the stars," Nova cried, burying her hands in Ryker's hair as his hot mouth grazed her other nipple, then moved over the star on her chest. He licked it with his hot tongue. His mouth illuminated as the star bloomed with celestial light. Nova whimpered at his touch.

What she'd give to do this with him over and over. She'd promised him she would go home once they were done, so she was safe, but how could she, after this? Ara couldn't offer her anything like Ryker could.

She'd give her heart fully to him if he'd offer his in return.

Ryker's teeth grazed her skin as he pulled back. "I want to feel you deeper. Do you think you can handle that?"

Nova had no idea if that was even possible. He was already filling her beyond her wildest dreams, but she was too curious to say no, so she nodded.

"I'm all yours . . ."

With a boyish grin, darkened eyes full of desire, Ryker gently eased Nova off of him. The absence of his body was sudden and cool, but the hum of pleasure still pulsed through her body.

"On your hands and knees, little star."

Nova did as he bade, sucking in her breath when Ryker placed himself behind her. It was so vulnerable, baring herself to him, but the way his hands traced patterns down her spine, across the dip in her lower back and over the rise of her ass, gave Nova all the confidence she needed, to stretch her arms forward, putting herself fully on display for him.

"You're so fucking beautiful," he hissed.

Without wasting another moment, he lined himself up behind her and plunged back into her warmth, sinking all the way to the hilt. Nova moaned as her inner walls stretched to accommodate his size once again.

"Does it hurt?" Ryker asked as he slowly drew out.

She was breathless with pleasure. "No . . . not at all, the opposite, in fact."

Calloused hands gripped her hips as Ryker started to pump into her, each stroke picking up pace. Ryker became consumed by his desire for her as he plunged into her faster and faster.

This was the missing piece of her journey. Ryker was the perfect send-off before returning to Ara, making everything else pale in comparison. Nothing she'd seen or done here captivated her like he did.

Nova felt the throb in her core building, heat rising to her cheeks. She knew with each thrust of Ryker's rigid length, the coil inside her tightened, readying itself to release at any given moment.

"Hound . . ."

"Yes, my little star." Ryker's breath came up short.

"I can't hold on," Nova gasped.

Ryker chuckled as he reached one hand to grip the back of her neck, angling himself so he could drive in deeper. "You let go whenever you're ready."

The sound of their bodies slapping together ricocheted off the walls alongside their moans and whimpers as their climax built higher and higher.

Ryker's hand found its place between her legs once more. Circling her clit. Bringing her intense pleasure with every stroke of his fingers.

One last rough thrust into Nova's warmth had her mind blanking as pleasure ripped through her and exited her body with an anguished cry. Her ears rang, drowning out any other sounds. Ecstasy pulsed through her over and over.

Ryker grunted, his cock twitching with pleasure as he found his release—-spilling into her. She clenched around him as he gently pumped. His hands still gripped her hips as he rode the waves of his pleasure. Her legs shook from the ebb of bliss that washed over her body.

After a moment, Ryker eased out of her, his seed trickling out and mixing with her own slickness. Nova didn't know up nor down, left or right as her legs finally gave way, sprawling to the ground, in a shivering heap. Ryker collapsed by her side.

"Are you alright?" Ryker nuzzled her ear and drew her closer.

Nova simply nodded. She couldn't even find the words to explain what had just happened. She also didn't need the pool of reflections to see stars.

Ryker had done that to her all by himself.

They lay together on the ground for a while, simply basking in each other's glow. Nova didn't want to move. Physically, she almost couldn't. Her arms and legs were languid to the touch.

The cloud of desire soon broke as Ryker got up to retrieve his trousers. "Let me help you dress."

Nova stood and reached for her clothes.

"Your knees," Ryker pointed. "They look red. Are you in pain?"

With a brush of her fingers over her skin, Nova shook her head. "What's a little pain in the name of so much pleasure?"

Ryker offered a small smile, but his face still held concern. "I don't want you to be hurt, though."

"But it was so worth it." Nova grinned at him.

She quickly dressed. Smoothing her hair down, Nova turned to face the male who'd just destroyed her for anyone else. She truly felt deep down that if she ever returned to this part of the world, she wouldn't be with anyone if she couldn't be with him.

He caught her staring and offered her a smile. He was irresistible standing there, half naked and messy hair. She took a few steps towards him, and Ryker met her halfway. He caught her around the waist as she looped her arms around his neck.

This kiss was deep, but it was tender. Slow and exploring—neither one wanting it to end. When they finally pulled apart, Ryker rested his head on her forehead, breathing her in.

"Thank you for bringing joy into my life even if it was only a blip in time," Ryker murmured, lifting her chin with one finger so he could look into her eyes.

The cave was dark when Nova woke.

Ryker nestled beside her, still slumbering. The worries of the world were not yet evident on his peaceful face. Nova traced a finger along his jaw and up to his ear under the curtain of his inky black waves.

"Morning, little star," he whispered.

Nova's hand shrunk back as Ryker's russet eyes found hers. Caught in the act of admiring him while he slept brought a tinge of heat to her cheeks.

"Morning, Hound."

Ryker grinned before leaning over to kiss her solidly.

Memories of his lips on other parts of her flashed through her mind and warmth blossomed through her body. He'd sparked a fire in her that she never wanted to see fade. It could blaze endlessly, and she'd never tire of its warmth.

He pulled away before rolling over and slipping from the bed. Nova watched as he dressed, knowing that this would be the last time she'd see him utterly vulnerable—and naked.

With clothing on, Ryker moved to make sure the fire had diminished. She took the cue to get dressed herself. She stood, shaking her hair free from its tangles. Running her hands across her torso and down her hips, Nova mentally took images of her human body. The way her skin felt under her fingertips—soft silk. It would probably be the last time she would look like this. Once in Ara, she'd take back her celestial form.

She picked up the discarded navy dress, a smile playing on her lips from the memory of Ryker undoing the buttons and easing it down her body.

She shook her head to clear her thoughts. If she kept thinking of him and the way his tongue—she really needed to stop, or her face was going to look like a bright red tomato.

Nova turned her gaze to the pool, its surface smooth and still as glass. The walls remained speckled with tiny blue lights, casting a soft glow. She let out a quiet sigh as she wandered to the edge, taking a moment to gather her thoughts while Ryker busied himself with packing up the bed.

Did she want to go home? Ara was a magical place, like no other, but if she was being truthful, there was so much about this part of the world that she was yet to explore. Perhaps they could travel further and be out of the king's reach forever. Maybe, just maybe, there was a chance.

Nova spun on her heel to face him. "Ryker?"

He stopped folding the woollen blanket, his eyes travelling over her face. "Is everything alright?"

"What if—"

Nova froze, feeling her brow knit together as something moved in the shadows behind him.

"RYKER!" she cried, but it was too late. A figure burst from the shadows and slammed the hilt of a sword into the back of his head, and Nova met him on her knees as he dropped to the cave floor.

A second figure emerged from the shadows, and Nova's heart lurched in her chest.

"Did you miss us?" Dante sneered.

TWENTY-FOUR

Squeaky wheels grated on his ears, a relentless noise that cut through the haze clouding his mind. Horse's hooves slammed against the rocky ground, their even pounding residing with the dull ache at the back of his head. Every jolt of the cart sent a fresh wave of pain coursing through his skull, making him wince involuntarily.

Muffled voices floated around him, indistinct and distant, like they were underwater. He couldn't make out the words, but the tones were harsh and urgent. He tried to focus, to grasp onto something concrete in the swirling fog that filled his mind. It was like trying to catch smoke with his bare hands.

Ryker's eyelids felt heavy, almost too heavy to lift.

He was no longer in the cave, delighting in the arms of a certain star—Nova.

The last thing he could remember was her crying out his name before black engulfed him. Trying to swallow against the dryness of his mouth, Ryker rolled onto his back. It was semi-dark inside the carriage, with only the smallest crack of sunlight coming through the door frame. There was no way of knowing how long he'd been inside, and there was no way of finding out either.

His hands and feet were bound to bolts on the floor, with just enough chain length to let him move his limbs and possibly sit up. However, standing was impossible.

His head throbbed, making him feel nauseous. Closing his eyes against it, Ryker took in a deep breath, trying to focus on Nova. Where was she? Was she okay? Whoever took him hadn't locked her in the carriage with him, so obviously they were after her and he was just in the way.

Why not just kill him?

He was grateful they hadn't, but you don't take a prisoner unless you're a guard or a . . . bounty hunter.

Well, at least that narrowed down who the culprits might be.

Ryker groaned as he rolled back onto his side. They must have dealt him a dose of dreamroot. He could taste the bitter taste on his tongue. The stench of it was all too well known. His body rocked with the sway of the carriage, lulling him into a state of unconsciousness once again.

This went on for days. At some point, a chunk of stale bread and a small canister of water had been tossed carelessly into the back of the carriage, though Ryker couldn't remember exactly when. It was far from enough to sustain his strength, barely enough to keep the edges of hunger from gnawing at him.

The only hope that held his sanity together was the flickering thread tied to one of his left ribs that invisibly tethered him to the woman with the floating white hair.

He would find her again.

There was no longer movement, or the sound of carriage wheels against the ground, as Ryker came to again. In fact, there was barely any sound at all, except for the agonising cry from someone in the distance, echoing through the silence. The smell of wet stone and burnt oil emanated from wall sconces, a pungent the first clue of where he was—a prison cell.

He slowly cracked his eyes open. The very dimly lit room was definitely that of a prison cell. The walls were damp, with moss creeping between the decaying stones. Iron bars lined one side, offering a view of a dimly lit corridor where shadows danced from the flickering flames of torches. A heavy, oppressive silence hung in the air, broken only by the occasional drip of water from the ceiling.

He shifted slightly; the chains clinking softly as he moved. His limbs ached from the restraints, and he could feel the rough texture of the stone floor beneath him. As his eyes adjusted to the gloom, he noticed the cell door—solid iron, with a small, barred window at the top. Escape seemed impossible, but

Ryker's mind was already working, assessing his surroundings, searching for any weakness or opportunity. Listening for any signs that might help him figure out his location.

How long had he been here and where was Nova?

Ryker forced himself to sit up, his muscles protesting with every movement. The stone wall was cold against his back, a stark contrast to the burning pain that coursed through his body. As he struggled to breathe, flashbacks of men hitting and kicking him—vivid and brutal—came rushing back.

He remembered the sharp pain of a boot connecting with his ribs, the dull thud of a fist against his jaw. He could almost hear their taunts, their laughter, as they beat him down.

Someone wanted to see him suffer. Unfortunately for Ryker, that could be a multitude of people. He needed to get himself together, and he needed to do it with haste if he was going to make it out of here alive.

Wherever here was.

Footsteps echoed outside the door and keys jangled as someone unlocked his cell door. As soon as the two guards stepped through, he recognised the kingdom's colours.

He was right back at square one.

Branoc's castle.

"Get up," one guard gruffly commanded.

With pain and a lot of struggle, Ryker used the wall as support to push himself into a standing position. He nearly blacked out, but managed to stay upright.

The other guard moved towards him and reached to chain his wrists. "The king wants to see you."

"I bet he does," Ryker uttered.

He refused to let them believe they'd broken him. There was nothing these guards could do to him that would make him bend to their king's will, but if they harmed Nova in any way . . . that would be a different story.

Ryker climbed the stairs with heavy footsteps, flanked by the two guards as the prison cell faded behind him. Rough hands pushed him through a wooden door into a grand hall. Noble men and women turned their gaze towards him—some with pity, others with judgement, as if to say you should have known better. But Ryker kept his head held high, walking forward with as much dignity as he could muster.

It felt like days passed as they walked from the cells to the throne room and Ryker couldn't help the exhausted relief that coursed through him when they finally reached it.

Large, ornately carved wooden doors were pushed open in the centre, revealing the grand throne room beyond. Ryker was a little disappointed; he had hoped for a more private visit with King Branoc. Instead, the room was filled to the brim with people—courtiers, nobles, and guards all gathered to witness whatever spectacle was about to unfold. The murmur of voices hushed to a whisper as the doors swung wide.

Of course, Branoc would have an audience.

A long red carpet divided the crowd into two, leading straight to the opposite end of the room where King Branoc sat on his imposing throne. One guard shoved Ryker forward as they started their journey from one end of the hushed room to the other.

Rage simmered beneath the surface of his skin as he flicked his eyes around the room, but he couldn't locate Nova. If they'd captured him, it was most likely they'd caught Nova too.

The trio reached the foot of the dais and the guards shoved Ryker to his knees before the king.

He kept his eyes glued to the floor while he waited for Branoc to speak.

"Subjects of the realm, today is a day of grievous disappointment. Ryker, the once-trusted bounty hunter, has betrayed not only his king but the sanctity of the kingdom itself."

The king's voice rang through the hall as he continued, his words laden with disdain. "I'd welcomed him into my service, and in return, he dared to steal away a jewel more precious to me than actual diamonds."

A heavy tension settled over the hall as a door behind the throne swung open. Ryker slowly glanced up to see a few ladies-in-waiting, hurrying through. In tow was a very forlorn-looking Nova.

Her appearance spoke volumes.

They'd piled her glistening white hair on top of her head, adorning it with ribbons and jewels. Rouge on her lips and cheeks hid what Ryker knew would be bruises underneath. The dark-green velvet gown swallowed her. It hung on her bones like fabric caught on the dead branch of a silver birch with a gust of wind threatening to carry it off at any moment.

Yet beneath the facade the king had tried to bury her in, Ryker saw it all.

Tear-stained cheeks. Sea-green eyes once filled with light sank into her skull—hollow and dark. They darted to and fro as she scanned the room. Her body was rigid in its movements, as if every step she took was pure agony. She looked frightened, like a deer running from the crushing jaw of a Lycan.

Every fibre in Ryker's being screamed her name. He wanted to wrap his arms around her and tell her everything was going to be okay. That he would get them both out of this situation. He wanted to bind his hands around Branoc's neck and snap it.

Nova's sad eyes met his from across the distance. A silent plea resonated within them. A cry of help, yet also comfort. He saw the relief wash over her face at the sight of him.

The courtiers exchanged uneasy glances as the king gestured towards Nova.

"Ryker, I believe you've met my soon-to-be queen," King Branoc proclaimed with a twisted sense of triumph. "She will wear the crown by my side, and she will be mine for as long as I live."

The announcement sent shockwaves through the court, and many exchanged uneasy glances. Nova closed her eyes against the king's words.

"Wife? No. Another trophy. Another show of power." Ryker tried to stand, but the guards held him firm. There was very little strength left in his body. Days without food would do that to a man. "You can trap her in a marriage, but she will never love you."

"It is of little consequence to you," Branoc sneered. "As for you, Ryker, the traitor who dared to defy a king, your fate is sealed. You shall meet the executioner's blade for your treachery."

"NO!" Nova cried as she rushed towards Ryker, but armoured hands held her back. "Let him live. I promise I will do anything you ask of me if you will just let him live."

Nova's voice cracked and Ryker's heart broke in two. Their eyes met, and he mouthed 'It's okay,' to her, but her eyes didn't believe him.

Gasps and whispers swept through the assembly as the king descended from his throne, saunting towards his prized star. "You will marry me, whether he lives or dies, do you understand?"

King Branoc turned to look back at Ryker. "Let this be a lesson for anyone who tries to defy me."

Branoc sauntered back towards Nova, gripping her frail arm in his hand. "Come, let us be gone from this filth." He yanked on her arm as they left the room, his grip cruel and unyielding.

Ryker tried to lurch after them, his heart pounding with desperation, but the guards held him back, their grips like iron shackles. He struggled, but it was no use. He would have to think of something, and fast.

King Branoc would not have her—Ryker wouldn't allow it, no matter the cost. Nova was more than a prize, more than a possession for a ruthless king. Ryker would find a way to set her free, even if it meant sacrificing everything, including his own life.

The guards dragged him to his feet and marched him from the room. Ryker's eyes scanned the room, frantically searched for something, anything that might help him get free. His mind raced with potential escape plans, but none seemed feasible in the moment.

Then, amidst the sea of faces, a pair of familiar moss-green eyes met him. His heart leaped in his chest, mending the fractures of despair. Pete. Pete was here. His friend and palace chef—there was hope for him yet.

As the guards pulled him closer to the exit, Ryker's resolve hardened. He refused to meet his end at the hand of King Branoc, whether by noose or blade. He'd fought too hard, endured too much, to let it all end like this.

He locked eyes with Pete, silently conveying his need for help. Pete gave a barely perceptible nod.

Ryker would live to see another day.

TWENTY-FIVE

THE BUTCHER'S BLADE

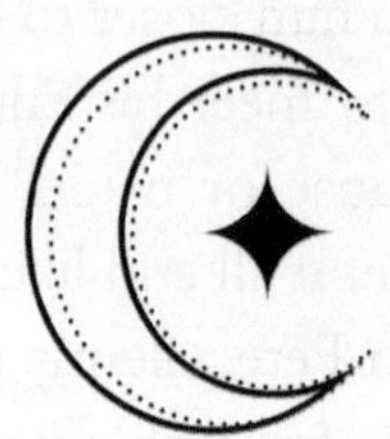

Hours passed.

Free of his chains, Ryker stretched his aching limbs though every muscle complained. He'd done his best to rest, hoping to gain strength for whatever he might face next.

The only sounds that pierced the silence were the distant cries of prisoners further down the hall. Some were begging for food, others water, and a few were moaning in agony. The echoes of their misery blended together, forming a haunting chorus that filled the damp air, growing alike from one another after hours of endless wailing. It felt like the walls themselves were mourning.

Somewhere in the distance, the heavy thud of the door echoed through the cold stone walls of the prison. Ryker felt the vibration through the floor. Soon, metal keys scraping against wood and iron screeched through the air.

Muffled voices drifted through the wood. "This is specifically to be given to the Hound. King's orders."

A narrow slot in the cell door slid open with a creak, and a guard carelessly shoved a tin plate through, sending it skidding across the floor. On it sat a hunk of what looked like fresh bread, a small wedge of cheese, and a bruised apple. Cautiously, he stood to gather the measly meal. If someone specified it for him, there was a chance they had poisoned it. Everything seemed normal. Yet, he couldn't be too sure.

With the plate in hand, Ryker sighed and sat back onto the cot. He picked up the bread, held it to his nose. It didn't smell like it had traces of anything deadly. Though that meant nothing. What if someone had placed blades or something worse inside? Waiting for him to bite into it.

Ryker smirked. He wasn't that dense.

He tore the bread in half and there, in the centre of the fluffy, wholemeal loaf, was a rolled piece of paper.

Ryker grinned as he tore it from its hiding place and unfurled it to see four words sprawled across the scrap of paper.

Be ready for tonight.

He scrunched the paper into a ball and shoved it into his trouser pocket before taking a large bite of what was possibly the most delicious bread he'd eaten in a long time. All he had to do now was wait for Pete to come.

As he savoured the morsels of food, his mind wandered to Nova. The moment their eyes met in the throne room; his heart pulled against the restraints in his chest. She'd looked at him the same way Yolanda had when Ryker held her against his chest for the last time.

A different kind of pain spread through his body, and Ryker allowed it to wash over him. He'd held it back for too long. Being alone, stuck, forced him to face the demons inside that clawed at him day and night.

He was used to being alone, though. It was what he deserved, wasn't it?

"... she wouldn't want you to be alone ... she'd want you to be happy."

Acute pain broke inside his chest. Ryker clutched at his heart. Fighting the emotions that hammered against the barricade of his mind.

Did he really deserve to be happy when Yolanda didn't get her happiness? Nova wasn't happy right now. Why did he deserve anything when both of the women who meant the world to him had experienced so much pain?

Ryker longed for silence in his mind. He ached for the day when the voices of accusation would forever hold their tongue. Could one soul live the rest of their days in torment? What kind of life was that? Was it a life at all?

He had to deal with them—with the pain. He had to deal with the ghost of her . . .

Tears welled and spilled, trailing down his sun kissed skin as Ryker quietly sobbed for the love he lost. She would forever be his firecracker. The one who tested his every limit but loved him fiercely. The life of the party wherever they went. Her dark brown hair billowing in the wind as they raced each other on horseback. How could he ever forget her laughter that could brighten even the darkest of days? The red rouged lips she wore just to tease him.

Yolanda had been his everything.

After her death, Ryker truly never thought he would love again.

His world went from watercolour sunsets and oil painted days racing through the fields on horseback, to charcoal sketch graveyards and black smeared memories.

Yolanda had been his colour . . . until Nova.

Sea-green eyes, hair like tiny diamond strands. Skin like ivory. Laughter like bottled sunshine. She was the stars, the moon, and the galaxies. The very thing his heart needed to heal, and she brought with her a sense of adventure and curiosity into his life again. Her zeal for life showed him that there was colour on the other side of his dark and desolate world.

Nova had stolen his lonely heart from the moment he saw her. It was never his to keep. Always hers to have. He just didn't realise until this very moment.

Another sob escaped his lips as the realisation washed over him.

"Thank you, Yolanda. Thank you for loving me and teaching me how to love deeply. I will always love you, but it's time for me to give my heart to another. Until we meet again," Ryker whispered to the cold, frigid cell.

Yolanda was gone, and she wasn't coming back. He would always hold space for the love they shared and for the life they could have built together.

Nova was here, and she was real. It was like the Creator smiled upon the broken, weeping heart inside its cage of Ryker's chest and gave it new life.

King Branoc would not have her.

Because she was his and he was hers. It was at this very moment Ryker felt Yolanda smiling down upon him from her place in the world of lost loved ones, giving him the courage to move on. He'd been holding back, thinking his heart only had room for one, but now he could see how untrue that was.

Once free, he would tell her how he felt, and that she had a place with him forever—should she choose that. Choosing a life with him in this part of the world would mean they'd never truly be free from danger. They would always look over their shoulder.

So, if she wanted to go home, he would take her back to the pool of reflections. After all, it was still her choice whether she should stay or go. He wouldn't stand in her way. But if she stayed, he would spend his life protecting her, no matter the cost.

He wanted her—no; he needed her.

Memories of how she tasted upon his lips and the touch of her hands threaded through his hair brought a soothing balm to the agony in his heart. The way she fit so perfectly in his arms, the little noises she made when he made her reach for the celestial realms by the fire that night. All of these moments together transcended into one and created a swell inside his heart that he knew was the birthing of new love.

A smile broke across his dampened cheeks.

Love . . .

He *loved* her.

The soft sound of keys turning in the lock jolted Ryker upright from the cot he'd been sleeping on. It was dark outside.

Not even the moon could be seen from the narrow barred window high above his cell. His senses sharpened as the door creaked open slowly. A mop of sandy hair and a friendly face greeted him, and his heart leaped with relief. Pete stepped inside, closing the door quietly behind him.

"Friend," Ryker pulled the man into a friendly embrace as the pair met in the centre of the room.

"Appears, you've gotten yourself into a spot of trouble."

Ryker checked over Pete's shoulder towards the door. "How did you get in?"

A smirk travelled across Pete's face. "Knocked the guards out cold."

"With what?"

Pete chuckled, "Sleeping elixir in their grape juice. They'll be snoring for a good few hours."

Ryker clapped him on the back. "Didn't know you had it in you."

"I've always wanted to be a part of an escape expedition." The keys Pete held in his hand glinted as he rattled them. "We must hurry before the change of guards. I'd say we have about half an hour before someone raises the alarm. There is a back passageway we can sneak through undetected if we're careful," Pete murmured.

"I'm not leaving without Nova," Ryker replied.

"Let's get you free and then come back for her? You're in no shape to fight," Pete whispered.

The thought of leaving the castle without Nova twisted uncomfortably in Ryker's gut. It wasn't an option—he couldn't abandon her, no matter the wounds he'd already suffered. She needed to be freed from the cruel grip of her captor, and he was determined to be the one to do it. He would find her, even if it meant facing every danger this wretched place held.

"I can't Pete, I have to go to her."

"Alright, well, let's think about this for a minute." Pete scratched his head. "Perhaps in the kitchens, where we will be undisturbed."

Ryker followed Pete out of the cell and up the stairs to the first floor of the palace. "Does the kitchen have weapons?"

Pete glanced each way down the dimly lit hall before looking back at Ryker. "It doesn't, but we've got some knives."

Ryker and Pete moved silently through the labyrinthine corridors; their footsteps muffled by the thick stone floors. Pete led the way, his familiarity with the castle's hidden passages and servant's entrances guiding them through the maze.

At one point, Pete pulled him into a small doorway where they both froze, until a woman carrying a basket of laundry passed them, disappearing around the corner. With a silent sigh of relief, the men returned to their escape.

Finally, they reached a small wooden door at the end of the corridor. Pete eased it open, revealing a narrow staircase descending into the darkness below. "This leads to the kitchens."

Ryker followed Pete down the stairs, the air growing cooler and more humid as they descended. The flickering torchlight cast eerie shadows on the stone walls. They emerged in a low-ceilinged room, the faint smells of dinner still lingering in the musty air. A small brown mouse darted across the floor, and Ryker could hear muted voices from somewhere in the distance.

Pete closed the large wooden door behind them.

"We will be undisturbed here for a while. I dismissed the servants before I came to you."

"How late is it? I fear I haven't seen the sun in days." Ryker rubbed his face with his hands.

"It's late. Most of the palace will be sleeping."

Ryker placed his palms flat against the wooden kitchen table and closed his eyes, taking a moment to breathe and gather his thoughts.

The air was thick with the mouth-watering aromas of roasting meats, simmering stews, and fresh herbs hanging from the rafters. Ryker's stomach growled. It had been days since he'd had a decent meal, and the gnawing hunger was clouding his focus. Would he have time to eat?

Pete hurried over to the fireplace, which held a solid black iron pot. He held a bowl in his hand. He dished up a large helping of stew and brought it to Ryker. "Sit and eat this. It's leftovers from dinner."

"Do we have time?"

Pete threw a cautious glance towards the internal kitchen door. "There won't be a guard swap for a bit. I think we have time."

"Thank you, friend." Ryker gratefully sat at the table and tore into the stew.

It was so flavoursome that it almost made his jaw ache the moment the broth hit his tongue. Within moments, it was all gone. Instantaneously, Ryker felt better. "You sure know how to cook."

Pete flashed him a grin. "So, what's the plan?"

Ryker shook his head. "Do you know where Branoc keeps Nova?"

"On the second level in the north wing, but I don't know what room."

This made his search difficult, but not impossible. He'd knock down every door in the damn castle if he had to.

Ryker stood from the table. "Whatever I decide, I'm going to need weapons. How about those knives?"

The guards had taken his sword and any blades he'd carried. Who knew where they were now—and he certainly didn't have time to find out.

Pete rose from the table. "Let me see what I can find." He disappeared into a small storeroom adjacent to the kitchen.

Ryker heard him fumbling around before he returned and released the handful of knives he carried. The metal blades clattered onto the wooden surface.

"Will any of these do?"

Ryker stood and surveyed his options. There wasn't much to choose from. He picked up the large butcher's knife, its hefty weight solid in his grip. The blade gleamed under the light, sharp and reflective, with a well-worn handle that fit perfectly into his palm. It had the marks of use—scratches along its surface—but the edge was keen, ready for work or slicing—whichever came first.

"That's a brutal way to leave this world," Pete said, eyeing the blade Ryker held.

"Let's hope I don't need to use it." For safe measure, Ryker gathered two small paring knives and shoved them into his boots for safe keeping. He'd gladly use them on anyone who got between him and Nova.

"So, second level, north wing?" Ryker asked as he pushed the butcher's blade into the leather belt around his waist.

"Or the throne room, but I doubt they'd be there at this time in the evening."

Ryker nodded, combing his hands through his inky waves. He would find Nova. He wasn't leaving without her—not until she was safe in his arms, away from the king's reach, and they were both free.

"I'll stay here in these kitchens and man the passageways. When you find her, bring her here and I can get you out. Just try not to bring a whole host of trouble with you, eh?" Pete murmured.

Ryker placed a solid hand on his friend's shoulder. "Thank you. I owe you more than a single whiskey . . . I owe you an entire bottle."

TWENTY-SIX

THE GOLDEN GOBLET

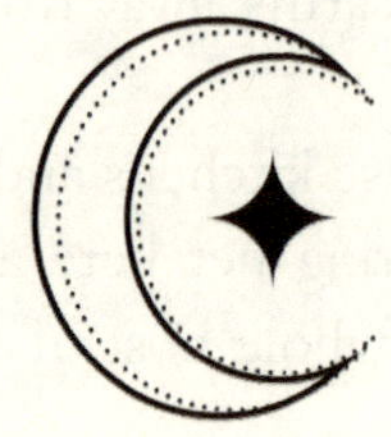

"Please miss, you need to eat," the maid serving Nova begged.

Nova took a few steps towards the balcony before glancing over her shoulder. "No. King Branoc will not have me now, nor ever."

"The king won't care; he will still harm you."

"He can try."

"Please miss . . ."

Nova shook her head at the woman's pleas.

The maid sighed, setting the tray down gently on the small table beside the bed, the dishes clinking softly. She gave Nova a brief, almost pitying glance, then turned and slipped out of the room, the door clicking quietly shut behind her.

How could she eat after seeing Ryker so bloodied and broken? The memory of his disfigured face flashed across her mind. Nova gripped the balcony edge and squeezed her eyes shut. Branoc was a wicked, wicked man. Surely there was something she could do. But what? Guards stood outside her door's day and night—keeping her trapped like a caged animal.

The only time she could leave her room was when Branoc summoned her. Even then, she wasn't free. She was practically dragged to his side and forced to replicate whatever jewels and treasures he so desired.

Nova knew all too well what punishment awaited her if she didn't.

A gentle breeze played with her hair as she collapsed to the ground. She drew her knees up and wrapped her arms around them, hugging them tight.

Ryker was here. Somewhere.

She wanted to run to him, yet Branoc had ordered his guards to never let her from their sight. Nova was surprised that there were no guards stationed on her balcony as well. It's not like she could climb down anyway—or could she?

Nova glanced between the marble railings. It was no use; the ground below was covered in a blanket of darkness. She'd likely break a leg trying to escape. Besides, she couldn't leave Ryker here—she wouldn't.

Pain ripped in her chest. This wasn't how it was supposed to be. She was going to declare her love to Ryker by the pool. She was going to tell him she couldn't possibly step into the water because she wanted to stay.

Tears rolled down her cheeks. Silent tracks of salted drops. She loved Ryker.

And she needed to tell him.

Her tears soon turned to anger.

How had the Twins found them? Had they been tracking them for a while? They'd laid in wait and struck so quickly Nova was bound before she could claw to Ryker's unconscious form.

Quite frankly, she was sick of all these men telling her what to do.

The journey down the mountain with the Twins hadn't been pleasant.

Finnian drugged Ryker with dreamroot and bound him with chains before throwing him into the back of the carriage. It was the last time she saw him until today in the throne room.

She'd wondered if she'd ever see him again at all. Her heart had fractured at the sight of his pain and exhaustion. Ryker had been brutally bashed all because she existed. She should have jumped into the pool of reflections when she had the chance. Then Ryker wouldn't be in the situation he was in right now.

A sob caught in her throat as she lay on the cold marbled floor of the balcony—crying out as her skin stung from the cold stone.

Dante and Finnian had ruined everything. Branoc had ruined everything.

As she wiped at her eyes, Nova wracked her brains, trying to think of some sort of plan. Ryker was trapped in the cells deep below the castle. Wasting away, waiting for the moment, Branoc decided his day of death. How could she get to him? What could she do? Multiple times she'd tried to summon her powers, but the moon had not been full enough for her to bask beneath it and no matter how much she tried, her powers would not do as she bade. Either the replication drained her more than she realised, or her heart was too heavy.

It was too much to bear. Nova lay on her back, staring at the murky skies above. Too many clouds were present, making it hard for her to see her sisters above.

"Tell me what to do," she whispered.

Tiny diamonds peeked through the grey, glittering in response, but it was no use. There was nothing they could do for her.

Another tear slipped down Nova's cold cheek, and she wiped it with the back of her hand. Surely there was something she could do to fix this.

A low creak filled the room as the door swung open. Nova quickly sat up, brushing her tears away. She refused to let anyone catch her crying. She had to stay strong for as long as she could.

For herself . . . for Ryker.

The maid from earlier stepped out onto the balcony. "The king wants you."

"Now? At this time of night?"

The maid nodded. "He's in one of his moods . . . I'm so sorry."

Nova dropped her head back and closed her eyes. What could Branoc possibly want? He never called for her in the evenings.

She sighed and stood to her feet. "Take me to him then."

Nova's footsteps echoed softly against the cold stone floor. Two stern-faced guards flanked her down the dimly lit castle halls. She kept her head down, her heart pounding in her chest, each step drawing her closer to the king's throne room, a place she desperately didn't want to go.

The torches lining the walls flickered, casting long shadows that seemed to dance with her growing dread. Nova tightly clasped her hands in front of her, fidgeting with the edge of her ridiculous dress.

She hated the way Branoc demanded she dress. Another reason to poke his eyeballs out.

Her stomach sunk to the floor as they approached the towering doors that led to the most hated man in Nova's life. She swallowed hard, forcing her legs to move forward even though everything in her screamed to run the other way.

No one was coming to save her—not this time.

Branoc was lounging on his throne when she entered the room. The air stunk of wine—he'd been drinking. Not a good sign. Nova knew she shouldn't test his patience, but seeing his sneering face and cold hazel eyes flicked a switch inside of her.

She ground her teeth together as she stalked towards him, her boots echoing on the stone floor. "What do you want?"

Branoc's brow rose. His fingers danced on the edge of his golden goblet that sat on the armrest of his royal chair. "That's no way to speak to your future husband."

Nova stopped in front of the dais; her fists clenched at her sides. "I will never marry you."

His brittle laugh sounded through the room. But as quickly as it erupted—he silenced it. His fingers gripped the stem of the gold cup. It was bigger than the ones she'd seen before. Glittering garnets, sapphires, emeralds and diamonds wrapped around the side in an ornate pattern. Red liquid sloshed over the lip as he stood. He took four steps towards her, gulping down the last of his drink before meeting her eye.

"You will do as you're told—whether or not you like it."

Heat washed over Nova's body. The sad fact was his words were true. She knew he would do whatever it took to lock her away from the world—to own her—no matter how much she denied him.

Branoc took another step, his nose inches from hers. "Now, I want more of these." He held the golden goblet up. "One for every seat at my table . . . Be a good star and make me some."

The king sauntered back to his throne and placed the cup down. "I'm waiting?" Branoc turned and held out the goblet. With an internal sigh, she closed her eyes and reached for the glittering cup. She knew the very little magic in her veins would only wield a handful of gems—how would she summon gold cups? All she could do was try. Hopefully, a few would be enough for one night and she could return to her room in haste.

The goblet was heavy in her hand, the weight of it a reminder of the pain and guilt she felt for Ryker rotting away in the prison cells. "Free Ryker and I will make all the treasure you desire."

Branoc's brittle laugh sounded through the room again. "My advice to you, star, is that you forget about his existence. He's as good as dead to you." Branoc's eyes bore into hers. "Now, make me rich."

Nova hung her head. She didn't have the energy to fight him. She would try her best to make the replicas. Return to her room. Formulate some sort of plan to free Ryker. Perhaps she could bribe the maid to help her. Nova could replicate some of the jewellery from the sparse collection the king had given her to make the costume she wore look more like a queen.

A faint thrum of energy built in her hand. Nova willed it into being as hard as she could, but the flutter of magic refused to produce any more than three new cups.

She faltered with the armful of gleaming metal. "Here, take these. This is all I can do."

Branoc snatched them from her hand. "It's not enough— make me more."

Nova fisted her hands by her side. "I cannot make any more magic. My body has been depleted of all my magic." The days of being abused leaking out through her words.

The king's rough grip found Nova's face. He held it inches away from his own. The scent of soured grapes watered her eyes and terror coursed through her veins as his fingers dug cruelly into her jaw.

Her heart raced, pounding in her ears, while her breath hitched in her throat. She could taste the metallic hint of blood where her skin had been crushed against the sharp edge of her teeth. She felt helpless, but fought to keep herself from trembling under his crushing hold.

"So, tell me, wife-to-be, how can you replenish what you have lost?" Branoc sneered.

Nova gritted her teeth and refused to speak. She didn't want to give him any part of herself anymore. Not if he was going to take the one thing that brought her joy.

"TELL ME!" Branoc cried. Spittle sprayed across her face. The act rendered her stomach in knots. To have any parts of Branoc's bodily fluids on her face made her stomach revolt.

Tears welled in her eyes as he gripped her face harder. "I need . . . I need to bathe in the moonlight," Nova whispered.

Branoc's eyes narrowed as he scrutinised her face, trying to determine whether she was telling the truth. After a tense pause, he seemed to accept her answer, loosening his grip on her momentarily. But before she could catch her breath, he seized her wrist, yanking her roughly as he dragged her from the room.

"Where are you taking me?" Nova sobbed.

The king's grip was iron as he dragged Nova out to the balcony, her heels scraping uselessly against the stone floor. Panic surged through her as she clawed at his arm, but he was too strong.

Tears streamed down Nova's face. "Please, stop!"

Branoc held her fast with one hand. The other ripped at her clothes, tearing them to ribbons. Clouds parted and moonlight cast an eerie glow over the scene. Though the moonbeams were weak, as soon as they touched her aching skin, a faint thrum seeped its way through her veins.

"Someone help me!" she shrieked, her eyes darting to the guards standing motionless nearby. They did nothing—no flicker of sympathy, no move to intervene. They stood there, indifferent, as if this was nothing unusual.

Nova wanted to fight, to run, but Branoc's strength was overwhelming. Desperation filled her chest, a hollow ache that spread through her entire body. Her breath came in ragged gasps as she tried to push him away, her strength waning. Each tear of fabric in her gown revealed a new crack in her heart.

Branoc finally freed the bodice of her gown by yanking it from her arms and letting it fall around her waist. Nova sobbed, her body shaking with fear and humiliation, her mind screaming louder than her voice.

He shoved her to the ground where she met the harsh cold marble, her palms splatting against the smooth surface. Branoc stooped down so his face was near hers. "Here is your moon, star. Let's hope your magic grows faster than my fury."

Nova dropped her forehead to the ground, trying to hide her face and chest from the eyes of the surrounding witnesses. What would her sisters say if they saw her now? They'd cry with her.

They'd tell her to get up and to fight back.

Could she do it? Could she keep fighting?

Her body hummed with energy as the moonbeams soaked into her skin. Every echo of Branoc's boot against the marbled floor as he paced back and forth gave her the strength to get back up. She had to. This would not be the life she'd live in this part of the world.

She refused.

The king stopped his pacing. He crouched down before roughly lifting Nova's chin in his broad hand. He forced her to meet his gaze. Cold, hard hazel eyes. Ones filled with so much greed, Nova didn't know how a human could live like this.

"Is that enough time under the moon?" His voice dripped with venom.

What was that word that Ryker liked to mutter sometimes? Often, he aimed it at people he didn't like. Branoc was certainly someone Nova didn't like.

"Fuck you, Branoc."

The glint in the king's eyes changed from greedy to livid. Nova knew she should have kept her mouth shut. But she was tired of being quiet. She was tired of being treated like she was nothing. Because she wasn't nothing. She was a celestial being from another realm. It was time to show the world what she was truly capable of.

A sharp sting spread across her face as the back of Branoc's hand met her cheek. Her head snapped sideways, pain blossoming through her head like wildfire.

Before she could gather herself, the king yanked her up by her arm, placing her on her feet. "Keep talking to me like that and there will be plenty more of where that came from."

Tears turned to determination as he marched her back into the room and shoved her against the throne. Nova caught the edge of it just before she fell. She turned to face him with fire in her veins.

Branoc swiped at the large glittering cup on the seat of his royal chair and held it out to her. "Put your dress back on properly and make it rain gold." His voice was low and commanding.

Nova slowly placed her arms back into her dress, never taking her eyes off the king. She calculated her next move. Tonight, she would be free of this wretched man. Branoc would no longer hold any power over her. She would see to it herself.

The sound of clashing metal and shouting erupted from the other side of the room, startling Branoc. The door flew open, splintering under the force of Ryker's boot as he stormed inside, sword drawn. Two guards rushed him instantly, and the room erupted into chaos.

Relief at the sight of him rushed over Nova. He was here in the room. Not down in the prisons. He'd escaped.

He was alive.

Nova held her breath as both she and Branoc froze, watching the scene unfold around them.

Ryker fought fiercely, blocking blows and cutting down one guard, but another stabbed him in the shoulder.

"Ryker!" Nova cried as she lurched forward, her legs kicking into action.

Branoc, enraged, screamed orders to his men. "If he leaves this room alive, I'll have your heads!"

A sharp grunt of pain escaped Ryker, but he didn't falter, slamming the guard back with his free arm.

Branoc spun to face Nova and reached for her. She dodged his grasp, but his fingertips brushed her skirts as she spirited away. A sharp yank on the fabric caused her to stumble forward towards the throne.

Her eye caught one of the empty golden goblets she'd produced earlier. Nova reached for it with a surge of energy. She whirled to face the enraged king. Rage filled his face. Eyes bulged, veins erupting from his temples, wrapping around like strangler vines choking the life from a tree.

Nova held the gold cup out in front of her, aimed at the king. "STOP!" she cried.

The king halted in his steps, a wicked gleam in his eye. "You will not escape me again, star. You will do as I wish."

"I would rather die." Nova's hand trembled, but her voice was unwavering.

The corners of Branoc's mouth turned up in an evil smirk. "I need you alive, but breaking legs never killed anybody."

Nova flicked her gaze towards Ryker as he fought multiple guards, his strength never ending despite the blood seeping from the wound in his shoulder. Metal against metal rang through the room as battle went on around her. Nova brought her gaze back to the King.

"You said you wanted it to rain?"

She held the golden cup higher. Branoc watched with monstrous eyes.

Nova's thrum of energy pulsed more intensely, enveloping her in a glowing cloud of ethereal viridian light. Her hair lifted, caught in the electric charge, and the very air around her vibrated with power. Fear left her, replaced by something raw and unyielding that awakened deep within her.

Branoc faltered, momentarily stunned by the shift in the room's energy, his hand frozen mid-reach. The smirk he'd worn moments before faded into uncertainty.

No more would he harm her. Nova's fists clenched, and the surrounding energy flared brighter, crackling with her determination. No more would they treat her like one of those marionettes from the marketplace, dangling at someone else's command.

Her gaze locked onto Branoc's, and for the first time, he looked afraid.

Nova lifted her other hand. "Well, I hope you drown."

She released the pent-up power coursing through her body. Golden goblets spilled from the magic in her hands, flying through the air and hitting Branoc in the face.

The room echoed with their metallic thuds as they piled up around the king, whose arrogant grin quickly twisted into a grimace of panic.

"You—stop this!" he yelled, his voice breaking as the pile grew higher. His arms flailed, trying to push the goblets away, but Nova wouldn't stop. She couldn't stop. Branoc cried out in anguish as the pile at his feet grew higher and higher. Rendering him helpless in movement.

Every slap across her face. Every hurtful word he spoke. Every time he forced her to use her magic. Each moment fuelled the fire erupting in her chest. Nova let out a guttural cry, her vision blurring at the edges as her magic strained against the limits of her strength. Each new goblet took more energy to replicate, and she could feel her power flickering, threatening to vanish completely.

Sweat trickled down her brow as the king became harder and harder to see. Branoc would learn his lesson.

"Never again," Nova whispered, pushing herself even harder. Her knees threatened to buckle, her head spun, but she couldn't give up. Not now.

She could hear Ryker still fighting guards and the thought of him losing blood gave her more determination. He would not die today. She would get them out of here and she would heal him.

The golden pile finally overtook Branoc, covering him up to his shoulders, then his chest, until only his arm remained, sticking out from beneath the crushing weight. His fingers twitched, grasping weakly at the air. The pile was massive, gleaming under the moonlight spilling into the room.

Nova swayed on her feet, her vision swimming as the world tilted. She could barely stay upright, her magic nearly gone, but she saw the arm twitch one last time before falling still.

King Branoc, buried beneath his own greed.

TWENTY-SEVEN

THE HARSH REALITY

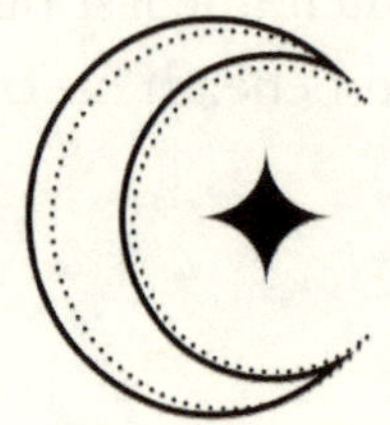

The last guard went down with a knife handle to the back of the head. The room spun as Ryker twisted, searching for Nova. He spotted her, unsteady on her feet and stumbling. His mind raced, urging his legs to move faster, and just in time, he reached for her as she sank to her knees.

"I've got you, little star," Ryker whispered against her head.

Everything around him melted away until all he could see was her. This was all that mattered. They were alive. Once they were free of Emberfell, he would let the barricade of emotions open that threatened to spill as soon as sea-green eyes met his russet ones. All the pain, the exhaustion, the tears—they would have their moment. However, he still needed to get them free of the castle.

A golden goblet slipped from the pile beside the dais and clattered to the marble floor, the sound echoing through the hall. Ryker was speechless.

Nova had done it. She'd buried the king . . . she'd saved them both.

"Ryker," Nova whispered.

"I'm here."

He held her tight, pulling her to her feet. What followed was a blur. Multitudes of guards lay sprawled on the ground. Some were still as death itself, some still writhing in pain. Ryker held her upright as they moved through the sea of bodies and left the throne room behind.

It was almost over.

Ryker's grip was firm. Holding on tight as the world swayed. He refused to let her go, even for one moment.

A figure loomed down the hall. "This way," Pete called to them.

Ryker stopped and placed his arm under Nova's knees, lifting her so she was cradled against his chest. He'd be able to move faster if he carried her—besides, she had no energy left of her own. Not after the ordeal with the goblets. Branoc never stood a chance.

He could feel her heart racing as she lay against his body. It was music in his ears. Her beating heart—alive and pulsing.

"Back through here," Pete whispered as they wound their way through a maze of corridors.

They reached the dark stairwell to the kitchen and headed down. Once they were inside, Pete closed the door behind them. A few soft whimpers escaped Nova's lips—she was fading. Ryker knew the urgency of replenishing her magic. He needed to get her out of the castle and under the moonlight.

Cool night air greeted them as the back door to the kitchen opened and they stepped out into the night.

"We need to head to the stables," Pete whispered. "I know Charlie is there. I saw him earlier today."

Ryker nodded, his eyes scanning the shadows for any sign of movement. "Did he seem well?"

"Perfectly fine."

They moved swiftly, sticking to the walls and keeping to the darkest parts of the courtyard. Most of the kingdom was asleep—or in the shambles of the throne room. As they reached the stables, Ryker gently placed Nova down on her feet next to Pete.

"Will you be alright for a moment?"

She nodded. Ryker knew she had little strength left. He just needed her to hold on for a few more moments.

Pete drew an arm around Nova's shoulder, supporting her as Ryker dropped to his knees. He searched the ground for something to jimmy the padlock open with.

There wasn't much around. Ryker glanced up and his eyes settled on Nova, who had her hair pinned in a mass of loose waves atop her head. He rose swiftly, boots quiet against the ground as he approached her. "Care to spare a pin?" he murmured, his gaze flicking toward her hair.

Nova nodded, managing a faint smile. "Of course. Take what you need." She carefully reached up, sliding a pin from her hair and handing it to him, the simple motion leaving her a little more drained. Ryker gave her a gentle nod before turning back to the lock.

He worked the pin into the keyhole, picking steadily until he felt the lock give. As the door swung open, they all slipped quietly inside.

The horses stirred but remained calm as Ryker and Pete quickly located Charlie. He whinnied at the sight of them.

"Hush boy," Ryker whispered as she led the shiny black stallion from his stall.

Pete brought a saddle and bridle over, helping to tack Charlie up swiftly. When they were done, Ryker held Nova into the saddle before turning to Pete.

"How can I ever thank you, Pete?" Ryker murmured.

Pete flashed a grin and tipped his head towards Nova. "Get her out of here and live a full life . . . both of you."

Ryker dipped his head in thanks. Nova offered Pete a weak smile. It was all she could muster. "I owe you my life." Ryker murmured.

"Let's just get that bottle of whiskey when you're settled somewhere safe."

Ryker nodded and shook his friend's hand.

Pete gave him a boyish grin. It gave him a sense of relief, knowing that he wasn't entirely alone in this harsh world. He truly had happiness here. He had people in this part of the world who loved and stood by him. That alone might make what he'd come to terms with easier for him—and for her.

Charlie moved through the night like a creature born under the light of a full moon. It was almost as if he knew the urgency of the matter at hand by the way he surged forward into the moonlit forest. His brilliant black hide glistened with sweat as he raced along.

They'd been travelling for a few hours.

He was certain no one would come after them tonight. Not when most of the guards would be too busy digging Branoc free from his gold prison—or they'll be lollygagging, hoping if they move slowly enough, Emberfell will receive a new king.

Ryker inwardly huffed at his own thoughts. He would figure out a plan tomorrow. For now, they needed a bath and sleep. Hooves pounded the Earth in sync with the wild rhythm of Ryker's heart. The inn—where he knew they'd finally rest—was just around the bend. Soon, he would hold Nova properly. He'd cradle her in his arms and never let her go.

No more would he hide behind his wounds. No more would he take for granted the things that mattered to him. No more would he avoid seeing his family because the pain was too much.

No more would he push the woman who'd fallen into his life away.

It was time to come home.

Faint orange glowed in the distance, and Ryker grinned.

Nova's head bounced against his chest as they raced along. She'd passed out not long into their escape. All that power she'd used to bury Branoc seemed to almost have taken her life. She truly was the most incredible woman.

Ryker urged Charlie on.

Nova stirred as Ryker brought Charlie to a stop. "Where are we?" she murmured.

Ryker slid from Charlie's back before easing Nova down. "We are at an inn. We will be safe here for the night."

His arm wrapped around Nova's waist as he guided her up the steps, careful not to disturb her torn gown. It was barely covering her as it was. She leaned against him heavily, battling the exhaustion. He pushed open the door, the warmth of the firelight and the rich smell of stew meeting them as they stepped inside. He helped her over to the counter, where a stocky, full-bearded innkeeper greeted them. "Evenin'. Need a room, do ya?"

Ryker gave a curt nod. "Yes. And someone to stable our horse. He's outside."

"Aye, I'll have the boy take care of him." The innkeeper motioned to a stable hand, who darted out the door hurriedly.

Ryker slid a few coins across the counter. "A room for the night—preferably one with a good lock."

Just for peace of mind.

The innkeeper raised an eyebrow but said nothing, handing over a key with a knowing look. "Up the stairs, second on the left."

With a grateful nod, Ryker pocketed the key and turned to Nova. "Let's get you to bed. You need to rest."

The stairs creaked under their weight as they made their way to the room. Ryker couldn't wait to be behind the security of a closed door. His fingers fumbled for the key in his pocket, and a wave of relief washed over him when the door finally swung open.

She headed in and Ryker followed, closing the door behind them.

"Ryker . . ." Nova whispered.

The sound of her voice was all he needed to close the distance between them and cradle her face between his hands.

Bringing his head down, he captured her lips in a passionate and hungry embrace. All the pent-up feelings over the last few days came flooding out, and it showed in the way his mouth nipped and kissed hers.

Nova responded with equal passion, as she slipped her arms around his neck and weaved her fingers into his hair at the back of his head. Groaning softly, Ryker moved his hands to encircle her waist, pulling her closer. Although, it wasn't close enough. He wouldn't be satisfied until they were naked and breathless in a world where no one knew they existed. If that was even possible.

Ryker drew his head back so both of them could breathe. His eyes met Nova's sea-green ones as tears slipped down her ivory cheeks. Their longing made him reach for her again.

His kiss was tender but full of need. He ran the tip of his tongue along the seam of her mouth, and Nova sighed softly as she opened for him. She tasted like honey and smelt like lavender. Ryker cupped the back of her head and fisted his hand through her diamond stands, pulling her head back to kiss her soundly. She felt so small and fragile in his arms.

The passion between them softened into slow, deliberate kisses—each one lingering as if to savour the moment. Their hands roamed over each other's bodies with a delicate reverence, tracing the curves and lines as if committing them to memory.

Both so aware of the desire for one another.

Ryker pulled away and rested his forehead against hers. "I'm so sorry."

She tipped her head to look at him. "Sorry for what?" she whispered.

"I'm sorry our trip to the pool wasn't quite the reunion you expected."

Nova shook her head. "It's not your fault." She cupped his face gently. "None of this is your fault."

Ryker reached up a hand to wipe her damp cheeks. "Why do I feel like I've failed you?"

"You haven't. The world has . . . but not you, Ryker."

He pulled her into a tight embrace, never wanting to let go. "I just want to forget it all."

Nova pushed against his chest softly. "Let's talk about this later. I don't want to think about anything but this very moment," she motioned to the washroom. "Care to join me?"

The bathwater was warm, steam rising in gentle curls around them as Ryker lowered himself into the tub behind Nova. She leaned against his chest, the heat from the water soaking into his skin, soothing muscles still sore from—everything. His arms wrapped around her waist, drawing her closer until her back rested fully against him.

Golden flickering flames from a few candles that sat on a wooden stool beside the bath gave the room its only light. Despite the danger that might await them in the future, Ryker felt a sense of peace. Nova was safe, he was alive. Together, they would decide what their future looked like, but first it was time to heal some wounds—physically and emotionally.

Ryker reached for the cloth that lay draped over the edge of the bath. He submerged it under the steaming water before gently rubbing it up and down Nova's arm. His fingertips brushed over her wet, mottled skin, trailing lightly across her flesh. Brown, purple and grey. Spots where fingers had grasped too tightly. Fingers that deserved severing. Fingers from hands that would never touch her again.

"How are you feeling?" he asked softly.

Nova tilted her head to the side, her damp hair sticking to her neck. "Better . . . thanks to you," she murmured, a smile tugging at her lips.

Ryker leant down and kissed her shoulder, his lips warm against her skin. "You were incredible back there at the castle."

Nova huffed, the sound equal parts relief and amusement. "I thought I was going to die."

Ryker tilted her face so he could see her. "I wouldn't have let you," he said, brushing her lips in a feather-light kiss.

Nova smiled at him, yet her eyes held a hint of sadness. Like she knew something he didn't, and she was too afraid to let the letters form into words, lest they tumble off her tongue. An unspoken truth that Ryker already knew. He just didn't want to admit it yet.

He brushed her cheek with the damp cloth. "What pains you so much?"

Tears gathered in the outer corners of her sea-green eyes. "I thought I was going to lose you."

Ryker dropped the cloth into the water, wrapping his arms around her waist, pulling her closer. "It's going to require more than that to take me down."

Nova nestled against his back, bringing a fresh wave of sudsy lavender. She glanced to the side briefly. "How's your shoulder?"

"It's fine. I only caught the tip of the blade," Ryker murmured. "Thank you for healing it."

Water sloshed against the sides of the bath as Nova turned to face him, her legs now straddling his lap. His blood surged as her nakedness pressed into him, but she seemed focused. Ryker tucked a piece of Nova's hair behind her ear. "What are you doing, little star?"

She picked up the cloth from the warm soapy water and wiped Ryker's chest down. "It's my turn to wash you."

Concentration etched her face as she trailed warm, soapy water over his sun-kissed flesh. Her sea-green eyes were in the room, but the depths of them dwelt elsewhere—somewhere far away.

The drag of the cloth against his skin was intentional and slow. Nova took her time, tracing every scar, every indent of muscle. He melted like butter under her touch. Fire bubbling at the surface of his veins.

Ryker gripped her ivory thighs as she shifted forward to wash his face.

"Close your eyes," Nova whispered.

Ryker didn't want to miss a thing, but he did as she bade.

Her touch was as light as a dandelion seed floating in the air as she wiped away the worry from his forehead, his nose, his cheeks. One hand threaded through the waves at the back of his neck as the other took its time learning the plains of his face.

The sound of the cloth dropping into the bath water opened Ryker's eyes. Nova's mouth was inches from his. Her gaze flicked down to it before she met his eyes again. No words were needed. Ryker knew what hung between them because he could feel it too.

She wanted him as much as he wanted her.

"You can have it all, little star. Every part of me," he whispered.

Ryker heard the faint hitch in her breath before they met in the middle, their lips colliding, becoming one and the same.

There was nothing soft about the kiss. It was fervent and erotic. Nova met him stroke for stroke, wrapping her arms around his neck and shifting further onto his lap. Her damp hair draped around her body like the flowing tendrils of a mystical meteor shower, each strand shimmering with a delicate dusting of stardust, cascading in soft, luminous waves that glowed faintly in the dim light around them.

Her pink lips trailed over his face, leaving fire in their wake. She pressed her mouth to his eyelids, his nose before finding her way back to his mouth. Every velvet touch sent a pang of pleasure down to the hardened length trapped between their bodies.

Ryker's cock had awoken the moment she undressed and climbed into the bath. He hadn't presumed anything would happen, though it was all he could think about. But as her slick warmth slid against his length. All forms of restraint left his body. He hardened instantly, throbbing against her core.

"Fuck, Nova," he whispered against her mouth.

She smiled, a sigh escaping as she pulled him closer. "I want you inside me."

Ryker didn't need to be told twice. He reached between them, shifting his cock so the tip of it slid between her warm folds. Nova let out a moan as she sunk down onto his length. She was tight around him and Ryker had to steady his breath to slow his release.

She was a vision. A star encapsulated in human form.

He gripped her hips, dimpling her skin as she slowly rocked back and forth, creating ripples in the water. Ryker's gaze wandered over her glistening breasts. Each droplet reflected the candlelight, making them look like beads of liquid gold as they trailed down her skin. Her pink nipples, taunt against the cool of the air, begged to be sucked.

He leaned forward to lick her neck as she thrust her hips. Pleasure ripped through his stomach and blossomed into his chest as he nipped at the column of her ivory neck. Nova's head fell back, allowing him better access. He slowly made his way down to the star on her chest. Its blue glow pulsed faintly.

Ryker placed a single kiss on top of it.

The star grew brighter, and he smiled.

One of his hands left her waist and found one of her ample breasts. Ryker massaged it, grazing his thumb over her nipple. Nova whimpered and arched into him, so the floating strands of her hair dipped into the water surrounding them. Ryker moaned as he dragged his mouth over her breast. His tongue swirling, nipping, and tugging.

"By the stars, Ryker," Nova moaned.

He flicked his tongue over her nipple. "Take all of me. Mind, body and soul."

Nova dropped her gaze, her sea-green eyes heavy with pleasure. As she bit her bottom lip and rocked back and forth, she created a friction that Ryker was doomed to succumb to at any moment. He wanted to last longer, not only for his pleasure, but for hers, too. The viridian glow pulsing from her skin enveloped them, and as Ryker watched in awe, her bruises healed under waves of celestial essence. The scars of the past faded, leaving only untouched radiance in their place.

"It's even better the second time around," Nova whispered.

Ryker grinned. "Wait until we do it, one after the other."

Nova's eyes widened. "Is that even possible?"

"I'm willing to find out if you are?" Ryker murmured as he slipped his hand between them.

Nova cried out as his fingers brushed against her most sensitive part. Circling gently. She brought her arms around his neck, pulling their bodies together as her hips moved back and forth.

Ryker didn't know what he enjoyed more; the feeling of her slick walls clenching his cock as she rode him, or the way her soft breasts rubbed against his chest with every stroke. Both had him biting his bottom lip in restraint. His release was building and the way Nova gripped him told him hers was too. Her warmth wrapped around his cock like a pool of sunlight, bright and all-consuming.

"Are you ready to reach for the stars?" Nova whispered against his mouth.

"Take me there."

Nova caught his lips with hers, teasing and biting. His tongue found hers and together they created a symphony of music as their bodies moved together, their moans tangling together in the small washroom.

As he kissed her, Ryker used his hand to trace circles over Nova's clit. She whimpered before tearing her lips from his. A cry escaped her lips, her fingers digging into the hair at the back of his neck. She dropped her head back as she rode the waves of pleasure pulsing through her.

Seeing her come undone was his undoing.

"By the stars." He couldn't hold back any longer and his release soon followed. Ryker let out a moan as his stomach muscles clenched over and over, spilling into her. Warmth spread over his body like a blanket. His limbs became limp with ecstasy as their heartbeats melted into one.

Ryker closed his eyes, gently resting his forehead on Nova's, their breaths mingling in the quiet of the night. The world around them seemed to dissolve, leaving only the sound of their heartbeats, the steady thrum of their shared exhaustion. They sat entwined, Nova's celestial viridian glow softly illuminating the surrounding space, casting shimmering reflections on the walls like a sanctuary made just for them.

Would this be their future?

For a moment, it felt as if time had stopped. He could stay like this forever—wrapped in her warmth, feeling the steady rise and fall of her chest, her presence so deeply comforting. It was everything Ryker had ever longed for, the peace, the sense of belonging. Her light wasn't just beautiful; it was healing, washing over him in a way that soothed the deep scars he carried within. In her arms, the weight of his past felt lighter, almost bearable.

But deep inside, in the corners of his mind where the truth always lurked, Ryker knew that this couldn't be their forever. His grip on her tightened slightly, a subconscious reaction to the ache in his chest. He couldn't protect her here—not fully, not forever. The dangers of this world would never leave them alone.

He opened his eyes slowly, looking down at her peaceful face, and his heart clenched. She was safe for now, in this fleeting moment, but he knew it wouldn't last. Not with the enemies who would never stop hunting them.

Nova smiled up at him, her lips slightly parted in bliss. How could he let her go? How could he live without her in this world? The idea of it sent a searing pain through his chest. Yet, he would bear the pain of losing her, though, if it meant she was never harmed again.

"What's on your mind, Hound?" Nova lifted a hand and brushed Ryker's hair from his brow.

He couldn't tell her his innermost thoughts. Not yet— tonight—but not yet. They would have this moment first. They would eat and then when she was laying in his arms under cotton sheets and woollen blankets, he would tell her everything.

"I'm thinking about how famished I am." Ryker smiled. "I've had my appetite for you satisfied—for a moment—but my stomach would love some food."

Nova flashed him a grin before placing a quick kiss to his lips. "Then let us eat."

Ryker had found the innkeeper at the bar downstairs. He requested some dinner, even though morning threatened to creep over the horizon at any moment. The innkeeper hadn't questioned and simply dished out a helping of steaming stew into bowls placed beside soft, wholemeal rolls.

Before he left, he'd inquired about some clothes for Nova, seeing as her gown was in tattered shreds. The burly innkeeper had checked his lost property box, returning with a simple grey gown, with a cream knitted shawl folded on top.

Ryker thanked him and headed back to the room.

He found Nova sitting on the bed, wrapped in a blanket.

"I found you some clothes."

Nova got up and moved across the room almost silently. "Thank you," she murmured as she took the clothes from the food tray where they were balanced. "Dinner smells wonderful."

Ryker placed the tray down on a small table in front of the crackling fireplace. "Let's hope it tastes good, too."

Nova flashed him a smile before she floated off to the washroom to change.

Ryker sat in one of the brown leather armchairs, angled towards the fire. He decided to wait for Nova before eating. She didn't take long. Soon enough, she reappeared, wrapped in the grey dress, the shawl pulled snugly around her shoulders as she swiftly crossed the room to join him.

She sunk down in the chair opposite him and together they ate, both relishing the flavour of the beef stew. Perfectly seasoned with spices, potatoes, and carrots.

Ryker flicked his gaze towards Nova. She was staring at the fire as she nibbled on her bread. The dress hung loosely on her frame, highlighting the dark circles under her eyes. But it would suffice for now. He'd find her something more fitting once they were back on the road.

"Where are you?"

Sea-green eyes met his. "What do you mean?"

Ryker placed his spoon back into the bowl so he could give her his full attention. "Your mind is not here in the room with me."

She was drifting again, her gaze unfocused, lost somewhere between here and a far-off place. Ryker could see it in her eyes—the turmoil, the quiet battle waging inside her. She was at war with herself, and all he could do was watch, powerless to pull her back from wherever her thoughts had taken her.

Nova's lip quivered. "I want to say something, but I can't form the words." Her voice came out in a whisper.

Ryker offered her a gentle smile. "Tell me . . . I can handle it."

"It's about Ara."

"You're going home, aren't you?"

It nearly killed him to say the words out loud, though his heart already knew what was on her mind. He'd seen it in her eyes when they'd escaped the castle, and he'd seen it when they found pleasure in each other's arms only moments ago.

A tear found its way down her cheek. "I don't want to. It brings me much heartache to even utter the words. But I can't ask you to put your life on the line every time we step outside."

"It's not asking if I give it willingly," Ryker murmured.

Nova shook her head, her white tresses shimmering under the light of the fire. "But it's so selfish of me, Ryker. My presence here on Earth puts you in so much danger."

Ryker traced the lines of her face. It wasn't his life he was concerned about. It was hers. He could endure whatever the world threw at them if she stayed here. He'd go to war for her. He'd fetch her the moon if she wished it so. Yet, despite the pain that gripped his chest. He wouldn't ask her to stay, because he knew she couldn't. She belonged in a world far greater than his.

"You never need to fear for my life, little star. I understand completely. Ara is your home, and you will be safe there. And that is all I have ever wished for you."

A sob caught in Nova's throat, her hand clasping her mouth as she fought back the surge of tears.

Ryker placed his bowl of food down and rose from the chair. He held his hand out towards her. "Come."

"Where are we going?" Nova sniffed.

"Dance with me," Ryker said quietly, a soft smile playing on his lips.

Nova blinked back tears as Ryker placed her hand in his, gently pulling her to her feet. There was no music, just the rhythm of their hearts and the muffled sounds of the night outside. Ryker's hands found her waist as Nova's arms wrapped around his neck, and they swayed together in a slow, easy motion.

"I thought you didn't dance," she whispered.

"I don't."

Sea-green eyes found him. "So why now?"

"Because I'd dance for you until my feet fell off and because you deserve to leave this place filled with joy . . . not sadness."

She offered him a smile before she rested her head against his chest, listening to the steady beat of his heart as they turned in small circles. He brushed his fingers against her back, pulling her just a little closer, and leaned down to whisper, "You are my joy, little star."

TWENTY-EIGHT

THE DREADED DECISION

The mouth of the cave was shrouded in darkness as Nova approached the entrance. Its dark maw was uninviting. She would be afraid had she not been here once before and knew what lay beyond the black, gaping mouth.

She hesitated, waiting for Ryker to hitch Charlie to a low-hanging branch of a cypress tree. The moon was full above her in the velvet night sky, as if it was already welcoming her home. In a few short moments, her time on Earth would come to an end. Life as she currently knew it would cease to exist.

Trees cloaked under the shadows of night stood tall and proud in the forest surrounding them. Nova took in a deep breath, the scent of nature intoxicating her senses. She'd never smell them again. Soil after rain. Fields of wildflowers. The salty air of the seaside. Farmlands laced with crops and animals.

Him—cypress and vanilla.

She glanced over at Ryker, her eyes lingering on him as he stood only a few feet away. His deep russet gaze rose to meet hers, and for a fleeting moment, the world shrunk around them.

Tears welled in her eyes. Nova didn't know the amount of times she'd cried on their journey from the inn, across the edges of Emberfell, through Pebble beach and up the Twin Peak mountain range.

She'd lost count.

But each time the salty droplets trailed down her cheeks, Ryker was there to catch them, his thumb brushing them away with a tenderness that soothed her pain. His embrace was steady, yet Nova could feel the tremor beneath it—an unspoken struggle as all the while he battled his own emotions. She could see it in his eyes, those vibrant brown orbs that had once held warmth and life. His gaze was distant, forlorn, and it broke her heart knowing that he was hurting just as much, if not more.

His heart had been shattered once before.

She knew it now, saw the cracks in the way he looked at her, as if she were both his salvation and the threat of his undoing. Could she do that to him? Could she be the one to break him all over again? The thought pierced through her chest, a sharp ache. She had come into his life, a star falling from the heavens, but stars didn't belong on Earth. They burned bright and disappear, leaving only darkness in their wake.

Ryker moved to her side and took her hand in his. "Are you ready?"

The inside of her cheek hurt where she bit it, fighting back the waves of emotion. Nova nodded, though her actions were a lie.

She wasn't ready—and probably never would be, but this was the right thing to do . . . for both of them.

She stepped into the cave with Ryker by her side, the familiar chill wrapping around them as they moved deeper into the darkness. The air was thick with the scent of damp stone, and the only sounds were the soft echoes of their footsteps on the uneven ground. Her heart felt heavy, each step an effort as the weight of what lay ahead pressed down on her chest.

She stole a glance at Ryker. His face was unreadable, but the tension in his jaw and the way his hands clenched at his sides told her everything. He was hurting, too. The silence between them was thick, not with anger or frustration, but with a shared sorrow neither of them could put into words.

Nova's fingers brushed the cold, rocky wall of the tunnel as they headed towards the pool of reflections. Last time she was here, she found pleasure with the man beside her. He'd shown her things with his hands, his body, his mouth that she'd only ever dreamt of feeling.

As they rounded the corner, her breath caught in her throat. She'd seen it once before, but seeing it again was still enchanting. The roof was scattered with millions of blue speckles that mimicked the galaxy above.

They came to the edge of the pool and stopped, their footsteps falling into a stillness that matched the quiet all around them. The water stretched before them like a sheet of glass, flawless and eerily perfect, reflecting the glittering ceiling. Not a single ripple disturbed the surface, as though time itself had stopped.

Nova turned to face Ryker as his gaze found hers. Their hands were still entwined, neither one ready to let go. "I don't think I can do this," Nova whispered.

He smiled softly, lifting a hand and cupping the side of her face. Nova leaned into its warmth, lingering for as long as she could. It wouldn't be long before she'd never feel his warmth again. She'd only have memories. She was afraid memories would never be enough.

Ryker brushed the single tear that stole its way down her cheek. "What can't you do?"

"Go home."

"Do you still want to?"

Nova buried her head in Ryker's chest, breathing him in. "No, but it's what I have to do."

Ryker placed a hand gently under her chin and lifted her face to meet his. Russet eyes—flecked with gold—held her. His gaze lingering as he mapped all of her features, committing her to memory. "If you stayed, I would protect you with my life," he whispered.

Nova shook her head lightly as fresh tears found their grave upon the hardened surface of the cave. "That's what I'm afraid of."

"I know. And I know you'll always be in danger here. That's what I'm afraid of."

It was true. Nova could see it in his eyes. He'd protect her and she would love him for it. There was no doubt in her mind. But she'd already asked so much of him, and she couldn't bear to see him hurt again—because of her.

She needed to go home.

Russet eyes met her sea-green ones again. "Promise me," she whispered. "Promise me you will look for me in the stars." A sob caught in her throat. "I will find you somehow."

Ryker cupped her face and brought his lips to hers in a whirlwind of passion. His mouth claimed her in ways that were only meant for him. Nova's arms instinctively wrapped around his neck, pulling him closer, as if being apart from him for even a second was too much to bear. His warmth enveloped her, grounding her in the moment, despite the tempest of emotions swirling inside her. His hands slid down to her waist, gripping her firmly but with a tenderness that made her melt into him.

They stood there at the edge of the pool, their bodies pressed together, the cool cavern air contrasting the heat between them. The soft, ethereal glow of the cave's blue and green hues bathed them in light, casting their reflections in the still water below.

Ryker gently broke the kiss, resting his forehead against hers. "I promise to always look for you. Whenever the moon shines, I will think of you and remember the light you brought into my life."

Sobs wracked Nova's body. The pain was unbearable. To never see his face again was pure agony. To never feel his skin or taste his mouth. To never make love to him again—all of it was agony.

Nova stepped from his embrace, her leather boots he'd bought her all that time ago sinking beneath the water's surface. The water babbled against her legs, triggering the glassy appearance to ripple out into rings.

She needed to go before she couldn't. Before her legs no longer moved and her feet cemented on the spot. Nova locked her eyes on Ryker. Just one more moment, so she didn't forget.

Ryker grasped her hand, stalling her, his eyes saying a thousand words. "Nova…" His voice was hoarse with emotion.

This must be what it feels like to love.

A gentle smile spread across her lips. All she had ever wanted was to love and be loved in return. To share her heart with someone, to weave her soul into another's. And she had done that. She had lived her wish—with Ryker.

Gone was the cold-eyed, gruff stranger. Here was warmth, safety, and a heart laid bare for the taking. She couldn't ask him to give away the last of him. It was cruel, but selfishly she wanted to take that warm, beating heart in her hands and place it in her chest, right next to hers.

Nova cupped the side of Ryker's face. "I love you," she whispered.

Ryker's brow knitted. "You love me?" A tear ran down the face of her kind, brave hunter.

Nova brushed it with her thumb. "I do."

Ryker's hand found the back of her neck as he pulled her in for a tender kiss. One that she would carry with her for eternity in a locket around her heart.

He pulled back, his eyes searching hers. "I think I've known this for a while, but I was a coward and didn't say it sooner." Tears gathered in his eyes. "I love you, Nova. And I'm so sorry it's taken until this moment for me to say it."

Nova beamed at him. He loved her. Ryker loved her.

His words sank into her heart, nestling between its human folds. She'd wanted to find a great love here in this part of the world, and she had. Ryker was her great love and hearing that he loved her was all she needed. She could go home now. Before the goodbye became even more unbearable——if that was even possible.

With one last kiss to his lips, Nova stepped back. Further into the pool. She took one last look into the russet eyes that would forever be etched into her memory and bravely smiled at Ryker. "Thank you for loving me," she whispered.

The water swirled around her knees, then her thighs. She stood in the middle of the water, beneath the cluster of star specks on the cave ceiling.

Nova's gaze locked onto Ryker's. "Go live your life. Promise me you'll find happiness . . . I'll be watching over you."

Ryker nodded, tears brimming in his eyes. "Don't forget me."

Tears from Nova's cheeks mingled with the water surrounding her. "I couldn't if I tried Ryker Thornbrooke."

He ran his hands through his inky waves, pain etched across his face.

"Veliar silea mynaris." Nova whispered.

The viridian hues seemed to pulse with each breath she took, growing brighter, as if calling her home. She could feel it, the pull from Ara, the celestial realm beckoning her.

"I'll always love you," she whispered, her voice barely audible over the soft hum of the cave.

The glow around Nova intensified, her skin shimmering like the stars she had come from. Slowly, she began to dissolve into the air; her form becoming ethereal, turning into light.

The warmth of her body faded as she became less tangible, the edges of her silhouette blending into the air like mist.

Ryker took a step forward into the water. "I will always love you, my little star," he cried out.

Nova reached for him as her body became nothing but glittering particles.

The last thing her fading vision captured was Ryker collapsing to his knees by the edge of the pool, tears carving paths down his sun-kissed face. His eyes, filled with sorrow, locked onto hers as he reached out, desperate to hold on to something that was already gone.

Then everything went dark.

TWENTY-NINE

THE 1ST MONTH

The porch groaned softly beneath Ryker's weight as he stepped outside. The sun had already dipped below the horizon, and fireflies flickered through the distant meadows, casting tiny sparks of gold. A gentle breeze swept through, stirring his curls and brushing against his skin.

Ryker looked up to the heavens where his eyes met a sea of glittering stars. "I hope you're happy back in Ara."

There was no way to tell which star might be Nova, but if there was even the slightest chance she could see him standing on the porch, searching the sky for her, he'd come out here and talk to her every night.

"I hope you're safe," he murmured.

The toe of his worn boot scuffed at the wooden deck. "I hope you haven't forgotten me already." Ryker managed a smile. "Although I wouldn't blame you if you had. You've probably got more important things to worry about up there."

He leaned his forearms against the porch railing, swirling the rusty tinted rum in his cup. The breeze continued to play with his hair. "I couldn't bear to live near Branoc's castle, so I moved." Ryker took a sip. "You'd like it here, little star. It's far from the noise and clutter of the city, but close enough that you don't feel isolated."

He'd bought the quaint little cottage in Sunriver, to be further from Emberfell and closer to his family. It felt like the right thing to do after Nova left. He'd been gone from his loved ones too long. He knew that now.

Ryker sipped his rum again. "I think I'll finish the canoe I've been working on."

He'd paid a handsome price to have it shipped from the old house to his new one. At first, he'd considered leaving it behind, but the idea of having a mind full of pain and empty hands had him paying the cost and not thinking about it again.

He was glad he'd done it. It was the perfect distraction.

Anything to keep from dwelling on the absence of her.

The galaxies glittered across the expanse of the black velvet sky. Ryker offered a smile; it was all his heart could muster.

Ryker finished his drink as his eyes drifted to the skies. "Goodnight, little star."

THIRTY

"I finished the canoe. It's been great for fishing on the lake behind the house." Ryker kicked a pebble into the grass.

Sometimes he wandered the fields at night, trying to find some source of comfort from the ache in his heart. The only thing that eased the pain, even if just slightly, was a glass of rum. He tried not to rely on it, but tonight was one of those nights he needed to drink and wander.

"The weather has been warm, so I go out on the lake early, before the sun. Feel free to let her know we don't need it any hotter." Ryker smirked at himself.

The pebble skittered away from his boot once again. "Oh, I planted some sunflowers for you. I think you'd like them."

Planting a field of sunflowers large enough she might be able to see them from the stars had cost him blood, sweat and tears. But it was worth it. The day he walked out of his house to find them blooming, their faces towards the sun, had brought him so much joy.

Just like she had.

He sipped his drink. "Branoc made a statement about you. Of course, the whole thing was a lie." His knuckles turned white as he gripped the glass. "He said that you'd impersonated a star and that he'd banished you from the kingdom when you tried to steal all his gold. Couldn't have been further from the truth, but at least now people might forget. Find other treasures to chase."

The sunflowers swayed on a warm breeze. "Not that I can forget about you . . . You consume my thoughts day and night." Ryker dragged his free hand through his growing curls, closing his eyes against the memories. "If I could do it all over again, I would . . . just to see you one more time."

Ryker stood in the knee-deep grass, staring up at the starry velvet sky. "I'm glad you're safe now . . . Goodnight, little star."

THIRTY-ONE

The usual clear sky was covered in a thin layer of silver cloud. Not a star could be seen. Even the moon had gone into hiding.

Ryker dropped to his knees in the middle of the sunflower field, fighting the sob in his throat. "Today, it's too much to bear. My heart aches for you," he whispered to the nothingness.

Why did he keep torturing himself like this? Nova couldn't hear him. She probably couldn't see him either. But talking to her somehow made the pain more bearable.

What he'd give for one more night. One more kiss.

She was safer in Ara. No one could harm her there.

Yet he dreamed she would return to Earth, and he'd spend the rest of his days protecting her and loving her until he was grey and old. Every sunrise would remind him of the warmth of her smile, and every sunset would be a promise of the memories they would create together. He envisioned lazy afternoons spent in each other's embrace, sharing whispered secrets beneath the stars, and laughter echoing in the quiet moments. "If ever you decide to come back to me . . . I'll be right here waiting for you."

Ryker's hands dropped to his sides, his knuckles grazing the burnt sienna soil. "Goodnight, little star."

THIRTY-TWO

"My sister is pregnant." The wooden rocking chair creaked under Ryker's weight as he rocked back and forth. "I'm going to be an uncle."

His eyes roamed the field to the left of the porch. "And the sunflowers have finished. The cold autumn winds are bringing the winter to my doorstep. I wonder if the lake will freeze over this year."

Rust tinted rum swirled in his glass. The liquid that left a burning trail down his throat warmed his stomach, but he still wore a coat. "How are Soliel and Tierra? I bet they're happy to have you home."

Ryker knew he should go and visit his friends, Chester and Pippa. Probably Pete too. He was the one who saved Ryker's life after all. He'd found Pete a well-paying chef's position at an inn located in Sunriver. Close to his folks' place. It was the least he could do.

"Did you tell your sisters about how you nearly stole a peach from the fruit stall that one time?" Ryker chuckled. "I'll never forget the look on your face when that boy asked you to pay for it."

The rocking chair creaked again. Ryker flicked his gaze to the matching chair on his right. "Do you think of me?"

Calloused fingertips, worn down from hard work, brushed against the oak armrest. After Ryker had finished his canoe, he'd set about making matching rocking chairs to sit on his front porch. One was worn already—the other had yet to be sat in. "There's not a day that passes by that I don't think of you," he whispered.

Ryker finished his rum and rose from his chair, pausing at the steps that led to the gardens. His russet eyes took to the sky. "I miss you . . . Goodnight, little star."

THIRTY-THREE

There was no rum tonight. Just a man in a field laying on his back as he stared at the black velvet sky. Tears streaked his face. "I thought I could move on, Nova . . . I'm trying to let you go. But it's been twelve months of living with a star-shaped hole inside my chest. What I'd give to see your sea-green eyes filling with wonder as you experience life for the first time. Or to taste your lips as we make love under the blankets of our bed."

Ryker smiled at the vision of Nova twisted in his sheets. Her hair a tangled mess of diamond strands. Cheeks flushed from the pleasure they'd shared. The scent of jasmine floating in the air. "Sometimes I think I hear your laugh, but when I turn around, the wind carries it away."

A star streaked across the velvet blanket above him. The sight of it stabbed him in the chest. It wasn't his star, but the memory of seeing her fall to Earth was still so vivid in his mind.

The wind rushed through the long grass. Blowing the fireflies higher above him. "I don't know how to live without you," he whispered.

But he had to. Whether he liked it or not. Nova had asked him to live his life, and he said that he would—he didn't promise that it wouldn't be easy.

Ryker got up, wiping his eyes with the sleeve of his shirt. He looked at the sky one more time with his hands on his hips. "I hope you know that I try to find you every night. I hope you're happy . . . I hope you feel loved."

He turned and headed home with a whisper on his lips. "Goodnight, little star.

THIRTY-FOUR

THE STAR COMES HOME

The soft glow of the oil lamp flickered by the front door, casting a faint, warm light over the small porch. Though it was too dim to make out details, Nova could see the figure of a man sitting in a rocking chair, slowly swaying back and forth.

A warm breeze played with her hair as it danced through the fields, collecting seeds and brushwood as it frolicked through the grass. Nova closed her eyes and drew in a long breath. As she released it, she opened her eyes, letting them wander over the world around her. It felt so good to smell the scent of Earth. Everything seemed so much richer the second time around. And though it was evening, she could still feel the end of the day's warmth. She'd missed the kiss of heat upon her skin, and she couldn't wait to have the sun's gaze forever on her moon-bathed flesh.

Crickets sang beneath her feet, their rhythmic chirps filling the air. Owls called out with their haunting cries, perched silently on branches at the forest's edge. The trees she had come to know swayed gently around her, their dark silhouettes blending together like charcoal strokes on a canvas.

Her gaze returned to the man in the chair. A familiar tingle coursed through the red blood in her veins and as the warmth seeped through her body, her skin came alive. She glowed, the azure blue light gleaming from her as she stood on the grassy knoll, her heart racing a million miles an hour.

Ryker—her love.

He stood from the chair and slowly made his way to the top step.

Nova stayed still, wanting to savour this single moment. For five celestial years, she'd watched over him, wishing she could be the one sitting at his side. She soaked in every sound, every scent, and every sight. This was the last time she'd experience seeing him for the first time again. Once she was in his arms, she was never leaving.

Ryker started down the steps torturously slowly, his gaze fixed in her direction. Every deliberate step he took towards her only made her glow brighter.

All the emotions bubbled to the surface, tightening her chest and causing her breath to hitch. She never thought this day would come, but it was here, and it was real, just like the grass that brushed against the skirts of her silver embellished gown. Real like the frogs she could hear down by the banks of the lake. Real like the man walking towards her.

The need to feel Ryker in her arms propelled her forward. She wanted to bury her face in his chest and breathe in all his essence. Her feet carried her willingly towards the Hound, and with every step she took, her celestial glow brightened.

A sob caught in her throat as Ryker ran. Seeing him race for her was all the permission Nova needed to do the same. She picked up her skirts and dashed forwards. The wind caught her hair, sending it around her in a whirlwind of swirling white strands. Each one glowing just for him. Tears spilled down her cheeks and mingled with the smile that had plastered across her face. Who knew one could cry and be happy at the same time?

Cypress and vanilla drenched her senses as Ryker's arms crushed her body against his chest. The world around her faded as she melted into his embrace. The sounds of the distant owl dissolved. No longer could she hear the crickets. Even the frogs were silent.

"Ryker," she sobbed as clutched her arms around his neck.

"Hello, my little star."

His voice was soft but laden with emotion as they sank to the emerald grass below. Their bodies mingling together to become a cocoon of shared tears and joy. Azure blue wrapped around them, sealing them from the world, creating a place where only she and her hunter existed.

After some tears had subsided, Nova gently pulled from his embrace. She brushed a tear from his face with her glowing hand and smiled. "Hello."

Russet eyes met her. "How . . . how are you here?"

"I could not bear to be from your side for one more moment. My sisters sent me back."

Ryker cupped her face. "But how? Have you been flying through the heavens all this time?"

Nova shook her head, her gleaming white hair brushing her shoulders. "No, I came through a portal from Ara straight to Earth."

"Does this mean no one knows you're here?"

"No one knows."

Ryker's brow pinched. "So . . . we're safe?"

"As long as I can keep my glow under control—we are safe."

Strong arms encased her once again. Nova breathed in Ryker's scent. She'd missed it. Woody aromas of cypress leaves mixed with the sweet smell of vanilla. She'd recognise it anywhere.

"I can't believe you're really here," Ryker whispered against the side of her head.

"I'm really here."

Nova sat in his embrace for a while, simply soaking him in. Not once did his arms ease their hold. She smiled against his chest. She didn't want him to let go.

He pulled back, tucking her hair from her face before his warm gaze found hers again. He glanced down at her lips. She wanted that, too. Nova had dreamed of this moment.

He pulled her face closer, his nose almost touching hers. The world melted away once again as Ryker's lips found hers in a tender kiss. He tasted just as she remembered. Warmth and rum. His tongue danced with hers and fingers became entwined in hair as they locked their bodies together.

Nova sighed contently as the kiss deepened. There was no place she would rather be. She belonged in this world with him, under the blanket of black velvet skies, while the moon shone down upon them.

The kiss didn't need to be full of passion. It was sweet, and it was true. Every movement of his lips on hers cemented the love Ryker felt for her. She knew how he felt by the way his fingers dug into the back of her neck, cradling her head with such a gentle caress. He held her as if she might suddenly shatter or worser yet—disappear.

Nova gripped him tighter, reassuring him she wasn't going anywhere. She was here to stay.

Their kiss broke, leaving her breathless and flushed.

Ryker reached out to smooth her unruly hair gently, then helped her to her feet. His hands enveloped hers as she stood facing him, her eyes lifting to meet his warm russet gaze. He smiled down at her. "I have so many questions."

"And I shall answer them all. Tell me what you wish to know?" Nova murmured.

He cupped her face. "Why did you come back here? I thought we agreed it wasn't safe."

"This had been my perception, too, until the portal. And I tried Ryker. I truly tried to be happy in Ara. But everything I did, or everywhere I looked, I would see you. I had to find a way to come back to you that kept us both safe."

Ryker's brow pinched. "So, the portal? . . ."

Nova nodded. "There is a portal that joins our worlds. Like the pool of reflections. It's not something that is widely talked about in Ara, for fear of too many stars might wish to come to Earth. But the elder stars could see how broken my heart was, and they offered me a way back."

"Did you travel here all the way from the Twin Peaks mountain range?"

Nova shook her head gently, a smile dancing on her lips. "No, this time I could choose what body of water to come from . . . You have a beautiful lake here."

Ryker's eyes grew wide as he glanced in the direction of the lake near the cottage. "But you're not wet?"

She grinned. "I was encased in a celestial orb. No elements could touch me."

"That's handy." Ryker grinned.

"I thought so too."

Ryker brushed his thumb over her cheek before he leant down and pressed a soft kiss to her lips. Then he rested his forehead on hers. "I watched for you every night." His voice was barely a whisper.

Nova placed her free hand over his heart. "I know you did."

"You saw me?"

Nova nodded. "Sometimes. But my position in Ara wasn't always where you were. It was torture to see you and then have to wait months to catch another glimpse. Five years was too long."

Ryker huffed softly. "I forgot our time is different. An entire year was unbearable for me."

Tears gathered in Nova's eyes again. "Let us never be parted again."

Ryker pulled her closer, his warmth seeping into her content heart and wrapping its way around every cell in her human body. "Never."

She stayed in his embrace for a few moments. Allowing the meadow breeze to wash over them. The sounds of Earth had returned, and Nova smiled. Every single syllable of nature's symphony was a song she never wanted to end. It was music she would cherish for the rest of her living days.

Nova eased back a little to look up at Ryker. She brought her hand up to brush the ends of his curls that sat around his neck, closer to his shoulders. "Your hair is longer."

"When I retired, I grew it out." Ryker smiled. "Do you like it?"

Nova tugged on the curls. "Do I like your hair or that you are no longer a bounty hunter?"

Ryker shrugged. "Both?"

A smile danced across Nova's lips. The idea that she would have him wholly to herself without the interruption of needing to return people to their rightful place was very enticing. "I quite like the idea of not sharing you. As for your hair . . . I love it."

Warm hands cupped her face again. "I can't believe you're here," Ryker murmured.

Nova smiled up at the hunter. "I can't believe it too."

"Will you stay forever?"

Nova didn't hesitate to answer his question. From the moment the elder star had offered her the choice to return to Earth, she knew she would never leave again. Not as long as Ryker was by her side, walking through life with her.

She placed her arms around his neck and stood on her tiptoes. "My home is wherever you are, Ryker Thornebrooke."

He grinned before pulling her close and covering her mouth with his. The kiss was more fervent this time—hungry. Warmth blossomed between her legs. Her body craved the pleasure only Ryker could offer her, and she couldn't wait for the moment until clothing would be discarded and together they would disappear into a world where only they existed.

Ryker broke the kiss gently. "Let me show you where we will live for the rest of our days."

The night was soft around them; the world bathed in silvery moonlight as Nova walked hand in hand with Ryker. Cool air whispered through the meadows, carrying the scent of blossoms and nectar, while above them, stars dotted the sky in a blanket of shimmering light. Her fingers intertwined with his, the warmth of his skin grounding her.

Nova nodded as she offered him a smile. "How's retirement treating you?"

Ryker grinned down at her as they strolled. "Just dandy. I finished the canoe I was building. Remind me to show you later."

"And Charlie? Is he here too?"

The Hound glanced off to the right of the cottage. "He's the proud occupant of the stable over there and a pasture full of grass."

Nova's heart swelled. She couldn't wait to see the black stallion who'd become her friend. "Take me to him in the morning?"

Ryker nodded. "I shall."

Ahead, the small white cottage waited, its windows glowing faintly with the light of the fireplace. The grass beneath their feet was barely visible, but Nova felt safe, as if the darkness couldn't touch them, not while Ryker was beside her. His thumb brushed softly against the back of her hand, and her heart fluttered, the simple touch igniting a warmth inside her that no fire could match.

She glanced up at him. His strong, familiar features were softened by the moonlight, casting shadows across his face. He caught her gaze and smiled, a small, quiet smile that made her chest ache with love and something bittersweet.

"You must be starving?" Ryker murmured.

Nova rested the side of her face on Ryker's shoulder. "Do you have any peaches?"

Nova sat beside Ryker on the porch step, their knees brushing together as they embraced the quiet of the evening. The sky above them was darker than when she'd arrived a few hours ago. Dinner had been a full meal of roast chicken topped with a dill and garlic butter. With a side of steamed greens and whipped potatoes. Ryker had even shown her how to make an apple pie.

In between the dinner preparations, Nova had found herself trapped in Ryker's arms, her face being peppered with kisses. The laughter that had rung through the room was like pure sunshine. She couldn't wipe the smile from her face.

"Your home is beautiful, Ryker," Nova murmured as she glanced sideways at him, watching the way his russet eyes reflected the heavens. His hand rested beside hers, fingers entwined together.

He looked down at her, a soft smile tugging at his lips. "Our home."

Nova wrapped an arm around his thick, muscular one. "Say it again."

Ryker chuckled before tenderly kissing the spot right above her temple. "This house right here is yours just as much as it is mine."

The cottage was small, cosy, with whitewashed wooden walls that had aged under the sun. The roof was made of black tiles, neatly covering the cottage and giving it a sharp contrast against the pale exterior. It was smaller than his last house she'd visited a handful of times over a year ago. It also felt different, in a good way. It was as if the home made him happier. His smile was brighter, and his eyes no longer tried to hide the ghosts of his past.

It was too dark to fully make out the gardens, but Nova was already excited to plan all the flower and vegetable beds with Ryker. She dreamed of having an abundance of produce, enough to overflow and share with the nearby villages. "Can we have ducks?"

Ryker's warm, russet eyes met her sea-green ones. "As many as you like . . . within reason." He stood, holding his hand out to her. "Come, let us walk."

Nova and Ryker eased through the tall, soft grasses of the meadow, their steps in perfect rhythm. The breeze swept gently over them, carrying the scent of wildflowers. As they reached the top of a grassy knoll, she paused, looking out at the rolling landscape beneath the soft twilight sky. The world felt peaceful, quiet. Ryker stood close, their shoulders brushing, and Nova couldn't help but feel that in this moment, everything was as it should be.

She reached inside her dress pocket and grasped something in her hand. "I have something for you."

Ryker's brow knitted softly as she pulled her hand from the folds of her skirts and placed the teardrop shaped moonstone pendant on his outstretched palm.

"I made this in Ara for you."

"But how?"

"It's from the seed of the star fruits, infused with a little celestial star dust—and magic," Nova murmured.

Nova noted the apparent emotion written on Ryker's face and she stepped closer to him. He took the gold chain from around his neck, placing the new silver pendant beside the ruby red one. Together they made an upside-down heart shape.

He gazed at them shimmering under the light of the moon.

Nova hugged his side. "Now, you can hold both Yolanda and I close to your heart."

A single tear stole its way down Ryker's sun kissed skin. Nova reached up to wipe it away, but he caught her hand, stilling it on his cheek.

"Thank you," he whispered. "This means more to me than you will ever know."

Nova smiled up at him. "You're welcome."

He looked down at her with such adoration, and she feared her heart would burst.

"Let me show you something," Ryker pulled her along.

They walked down the small grassy knoll towards the lake. At night it was a mirror of darkness, its surface smooth and still, reflecting the silver glow of the moon above. Ripples from the breeze shimmered like liquid light as the moonbeams danced across the water, creating a soft, ethereal glow. The edges of the lake faded into shadows where the trees hugged the shoreline, their silhouettes barely visible in the dim light.

There was something about water that captivated Nova. Perhaps there was so much of it she'd seen from high in the cosmic, but could never actually touch it. Now, not only could she touch it, but she could smell and swim in it. "It's so beautiful Ry—are those fish I see?"

A flash of something darted across the edge of the water. Silver scales glinted in the light.

Ryker chuckled. "They certainly are."

Nova glanced up at Ryker and grinned. "What are they?"

"Little minnows."

The silver flash caught her attention again. "Do you hunt them?"

Ryker crouched down, his hands resting between his legs. "No, these are purely for you."

Nova crouched beside him. "I could sit here and watch them all day."

"They reminded me of you. Of that day in the forest when you couldn't look away from them. Actually, Yolanda always enjoyed watching the fish in my father's pond too— sorry. I probably shouldn't talk about her."

Nova turned to face him. "Never apologise for talking about your first love. She was real, and those memories will never go away. Don't shut them out. Just bring me with you when you talk about them."

Ryker stood, drawing her up with him, gently cupping her face. "How are you even real?"

She reached to entwine her fingers into Ryker's hair, pulling him closer. "Why don't you kiss me and find out?"

"I'd be delighted," he replied, leaning down to kiss her.

The kiss was thrilling. All their kisses were intoxicating, but something in this one was so pure and wanting. She opened her mouth for him and moaned at his taste.

Rum and apple pie.

Ryker's hands slowly slid down her back to grasp the back of her thighs. He gently lifted her so she could wrap her legs around his waist. Their mouths and breath were tangled together in a dance of desire. Heat pooled at the most sensitive part of her body.

She broke the kiss and pulled back, her arms still around his neck and his arms around her waist. "Does that feel real enough to you?" she whispered.

"Not quite. I think we should do it again," Ryker answered in a low voice that had Nova trembling with delight.

He sat down amongst the flowers and Nova straddled his lap. "It's beginning to feel much more real now," Ryker murmured into her neck as he nuzzled it.

The feeling of his teeth scraping against her pulse and his lips sucking at her skin brought little bumps to the surface of her skin. Throwing her head back, Nova looked towards the stars as Ryker explored her neck and ear with his lips and tongue. Arching into his chest, Nova tried to press them closer, but it wasn't enough. She needed to feel his skin against hers.

She dropped her head back down to face him, reached for his face and clasped it between her hands, kissing him like it would be their last. He groaned into her mouth, and she grinned. Her fingers found the buttons on his shirt, and she undid them one by one, allowing the fabric to ease from his shoulders and fall onto the surrounding grass.

Nova pulled her lips from his and took in Ryker's naked torso. By the stars, this man was incredibly beautiful. Exploring hands found their way to his chest as she drew a finger across each crevice of carved muscle on his stomach. She wanted to kiss each one of them.

Ryker stilled, holding her hands in both of his. "Nova . . . I love you."

Nova's heart hammered in her chest.

"I want you . . . And I must have you as my own," Ryker murmured.

Tears welled in Nova's eyes. He'd said he loved her before she left. But hearing them again on her return was even sweeter. "I love you too and I'm all yours," she whispered.

Light flashed across the sky in the distance, drawing Nova's attention. A storm was approaching. Her eyes travelled to Ryker's ruby pendant. She waited for him to reach for it, but as the sky lit up and thunder rumbled in the distance, his eyes stayed focused on her.

The heavens lit up again. Surely, he would grasp his pendant now. It was the only way he could calm the turmoil in his mind. Yet his hands did not reach for it. Instead, Ryker reached for Nova, tucking a stray hair behind her ear.

"Do you want to go inside?" She whispered.

Ryker gently shook his head. "No . . . No, I do not."

"But what about—"

"You are my peace, Nova. You are my anchor in the storm and right now I would like to make love here in this field. You will be mine and only mine and I will be yours and only yours."

Tears welled in her eyes.

She knew the enormity of marriage to Ryker. It wouldn't be something he would consider lightly.

"What are you saying, Ryker Thornbrooke?" Nova smiled through her tears.

Ryker leaned to his right and pulled a grass stalk from the ground. He twisted it around his pinky a few times before tying both ends in a knot. Reaching for her left hand, Ryker looked her deep in the eyes and as he slipped the ring of grass onto her finger. "Nova Seraphine, will you do me the honour of becoming my wife?"

This was it. This was the moment Nova had witnessed many times from her celestial realm above. When a man asks a woman to pass through life at his side—as his partner and lover. Nova smiled at Ryker, who looked as if he might die if she didn't answer him soon.

Nova drowned in his russet eyes. "Yes, Ryker Thornbrooke. I will gladly marry you."

The Hound grinned and pulled her lips to meet him, but before they could touch, she stopped him. "Promise me one thing."

Ryker lifted a brow. "Anything, my little star," he said as his warm breath tickled her jaw and ear.

"That you will take me on adventures. Show me the world and while we are exploring it, you will teach me all the ways we can please each other," Nova whispered as she leaned forward and kissed a line across his jaw. "I want to experience life with you in all its forms." Her lips kissed his closed eyelids and travelled over the bridge of his nose. A soft groan escaped Ryker's throat as his hands found her backside and squeezed it.

Nova arched into him. "I want to go on adventures during the day, and at night I want to feel your hands all over my body while we moan each other's name."

Ryker's rough yet tender fingers worked at the buttons along the back of her dress, his eyes darkening with desire as he slowly slid the fabric from her skin. It bunched at her waist, leaving Nova's torso bare to the cool touch of the night air.

"Starting now?" Ryker whispered as he pressed light kisses across her collarbone.

Nova nodded, illuminating strands of hair floating around them. "Right here and right now."

Ryker dragged his fingers up her spine. "Is this good?"

A small moan escaped her lips at his touch. It felt incredible, but it wasn't enough. She gently eased from Ryker's embrace and stood, letting the rest of her dress fall to the ground. "It is, but—no fabric, get naked," she ordered.

Ryker obeyed, hastily removing his boots and trousers.

Nova stood in only the bottom half of her undergarments and took in the hunter's fully naked body. Ryker's well-defined chest looked as if it had been carved from marble. The way the moonlight hit his skin, creating shadows along the dips and grooves of his muscles. The sharp v shape that guided her eyes down further caught her breath. His cock stood tall and proud.

The last time Nova saw it and how it fit so beautifully between her legs came to her mind. It wasn't the first time she'd seen him naked, but it was the first time seeing him as her future husband.

He caught her gaze. Warmth flooded her cheeks as it travelled over the length of her body. "Like what you see, Hound?" she murmured.

Ryker grinned up at her. "Yes, I do, little star." Nova slowly eased the lightweight fabric of her undergarments down her hips, then to the floor. Stepping out of them, she stood fully naked before him, relishing his obvious pleasure with what he saw.

He held out his hand and beckoned. "You need to come back over here and sit on my lap again because I would very much like to do some things to you." Ryker's voice was low, sending a shiver up her spine.

Nova took a few steps towards him and climbed back onto his lap, her knees digging into the soft bed of flowers beneath them.

His arms encircled her waist, and his lips found hers with hunger and need. She breathed him in. This is what she'd been craving since the moment she saw him sitting on his porch. The feel of his lips upon her skin, searing heat with every touch. It was different this time, knowing she was his, and he was hers.

Ryker's teeth nipped at her bottom lip before he sucked it between his lips. She whimpered into this mouth as his hardened length rubbed against the sensitive part between her legs.

"I need more, Ryker," Nova cried as she pulled her mouth from his.

"What is it you need, my little star?" He asked as he gently cupped one of her breasts and rolled her nipple between his thumb and finger. Nova arched into his hand and cried out with pleasure.

"You," she whispered in response.

Ryker chuckled and dropped his mouth to the nipple he'd been toying with. He sucked on it softly and flicked it with his tongue. Nova cried out in pleasure again as she dug her fingers into his hair. Pulling his head up to meet her gaze, she held him there. "It's my turn."

She pushed on Ryker's chest until he lay back against the flowers. Nova remained straddled over his hips. The sight of him beneath her with the moon's glow upon his skin was almost more than she could bear. This perfectly sculptured man was her and hers forever. She leaned down, scattering kisses across his chest. Her fingers lightly scraped his skin. The hunter groaned and Nova grinned as she kissed along the line where the belt on his pants usually sat.

"Oh, my sweet girl, I'm not sure how much more of this perfectly wonderful torture I can take."

Nova giggled as she crawled her way back to his face. "Then shall I show you what comes next?"

Ryker nodded.

Nova dipped her head lower, catching the tip of his cock with her tongue. Ryker's moan vibrated through his body. Nova smiled at the sound. She was going to make him come undone.

She wrapped her delicate hand around the girth of his length and squeezed it, slipping the head of his cock between her warm lips. Sucking him as she slowly pumped her hand up and down. Ryker's hips bucked off the ground as Nova's pace quickened. A hint of a salty flavour touched her taste buds, and she swallowed it down.

Ryker moaned with pleasure, his hands fisting into the grass beneath them. "Fuck, Nova."

She flicked her gaze up towards him as he supported himself on his elbows, watching her take as much of him as she could fit into her mouth. His russet eyes were heavy with pleasure, and Nova felt the warmth between her legs grow. She pumped his cock a few more times as she gently sucked it before releasing him with a light popping sound.

Nova sat back on her heels. "Did I do that alright?"

"Any longer and I was going to find my release a lot quicker than I'd like too," Ryker growled as he wrapped his arms around her waist and flipped them so Nova was now under the weight of his body. Warm lips found her breasts again, and she arched into his mouth. His hand slid effortlessly over the smooth skin of her stomach and hovered just between her legs.

"Please . . ." Nova whimpered.

"Please what, my little star?" Ryker asked as his fingers grazed her skin.

Nova groaned. "Please don't stop."

Ryker dipped his fingers into the slick warmth between her legs and Nova cried out. He covered her mouth with his to quiet her sounds as his fingers gently plunged in and out.

"You're so ready for me," he whispered against her lips.

Nova nodded, her eyes begging him for more. Disappointment filled her as he removed his hand, but she was quickly pleased again when Ryker placed his hands on either side of her head and softly pressed his tip against her entrance.

"Tonight, I'm going to make love to you," Ryker said as he smiled down at her.

Nova nodded again. "Over and over, I hope."

Slowly, he pressed into her, and Nova sucked in her breath. The feel of him inside made her dissolve on the spot. With a gentle thrust, he buried himself inside her and Nova cried out.

"By the stars," he murmured.

Nova arched her back, baring her breasts to the moon's glow. She could feel the silver rays penetrating her skin and filling her veins with life. The thrum of energy reverberated through her and in its wake, the star in the centre of her chest pulsed with light. She couldn't hold back any longer, allowing her powers to ebb and flow, casting out of her in waves of blues, purples and greens.

She reached for the Hound and brought his lips to hers. "I love you, Ryker."

Ryker chuckled and kissed her as he pulled out and thrust back in. Nova whimpered against his lips each time he did. The coil inside her wound tighter and she knew it wouldn't be long before it would spring free and send her mind and body to the stars.

"I love you, Nova Seraphine."

The pace quickened, and Nova gripped Ryker's back, his muscles flexing with every thrust.

"Ryker," she whimpered.

Ryker grinned. "Let's go over the edge together, my love."

Love. There was that word again. It was music to her soul.

A cold, sudden breeze swept through the meadow, setting the flowers into a gentle dance as the draping boughs of the weeping willows swayed gracefully. The crickets sang their evening serenade, a soothing melody that harmonised with the frogs croaking on the banks of the lake.

Above them, millions of stars glittered in the darkened sky, their light shimmering like diamonds scattered across a velvet canvas. Nova basked in all of it. Here, on Earth, was exactly where she wanted to be.

Come what may.

"You know how stars bring joy when they fall to Earth?" Ryker asked as he pulled out ever so slowly and thrust back into her warmth.

Nova whimpered as the walls inside her clenched around Ryker's rigid length. "Yes," she answered, sounding breathless.

"You are that joy Nova . . . my joy."

Ryker slammed into her over and over. His eyes rolled back into his head as his climax built. Nova was lost in him, in the heat and power of his touch, in the way he seemed to light up from within. The sensation of his body moving against hers, the rhythm of their shared desire, sent waves of pleasure crashing through her. She was radiating with him, feeling the overwhelming energy between them intensify to where she thought she might explode into a million tiny pieces, scattering like stardust across the sky.

It was all she needed. Those two little words with the man she loved making love to her beneath the vast, starry night sky pushed her over the edge. Her whole body felt a powerful surge of pleasure, shaking and arching as she reached for the stars, as if she could touch the sky.

Nova cried out as a wave of pleasure washed over her body, pulsing like electricity. Colours in her mind burst as she whispered, "You are my joy, Ryker Thornbrooke."

Ryker thrust a few more times and then softly groaned as his pleasure took him. His cock pulsing inside of her as he spilled himself into her warmth.

Nova trailed her fingers over his chest, making her way up to his face as he caught his breath. His skin was clammy beneath her touch and glistened in the moonlight. He was perfect.

Ryker collapsed against her body, and she smiled as her eyes flicked to the stars above. Two bodies entwined in a heap of ecstasy and bliss. Hundreds of tiny specks shot across the sky. It was almost like her sisters were celebrating with her. What once was her home in the heavens above was now wherever he was.

Nova glanced down at the hunter, who lay against her chest. Nova reached over and brushed the hair from his sleepy eyes. "How long until we can do that again?"

Ryker chuckled as he propped himself up on an elbow. "At least give me five more minutes."

Nova smiled as she pulled him close.

Life here was definitely going to be fun.

"Ryker . . . ?"

"Yes, little star?"

"Thank you for being my last first kiss."

ACKNOWLEDGEMENTS

I remember when I was younger; I wrote a book that had about five words on each page and my friend Anna drew the pictures for me. To this day, I still have it.

I always knew I wanted to write stories from a very young age, it just took until I was thirty-six to find the stories inside me. The day I took the leap into making this happen was the day I finished reading a fantasy romance I'd randomly bought in a bookstore one day. That book helped me rediscover my love for fantasy and the endless worlds that could be imagined. Magical tales woven with romance, action and mysteries. A place where powerful men and women went on adventures, and where I could escape reality and join them.

To my readers. I hope you know that no matter what stage in life you are at that you are always worthy of love. I hope you read this and find joy, spreading it to others around you. Thank you for encouraging me to keep writing my cosy, romantasy books.

To my husband Jared. My rock and my safe place. You have held me when I've cried and almost given up. You have encouraged me to keep going and always supported my dreams. Thank you for believing in me, even when I didn't believe in myself. You have shown me that the men I write in my stories are actually real. You are my perfect man. Without you, I wouldn't be where I am today. Thanks for all the donuts. I love you.

To my beautiful children, Charleston and Meadow. Thank you for being patient with me through the tough times. You are both sunshine in my days and I love the joy you bring to everyone around you. Never give up on your dreams. I love you both so much.

To my darling Megan. I would need thousands of pages to write everything I would like to say to you. You've changed my life in ways I can't explain. Thank you for walking with me on this journey, for your endless support and your beautifully intricate mind. Thank you for staying up until the early hours of the morning with me, and most of all, thank you for every word you suggested and every comma you added to this story. It wouldn't be where it is now without you. You are pure sunshine. I love you.

To my Kindred Spirit Alex (AllyCat). Who would have thought that an image of a Motionless In White concert would join two souls together. Both which have a love for emo music, writing and staying indoors with a cosy book. You have such a gift when it comes to writing, a gift that doesnt go un-noticed. Thank you for all your incredible input into this story and for encouraging me when I wanted to give up. I'll leave the light on for you. I love you.

To the Coven, Jems, Leah, Steph, Diana, Iesha and Chelle. Thank you for your friendships, for your encouragement and for helping me to believe in myself. Our silly conversations have been a breath of fresh air, exactly what my heart has needed. Thank you for being the best beta readers an author could ask for. Thank you for all the wisdom and joy you bring to the book world and mine. I love you all.

To Lucy and Keziah. Thank you for always supporting me no matter what new project I started or became obsessed with, despite the other thousands I already had on the go. The interest you have both continually shown in my stories hasn't gone unnoticed. Thank you for always showing up for me and for loving me right where I'm at. I wouldn't be where I am today without you both. I love you.

To Jenny. Thank you for taking a chance on me and introducing me into the world of books. Thank you for all of your guidence and wisdom as I have travelled this path, and most of all. Thank you for your kindness.

About the Author

Sarah Davies lives in a cottage by a stream that runs through a meadow at the base of a grassy hill. Her garden is filled with every flower imaginable and white ducks with orange beaks and webbed feet, pitter patter in puddles of mud. A beehive is nestled beneath the branches of a pink crepe myrtle tree that provides shade for all her cats and inside her kitchen, the kettle is always warm.

She doesn't really live there, but in her mind, that's where she goes to find inspiration. It's in that magical place where all her stories are formed and she puts them down on paper. One day she hopes to make this dream a reality, where she will live peacefully with her husband and two children.

Sarah is a self-labeled "Cosy, romance, fantasy" author, writing predominately fantasy romance from her home in Queensland, Australia. When she's not dreaming up a new story or chipping away at current ones, you can find her sipping on tea, gardening, painting, sewing, or simply being with her family.

OTHER BOOKS

KEEP IN TOUCH

INSTAGRAM @SARAH.C.DAVIES

TIKTOK @SARAHCATDAVIES

EMAIL SARAHCATDAVIES@GMAIL.COM

FACEBOOK GROUP SARAH C DAVIES AUTHOR